The Darkest Edge of ⟩
THE BETTER
. . . the
"star on the r

"This gritty urban fantasy . . . is extraordinary."
—*Booklist*

"Intricate world-building and richly complex characters mix with a fast-paced plot to create a standout start to a new series." —*Publishers Weekly*

"What sets this book apart, besides the great writing and the unique world-building, is the fact that our heroine is a single mom. . . . The love and protectiveness of a mother for her child as well as her family just gave so much depth to the situation as well as a real sense of urgency." —Night Owl Romance

"Charlie Madigan is an awesome character. . . . I could not put this book down." —Fallen Angel Reviews

"Her dark urban setting is so gritty, vivid, and original that it flaunts one of the greatest qualities of good fantasy: utter believability. . . . Kelly Gay whisked me into a dangerous world and made me want to stick around. . . . I can't wait to spend more time with Charlie Madigan." —Vicki Pettersson

The Darkest Edge of Dawn is also available as an eBook

ALSO BY KELLY GAY

The Better Part of Darkness

THE
DARKEST
EDGE OF
DAWN

KELLY GAY

POCKET BOOKS
New York London Toronto Sydney

The sale of this book without its cover is unauthorized. If you purchased this book without a cover, you should be aware that it was reported to the publisher as "unsold and destroyed." Neither the author nor the publisher has received payment for the sale of this "stripped book."

Pocket Books
A Division of Simon & Schuster, Inc.
1230 Avenue of the Americas
New York, NY 10020

This book is a work of fiction. Names, characters, places, and incidents either are products of the author's imagination or are used fictitiously. Any resemblance to actual events or locales or persons, living or dead, is entirely coincidental.

Copyright © 2010 by Kelly Gay

All rights reserved, including the right to reproduce this book or portions thereof in any form whatsoever. For information, address Pocket Books Subsidiary Rights Department, 1230 Avenue of the Americas, New York, NY 10020.

First Pocket Books paperback edition September 2010

POCKET and colophon are registered trademarks of Simon & Schuster, Inc.

For information about special discounts for bulk purchases, please contact Simon & Schuster Special Sales at 1-866-506-1949 or business@simonandschuster.com.

The Simon & Schuster Speakers Bureau can bring authors to your live event. For more information or to book an event, contact the Simon & Schuster Speakers Bureau at 1-866-248-3049 or visit our website at www.simonspeakers.com.

Designed by Jill Putorti
Cover design by John Vairo Jr.
Cover illustration by Chris McGrath

Manufactured in the United States of America

10 9 8 7 6 5 4 3 2 1

ISBN 978-1-4391-1004-1
ISBN 978-1-4391-5547-9 (ebook)

For Allen & Cheryl Hogan
(*aka Al & Dinky*)
(*aka Mom & Dad*)

They say that at dawn, on the winter solstice, the top of Helios Tower burned brighter than the sun and dragons fell from the sky . . .

~~~~~

December 24th
From the journal of Emma Garrity

I

"Okay. I'm ready. Give me a leg up."

With my right leg bent at the knee, foot poised in the air, and my fingers grasping the brick ledge below the broken window, I turned just enough to fire a withering glare at my partner. "Hank! A little help here?"

He didn't budge.

My eyes narrowed to slits as he stood there frowning at me like usual. I shook my foot at him and reached higher, my arm and shoulder muscles burning. "Oh, just forget it," I muttered, dropping my hands from the ledge and hopping back, giving my partner a push toward the window. "You're taller, you try."

A dark blond eyebrow rose, and he shifted his weight onto one foot. Two seconds passed before he let out a dubious sigh and graced the world with his rich baritone. "I'm going to take a wild guess, Charlie, and say the chief doesn't know about our afternoon detour."

I glanced at the derelict parking lot, forcing down a shiver. "Your powers of observation are mind-blowing."

"I have been called 'mind-blowing' once or twice," he said, completely ignoring my sarcasm as he removed a few chunks of broken glass from the bottom window frame.

"Once or twice, that's all?" I teased. "Wouldn't go around admitting that if I were you. Might give all sirens a bad name."

He shot a glower over his shoulder. "I was *trying* to be modest. Now, if you want to get technical, the number is quite—" The light atop the corroded steel pole behind us blinked out with a loud electrical buzz.

Five seconds passed in darkness.

The unusually mild December wind sent brittle leaves dancing like skeletons over the concrete parking lot. The echoes of their skip and scratch made the warehouse district seem even more desolate and remote despite the distant sounds of Atlanta's midday traffic. "Let's just get in and get out. This place gives me the creeps."

The light sizzled back to life, illuminating the heavy gray clouds undulating above us like whitewater rapids in slow motion. Occasionally a bottle-green flash would light up the sky—silent and strange—each burst never quite the same. I frowned, wondering if I'd ever get used to the darkness that hung above the city for the last two months.

"Why the hell did Ebel-whatever-his-name-is lock the place back up?" Pieces of glass hit the concrete and shattered into small bits as Hank finished clearing the window.

"It's Ebel*wyn*," I said. "And I doubt he was thinking straight. You know . . . saw dead body, ran, locked the door behind him. That's what real estate agents do; they lock the door behind them. Creatures of habit, I guess."

"Could've told him to meet us here with the key."

"I did. He was so spooked, he wouldn't come back."

The tip I received earlier had come from a darkling fae, a Charbydon who'd stopped by the warehouse to check out the property and put up a *For Sale* sign. Not surprising he hadn't called the ITF—relations between Charbydons and law enforcement were on pretty shaky ground right now, as were relations between Charbydons and Elysians. The darkness made everyone edgy. Anyone with a scrap of common sense would've known calling the ITF to report an Elysian body inside of a Charbydon-owned property meant trouble.

Hank moved aside and brushed his palms lightly over his cargo pants. "The window is too small for me to fit through. You'll have to go."

He bent low, linking his fingers together to hoist me up. I placed both hands on the cool leather jacket that covered his shoulders and put my foot in the cradle of his hands, getting a whiff of the same herby scent that perfumed The Bath House in Underground. I glanced down.

Dark sapphire orbs stared up at me, set in features that remained mostly grim ever since the night his voice-mod had been fused together, stuck on his neck and subduing his greatest power—his siren's call.

Of course the voice-mod did nothing to stifle the sensual quality of his voice or the natural siren magnetism that constantly emanated from him. Nor did it stop him from using his other natural abilities—healing, sensing energies, and being a superb wiseass.

I reached for the ledge. The sharp brick edges scraped my wrists, pulling my attention back to the job at hand. Once up, I balanced on my stomach and swung one leg over, then followed with the other until I was looking down at my partner's upturned face. "I'll see if I can open the side door from the inside. Meet me over there."

"Careful, Charlie," his voice came out low, "there's negative energy all around this place."

"Yeah, I know."

I dropped down into the darkness of the two-story warehouse, my boots slapping hard against the concrete floor and echoing through the lofty space. The flap of startled wings sent my heart to my throat, and my hand to my Nitro-gun. It slid from the harness with a comforting whisper.

Owls. Just owls.

Regaining my composure, I pulled the standard-issue flashlight from my belt with my free hand and clicked it on, liking the weight and the chill of the metal. I didn't bother looking for a light switch—Ebelwyn had said the lights didn't work, and he'd never made it to the main fuse box to trip the breakers. He'd gotten as far as the body, dropped his flashlight, and ran like hell. And if the flashlight was still on, I couldn't see it from this distance.

The inside of the warehouse was massive, a long, hollow tomb. Owl eyes blinked at me from steel beams high overhead. Part of the ceiling was gone in places, exposing the inside of the warehouse to the elements. Many of the second-story windows were cracked or broken, and the floor was littered with glass, dust, and an odd assortment of trash, wooden pallets, and steel parts.

My light beamed over graffiti—names, faces, cityscapes, and a life-size rendition of Mary Magdalene. On the other wall were the spray-painted symbols of black crafting; pentagrams, spirals, zodiac signs, planetary symbols, and Enochian script.

The warehouse was too deep for my light to penetrate the blackness completely, but I sensed there was something down there—not a physical presence, but something that made my instincts fire off warning signals.

A body. A nymph, I think, Ebelwyn had said, shaken and breathless over the phone. *Can't fucking miss it*.

I focused, using my senses to get a clearer picture of what lurked in the darkness, proud of myself for remembering to try in the first place. Thirty-one years of being human and relying on human instincts made it difficult to switch gears and rely on the off-world abilities I'd recently been given, especially out in the field.

Regulate your breathing. Sharpen your focus, Aaron's voice echoed in my mind. My teacher had done nothing but drill me in focus and concentration for the last two months, something that bored me to tears most sessions. But I *was* getting better at it.

As soon as my concentration peaked, my throat closed.

A smothering, vile sensation gripped me so hard I stumbled, grabbing my neck, instantly panicked by the feel of thick sludge filling and stretching my throat. My pulse hammered heavy and quick.

It's not real. It's not real. It's not real.

All my instincts, both natural and engineered, propelled me away, and I stumbled again, scrambling backward to the side door.

Fear had ignited my entire body, making it hum, making me lose control as my hand flailed around for the doorknob, losing my hold on the flashlight. *There.* A wave of hot power surged from my core and down my arm as I yanked on the knob. The door broke open, snapping the bottom steel hinge in half.

A blink later, the sensation vanished.

Oxygen filled my lungs as I bent at the waist,

bracing both hands on my knees, my right hand still curled around my weapon, trying to reclaim those lost moments of precious air and shake away the mental fuzziness. So fast. It all had happened so fast.

A long shadow across the warehouse floor shifted. I glanced up as Hank cleared his throat, giving me a raised eyebrow and then stopping the door from swinging with one hand as he ducked under and stepped inside.

"Might want to prepare yourself," I said, picking up my light. "It's worse in here."

He straightened and scanned the area. "What's that smell?"

"Not sure. Dead rat, maybe? There are owls here. Could be their leftovers."

Whatever happened, it was just me and Hank. We worked on a need-to-know basis with the ITF, which meant they didn't *need to know* what the hell we were up to unless we wanted them to. We were the only 5th Floor agents in Atlanta, and if we bought it, two others—willing or blackmailed into it—would take our place, going outside the boundaries of the law to bring down the most vile and vicious off-world criminals in the city.

To our covert supervisors in Washington, we were replaceable. And, for now, we were on our own.

"You feel anything?" I asked.

"No substantial presence. Nothing but smut," he said, using our popular term for negative energy signatures.

"Nothing but smut," I echoed softly and took a step forward.

The whining charge of Hank's Hefty filled the cavernous space. Until we knew what we were dealing with, an Elysian or Charbydon threat, we each drew separate weapons. My own Hefty was safely tucked against my left side and on my hip was a human firearm—a 9mm SIG Sauer. Three weapons for the races of three different worlds.

Both of our lights crisscrossed the darkness as we moved down the center of the warehouse. The force of whatever lurked beyond was so strong, so negative that it felt as though we were trudging through knee-deep mud. We passed old sleeping bags and shopping carts, cardboard boxes that were once used as make-shift shelters. Who knew how many homeless had lived here at one time—or who might, even now, be watching us from the dark corners beyond our flashlights and vision.

"It's getting thicker. Damn eyes are burning," Hank whispered.

I felt the weight of the energy, but not the sting. Hank, being one hundred percent Elysian, was *way* more sensitive to smut than I was. I glanced over my shoulder. We were so far in now that the darkness had closed in behind us, wrapping us in a cocoon of noxious black energy.

I jumped as Hank's hand touched my arm. He'd stopped cold. I returned my light to the path in front of us. "What the hell is that?"

A mountain of debris. The source of all the negative energy.

I covered my nose as we approached; the smell of something rotting was bad enough to trigger my gag reflex. Our lights beamed against the jumble of trash and debris and—*dear God*—limbs.

With a sinking realization in my stomach, my trembling light traveled slowly over the pile, revealing pieces and parts of several corpses mingled with the debris. Tendons. Flesh hanging off bone. A torso. An arm. A mass of curly blond hair.

"Looks like we found our missing Adonai," I said, stunned.

"Hold on," Hank muttered. "There's an office . . ."

I backed away from the pile as Hank made his way to a glass-enclosed office. He shoved a desk end over end, tossed a mattress to the side, and found his target—an electrical box.

The switches Ebelwyn never found, four in all, echoed loudly in succession like church bells tolling the dead. Large round lights, running in spaced intervals down the length of the warehouse ceiling, sputtered to life. Some bulbs popped, some didn't work at all, but enough blinked on so that the mound in front of us lit up like a Broadway stage from the depths of hell.

As Hank returned to my side, I gestured with my flashlight to the top of the pile. "They're fresher at the top."

No need to say more. I think we both understood

what we were looking at. A dumping ground, a place to toss the latest victim like they were garbage. Not even buried or hidden. Not even worth that much.

The horror of it made me turn away, and I wondered if I'd ever be able to wash away the smell, if I'd ever get the burn of it out of my nose and throat.

My eyes began to water. "Okay, I'm done."

"You see those symbols?" Hank asked, not hearing me. "There, on the wall? It's a charm. Probably to hide the stench. Otherwise, we should've been able to smell this place a mile away."

"What about those?" I pointed to an odd batch of symbols on the opposite wall.

"Not sure. Never seen script like that in vertical rows before. Some of these letters or symbols look like ancient Elysian, but the others . . ." He shrugged. "Could be Charbydon."

"Aaron or Rex can probably tell us." I took out my camera phone and snapped a few photos of the unusual script that also bore echoes of Enochian, Egyptian hieratic, and Aramaic. Definitely odd. Bryn probably knew what this was, too, but the last thing I wanted was to bring my sister into another investigation—the last one, fighting Mynogan and his followers to save my daughter, had nearly killed her, and left her with an addiction to *ash* that was making her life miserable.

"I'll call the chief." Hank walked away, cell in hand.

Our medical examiner, Liz, was going to have a field day with this one. She and her team would need months to sort through the carnage.

From the very beginning, from the moment we learned that six members of the Adonai race had simply vanished, I knew the outcome would be bad. Adonai were the ruling elite of Elysia—some called them divinities or angels, and for good reason. They were the most powerful beings from that heaven-like world; they didn't just vanish into thin air, not without a fight. Whoever had done this was very powerful— a butcher who, until now, had left no trace of his or her crimes.

Was it carelessness to leave the bodies here like this? Or had the killer wanted us to find them? Or maybe it was just complete and total arrogance. Maybe our perp didn't give a shit either way, so sure of his power and right to kill that law enforcement really didn't factor into the equation.

I went to turn away, but a flash of pale skin caught my eye. A hand, palm upturned, on the floor near the edge of the pile. I moved closer.

"Hank!"

I dropped down next to what appeared to be the remains of a female nymph. Her tanned skin was sunken, as though every ounce of moisture and fluid had been sucked from her body. Her dark, wavy hair was matted and held bits of debris, possibly due to a roll from the top of the pile.

Ebelwyn's nymph.

He must've kept his light trained on the ground in front of him, the light beaming on this body first. And then he ran, never knowing what else lurked in the debris pile. His broken flashlight lay nearby.

I grabbed a pair of latex gloves from my inside jacket pocket, pulled them on, and then reached into the front pouch of her thin hooded sweatshirt. A few dollars. A set of keys. A gym ID with her picture and name: *Daya Machanna*. No purse or wallet that I could see from a quick scan around the body.

Hank knelt next to me, intelligent eyes scanning the body. "She looks mummified." He placed two hands on her neck. "That's odd—she's still warm."

A rush of hope blew through me. "I'll call Liz." I jumped up, removing the gloves as I walked away, mentally praying that this was the break we needed.

A few steps in, I froze, the hairs on my arms standing straight, instantly gripped with the sense that something new had made its way into the warehouse, something that brought with it the scents of the darkness outside.

A low growl confirmed my suspicions.

I spun slowly on my heel to see two red orbs approaching from the shadowed side of the debris pile. Hank was on one side of the body and the hellhound on the other.

I let the gloves fall to the floor. My hand moved for my Nitro-gun. Hank eased up, inch by inch, to his full height, his arm slowly going back for his weapon.

The hellhound stepped forward.

Jesus, it was huge. Bald, gray head hung low between muscled shoulders, muzzle drawn back in a snarl.

This was its territory. Now the carnage made sense. It had been feeding on these discarded victims.

And Hank was standing over its freshest meal yet, directly in my line of fire.

I pulled my weapon. The whisper to tell him to get out of the way was on my tongue, but I dared not. The slightest move or sound could trigger an attack. Hank's thumb flicked the snap to the holster strap. I winced. It might as well have been a bomb going off. Shit.

The hellhound leapt.

"Hank!"

His half-drawn weapon clattered to the ground as the hellhound slammed into him. They fell to the floor, the hound's teeth snapping inches from Hank's face. *"Shoot it, Charlie!"* His big hands squeezed the beast's jowls, holding it at bay.

I ran to the side, trying to get a line for a clean shot. "I'm trying!"

"Try harder, for Christ's sake!"

I ran closer to the debris pile, my attention so fixed on the two that I tripped over a small piece of plywood, landing hard on my hands and knees. The hellhound lifted its head and stilled—perfect time to shoot it if I hadn't been on all fours, the wood angled between my calves.

The wide nostrils flared intensely. In and out.

Oh shit.

I rolled, kicking out the board and then scrambling to my feet, adrenaline firing as Hank's warning shout echoed through the warehouse. I didn't look back, didn't have to. I just ran, arms pumping, leaping over debris and trying to get a lead so I could turn and fire.

Too late, though. No one could outrun such a creature.

Paws landed on my shoulder blades. Warm, moist breath breezed across the back of my neck an instant before my face met the floor. I struck with at least two hundred pounds of hellhound on my back, every ounce of air forced from my lungs as my forehead smacked the concrete with a loud crack. Pain surged over my skull like a shockwave—hot, consuming pressure that stunned me for several seconds and stole my vision.

Wet jowls smacked eagerly, the sound of an eating frenzy that finally terrorized some sense into me and made me gasp for what little air my squished lungs could hold. It had straddled me, paws on floor, belly grazing my back, and its muzzle nudging and pressing and licking my neck. I closed my eyes bracing for the killing bite . . .

. . . that never came.

No fangs, no broken skin, no scent of blood; just an intent, slobbery licking at the back of my neck, drool running down both sides.

And then it hit me. Of course. Brimstone. *Sonofabitch!* I had a rescued hellhound living in my house. Brimstone's scent must be all over me . . . at least to the beast on my back it was. Slowly, I lifted my aching head and rolled slightly to look over my shoulder, but a bright flash stopped me cold. Everything became suspended, but my mind burst with color. Colors that soon became images . . .

Hank behind the beast . . .

Firing . . .

Four small fetuses curled within the womb of this terrifying animal . . .

And then just as quickly as it came, the vision ended and reality rushed back in, the yell already in my throat. "Don't kill it!" I didn't need to look beyond the beast to know my partner's dark silhouette was already there, weapon raised for a clean shot. "Low stun, Hank! Don't kill it!"

A nitro capsule sank into the beast's hip to the sound of Hank's curse. She leapt straight up, yelped, and bounded away, each stride becoming slower and slower as the nitro spread through her muscle. It didn't take long before she fell onto her side, her distended belly pushed skyward and her entire torso rising and falling in quick pants.

The cold would paralyze her long enough to figure out a plan of action, but it wouldn't kill or damage her permanently. No doubt the healing process was already beginning—something all off-worlders, beings and animals alike, were blessed with. Pump too much nitro into a Charbydon, though, and no amount of natural healing would help. They were particularly sensitive to the cold, just as most Elysians had a severe reaction to high frequency sound waves.

I rolled from my side onto my back, staring up at

the dark ceiling and taking several more deep breaths to calm my pulse. That's when my sense of smell kicked in, and my gut clenched into a hard, sour ball at the foul, rot-scented saliva encasing my neck and dampening strands of my hair. *Nice.*

"Goddamn, Charlie," Hank said, stunned. "You okay?" He reached down with an outstretched hand.

"Peachy, thanks. Who wouldn't love a tongue bath from a hellhound feeding on body parts?" I slapped my hand in his and let him pull me to my feet, realizing my words only made me more nauseous.

Once upright, dizziness swamped me and pain stabbed my brain in hot pulses. "Fuck." I squeezed Hank's hand and bent over as bile stung the back of my throat and the mother of all migraines descended.

"Breathe." Hank peeled my fingers away from his hand. "You can heal now, remember?"

"Oh, yeah, right." My response came between small, quick breaths. "That's a little hard to do when your breakfast is about to come back up." I closed my eyes as his footsteps retreated toward the direction of the hellhound, using the time to refocus and reach beyond the pain.

Hank was right. Thanks to my new genetic make-up, I had the ability to heal courtesy of *both* the Elysian and Charbydon DNA that now ran through my system. Double whammy—and something those in my small circle of friends believed made me indestructible. Of course, there was the little problem of figuring out *how* to use those abilities. Unlike my partner, it wasn't second nature for me to heal or manipulate the natural energy that existed all around us. It took concentration and effort. Two things that were kind of hard to do when you're in pain and about to barf.

"Here."

A cloth hit me on the left side of the face, bringing with it a burst of machine oil aroma. I straightened and pulled the old work rag off my shoulder. It was better than nothing to wipe the slime off the back of my neck. I tucked the rag between my knees, twisted my disheveled hair and then tied it into a knot, my band lost in the hellhound lovefest. Then I set to work slowly wiping the slobber from my skin, eyes closed, and focusing on sending healing messages to my aching head.

Cool breezes. Laughter. Peace. Joy. Love. Strong emotions that I tapped into, that gathered in my chest with each long, controlled inhale until a faint tingle spread out in all directions. My toes wiggled in response. Once the healing energy was alive within me, I zeroed in on my head, pulling the energy up, directing it, and letting it take over.

A deep, accusing voice broke my concentration. "She's pregnant."

I cracked one eye open to see my partner standing in front of me with his brow raised, one corner of his mouth drawn down, and both hands on his hips, drawing back the sides of his black leather jacket. The stark white of his T-shirt was almost too bright for my head to bear. I finished with the rag. "And your point?"

A flash of exasperation widened his eyes. He flung a hand and a glance back at the hellhound. Anyone seeing her lying there like that could tell she was expecting. "You knew it was pregnant."

I shrugged in answer. How in the hell was I supposed to explain? And why even bother? So I could feel more freakish than I already was? No thanks. Those closest to me *knew* I was changing, still morphing into something no one had ever seen before thanks to the gene manipulation. Two months had passed since I learned the truth behind the strange evolution taking place inside of me, but damned if I wanted to talk about every weird-ass side effect. Healing. Making nightmares a reality. Throwing bolts of power out of my hands. Eating like a sumo wrestler. Why not visions? A sharp laugh burst from my throat and I rubbed a hand down my face.

Might be cool if it wasn't going to kill me.

I finished with the rag and tossed it into a nearby trash pile. "I'll call Animal Control and have them send her back to Charbydon."

"They never send them back, Charlie. It's policy to euthanize them. You should've let me kill her."

There was a time I'd have agreed wholeheartedly with my partner. Having Brimstone around must be making me soft. I blew my long bangs away from my eyes. "Why? Because some asshole brought her here for God knows what reason and then abandoned her?

She's not evil, Hank. She's just an animal trying to survive." I brushed the debris from my raw elbows and hands. "I'll make sure they send her back."

I marched away, tracking down my Nitro-gun, which had skidded down the warehouse floor when I hit the ground, glad for a reason to get out from under Hank's curious gaze. Once I located my gun, I holstered it and then called a friend at Animal Control.

My next call was to Liz. We had a body to raise from the dead. And this was just the break we needed.

2

Liz made it in fifteen minutes. Not bad for her day off. But then, Liz was one of those people always prepared, always organized, and always on time. I'd hate her for it, except that she'd weaseled her way into my heart a long time ago with her wry sense of humor, dedication to the job, and pitbull tenacity. I'd learned just as quickly as the other new officers, when meeting the chief medical examiner for the first time, that the small-framed doctor and licensed necromancer with the striking Asian features had balls of typanum-infused steel. Everyone respected her. *Everyone*.

And a natural-born necromancer like Liz was rare—only one in every major city, if you believed the statistics. Having her on the ITF payroll was a major bonus to the department.

I remained crouched near the nymph's body as

Liz's telltale footsteps—quick and determined—grew louder. She stopped behind me as I glanced over my shoulder to see her in a plum-colored velour jogging suit, her large black duffel bag hanging off one shoulder and a canvas gurney rolled up under her arm like a yoga mat—she always kept one in her trunk because, hey, you never knew when you might need to move a body, right?

"That knot on your forehead is the size of an egg, Madigan. Kind of looks like a third eye."

"Don't you ever say hello? You know, actually *greet* a person before pointing out their flaws?" Rhetorical question. We both knew she never did.

She squatted down next to me. "Eh. Greetings are a waste of time. You know a person wastes seventeen hours of an average lifespan just on greeting people they already know?" Her bag rested on the floor between us. Her straight black hair fell forward, curving just under her chin, but held away from her vision by the corners of stylish horn-rimmed glasses.

"No kidding, really?" The faint scent of gardenias tickled my nose, a welcome break from the decay all around us.

"No. I just made it up. But I bet I'm close. You also smell really, really bad. Could use a charm like the one put on these corpses."

"Thanks. Your honesty is touching, really."

"Mmm. So I take it the fact I'm here on my day off means you don't plan on calling the ITF?"

"By the time the ITF gets here, secures the scene,

and debates on whether or not to raise the dead, our victim wouldn't have anything left to tell us. I'll make the call after we're done."

Unable to argue the truth of my words, Liz turned her attention from the pile back to the intact victim on the floor, leaning closer and closing her eyes as she ran a flat palm a few inches over the body.

I was antsy. Every moment we waited was another moment Daya's last memories slipped away. Liz couldn't bring back the nymph's spirit, but she could reanimate the corpse long enough to engage what was left of those final memories. The longer the dead stayed dead, the less of a chance one had to learn anything useful at all.

"Patience, Madigan," Liz murmured, sensing my energy. "Have to sweep the body, get a good look at everything first. You know the drill . . . No energy signature on her. Never seen this kind of drain before; looks like she's been sucked dry. Practically mummified, and she's stiff, yet her skin isn't cold. Bizarre. You do know," she said, tilting her head to look at me, "the ITF has been working the Adonai missing persons case . . ."

"I know. *I'll call.* We've been monitoring this case, too." I turned my attention back to the gruesome pile. "And now that they've been found dead, DC will want us to look into it."

"You mean take out the killer. That still doesn't bother you, does it?"

We'd had this discussion before. Liz was privy to

our cases and the truth of what we did because we needed her and we trusted her. But from the beginning she'd made it clear she was uncomfortable with the power we'd been given.

"Depends," I answered, "on who or what killed these people. You know as well as I do some things can't be locked up, or reformed, or tried in a court of law. Hank and I do what needs to be done."

A heavy sigh escaped her red lips, and her attention went back to the body. "And so do I."

There were no illusions about what Liz was referring to. Raising the dead came with a hefty price. Every time a corpse was raised, it cost the necromancer a little bit of life force. And once it was gone, you couldn't get it back, couldn't recoup it like blood loss. How much loss depended on a lot of factors: how long the victim had been dead, how long the necromancer kept the dead animated, and how skilled the necromancer. Fortunately for Liz, she was the best. But still, I asked, "You sure about this?"

A soft snort came with her answer. "Serial killer powerful enough to prey on Adonai? Yeah. You need me. I'm sure. Where's Hank? We need to get started."

"Checking the perimeter." I stood and brushed off my palms.

"And the hellhound you told me about?"

"Over by the office. We should have enough time to do this before Animal Control gets here."

Liz surged to her feet. "All right then," she said,

unrolling the canvas, "let's do this while it's still worth it."

Hank's footsteps echoed through the lofty space as I helped Liz roll out the canvas and place it on the floor alongside the body. "Perimeter is clean," he said, approaching. "Doubt the killer uses this for anything other than a dumping ground." He gestured to the corpse. "We're not going to do it here?"

"No," Liz said. "We need to raise her away from the others. That empty storage room I passed up front should work." Her voice dropped to a low mutter as she bent to grab Daya's shoulders. "Wouldn't want any residual power to raise a body part . . . or a dead cockroach. Trust me, that's *no* fun."

Hank and I exchanged incredulous looks over the sunken, dead body we were about to raise, not sure if she was serious or joking.

Liz tossed us two extra pairs of gloves. "Charlie, get her ankles."

I cleared my throat, pulled on the gloves, and then grabbed both ankles. They felt wooden; no shift or give. The only thing that moved was the tangled mass of dark hair that dropped away from the shoulders as we lifted Daya onto the gurney.

Hank took over Liz's spot, threading his fingers through the canvas handles as Liz picked up her large duffel—the bag, I knew, held all of the ritual equipment needed to raise the dead—and began leading the way to the front of the warehouse and into the empty storage room.

Once inside, she bolted the door and then set to work, using a canister of salt to make a large circle on the dusty floor. Then she used what looked to be a very old compass to draw a salt pentagram inside the circle, three of the points touching the circle at what I guessed to be the north, east, and west compass points. At each point of the pentagram, she placed five black candles.

"Now," she said, straightening to survey her work and shove her eyeglasses back up the bridge of her nose, "we need to lay her on top of the pentagram, head on the east point there."

I'd seen enough dead bodies in my line of work, ones in worse shape than this, but knowing what we were about to do . . . Hank let out a heavy sigh, his expression resolute. It didn't take a genius to see he was about as thrilled as I was with the prospect of disturbing the dead.

As Liz removed her ritual bowl from the bag and set several additional items on the floor, we stepped over the salt circle, careful not to touch the lines, and placed the nymph in the center of the pentagram as Liz had instructed. As I straightened, the sight made me shudder—the way the body remained manne-quin-stiff, not melding against the floor like a living body would.

"Out of the circle. Here." Liz held out a lighter. "Charlie, light all the candles."

I removed the gloves, swiped the lighter, and tried to shake off the willies. Necromancy had the uncanny ability to spook the hell out of the most seasoned officers. And I was no exception.

When I finished lighting the candles, Liz took back the lighter, tucked her black bob behind one ear, and proceeded to light a bundle of belladonna. Once the dried leaves caught, she blew the flame out, letting the ends smoke and propping it in the ritual bowl.

"If something goes wrong, break the circle immediately."

Hank and I nodded.

"There's a video recorder in my bag. Hank, please set it up and turn it on. I'll ask her questions. Sometimes I'll get a vision in my head, too, so don't get discouraged if what she says doesn't make sense. Once we're done, we can piece together her death, and hopefully get a lead on her killer."

Hank stepped to an empty, built-in shelving unit and, after rolling the recorder around in his big hands and doing a fair bit of frowning, he found the on button and made sure everything was functioning properly. He set the camera on one of the shelves at the correct angle before returning to stand at my side.

Liz took the bowl, the smoking belladonna, and a sheet of papyrus paper into the circle, sitting just inside the north point. A curtain of confidence and serenity fell over her as she centered herself. A low hum began in her throat, which slowly turned into a deep, resonant chant.

The room grew cold. So cold that my breath floated into my line of sight.

Liz selected a stem of the smoking belladonna, and used the charcoal end to scratch out symbols on the paper, all the while chanting her dark, necromantic song. When done, she leaned forward, pried the corpse's mouth open, and matter-of-factly shoved the paper inside. Very much like a medical examiner who'd seen it all.

The mouth stayed open.

I was really starting to regret ditching the ITF Necromancy Seminar last spring. Maybe if I hadn't, my heart wouldn't be pounding like a Charbydon drum and my skin wouldn't be crawling like a nest of scattering spiders.

Liz took the belladonna bundle and blew the smoke all over the body. As it drifted up, it stayed within the invisible dome of the circle, which was a very good thing. Too much in the air would cause me and Hank to drop unconscious onto the hard cement floor. Liz, however, was immune thanks to her unique physiology—a few gifts passed down from an off-worlder somewhere deep in her family tree. It had made her future as a necromancer a no-brainer.

I chewed softly on the inside of my cheek as she grabbed a small dagger from its sheath and then sliced her palm without hesitation. Blood flowed bright and red into the bowl. After enough collected, she leaned forward and poured the blood into the corpse's mouth.

The paper inside crackled as though on fire.

Carefully Liz made an unbroken blood line from the corpse's mouth, down the neck, along the shoulder and arm to the palm. Then she sat back down and placed her own wounded palm into the corpse's, making an unbroken blood link—her living blood flowing into the body of the dead nymph.

The blood line began to glow. Very subtle, but there. The connection was made. Liz was feeding her life force through her unique blood, reanimating the dead.

Slowly, very slowly, the body softened against the floor, no longer stiff but still gray and sunken and . . . dead.

The nymph's jaw popped suddenly, and she gasped, drawing in a long, wheezing breath as air filled her collapsed lungs. Liz continued chanting, her eyes closed, and her posture confident.

Like a puppet on a string, Daya Machanna sat up straight. Several vertebrae cracked, each sickening pop echoing off the walls and making me wince.

Hank's arm rubbed against my shoulder. My fists closed at my sides as I resisted the urge to grab his hand out of pure horror. The corpse's eyes snapped open, unfocused and grayed over. A ring of blood painted her lips, a trickle forming at one corner.

"Tell us what is left," Liz said calmly, opening her eyes. "Tell us your last moments."

Daya's jaw worked, opening and closing with a horrible breaking sound. Her blood-wet lips smacked together like a fish. Sounds tried to come out, humming deeply through her throat, but not reaching fruition. After several disgusting seconds of smacking and moaning, she had voice. Scratchy, wheezing, but audible.

"Darknessssss . . . hurtsssss . . ."

"Your life was taken from you, Daya," Liz told her. "You must remember what happened. What do you see?"

After a false start and blood spurting out of her mouth like spittle, she murmured, *"Terrace. Touching the sky. The darkness. Red like fire . . . like fire."* Daya coughed up blood. Her hand moved slowly to push some of it back into her mouth, her expression appearing more sentient, more aware that she needed to keep this blood, that she *liked* this blood.

"Then what happened? What came next?"

"Light." Gasp. *"The ring and . . . the light . . . mine . . . it's mine . . . into the hand that . . ."* She froze. *"DAMN YOU!"* Hank and I jumped. Red spittle flew across the circle. *"I DON'T WANT TO DIE!"*

The blood line glowed brighter.

"EVEN FOR A CAUSE! FUCK YOUR STUPID CAUSE! I WANT MY LIFE BACK!" The nymph's body doubled over. Liz's face became strained. I stepped forward, but she put out a hand, signaling me: not yet.

A dirty haze began to grow in the back corner of the room.

"What cause?" Liz pressed. "What cause, Daya? Tell us and he will answer for your death."

A wet, guttural scream issued from the nymph's throat. Her hair covered her face. She remained doubled over, her voice a hostile whisper. *"For the star, he says . . . the star, the star, the stupid, fucking star."*

The cloud in the corner grew thicker and brighter. I leaned into Hank, sensing the presence of smut. "I don't think that's supposed to happen."

"Yeah. Me neither."

Daya began mumbling, her head still down, forehead against her knees, her hand still in Liz's and the line glowing a bright, angry red.

Liz's face paled.

Something was wrong. My fingernails dug into my palms. Shit. I realized we were witnessing a very rare event, one of the cons of raising the dead—the birth of what some might call a zombie. If the dead had arcane knowledge, if somehow that knowledge remained in their short term memory, they could suck the necromancer dry and raise themselves. And, in most cases, there was no way to tell beforehand if the dead had that kind of knowledge or not. "Daya must be a mage," I said. "She still has some of those memories. She knows how to reanimate herself. Liz!"

Hank and I ran to the circle, scattering the salt with our shoes. Nothing happened. "Break the link," I said. "We have to break the link." I grabbed Liz's hand, smudged the line, and pulled her away from the nymph's grip. Their hands wouldn't budge and the blood line kept repairing itself. *Damn it!*

I got behind Liz and wrapped both arms around

her slim waist, prepared to pull her entire body out of the circle, when the nymph lifted her head and glared at me. Bits of the bloodsoaked paper stuck to her lips and chin. Her dry tongue darted out and licked at the lifeblood. Daya's eyes burned red and scornful.

And then she smiled. She fucking smiled at me. A *corpse.*

"*I'm coming back,*" she hissed.

3

Liz went limp. I screamed at her to stay awake as Hank nudged me aside, attempting to pull Liz's hand away from the corpse's steel-like grip. The rest of Daya's body remained bent over so far, her head touched her knees. Hair covered her face from view, but it was the raspy, guttural chanting that made me worried. I scrambled out of the way on my hands and knees as Hank leaned over, his strong arms wrapping around Liz's tiny form.

The smut cloud in the corner drew closer. Daya was drawing on negative energy to aid her cause. The hairs on my arms stood. My heartbeat thudded loud and heavy in my eardrums as I pulled my 9mm from the holster and fired at the corpse, thinking it might be enough to distract her while Hank pulled. Each bullet slammed into her torso with a thunk.

Three shots and nothing happened.

"Goddammit!" Hank pulled at Liz so hard he had her off the floor, his feet slipping in the dust and salt. Daya was not letting go. The only way to stop her was to break the link.

I scanned the room, betting my ass the ITF seminar had never covered this. Not knowing what else to do, I grabbed the corpse from behind, hands under both armpits, and pulled. She reeked of rotting flesh from the debris pile and her own decay. My stomach shriveled into a hard, tiny knot. Her tangled, matted hair stuck to my mouth. I spit the hair away from my lips and then gritted my teeth, pulling hard. Daya's dead ass rose off the floor, but she refused to let go of Liz's hand.

One look at Hank's widening eyes, and I knew the smut cloud was right behind me, drawn ever closer by the chanting. *Shit!* I released my hold and pulled the Nitro-gun, doing the only thing I could think of and hoping I didn't injure Liz in the process. I pressed the nozzle against Daya's bicep and fired twice.

The newly designed nitro capsules sank into her flesh, the housing disintegrating as it went, releasing a shot of nitro into her body and instantly freezing the skin.

The nitro spread, traveling up and down her arm lightning fast. Just before it reached her wrist, I stepped down with all my might, severing the frozen limb at the joint. Severing the bloodline.

Hank and Liz fell back, the dead hand still gripping Liz's.

The corpse's red mouth slowly dropped open, milky eyes trained on me, as a desperate, enraged scream pushed out of her mouth along with bits of blood and paper. The sound raised goose bumps over much of my skin.

Despite the fact that my entire body was begging me to physically shake off the traces of her that clung to my skin, hair, and clothes, I stood my ground, breath coming out ragged, and kept my weapon trained.

Daya turned in despair, her gaze seeking the energy that would've helped reanimate her. She groaned and reached out with her good hand, her look becoming heartbreaking as she realized her chance at rebirth was slipping away. Blood tears swam over her eyes as they turned opaque, and her body hardened, collapsing to the floor.

For a long time no one moved or spoke.

"Get this fucking thing off of me," Liz muttered, weakly flinging at the severed hand latched to hers. Hank raised them both to a sitting position, his arms still wrapped tightly around her. Once they were up, he scooted out from behind her to pry the stiff fingers from Liz's open hand.

I holstered my weapon, hands shaking, and grabbed my phone to call paramedics, squinting at the numbers and the blurry display.

"What are you doing?" Liz asked.

"Calling the medics."

She shook her head, looking like I'd felt earlier after the hellhound jumped me. "No. No medics. Elliot will be here soon. I called him earlier . . ."

A crack of bone made me jump. Hank's skin went a shade paler and his throat worked with a hard swallow. He'd had to break the corpse's finger bones. "Sorry," he murmured, finally freeing the hand and tossing it toward the rest of Daya as though it was a hot potato.

"Who the hell is Elliot?"

"My new apprentice." Liz made a slow fist, opening and closing several times to aid in circulation. "And I'm fine, okay? You don't need to call the medics."

"You're not fine. That . . . *thing* . . . almost killed you and—" My sight went blurry again.

"Don't tell me you're gonna cry," Liz joked, but her ragged breathing and pale skin told me she was putting up a brave front.

"Ha ha." Yeah. So the shock of nearly raising a zombie and losing my friend made my eyes a bit glossy. I didn't feel like crying; more like decimating the damn wall with my bare hands. The thought manifested in a warm wave of humming energy through my veins. My fist closed around my phone. I heard a small plastic crack and eased up. Now was not the time for one of my accidental power surges.

"Hell no, I'm not going to cry." I shoved the phone into its holster on my hip. "Why? You still have that stupid bet with the cold cell nurse? Whoever sees Charlie cry first wins?"

She gave a small laugh. "It wasn't my idea. But, hey, odds *are* in my favor. Figure I have a better chance of witnessing the monumental event than she does. You could *try* to squeeze out a tear. Mama needs a new pair of Donna Karan featherweight frames in brushed copper."

I rolled my eyes. "You have enough eyewear to open your own LensCrafters."

The banging on the door made me jump. A voice shouted Liz's name.

Liz sighed. "That would be Elliot. Hank, would you let him in?"

Once Hank unbolted the door, Elliot rushed in with a gallon jug of orange juice in hand. He looked wide-eyed and rumpled like a kid who'd just gotten out of bed, but ready and willing to take on the world, despite the fact that he also seemed scared shitless.

Smart kid. I liked him already. It was the people who *weren't* scared of anything that worried me.

"Shoot," he breathed, surveying the scene. "I missed everything." He bent down to help Liz to her feet and I saw one corner on his shirt had been tucked into the edge of blue-striped boxers. "Man." His wide eyes were locked on the corpse. "What happened to her hand? And why is she all wrinkly?"

"How old are you?" I asked.

He straightened, his hand on Liz's elbow to keep her balanced, to a height just shy of six feet. "Eighteen."

"Don't you raise your eyebrow at me," Liz said at my pointed look. "The kid begged me for two *years* to apprentice. Kept telling him, when he was eighteen." She threw a frown his way. "Thought he would've given up, but as you can see luck was not on my side."

Elliot grinned, revealing white teeth and a cute, boyish charm that probably got him into loads of girl trouble. "That's really code for she loves me."

Liz snorted and swayed on her feet. Her fingernails dug into Elliot's arm. "Okay. Wow. Seeing stars here."

"Come on, let's get you out of this room and into some fresh air," Elliot said.

After they were gone, I stepped to the built-in shelving unit and snagged the video camera, leaning my hip against the counter and rewinding the tape, trying to concentrate on the task as the guilt formed in my gut. "I should've known she was a mage," I said.

"It's a risk every necromancer takes. No one can see auras on dead people, Charlie. Not even you. And it's not like we had time to find out who she was beforehand. If we'd done that, we wouldn't have gotten any information from her at all."

Hank wasn't looking at me. He was staring down at Daya's corpse. I knew how he felt. Powerless. Daya wouldn't have died in the first place if we'd been able to do our damn job and figured out who was kidnapping and killing Elysians. Seeing her wanting her life back, wanting what anyone would want . . . Yeah. Been there. Knew what that was like.

"At least we got the call instead of the ITF," I

muttered. Score one for the new federal agents.

Except for one "capture alive" case, the only other case we'd worked since taking on our new role two months ago had been a "kill or be killed" situation. Sounded harsh, but I—and obviously a lot of other people—believed that what we did was a necessary evil. There were things, even after thirteen years of integration, that posed too much of a threat to society, things that didn't require capture or a trial, things that often preferred to fight to the death, things better left to . . . well, us.

The tape stopped rewinding. I turned the power off to save the battery.

"So now we know where our missing Adonai went. This"—Hank stared down at Daya—"is the seventh body in less than two weeks. Dumped in the trash . . . discarded."

His profile went grim and utterly determined, lips drawn into an angry line, the muscle in his jaw flexing beneath day-old stubble. He dragged his fingers through his hair and then propped both hands on his hips. The air became charged with rage for these victims. He stood there like some dark avenging angel.

Like all sirens, Hank's beauty bordered on fantasy, and he oozed masculinity like a sweet, beguiling perfume, but the last few months of being cut off from his siren power, had done something to him, had made him colder, harder, unpredictable, and, if I wanted to be honest with myself, scarier.

★   ★   ★

My friend at Animal Control arrived as Hank and I were leaving the warehouse. After showing Tim the hellhound and making him swear on his entire collection of autographed Atlanta Braves baseball memorabilia to send the beast back to Charbydon, I joined Hank in the parking lot with Liz and Elliot.

It was drizzling.

I sensed it before I ducked under the lopsided door.

Interesting phenomenon, the rain. It had to pass through the darkness, and each drop carried with it some gray, some primeval Charbydon power. When a drop hit the ground, it dispersed the darkness in a tiny puff, like smoke. The thing was, there were so many drops going on at once that it created a fog over the ground. And as long as it rained, those little whiffs of "smoke" kept being hit back down, or trapped once more into the rain. The more rain, the more "Charbydon Fog" as we'd begun calling it.

I turned up the collar on my jacket and hunched my shoulders, not happy at the thought of darkness splatting on my head and shoulders, not happy that my body responded, got a little energized by the raw, arcane power around me. Part of me was Charbydon now. And there was nothing I could do about the near-constant tingle I got from the darkness overhead. Made me wonder how all the other local Charbydons were feeling. Probably pretty damn good.

Atlanta had become a paradise for the Charbydon

races; the forty-mile radius of darkness that spread from the grounds of Mott Technologies and outward made the city a dark replica of their home world. They'd tolerated the sunlight before, but this . . . this was like their own little hell on earth.

My feet stirred the thin layer of fog on the ground as I made my way across the derelict parking lot toward the dark silhouette of Liz's van and the small overhead light spilling out from the vehicle, leading me like a lighthouse beacon. I rolled my neck, trying to ease the anxious feeling the darkness spawned in me.

All I wanted was to get out of this and somewhere I could think straight without this constant reminder that I was different, genetically altered to bring darkness to Atlanta.

Yeah. City in crisis? That was me.

Despite the press conferences and the constant assurances that the darkness had been the work of one power hungry Charbydon noble, many here held the entire Charbydon race responsible. And that idea was constantly fanned by those who'd been against the integration of our worlds from the beginning.

The tension wasn't as bad as it had been in the first few weeks, but two months wasn't a long time; the tension was still here like a living current just below the surface. Recently the focus had turned to asking: how does a city survive without sunlight? And that question was being addressed by the world's best and brightest—Titus Mott.

Since most of our food sources came from other places anyway, we didn't have to worry about produce and fresh foods; those continued to be trucked in as usual. But we did have to worry about sunlight deficiencies, the effect on sleep cycles, and the constant drain on electricity. The government was urging citizens to take frequent trips outside the forty-mile radius, and depending on where you were, that could happen almost daily or only on the weekends. The point officials tried to make was that it was doable. We *could* handle this until a way to get rid of the darkness was found. Travel outside the city. Sunlamps. Vitamin D pills, mandatory lights-out for residential districts and businesses on off-hours to save on power . . . Whatever it took.

And I refused to believe that Atlanta had become the new hell. The light would come back. My genetically altered blood had brought the darkness into this world, and it would be my job to take it out. I just wasn't sure how to make that happen . . . yet.

Liz sat in the passenger seat of her van, Elliot hovering nearby. Her white throat bobbed as she chugged the OJ, drinking like a person starved. A third of the gallon was gone before she stopped and noticed me standing there. "What? I need vitamin C."

A deficiency all natural necromancers were born with and one that got worse after a ritual. She seemed none the worse for wear except for the big elephant lurking over us that no one spoke about—how much of her life force this had cost her.

"You get a picture of her death?" I asked, folding my arms in front of me and trying not to look like I was hugging myself against the drizzle.

Liz angled in the seat to face us, took one more long drink, then: "Just flashes that corresponded to the things she said. Her life force was sucked out of her body. I felt that part. The ring Daya mentioned could be an object of power, the murder weapon possibly, a container for her life force." Another long drink. "Didn't get a face. I did get a halo of red. Fiery red. Power. Aura. Can't say for sure."

"What about location?" Hank asked.

"A terrace, definitely. Downtown view. Didn't see the actual building, but the view was downtown. And I didn't get a sense if it was her apartment or just the place where she was killed. That's it. I wish it was more." Another drink. "Oh, and guys? She wasn't just a mage—she was a Magnus."

"Perfect," I muttered. "So our killer is going after high-level mages."

"If he wants to keep on killing, yes," Hank said thoughtfully. "Whoever is doing this must be after power. Think about it. The Adonai are the most powerful of all Elysian races, right? They're top of the food chain. But most all of them have left the city or gone back to Elysia because they prefer light to darkness. So the killer's pickings are slim."

I picked up his train of thought. "Right. And next up in the Elysian power chain are sirens and nymphs. Add an Elder or a Magnus-level crafter to their résumé and you've got the next best thing in power sources."

"Exactly. And he had to target a Magnus-level crafter because the Elders are virtually untouchable within the confines of the league."

"True," Liz said. "The Elder crafters are like hermits; they never leave the safety of the Mordecai House."

"Okay," I began, my thoughts turning. "Well, we have a workable theory. We've found our missing Adonai, and we've got one powerful nymph sucked dry. Let's assume, for now, that the others in the warehouse met the same end. We've got a killer preying on power, but only Elysian power. He's not targeting Charbydons, because if he was, he'd be going after the nobles next; they're just as powerful as the Elysian Adonai."

"Which tells us one of two things: either the guy's got something against Elysians of power, or Charbydon power is of no use to him." Hank snorted. "Or both."

"Well, he can't be feeding on all that power alone," Liz said. "A body, no matter where it's from, can't hold that much."

"So who is powerful enough to kill a bunch of Adonai?" Elliot asked, getting into the spirit of our brainstorming.

Good question.

I glanced around the group, and saw the answer on their faces. Charbydon noble. In Elysia the Adonai were the most powerful, but in Charbydon, the nobles had that distinction. The two races also happened to be enemies since before Man walked this Earth. And most still were despite the peace pact they'd agreed upon when the two worlds had been discovered thirteen years earlier.

"But anyone can rise to power, enough to rival an Adonai or a noble," I said. "It'd take centuries of study and training, but there could be others in this city capable of taking down an Adonai."

Hank's brow lifted in agreement. "And this might be the perfect setup for starting a war."

The Adonai had recently bowed to government pressure, agreeing to stay quiet about their missing members in the interest of public relations. But once they learned the missing had turned up dead, it was highly doubtful they'd remain quiet. They'd blame the Charbydons.

Elysians versus Charbydons. Heaven and hell at war. Again. Only this time Atlanta would be the battleground.

"Sure hope he's not a Charbydon," Liz broke the silence, saying what we were all thinking.

"So we find him," Hank said in a deep, determined tone. "And shut him down before he fucks up life as we know it."

"Elliot and I will take care of the bodies."

"And we'll talk to the chief," I said. "See if he can convince the ITF to keep this quiet for as long as they can."

Liz's expression turned grave. "I guess you'll be going to the Grove next."

I nodded. "We need to find that terrace."

"Well, good luck. He's going to want her body. Tell him I'll have it to him by tomorrow morning and not to storm my morgue."

Easy for you to say, I thought. Liz wasn't about to stand in front of the Druid King and tell him one of his Kinfolk had been murdered.

4

It was a two-and-a-half-mile drive north from the warehouse district to Tenth Street. Downtown passed by in a quick stream of lights, lights that never went out. The clock on the console read 4:38 P.M. But outside it didn't matter—it could've been predawn or late dusk during one of the darkest thunderstorms you ever saw.

I sighed, staring out the wet window. Some days, it was hard to tell the difference between night and day.

"You pick up a sunlamp yet?" Hank asked.

"Yeah, Rex got two yesterday. Last two at the hardware store. Supposed to be a new shipment coming in tomorrow. You get yours?"

Hank nodded and slowed the car, turning onto Charles Allen Drive. "I hear the schools are going to replace some of their overhead fluorescents with those new sun bulbs Titus is hawking."

"That's good. They're supposed to draw less electricity, too."

"Well, good thing it's winter and Mother Nature is in hibernation right now. Hopefully we can figure out how to bring the sun back before spring."

The time of year was one bright spot, but it had also been unseasonably warm ever since the darkness. Many things continued to grow, trees, shrubs, and grasses keeping their leaves and color. And that color was starting to fade . . .

Hank parked the car against the curb, turned off the engine, and then proceeded to check his weapons. I did the same. It was a ritual at this point, but sometimes double checking or triple checking could save your life. Plus, it gave us both a moment of quiet time in which to switch gears into work mode.

The drizzle had turned to a fine mist, which did nothing to ease the faint sensations coursing through my body as I stepped onto the sidewalk and walked alongside the black cast-iron fence that enclosed the nymphs' territory.

It was quiet here, the sounds of the city drifting into the background and the streetlights giving off a dim, hazy glow. We stopped in front of the gate.

Fourteen-foot-tall iron bars spanned eight feet across, attached to enormous stone anchors. Not that a gate would keep out enemies. It was a statement.

A line drawn in the sand. Cross it without permission or invitation and all bets were off—you might be risking life and limb.

About five years ago, the nymphs had purchased part of Piedmont Park. Their territory consisted of the eleven-acre Clara Meer Lake and all the land south and southeast—what used to be Oak Hill and the Meadows. Nearly a hundred acres of lake, meadows, and woodlands smack dab in the heart of the city—the perfect home for the only beings from Elysia born with the ability to shape-shift into animal form.

Nymphs had a passionate and devoted relationship with nature, and they, along with the sidhé fae from Elysia and the darkling fae from Charbydon, had been the foundation for much of Celtic mythology when they settled in parts of the British Isles and Europe during the Neolithic Age.

A dark figure appeared on the other side of the gate. Black T, black jeans, black boots. Male. Angular face. Wiry. Lethal.

We flashed our shiny new federal ID badges.

"Hold on." He drifted back into the mist and darkness, returning a few minutes later to open the gate. The loud whine of the iron hinges made the fine hairs on my body rise. "Follow the path straight ahead to the lake. Don't stray from the path."

A thin layer of fog hugged the ground, covering the path, but we didn't need to see it since the way was lined with tall wooden torches carved with Celtic-style symbols and animals.

I knew from coming here as a child that it was a straight shot to the lake, but now the old pavement had been pulled up and replaced with quarried stone. Asphalt was not favored within Kinfolk territory.

Still, it was a long-ass walk to the lake.

The nymph closed the gate behind us, and then blended into the misty darkness.

"Guess we're footing it." Hank shoved his hands into his leather jacket, and started down the path.

"It's *hoof*ing. We're *hoofing* it." But he was already a few feet ahead of me.

The air was cooler and wetter in the park, reminding me of the lake at Mott Technologies and the unconsecrated Civil War burial grounds—the place where I'd called the darkness. The scents immediately triggered images. Iron dagger. Blood. Mine. Mynogan's. My daughter's face. The grass and the night sky shifting to gray.

And just as quickly as they came, the memories were gone, gone without having altered the rhythmic brush and scrape of our boots against the stone, but it did leave my heart knocking fast against my rib cage. I blinked hard and regulated my breathing, focusing on the tall skyscrapers that edged one side of the park like a mountain range of steel and lights.

My gaze traveled down and left, where the land rose, giving me a glimpse through the trees of the enormous gray monoliths of the nymphs' stone circle, a Stonehenge in the heart of the city. But unlike that dead, crumbling circle, this one was alive with power. A slow, pulsating beat that resonated so low it wasn't heard but *felt*.

Going into the Grove was like stepping back in time. Any minute I expected a naked nymph to go skipping by with her signature dark hair flying out behind her, calling herself Titania, Queen of the Fairies.

But no such creature appeared.

"You ever meet him?" I asked Hank, feeling the need to break the quiet and inject some humanity into the space.

"The Druid?" He shrugged. "Once or twice."

"And?" Leadership of the Atlanta Kinfolk had changed hands last year just before my little brush with death. I'd yet to meet Pendaran, the new Druid King, in the flesh, but I'd heard stories. Hank, however, was a bit more submersed in the off-world community than I was, so I wasn't surprised that he'd met the guy before.

"Let's just put it this way: if you put him and Grigori Tennin in the ring and let them pound each other, no powers involved, I'm not sure who would win."

"That's comforting." Grigori Tennin was the jinn tribe boss here in Atlanta. Think mob boss on steroids and you get the general idea. The jinn were a warrior culture where both males and females were the color of smoke and gunmetal and built like linebackers with glowing violet eyes. Some held positions as bodyguards to the Charbydon nobles.

The nymphs' temple by Clara Meer had been built

with huge oak columns and timber beams, nearly every inch carved with symbols and scenes of battles, heroes, beasts, and idyllic landscapes. It was a sprawling complex, all one level and large enough to support the entire Kinfolk of Atlanta. The buildings meandered through the woods, incorporating the trees into the structure.

Through the columns and courtyards, I could see some of the city lights blinking off the smooth, dark surface of the lake. I'd been here before, and had been just as awed then as I was now. There was a distinct serenity to the place that existed alongside the majestic structures and the trees, which had grown to incredible sizes since the nymphs had taken over the park.

Some sort of enhancement on the nymphs' part, no doubt.

The entrance to the main temple was a two-story, open-air colonnade of oak poles supporting a peaked roof. It led straight out over the lake, where a dock had been built. In fact, there were several docks and rooms built over the water. Nymphs, like most Elysians, had an affinity for water. A fire burned in the very center of the temple and to the left and right were the two main altars of the Mother and Father, two gigantic wooden carvings with their bases acting as altars, which held fruits and vegetables, votive candles, handmade jewelry, and small, gem-encrusted weapons.

A figure appeared from one of the many halls that spread out from this centralized area.

She was slim, dark haired. The Titania I'd expected

a few moments ago, though this one was clothed in a light blue gossamer dress. Her hair had been left down, long and wavy and dark. She had a lovely oval face with large olive-green eyes, pert nose, and pale mouth. In other words, your typical nymph. "This way, please."

We followed her down several hallways before coming to a massive set of wooden doors. Once they opened, a sense of trepidation gripped me. Everything here made me feel small, like I was in the hall of the gods and humans were trivial in the scheme of the universe.

"This is the Druid's private hall," she said. "Come."

The end of the hall was open to the lake and once we stepped outside again, I realized that it stretched over the water and we were far from the main temple in a secluded spot.

The nymph stopped and waved us toward the long walkway extending out over the lake. Poles supported the dock, rising through the platform about seven feet high and topped with burning torches. We stopped at the end, nothing before us but the mirror-like surface of the lake and the outline of downtown's skyline hovering over the park.

"So what now?" I scanned the area, resting my right hand on the hilt of my hip weapon, and casting a glance back at the nymph.

"Federal agents!" Hank called out. "We have news about one of your Kinfolk!" He lowered his voice. "There. That should do it."

A faint splash made us turn. The water rippled.

A figure floated forward from a shadowed area of the lake, arms hugging a small blow-up raft. The torchlight bounced off the edge of the plastic, but the being relaxing in the water remained hidden. The left hand and forearm, however, caught some of the light. Strong. Tan. Covered in inky Celtic-style symbols.

Nymphs had a hierarchy just like most races from both worlds, but their leaders were chosen not by birthright, or council, or vote. Druid was a title earned, taken only by those capable of leadership and judgment. The Druid of the Kinfolk was king and high priest simply because he was the most powerful, biggest, badass nymph in the city.

"You may go, Grainne," a rumbling voice said.

The nymph lurking behind us bowed her head and moved swiftly down the dock and back through the private temple. I cocked one hip, hand still resting on my weapon and quite frankly a little nervous. Hank and I pulled our badges at the same time.

"What news do you speak of?" Pendaran, the Druid King, asked from the shadows once Grainne was gone.

Why did I have a feeling this was going to be bad? I drew in a deep breath, really not liking this whole pins and needles thing. "I'm sorry to inform you that a female nymph by the name of Daya Machanna was found dead a short time ago."

His hands slid back over the curve of the raft, disappearing beneath the lake. I stood a little straighter. My grip on the weapon and badge tightened.

"Great," Hank muttered, releasing an unpleasant sigh. "Should've brought a fucking umbrella."

As the last word came out of his mouth, a plume of water shot up from the lake and, with it, a beast straight out of myth and lore.

"Jesus!" I scrambled back several steps, heart in my throat, wanting desperately to aim my weapon just for some measure of protection. It was halfway up when Hank's hand pressed it back down.

"No, Charlie."

Wings the size of a jetliner shot out. The trees around the lake rustled in the sudden wind. A black chest puffed up, and a long, corded neck stretched to the sky. Huge jaws opened and let out a piercing, angry shriek that shook the dock, the temple, every bone in my body, and probably much of downtown Atlanta.

Droplets of water began to fall. Shit. There was only time to turn my shoulder before the deluge fell upon us and flattened my hair to my face.

As the roar died down, I whirled on Hank, threads of water streaming down my face, pulse thumping with adrenaline and disbelief. "Dragon?! He's a goddamn *dragon*!"

5

Another roar rent the air and shook the boards at my feet, making my legs wobble. I wiped the water from my eyes and then tilted my head back.

Well, no wonder he was the Druid King.

Torchlight glistened against black reptilian skin. The underside of his wings shimmered with blues and greens, like an abalone shell. My mouth had gone completely dry despite much of my top half being drenched with lake water. At least the treated suede of my jacket kept the wetness from sinking all the way through. I wanted to take another step back, but held my ground, really hoping this wasn't going to be a case of "kill the messenger."

Hank, on the other hand, seemed unfazed by the show. He swiped a hand down his face, readjusted his shirt, and then dragged his fingers through his wet hair, looking part bored and part annoyed. Business as usual.

The dragon lifted its head to the sky once more and let out a sad moan that reminded me of a whale call, before sinking down into the lake.

Once he was gone, I wiped my forehead with the sleeve of my jacket and then rested my hand back on the hilt of my weapon. "You could've warned me."

Hank shrugged, his gaze on the lake. "Where's the fun in that?"

Ten seconds later, Pendaran slapped his big hands on the edge of the dock, pulled his hulking body out of the water, straightened, and strode past us buck-ass naked. "Follow me."

What was left of my breath whooshed from my lungs as I turned slowly on my heel, watching him go, his tanned, wet skin practically glowing from the reflection of the torchlights. The entire left side of his body was covered in swirling black tattoos. The ends of his black hair stuck to his neck. Water dripped down his back.

"Close your mouth, Charlie." Hank's unamused tone barely registered over my sudden state of distraction as he brushed passed me and followed the Druid King down the dock and into his private sanctuary.

I'd seen a lot of things in my time, but this . . . A dragon *and* a naked god all in the span of five minutes. File this one under: unforgettable. I shook off the daze and hurried after them, falling in step with

Hank and eventually entering what appeared to be private quarters.

The far wall opened to the lake via accordion doors. Sheer white curtains billowed in the faint breeze. Pendaran grabbed a towel from the back of a white couch, turned to us, and began drying his hair. His pecs bulged with the movement, leading my gaze to the black ink curling around the muscle. The lines and spirals and animal heads all interconnected from the top of his left foot, up his leg, hip, torso, shoulder, down his arm, up his neck, over his left ear, and finally disappearing into the hairline at his temple.

Looking at him was like standing in some natural history museum, staring at a larger-than-life exhibit on Celtic gods and warriors. His face was both beautiful and brutal, a visage that spoke of strength beyond measure, intensity I could not begin to fathom, and a lethalness that could fell a rhino.

And, obviously, like most Elysians, the guy didn't have a problem with modesty. But then, why would he?

His cool, measured gaze fixed on Hank. "Long way from home, aren't you, siren?"

Hank went noticeably stiff. "Could say the same for you . . . *Druid.*"

"Ah, but no one is missing *me.*"

I frowned, obviously not getting the innuendo. My mouth opened as I turned to my partner, but he cut me off before I could speak, his unreadable gaze still on the Druid. "Maybe you should go put some clothes on. My partner can get pretty sensitive to guy parts."

I did a double take, sucking in an astonished draft of air. Heat stung my cheeks. My fingernails dug into my palms.

Count. Count to three and breathe.

I swallowed down the hot, dry lump in my throat and gave a careless shrug to Pendaran. "Seen one, you've seen them all," I said. "Makes no difference to me how you want to conduct this interview."

A glimmer passed through the Druid's irises, revealing the same brilliant abalone color that had shimmered along the underside of his wings. He kept his thoughts to himself, tossed the towel on the glass coffee table, and then disappeared into another room. At least *one* guy around here knew when to keep his mouth shut.

The second he was gone, I whirled on Hank, trying to keep my voice to a low, infuriated whisper instead of the scream that pushed at my throat. "What the hell was that?! I have a job to do, same as you—" I stopped and closed my eyes. Showing any kind of weakness, especially feminine weakness, would completely diminish me in the eyes of the Druid, and Hank *knew* that.

I opened my eyes to see my partner's lips pressed tightly together, and something like regret passed so quickly through his dark expression that I wondered if I had imagined it. A hard, unreadable mask slid over his features. The only sign that he felt anything at all was the repeated flex of his jaw.

I couldn't read his face, but I sure as hell could read his aura, and the tense energy coming off of him was unmistakable. But whatever was going on with him, or had prompted him to act like a first-rate asshole, was no excuse to say what he had.

"If you *ever* put me down or diminish my abilities again when we're working," I hissed, "I swear to God I'll lay you flat on the floor right then and there, or die trying."

His only response was a curt nod.

I gave him another astounded look, shaking my head, because as bad as Hank got sometimes, he'd never done anything like this before. Ever.

I didn't have time to speculate more because Pendaran returned, barefoot, but dressed in black drawstring pants and a white T-shirt. And yeah, I wasn't going to lie—him being dressed was going to make this a hell of a lot easier.

He went behind the granite countertop in the kitchen area, opened the fridge, and grabbed a beer, sticking the end in his mouth, biting off the cap, and then spitting the cap into the trash can. After a long drink, he set it on the counter, one hand wrapped around the bottom of the bottle and the other flat on the countertop.

"I see it hasn't taken you long to acclimate," Hank noted.

He pierced us with a hard stare, black eyebrows

furrowing together, and ignored Hank's comment. "Daya is dead." Another drink. "How?"

"That's what we're trying to find out, Pendaran," I said. "When was the last time you saw her?"

"Most call me *sire*." A flash of arrogance tilted the corners of his mouth. "Last time I saw Daya was yesterday morning in the temple."

I kept quiet, letting Hank take the next round. "She work in the city?"

"At the Fernbank Museum, yes. Daya restores art." I saw it the moment he realized he'd spoken in the present tense, as though she was still alive. His jaw clenched and he took another swig. "Daya just received her Magnus level in crafting. She was three hundred and eighty-nine years old, never mated, has one sibling, and no children. Anything else?"

"Was she in a relationship?" Hank asked. "Have any friends outside of the Kinfolk that she hung out with?"

Pendaran shook his head, straightened, and leaned back against the counter behind him. "No."

Completely absolute. His response was like saying grass is green, so sure he was in his knowledge. But then, he wasn't the Druid King for nothing. Nymphs in general didn't exactly make a big attempt to foster any ties outside of the Kinfolk, and they rarely mated outside of their own race. Their pack-like mentality meant that whatever happened within their circle, Pendaran would know about, even something as mundane as who liked who.

Fine. Moving along. "And the sibling?"

"A brother. Orin. He moved here from Elysia last year."

"Did she keep an apartment in the city?" Hank asked. The only thing we had to go on was the apartment from Daya's final memories. I wanted to cross my fingers that he'd say yes.

Pendaran let out a snort. After another swig, he tossed the empty bottle in the trash can. "Kinfolk do not live outside of the Grove unless they're loners. She lived here like everyone else." His eyes narrowed on us for a hard, calculating second. "How did she die?"

My thoughts went back to the dragon screaming at the sky. The last thing I wanted was to have him go all medieval and scaly again. "We're not sure yet."

"Murder?"

"It's too early to say, but we'd like to take a look at her apartment."

One corner of his mouth dipped down. He knew I was bullshitting him. But he let it slide and pushed away from the counter and marched to the door. "Come."

We followed him from the private apartment to the main hall surrounding a large open-air courtyard with trees, gardens, and a fountain in the center where several nymphs were gathered. Heads bowed in respect as he strode by and stepped onto a raised area topped with a vine-covered pergola and fire basins on each side. Within the pergola there were chaise lounges and chairs but he remained standing, a commanding presence over the courtyard.

All eyes fixed on their king. No one spoke. The sound of the fountain became extremely loud, and the faint sounds of traffic invaded the courtyard.

Hank and I waited.

"Daya is dead," he announced without preamble.

Horrified gasps lifted in unison. Immediately a male nymph shot to his feet, his face draining of color. "No."

I focused on him, taking in his body language and aura. "Did you know her well?"

The nymph flicked a questioning glance at his king, waiting for the slight nod of approval before answering. "She . . . was my sister." His voice broke, but his chin lifted a notch. "My twin."

My entire brow rose, and my gaze went to Pendaran. Orin's sister was dead and *this* is how he tells the poor guy? Guess leadership and empathy didn't go hand in hand here in nymph territory.

"Orin," I began, allowing the sympathy I felt into my tone. I'd had a twin. I knew what it was like to lose your other half. I'd never get over Connor's death. Never. And I knew that, after the shock wore off, Orin was in for a lifetime of grieving where Daya was concerned.

Hank took over when I failed to expand on the sentence I'd started. "Did your sister have a second place outside of the Grove or maybe a friend she stayed with sometimes?"

Orin's glassy gaze went from me to the ground where he stared intently at the grass cradling his bare feet. A tear slid down and hung off his chin before he sniffed and swiped it with the back of his hand. "No." His answer was barely audible.

"Was she seeing anyone?" Hank asked.

Orin's eyes closed slowly. His face went a shade paler. The air in the courtyard flared from grief to fear, and panic. Underlying it all, I detected a faint wisp of aura gathering. It pricked the hairs on the back of my neck. I glanced around and my gaze found Pendaran. His nostrils flared slightly. His arms were crossed over his chest, legs braced apart. "Answer the question," he said.

What seemed like a simple command came across as a power-laced demand that echoed soft and deadly through the courtyard.

Orin dropped to his knees, head bowed so low his forehead touched the grass, trembling like a leaf in a windstorm. "Yes, Sire, she was involved with someone. I'm sorry. She asked me to keep her secret, and I did. I'm so sorry."

The guy's anxiety didn't sit well with me. I'd learned a lot about the nymphs and their culture through the years, but being ruled through fear was not one of them. I shifted my attention back to the Druid. "Is having friends outside the Kinfolk a crime?"

"No." His gaze leveled at me. "Cavorting outside of the Grove is not a crime. However"—he turned back to Orin—"lying *is*. If Orin has lied or withheld knowledge of a broken law, I have no other choice but to punish him. He knows this. It has been our way since before you humans started drawing on cave walls with sticks."

I returned the arrogant smirk that accompanied Pendaran's words with one of my own, only making it *way* more obvious than he had. Subtle, I was not.

"If Orin is too afraid to speak," Hank said, "then it's quite possible more of your Kinfolk will die . . . because whoever killed her is not going to stop."

Well, that was just great. He just told the Druid King and everyone here that Daya had been murdered. What the hell was he doing?

My heart pounded, low and deep, so deep it felt as though the entire grove pulsated. No. It wasn't me. Was it the henge? The Druid King? Feeding off one another? I didn't know. Hell, I didn't care.

Pendaran's stance remained the same, but somehow he seemed to have stilled even more, going absolutely quiet; the only movement was the shimmering wave within his irises.

Please don't shift. Please don't shift.

I didn't realize my hand rested on my weapon until my fingers flexed around the hilt. Pendaran finally pulled his ancient gaze off Hank and turned to the courtyard as a whole. "Orin will do service." His eyes found mine. "That is the best I can offer."

Great. Wonderful. The pulse in the courtyard dimmed, but not entirely. I turned my attention to the prone nymph, wanting to get this over with so we could get the hell out of there. "Orin?"

"Forgive me, my lord," he mumbled before looking up at us, his Adam's apple bobbing with a hard swallow. "Daya was sharing an apartment . . . in Underground . . . with someone." He paused. "A jinn."

The shockwave that swept over the courtyard left everything in its wake motionless and dead quiet, so silent that the pulse was gone and the distant sounds of the city trickled back into the bereft space. A jinn. Jesus, no wonder Orin was terrified! A nymph going outside of her own kind wasn't unheard of, but going over to a completely different world, a Charbydon? A *jinn?* Yeah. This was bad.

"Where, Orin? Where did they meet?" Hank's soothing tone invaded the space like it was the most natural thing in the world, creating a faint but calming shift in the volatile atmosphere.

"They kept an apartment somewhere near Underground. That's all I know." He sniffed. "She was a good person. If the jinn found out . . . Dear Dagda, they killed her, didn't they?"

"I don't think this has anything to do with the jinn," I said. And I prayed to God it didn't. I pulled out a card with my contact info and handed it to Orin. "In case you remember anything else."

"I expect her body to be returned to us immediately," the Druid said.

I flinched inside, thinking about the hand I'd severed, though it was no worse than the rest of her. "We'll see that you have it by morning."

"You have one week," Pendaran announced. "One week to find Daya's killer."

I blinked. "Excuse me?"

"Seven days or we seek retribution from the jinn."

A disbelieving half snort, half laugh sprang from my mouth. "Seriously? Because I didn't peg you for an idiot."

The nymphs fled the courtyard in a blur of gossamer and bare feet, disappearing into the darkness and mist, and leaving me with the sudden realization I'd said that thought out loud.

Shit.

The eerie abalone glow passed through the Druid's eyes again. I swallowed as he unfolded his arms and stepped off the dais, striding slowly forward. Toward me. My stomach dropped to the bottom of my gut. Hank cleared his throat, and I cast a quick glance to my right to see his hands clamped behind his back, and his attention on the ground in front of him, a small grin tugging the corner of his mouth.

Well, apparently my partner wasn't too worried I was about to be dragon flambé.

Pendaran stopped in front of me, forcing me to crane my neck. The guy was tall. "You seem to understand very little about the Kinfolk, Detective. And even less about etiquette . . . off-world *or* human."

My lips twisted into a cynical smile, and I bit off the smart-ass reply on the edge of my tongue because, quite frankly, I couldn't argue with that assessment. I gave a quick, indifferent shrug. "That may be so. But you're well aware how tense the city is right now. If you go storming into Underground, an Elysian pointing the finger at the entire jinn tribe, that's it . . . it's game over. For all of us."

He crossed his large arms over his chest, jaw set and freakish eyes turning hard like cold, polished stone. "One week."

The finality in that imperious tone made my teeth clench hard as I tried to maintain control and prevent another outburst. But, damn, how I wanted to wipe that overbearing superiority off his face. "Then we expect complete and total cooperation. That means no contact with the jinn from you or any of your Kinfolk while we investigate. *None.*"

"Done."

After Pendaran's ultimatum, Orin led us to Daya's apartment in the Grove, where we found squat. Not a single shred of evidence. With every step back toward the gate, my mood plummeted. I was still riled by Hank's comment earlier, and the Druid's unyielding manner. Then my cell rang. The number on the display only made things worse. *"What?"*

"Oh, good. Listen, Charlie, I need you to pick up some toothpaste, a can of diced tomatoes, and garlic—not the powder stuff, the whole head. Oh, and can you get a few pounds of meat for Brim?"

"Rex. I am working right now."

"So? What do you think I've been doing all day?

Who do you think does the laundry and the cleaning and the cooking? Revenants can't just point a finger and say 'presto' and everything is clean." A loud sigh blew through the phone speaker. "What time will you be home?"

I closed my eyes. *Deep breath, Charlie.* "I have no clue."

"Well, just an idea. So I can have dinner ready . . ."

I rolled my eyes and tossed up an annoyed hand, plucking a time out of thin air. "Six forty-seven."

"Oh, funny. Ha, ha. Just make sure you stop by the store."

"Fine."

Hank was already clearing his throat before I could get my phone back on my hip. As if Rex didn't add enough disorder to my life, my partner seemed to take great pleasure in razzing me about living with a Revenant who thought he was the love child of Laurence Olivier and Julia Child, a Revenant currently occupying the body of my ex-husband. And, to top it all off, I still hadn't found the right way to tell my daughter that Daddy wasn't really Daddy anymore.

Hank's mouth opened, one syllable came out, and I said, "*Don't* talk to me."

Rex's call hadn't detracted from my absolute fury at Hank. In fact, it just added fuel to the fire. We went a few more strides and then I changed my mind. Screw this, I wanted an explanation. "You mind telling me what the hell that was back there? And for the record, I've seen *plenty* of naked men in my time, okay, and I can do my goddamn job just fine."

He shoved his hands inside his jacket pockets and let out a tired breath. The drizzle was slowly turning to a soft rain. Fog swirled at our feet. "You wouldn't understand."

A sharp laugh burst from my throat. "Oh, right. What is it?" My stomach was already sinking before the words rolled out of my mouth, but I couldn't stop myself. "Feeling a little emasculated now that your powers are gone, so you have to make me powerless too?"

He stopped and grabbed my shoulders, scowling down at me and barely containing the firestorm behind that tight, furious mask. Heat leaked from his being, swamping me into a startled silence. "Do I *look* emasculated to you?"

I swallowed and looked. Six-four. Two hundred pounds. Radiating a thick haze of wrath that would've cowed anyone else. For the most part, I was fairly immune to the natural lure of sirens. Yeah, they drew my eye, but they drew *everyone's* eye. I'd gotten used to my partner's I-was-made-to-seduce-you-and-please-you appearance . . . unless he made me take another hard look. Like now.

"Yeah," he practically growled. "Didn't think so."

The cool night air washed over me as he stepped back and then stormed down the path. I released the breath I hadn't realized I'd been holding, surprised by how fast my heart was beating, and how quickly I could turn the tables and become a first-rate asshole just like he'd been earlier.

Way to go, Charlie.

I hunched my shoulders against the rain, folding my arms in front of me and quickening my pace.

The sirens living on our world were required by law to wear a voice-mod, a torc-like device, around their necks for everyday public interactions, since the power that often leaked into their voices was far too entrancing and distracting for the rest of us to function properly, and it was difficult for most sirens to control it, or to remember to control it, on their own.

It made me feel like shit to know Hank's greatest power, the very thing that made him who he was, had been caged inside of him. Hank was my lion— big, intensely beautiful, exuding an easy confidence and mellow demeanor that could only come from being near the top of the food chain. Except now he was shackled by the voice-mod and way more ill-tempered than usual.

The same dark figure that had guarded the gate before stepped out of the shadows at my approach, the tip of a cigarette glowing bright and orange, then slowly disappearing. He pushed open one side of the gate for me to pass. "Your friend already left," he said with an amused tone. I stopped, spinning on my heel as he gave a low chuckle. "Wouldn't want to be you right now . . . or him, for that matter." The gate shut, and the dark-clad nymph disappeared.

No car. Hank had deserted me.

Fucking hell.

Not that I didn't deserve it.

After standing there, hands on hips, for a good ten seconds, I released my damp hair to re-knot the long length tighter and more orderly than before—no thanks to Pendaran's dragon-out-of-water routine. I then began the hike down Tenth toward West Peachtree to catch the MARTA.

The constant darkness, the constant tingle, the constant volatile mood coating the entire city had become exhausting. I needed another lesson with my warlock teacher, Aaron. And no meditating. I needed to fight, to release some of the built-up power in my body, or I was going to completely lose it.

That, or lose my life like those other poor souls who'd been lab rats for Mynogan.

They'd come before me, but had been unable to handle the DNA of two different races injected into their bodies at once. It tore them apart from the inside out. So far, my body was handling it due to ancient bloodlines of both Elysia and Charbydon DNA already in my family tree. Mynogan's gene manipulation had been successful, had brought me back to life, and had created a being capable of summoning primal darkness with a gift of blood. I'd done what I'd been created to do, but one day, just like all the others, the two opposing powers inside of me would take their toll. It was just a matter of time.

Relax. Center yourself like Aaron taught you.

The walk helped ease some tension from my shoulders, despite the rain. I loved my city, the people, the traffic, the noise. Yes, there was a freakish, supernatural mass of gray overhead that was making life pretty difficult, but beneath it, Atlanta still thrived in a sea of colorful lights that burned day and night. The darkness would never change the fact that this was my home, and I'd love it regardless.

I decided to get off at the Five Points Station and head into Underground before returning to the station. Hank was probably sitting in his office chair with a mug of coffee and his face planted in front of his computer screen, thinking I'd show up at the station any minute.

Whatever. I didn't care.

Okay. I did care. And it pissed me off.

I replayed the scene over in my mind, trying to figure out why he'd even say such things about me. And then a thought occurred. He'd thrown me off the scent. Distraction Techniques 101. He'd known the right words to say to get me to stop the questions that had been gathering about him and Pendaran. How it seemed like the Druid knew Hank, or knew *of* him. That had to be it, because Hank being a jerk just for the hell of it didn't sit well with me. The stuck voice-mod couldn't have changed him *that* much.

Maybe his reputation in Elysia preceded him. Charbydons came to Atlanta for obvious reasons— their world was a hot, crowded, hellish place, and it was slowly dying. Elysians, on the other hand, lived in a heavenly paradise. Didn't seem like a place anyone would want to leave, unless you were running from something, or wanted an escape, or your own territory, or were simply following leaders or loved ones.

I never really questioned why Hank had left Elysia. Maybe I ought to start.

6

The minute I crossed the plaza where Mercy Street, Helios Alley, and Solomon Street converged, a huge sense of relief washed over me. Out of the drizzle, thank God. At least here in Underground, the darkness only rolled in via the fog when it rained heavily.

Underground was the largest off-world sector in Atlanta, with three main streets that divided the population. Elysians had claimed much of Helios Alley and a few areas Topside, just as the Charbydons had filled Solomon Street to the brim—the jinn, the Mafia of Underground, going so far as to carve out their own territory in the bedrock beneath the streets of Underground.

I headed for Mercy Street, the dividing line, the buffer between the two off-world factions. Mercy Street provided a nice balance of human, Elysian, and

Charbydon businesses run and patronized by those who cared more about making money (or spending it) than old wars and endless grudges. Restaurants, shops, nightclubs, bars, spell shops, apothecaries—everything existed down here, and if your need was the slightest bit peculiar, supernatural, or off-world, you'd find it on Mercy Street.

As I strolled over the brick pavers that made up the carless street, my thoughts turned to my sister, Bryn. I hadn't seen her in two days. And she hadn't bothered to return my calls, though I knew from Aaron that she was okay. It was time for a visit.

I stepped around a sales cart on wheels that held an assortment of rough-cut off-world stones, and shook my head to the vendor, a goblin. For a second, my heart contracted. Auggie, one of my informants, had been a goblin—a bony, yellow-eyed, blunt-toothed, cash-loving guy with a penchant for spellmongering and gossip. I missed him calling my name from the shadows. In the end, he'd tried to protect me from three jinn warriors pushing *ash* on the street. He'd died for the effort, and I'd never forget him.

I went to open the door to Hodgepodge, my sister's variety shop, expecting the tinkling of bells and to hear Gizmo's squawk as he patrolled the comings and goings from his perch atop the bookcase by the door. I was slowly warming to the little gray gargoyle even though I held my ground on the fact that a spell and a gargoyle were no substitute for a *real* security system.

The door didn't open.

Frowning, I pulled again, realizing it wasn't stuck, but double-locked. What the hell? I tried my key, but it didn't work. I cupped my hands and peered inside, then stepped back and noticed the small sign in the window.

"Closed until further notice?"

"Been closed three days now," the goblin's sandpaper voice called from his cart. Three days? My stomach dropped out, and he must have seen my alarm. "Oh, she's fine." He glanced up at the apartment windows over the shop. "See her shadow passing every once in a while."

I stepped away from the door and approached the cart. "How often does she leave the apartment?"

He wiped the stone dust from his long, skeletal fingers, leaving shimmering gray streaks on his dark apron. "More information will cost you."

The anticipation of money set his dull yellow irises aglow, and I smiled in spite of myself as I reached into the back pocket of my jeans with a brief second of hesitation. I was about to buy information on my own sister.

Bryn hadn't been the same since waking up in the hospital after her forced *ash* overdose, and I was getting increasingly concerned.

"Here's a ten."

He licked his cracked lips and reached out, carefully pinching the corner of the bill. Once he had it, it went to his large nose, where he drew in a breath so deep that it sucked the ten against his nostrils. "It's old." He folded the bill and shoved it into his pocket.

"The new ones are for serious info. All I want to know is if she comes and goes and how often."

"The Hodgepodge woman comes out once a day to take pizza delivery or delivery from Abracas." He motioned to the popular restaurant and pub across the street. "No more, no less."

Damn it. "Thanks." I paused and turned back to the goblin. "What's your name?"

His eyes went narrow, assessing, deciding if there was worth, a monetary future, in telling me. "Otto."

I nodded and then walked past the shop's main entrance, past the display window and a span of brick wall to the door that led to Bryn's apartment over the shop. I had a key, but I didn't use it. Juvenile, maybe, but I wanted my sister to get up, to show some fire, some interest in life. I pressed her buzzer and held it for a count of five. I was about to press it again when her voice came over the intercom.

"What?"

"It's Charlie; let me up."

"Use your key."

"Just buzz me in."

Silence. And then, "I'm busy . . ."

"What, taking the day off? If you don't let me—"

The door buzzed. I growled, jerked it open, and then jogged up the steps. As I reached the small landing, she opened the door.

"Damn it, Bryn . . ." She was pale. Hair in unwashed tangles. Wearing boxers and an old Georgia Tech T-shirt. Dark smudges cradled her eyes. She looked . . . muted. Grayed out. My chest hurt.

A spark of annoyance lit her eyes, but she stepped aside, letting me into the gloomy apartment, the only light coming from the spastic blue glow of the television set.

Immediately I began opening the blinds for some street light as she plopped on the sofa and watched me with indifference before grabbing the remote and flicking through stations. Once the blinds were open, I grabbed a towel from the bathroom, dried my hair, washed my neck the best I could, and then replaced my shirt—since the collar was damp and reeked of hellhound breath—with one of Bryn's clean, dry ones.

Her fridge held nothing but condiments and spoiled leftovers and a few bottled waters. I grabbed one, noticing the trash was overflowing with takeout boxes. Gizmo had curled his cat-sized body into an open pizza box on the floor and was snoring away.

I went into the living area and handed her the water.

Bryn opened the cap and took an angry drink, before leaning back into the cushions and drawing her feet up under her. I couldn't stand it. I wanted to shake her, to yell because the change in her was so extreme and I had no idea how to help her. I wanted my sister back, the vibrant, auburn-haired, freckle-nosed earth mage who walked around in flowing skirts and tinkling ankle bracelets.

"Please make an appointment to see someone."

She laughed. "Who would you like me to see, Charlie? I don't think there's a shrink who deals with forced drug addiction."

"So?" I sat on the arm of the love seat. "The point is to talk. You used to love to talk. All the time. About anything."

A snort came from her pale lips, and she scratched her dirty scalp. "Yeah well, that was before I became hooked on *ash*."

"Will you stop it?" I jumped to my feet. "Just stop it. You're on *ash* because if you don't keep taking it in regulated doses, you'll drop into a coma and die. Just like Amanda and everyone else who survived using the drug in the first place." I paused, trying to sound calm. "A few of them have formed a support group. Why don't you go? Talk. There's a meeting tomorrow. I can take you." I sat back down on the arm of the loveseat. "Doctor Mott is going to figure out a cure, but letting yourself shrivel away like this"—I slid from the arm into the seat—"it's not you."

My head fell back and I shut my eyelids tightly against the rising tears, repeating that last sentence over again in my head.

I hated this.

The frustration made me throw up my hands and give her a defeated look. "I'm sorry. I'm sorry this happened to you. I'm sorry that it was because of me and Emma—"

"Oh my God. Enough with the guilt routine, Charlie. If you say you're sorry one more time, I might actually vomit." She got up and walked behind the couch, her hands braced on the back. "I knew the risks. I love Emma. I love you. It was *my* choice to go to that bath house that night, my choice to fight, and I'd do it all over again. Just . . . let me deal with this on my own, okay?" Her eyes drifted closed for a moment. Her shoulders lifted and fell tiredly. "I'm tired. Can't you just come back later or something?"

I stared at the wall for a long second. "Sure." I shook my head, feeling exhausted myself. "I'll bring some groceries in the morning. Before I take you to the meeting."

"Whatever you want." She shuffled into her dark bedroom and closed the door.

I left Bryn's apartment, keeping my head down and my gaze averted as I passed the goblin, letting my steps carry me toward the plaza on autopilot, too overwhelmed with worry and frustration to notice much around me, just knowing I had to fix things.

The despondent aura surrounding her was eating away at her light, her spirit, at everything that had made her Bryn. My sister. The earth mage. The independent business owner. The much-loved aunt.

I didn't go back into the office. Instead, I got my Tahoe from the back lot of the station and drove down I-85 to the outskirts of the city, to the grounds of Mott Tech.

The guards at the gatehouse waved me in now that I had a full-clearance badge.

The complex was Titus Mott's baby—the underground research facility that allowed him to work on all of his off-world and human inventions. After he and his team had discovered the alternate dimensions of Elysia and Charbydon, he'd acquired the massive funding needed to create his scientific empire. But I didn't plan on seeing Titus. Not tonight. I'd been coming here on and off since I'd brought darkness to the city, not even sure why I chose this place of all places to come.

The cool night air made me pull my jacket closer around me as I got out of my vehicle and headed across the parking lot, grateful that the inside lining was dry and warm. My footsteps shuffled over the flagstone pathway that led through the manicured grounds to the romantic Victorian-style pavilion perched on the edge of a calm lake.

The breeze was heavy down here, like always. I rounded the grassy edge of the water, coming to the idyllic bridge that spanned the small creek that fed the lake and led to the pavilion. A bench had been placed near the bridge and I sat in my usual spot, on the right side, facing the circular meadow where I'd first called the darkness. Where I'd fed on Mynogan's blood, the blood of an Abaddon elder, killing him.

The center of it all.

I didn't know why I kept coming here, envisioning the past, replaying that night over and over in my head, and taking out Grigori Tennin's card from my inside jacket pocket. *I like what you've done with the place*, it said.

The small card had come with the flowers he'd sent via florist to the hospital just as I was leaving. The flowers were long gone, but the card I'd kept. It was wrinkled and bent now, but it reminded me of my place in this game. Grigori had had a hand in bringing darkness to the city; I just didn't know the part he played. His card reminded me to be vigilant, to always watch my back because he wasn't through with me. And I sure as hell wasn't through with him.

I stared at the meadow, my gaze not really focusing on any one thing as I flipped the card slowly through my fingers, thinking about the victims in the warehouse. All Elysian. There'd be no one who would benefit more from a war than the jinn tribal boss. The entire tribe would be eager to fight and get back to their warlike ways. And while the jinn and other Charbydons would be battling the rest of us, Grigori would, no doubt, benefit from the distraction. Law enforcement would be completely overwhelmed, leaving Grigori to expand his many illegal endeavors.

That was worst case scenario. And Pendaran would play right into Grigori's hands, starting a battle with the jinn over Daya.

A green flash snaked through the darkness above, lighting the meadow for a moment in a soft green glow.

I tapped the edge of the card against my cheek,

opening my mind, letting in all the possibilities, all the paths this case might take, and where they might have originated. My thoughts turned to Llyran, the Adonai serial killer, a Level Ten felon who had escaped Titus Mott's lab around the time I'd brought darkness to the city. Llyran had disappeared. No word. No sightings. He could be back in Elysia by now or right in my backyard, laying low.

Or—goose bumps sprouted along my arms—he could be killing his own kind. I hugged myself against the sudden chill. An Adonai killing his own kind? His own race? Seemed shocking, but why not? Humans had been killing humans since the dawn of time. The question was: did he have a motive? Or was he simply killing for the love of it, for a reason only understandable to the serial killer mind?

Pendaran's ultimatum of one week—one week to find Daya's killer before he confronted the jinn—grated on every last nerve. One week to find a serial killer powerful enough to kill not one, but seven of the most powerful beings in the city.

Hardheaded dragon bastard.

It was either lock the Druid King up and prevent him from waging war—which was *guaranteed* to cause *serious* injury to all parties involved—or find the killer. Or, I thought, biting the inside of my cheek, find something or some way to convince Dragon Boy to back off and let us do our job.

I slipped the card into my pocket and slouched further down the bench, bracing my boots in the grass.

A chuckle stuck in my throat as the realization of why I kept coming here, given the circumstances, dawned on me. This was the only place where I could just sit and not be bothered or worry about anyone else. This was the only place where I felt like I belonged, because, really, who else would belong at such a place except me?

This was the site where the warring genes in my body converged, melded, came together in one cohesive, perfect moment. Did I know that for certain? No. But it had *felt* like it. Thinking back on it, I was pretty certain Mynogan's ritual was what gave me that sense of oneness. I'd heard the drumbeats in my mind and body. I'd been thrown back to a time so ancient it felt like the beginning of time itself, and in that moment I was whole, not fractured like I'd felt before or after.

So, yeah, I thought, looking up at the darkness moving slowly overhead, this was my place, my . . . creation.

I was an hour and a half late for dinner, but I came home decompressed and back on track. And after I ate and showered, I planned to log on to the ITF database and pull Llyran's file. My footsteps echoed on the porch steps of my Candler Park bungalow, my stomach taking note of the warm spices leaking from the open window. The tap, tap, tap of claws on wood sounded beyond the door as I reached for the knob, preparing myself for yet another odd night at the Madigan home.

Brimstone greeted me from a distance, in the center of the hallway. His hairless gray body was still as his red eyes assessed me. His ears were up this time, instead of pinned back against his thick skull like usual, but his throat rumbled with uncertainty as he held his ground.

He shouldn't be in the house. But then again, if Rex hadn't routinely gone against my rules and let him inside to begin with, his scent wouldn't have been on me earlier when the pregnant hellhound attacked, and I'd be just another body in the debris pile.

I sighed, ignoring the beast and removing my jacket, which desperately needed a trip to the cleaners after today, placing it, along with my weapons harness, on the rack inside the closet door. Brim sniffed the air behind me, no doubt scenting the female despite my dragon bath at the Grove and changing my shirt at Bryn's. The smell was in my hair, on my jeans, probably on my boots.

"Brim! Come!" Will's voice called from the kitchen, followed by a quick whistle.

The beast's massive head turned for a quick second, and I could see his indecision. I pointed down the hall and took a step forward. "Go. Go on."

He didn't move. Another slow growl issued from his throat and he leaned back, bracing himself, his giant front paws spreading as they slid forward on the hardwood floor. The dark gray skin blended into the dimness of the hall, making his red eyes stand out.

"Move it," I ordered, deeper, snapping my fingers and continuing forward. He turned tail and loped his tiger-sized body toward the light of the kitchen. "I'm going to turn him into a doggie popsicle if he doesn't cut it out," I said loudly, approaching the kitchen.

Rex stood at the sink, wiping his hand on a dish towel. He wore my ex-husband's old State T-shirt. Loose jeans hung low on his hips, and his feet were bare. A defeated sense of loneliness and sorrow spread across my chest and squeezed.

It was hell sometimes—those first glances after a long day or after getting up in the morning. Seeing the body of my ex-husband walking around, his expressions, his smiles, the way his eyes crinkled at the corners, the deep southern drawl in his voice when he spoke . . .

There were moments, brief flashes, where I'd forget that a Revenant, a spirit entity, was in control, and I'd just see Will Garrity there—tall, athletic, and always with the smile that could melt snow.

Those moments hurt the most, and I tried not to let it show—how much I missed the real Will, and how much his decision to barter his body and soul to Rex, whatever the reason, had hurt. No matter what, no matter if we found a way to bring Will back, I knew now that it would never work, me and him. This final betrayal had broken the thin link between us.

"Hey, Charlie." Rex turned around, bracing both hands on the sink ledge behind him.

"Brim is supposed to be in the kennel." I snagged a water from the fridge and cracked it open, giving myself a moment to regroup before I turned back around. "That was the deal. I pay six hundred dollars for a reinforced mini version of Alcatraz, and you keep him in the kennel. Do you remember that at all?"

Brim had parked himself at Rex's side, his jaw resting easily on the granite countertop as Rex patted his bald head. Was I the only one who got grossed out by the slobber trail on the countertops?

"Well, that was just in the beginning, Charlie. It's cruel and unusual punishment to keep him back there all by himself when we're in here. He wants to be with us. We're his pack."

I leaned against the edge of the kitchen table, the rim of the water bottle paused at my lips. "His pack? That damn thing growls at me again, and he's on the next transport back to Charbydon."

Rex shot me a nasty look and let Brimstone out the back door. "He's not a *thing*. He's a hellhound. He has a name."

I rolled my eyes as he popped the lid to a canister of antibacterial wipes, snagged a sheet, and wiped up the slobber. He chucked it in the trash and then placed one hand on the countertop and one on his hip, frowning expectantly like Will used to do when I'd done something wrong.

"What?" I asked. He huffed in response, waiting for me to magically understand his problem. So I took a wild guess. "Um . . . sorry I'm late?"

An impressive snort came out of his mouth and his eyes rolled. "You're always late—that's why I always start dinner an hour *after* you say you're going to be home." Rex's eyes grew round and exasperated as I still had no clue. "The garlic? The tomatoes? I asked you to get a few things . . ." He marched to the oven to check on dinner. The smell that erupted was wonderful. Lasagna or baked ziti, I guessed. "You know, I work all day long in this house and the least you can do is remember when I call."

I heard the footsteps on the stairs and bit back my reply, waiting for Emma to come around the corner and into the kitchen. The mini bowling ball in her hands was a surprise. "Oh, hey, Mom."

I stopped her as she passed, pushing her long, wavy bangs back to kiss her forehead. "What's with the bowling ball?"

"It's Brim's. He's torn up the other dog balls we got and—"

"Whoa, whoa, whoa." I stepped back. "You've been playing ball with the hellhound?"

I turned a murderous gaze on Rex as he pulled on oven mitts. "Well, they get along great," he muttered in defense, knowing I was about to go nuclear.

"Mom . . ." Emma started in a tone that said she knew it, too, but I didn't let her finish.

"No, Emma. I don't care how *great* you get along.

He's a *hellhound*. They are trained to kill. They're born with the instinct. I was attacked by one today—"

"You were? Did you hurt it?"

"What? No, I had her sent back to Charbydon."

"Mom! That place is dying and—"

"How do you know their moon is dying?"

"Don't you ever watch TV? And it's not *really* a moon. Everyone just calls it that; it's more like a white dwarf star. Or that's the theory anyway. And now we have to do some stupid science report at school . . . Everyone has to come up with a hypothesis on how to . . ." She shook her head, realizing she was getting off track. "Sooner or later, someone's going to have to go in there and rescue all those poor animals anyway. You should've brought her home. We could've set up another kennel next to Brim."

I blinked, wondering if my daughter had lost her mind. Or maybe whatever the hell made Rex such a kook was catching. "This *isn't* a hellhound sanctuary, Em. You can't trust them. You turn your back on Brim for one second or look at him the wrong way, and he'll remember he's not Fluffy the Dog, but a killer, and I don't want you to be in his path when he does." I fired a hard look at Rex. "It *stays* in the kennel."

"Mom!"

I didn't answer, instead letting my angry footsteps carry me up the stairs. I refused to argue about it. The beast needed to go back to Charbydon. I was too pissed off to stay in the same room with Rex right now. He continually went behind my back and broke all my rules. What the hell was that going to teach my kid?

I removed my boots and jeans and then pulled on a pair of Lycra yoga pants and sneakers, stopping to look at myself in the full-length mirror to put my hair into a ponytail. Though my appetite had been insane the last two months, I'd still lost weight since the darkness ritual. Shadows lurked beneath my eyes, and I knew it wasn't just weight I was losing. My body was worn out, tired of fighting on the inside. Having two opposing powers inside of me was taking its toll, exhausting me.

I gathered the long, wavy hair that fell to the small of my back. It was darker than Emma's auburn-brown locks, but it fit my personality, and I liked the way the copper and mahogany tones mixed with the brown and matched my eyes. My lips pursed, taking the natural fullness out of them as I examined my reflection. My skin was paler. Hips a little thinner. But otherwise, I looked like the same old Charlie. Only exhausted.

A long exhale breezed through my lips, as my reflection dimmed.

What the—

My image completely disappeared along with the mirror, until I was looking at the wall beyond. I blinked hard, seeing strange linked patterns behind my eyelids. Damn. I must be more tired than I thought. I shook my head, knowing it wasn't possible to see *through* the mirror; it was just my mind playing tricks. When I chanced a look again, the mirror was there and my reflection scowled back at me.

The back door slammed, echoing through the house. I stepped to the right, leaning toward the window to see Rex's shadowy form in the yard below, leading Brimstone to the kennel. Emma's door down the hall slammed, too, this one rattling the walls and making me flinch. Terrific. Now everyone was pissed.

I rubbed my hands down my face, hearing Rex return from the kennel. I thought about going downstairs to reinforce my argument. But it was pointless. I was right, he was wrong. And we'd do nothing but go around in circles. I was the parent. Emma might hate me for it, but my job was to protect her.

Trying to get through to Rex might be pointless, but my kid was another matter.

My need to have her understand propelled me down the hallway to her room. I knocked softly, wondering what had happened to the old days when she thought I could do no wrong and sought me out for the smallest comfort. She didn't answer. I pushed the door open to find her lying on her stomach across her bed, using the large, brown, stuffed bunny Will had given to her last Easter as a pillow.

I sat on the bed. "Emma, you have to think rationally about this."

She rolled onto her side, raising up on one elbow and looking down the length of her thin body to where I sat. Her finger twined around the bunny's ear. "Mom, you don't know Brim. You can't say that unless you spend some time with him." She sat up, cross-legged, pulling the bunny into her lap. "You're the only one of us who hasn't and that's why he doesn't trust you yet."

"Can you hear what you're saying? That thing has to trust *me*? You're talking about a *hellhound*, Emma. Trust doesn't exist with them."

Her full lips went thin and her chin lifted, the stubborn expression reminding me of Bryn from earlier. She cocked her head as her eyes took on a challenging copper gleam. "Well how about trusting *me*, then? I'll be twelve next month. I'm not stupid. I wouldn't put myself in danger."

"Not on purpose, no."

Her mouth dipped. "He's calm around me. I've been reading about hellhounds and they're loyal to their packs, so loyal they'd die for them, and—"

"But we're *not* his pack, kiddo."

"We *are*," she stressed, growing upset that she couldn't break through to me. "He's probably never even had a pack before. Daddy said they probably got him as a puppy and just kept him chained up all alone."

"That's even more reason to be wary of him. If he's never been around a pack before, he doesn't even know the rules, how to act, the boundaries . . . He's a dangerous animal and should go back to Charbydon."

I tried to soften the reality of what I was saying with my tone, but she just shook her head, tears shining in her round eyes, her cheeks flushing. "He wouldn't know how to survive in the wild! Can't you just try? For once, just try something someone else's way? How about my way? I'm part of this family, too. I should have a say like everyone else."

"Emma."

"We'll vote on it."

"No, we won't vote on it. This is my house, and my money that's paying for Brim's food, which he isn't even eating by the way."

"He doesn't like dry dog food. Daddy even told you, but you don't even listen to him."

"Yeah, well, *Daddy* doesn't know everything. Maybe you should start listening to your mom once in a while. I know some things too."

She stood, clutching her stuffed animal and letting out a hurtful laugh. "No, you don't! You don't know when to trust your own daughter! Like, when were you going to tell me about Daddy, huh? I know something's wrong with him. He's not himself . . . and you know it!"

With that she flung the bunny at me and ran out of the room, slamming the door and leaving me sitting on her bed in stunned silence.

I hugged the bunny and glanced around at the room, the room of a very small girl—lilac walls, white furniture, floral quilt—but she wasn't so little anymore. She wanted some independence, to make her own choices, and even to make this room her own by hiding what she called the "childish" wall color with posters.

My fingers curled around the bunny, digging into the soft fur.

Here I was spouting off good parenting, and I was still lying to my own kid.

All this time . . . there just never seemed to be a right time to tell her the truth about her dad. And then Thanksgiving had come, Christmas was approaching . . . There were so many reasons *not* to pull her world out from under her. And they were all excuses. In the end, there were no good reasons for delaying the truth.

And if her father had had an ounce of patience and a fucking spine and hadn't sold his soul to a Revenant in the first place, we wouldn't even be in this situation.

I wanted to choke him, to squeeze him into a little ball, to scream and cry and let it all out. But he'd taken that away from me, too. One final betrayal to mark the end of our relationship. My throat thickened and I blinked hard, blocking the tears from spilling over, and glanced down. What I saw made me throw the bunny into the air and leap off the bed with a shout.

My back hit Emma's desk, almost knocking over her chair. The *bunny* landed on the bed and bounced, falling onto the carpet. What was once a stuffed animal was now a solid, fur-covered ball. Just like I'd imagined.

A hard shudder ran through me as my brain floundered to make sense of what I'd done. Same as the Abaddon chick I'd turned to ice for kidnapping my child. Hadn't meant to, it just happened. My Charbydon powers went far beyond creating nightmares in the mind of my opponent, to being able to actually manifest those nightmares.

I hadn't meant to. I lifted my trembling hands and stared down at my palms. What if I'd been holding my kid? My stomach knotted, and a cold sweat broke out on my skin. *Dear God.*

I raced from the room, down the steps, and headed outside, aiming for the track that ran around the soccer and baseball fields across the street.

Run. Just run. Don't think, just run.

7

Forty-five minutes later, I returned to the house sweaty and spent.

Muffled voices came from the living room. A quick glance as I passed showed Emma and Rex practicing her lines for the school play. There were four lines, but Rex was determined to make Emma the best Cobweb in *A Midsummer Night's Dream* that Hope Ridge School for Girls had ever seen. I left them alone, swiped a piece of garlic bread from the baking sheet atop the stove, shoved it in my mouth, jogged up the steps, and then went through the motions of stripping down while devouring the bread.

As I stepped into the shower, my stomach twisted irritably, wanting more food. From the looks of the kitchen, Rex and Emma had already eaten, but there were probably plenty of leftovers in the oven, since

Rex had been making extra lately to accommodate my ravenous appetite.

I turned up the heat, letting the hot water work its magic on my muscles and stress level, and leaving myself wide open for the guilt to worm its way in. I gave Rex a lot of hell, more than he deserved. It was just hard to pull my emotions out of the equation when everything he did and said was being done by Will's body.

I scrubbed my face with the washcloth, deciding to hurry because the heat was starting to turn my hungry stomach into a nauseated one.

I washed and conditioned my hair, rinsing and then quickly shaving my legs, spurred on by the thought of dinner. When the voice spoke beyond the curtain, it scared the shit out of me and made me jump.

"I hear you found a few bodies today, Charlie. Any leads. Any . . . *theories?*"

I stilled, the razor on my calf, the ball of my foot resting against the corner of the tub and hot water beating down on my back. *Jesus Christ.* I knew that voice.

A serial killer was in my bathroom.

Dear God. Emma! A jolt of adrenaline-fueled fear shot through my body. Pulse, blood pressure, muscles . . . Everything readied as I prepared to run for my kid and get her into her bedroom, the only room in the house with additional wards, ones made in blood—that of myself, Magnus mage, Aaron, my earth mage sister, Bryn, and two of the powerhouse

Elders at the League of Mages. The amount of blood it had taken made it the equivalent of a Fort Knox panic room. It was the first thing I'd done after getting home from the hospital two months ago.

"Relax, Detective. This is just between you and me. And for the record," Llyran said in a conversational tone steeped in haughtiness, "killing children holds little to no value. It's a question of payoff. The effort expended is more than the return. And killing that Revenant in your living room is a waste of my time. He'll just flit away and find someone else's life to ruin. Might want to work on your aura, though."

Relief flowed through my veins, so strong I nearly dropped to my knees, not caring that he had read my strong emotions; they'd been too swift for me to block anyway.

Calm down, Charlie. Focus on Em.

One of my most frequent lessons with Aaron had been learning how to forge a link with my child, a way to connect with her emotions, to feel her presence and state of mind. And after her kidnapping by Mynogan and his thugs, there was no way I ever wanted to feel that helpless again, to *not* know if she was okay. I wasn't as calm or as focused as I should be, but this was one thing I'd semi-perfected. I closed my eyes and summoned the link, that joyful, unbreakable bond with my child. It wasn't as strong as usual, but when the emotions poured in—humor, determination, nervousness—I knew she was still practicing her lines downstairs. Neither she nor Rex had any idea Llyran was here, in my bathroom.

Envisioning a slamming door, I severed the link, releasing a controlled breath and returning my attention back to Llyran. He was telling the truth about not harming my family. Was he also telling the truth about the rest of his statement, that he only killed for reason and motive? He knew about the warehouse murders. Was he the killer, an accomplice, or was he just taking credit?

"What do you want, Llyran?"

I was completely bare. No weapons. No way out. My grip on the razor tightened. His outline moved beyond the white shower curtain, pacing from one end of the floor to the other.

Llyran ignored the question as though I hadn't uttered a word. "I suppose you're wondering what I'm doing here in your bathroom."

"That, and how the hell you got into my house." My mind scrambled for a plan, any plan, but I didn't have much to work with, unless stabbing him with the blunt edge of a Wonder Smooth Vibrating Razor was a plan.

"Oh, that part was easy, Charlie. I can mask myself . . . make myself into an undetectable wisp of air. You can't see me, smell me, sense me . . . until it's too late." His outline stopped at the sink, his height, slumping somewhat, giving me the impression that he was leaning back on the countertop.

"So you broke into my house just to tell me that?"

I reached for the bar of soap with my other hand. If he came for me, it was going right into his eye. Might give me a chance to make it to the bedroom and the night table drawer where I kept an extra set of weapons.

Small clinks and movement echoed above the shower spray. The faint scent of my perfume reached my nose, and I knew the creepy bastard was going through my things, examining my toiletries, picking them up, setting them back down. "Nice," he muttered. "You see, the thing is, Charlie, you and I are a lot alike. Unique. Determined. Powerful. We both kill for reasons we believe in."

"I'm not a murdering sonofabitch."

"Necessary evils," he said simply. Another glass bottle clinked onto the marble countertop. "I came to make you an offer, Detective . . ."

My fists tightened around my so-called weapons. The soap shot from my grip and hit the shower wall with a loud bang. Shit.

Okay, calm down.

He was here. The shock was over. My weapons were stupid, and I had to concentrate. I closed my eyes and began to focus, to seek out the Elysian part of me that I was just learning how to use.

"Let me inside of your mind, and I'll stop playing badly with others."

I swiped away water from my face, my focus momentarily interrupted. "What?"

"It's simple. I can't promise it won't hurt, but you

give me access to that pretty little head of yours, and if I find what I need, I'll leave the city."

His words made me cringe. Llyran was not getting anywhere near my brain. "Stop killing? Just like that?"

The shower had turned lukewarm, but I'd started to shake as though it was freezing, taking a small step back so the spray hit below my thighs, totally baffled that Llyran had invaded my home to make me a deal. A freaking deal. I almost laughed. History proved I sucked at making deals.

I rubbed a hand down my face and tried to focus again while keeping him talking. "Why don't you just take what you want?"

"It's just easier this way."

Focus, Charlie. Focus on the light. You know it's there. It's there in your blood, in every part of you, just waiting for you to say the word.

The small drops of water that bounced off my skin began to hover. I no longer felt chilled because the warm vibration of power began to hum through me, growing, strengthening, becoming attuned to my thoughts and my wishes. If I could keep him here long enough to gather my strength, I had a shot at ending his playtime for good.

"Well?" he asked.

"You know what I think, Llyran? I think you're a schizophrenic sicko with a massive ego problem. I'm surprised you even got into my house with a head as big as yours."

I let my hands fall to my sides, still gripping the

razor, and closed my eyes, completely immersed in the thrumming line of power that ran through me, like a live wire just waiting for a signal.

Visualize your thoughts. Give direction to your power. And . . . now!

The bathroom door slammed shut as the spray of the shower amplified, directing outward and blowing out the shower curtain. It flew straight for Llyran's shadowy form, covering him. He cursed and flailed, struggling to remove it and slipping on the wet floor as the water swirled around the room.

His surprise would only last a second. I stepped onto the ledge of the shower and then dove at his curtain-covered body. We both went down to the wet floor, sliding to the wall. Elbows, legs, and shower curtain flailed. I absorbed the pain of random jabs and punches, trying my damnedest to wrap him tighter in the curtain. He growled, shoving me off. I spun across the tile and slammed into the wall.

Llyran tore the curtain away and sat up, furious. And there I was, on the floor, naked, the razor gone, both hands flat on the tile, sitting on my hip, facing him, my breath coming hard and fast. My eyes bored into his as I tried to gather my power again.

His red hair was in disarray, but the sight of him awed me just the same, despite the fact that I knew what he was, what he was capable of doing to another living being. He was a mass murderer masquerading in the gorgeous body of a Viking angel, his heart as black as iron.

He blinked, obviously shocked by the sight of me. But his aura practically glowed; he could unleash his own gifts any time he wanted.

"You are remarkable, Charlie."

I sat back and angled slightly, so he only had a side view as his gaze flicked to my breasts. Asshole.

"Why are you killing Elysians?"

"Because it is necessary to my cause."

I cocked my head. Daya had mentioned a cause. "And that would be?" My hip was starting to hurt. I'd have to move soon.

He pushed to his feet, his black tunic and jeans soaked, shaking the water from his red hair. His blue eyes were so light they appeared almost white. He smiled again as I copied his movement, pushing to my feet and standing—hell if I was going to sit on the floor while he stood over me.

Being bare like this, having to endure his blatant ogling, brought the dark power of Charbydon coursing through my veins. So easy and swift to rise, this dark energy of mine.

A ruddy eyebrow cocked and he grinned. "I have to admit I didn't think I'd be seeing this much of you . . . so soon, anyway."

"What is it with you Adonai? Not every female is going to fall down at your feet."

A perverse smile tugged his generous mouth. "They all bend in the end, Charlie. And we hardly have to lift a finger. That's why, when someone like you comes along, it makes the chase . . . thrilling."

A shiver shot up my spine, but I kept from flinching. "Is that what this is, a chase? Let me tell you something, you fucking scumbag, not a single thing about you appeals to me on any level. I hunt and destroy degenerates like you on a regular basis, and I love my job."

A deep, disappointed sigh whispered through his lips. "I know."

Let's see how he liked a little Charbydon justice.

I drew the power from every part of my body, sucking it into a tight ball in the center of my chest and then sending the dark energy surging down my arms. I clapped my hands together, forcing the power into a single bolt aimed straight toward Llyran's chest. Rex taught me that one.

The Adonai tensed, his eyes narrowing. Just before it hit him, his big hand whipped out and snagged the bolt. He flicked his wrist, slinging the energy backward like a whip. The bolt wrapped around me, and then Llyran gave a big yank.

I screamed, slamming into him, blinking in shock at how he'd grabbed my power. *Grabbed it.* I still had so much to learn. He tried to seize my wrists, but I slapped and kicked, able to evade a firm hold because of my slippery skin.

For whatever reason, he wasn't using his powers, and I wasn't complaining.

His curses filled the air as he lost balance and slipped, landing on his ass, his back against the tub. Finally he got hold of both my wrists, my stomach pressed flat against his chest and kept there by the fact that he held my arms wide, straight out on either side of me.

And then it started. The push at my mind. I cried out, shuddering at the searing violation as his will shoved its way into my head, too powerful for me to stop.

I never had a chance.

Completely immobile, I was caught like some terror-frozen animal as pieces and images of my memories flashed before me—the most stunning, unique pain I'd ever felt. The images slowed on Mynogan, on the night I'd killed him, sucked the blood from his body, and then he went deeper into those images I'd had during that horrible moment, as though I'd been inside Mynogan, inside the monster.

Please stop. Please stop.

The desire to fold in on myself—to curl into a ball and rock, to scream and deny what was happening—tore through me. My chest was on fire with the scream, with the denial until, finally, it physically burst from me, making Llyran pull back and out of my mind.

My nose was inches from his face and I was panting hard, disoriented and weak.

"Well, well, well . . . The more I learn about you, Charlie, the more I'm intrigued. You have great power in you. Great . . . potential. I believe my plans have just changed. In the end, we'll see exactly what you're made of." His eyes took on a fanatical glow.

"In the meantime, I'm going to cut a path across your dark city until the streets bleed red. My next one will be just for you."

"No," I said, "there won't be a next one, you bastard."

I reared back, gritted my teeth, and slammed my forehead into his face, hoping I was strong enough to cause some damage. Pain shot through my skull, but he released my wrists, cursing. He shoved me so hard that I slipped off him and slid back across the tile on my bare bottom as his eyes rolled into the back of his head.

Llyran's hand covered his nose. Then he closed his eyes and began chanting. The air changed, making the hairs on my body stand, even the wet ones.

The bathroom window smashed in, the stained glass panes shattering. I covered my head as glass rained down . . . and then my attention was snagged by the wind. The lamppost outside the window illuminated the darkness whirling overhead.

A small tendril of darkness snaked downward, enchanted by Llyran's summoning.

My eyes widened in total disbelief at the realization of what I was seeing, what it meant.

Llyran could manipulate the darkness. Fuck.

I panicked; any power I had was completely lost. The only thing left was physical strength and that was waning fast. The darkness snaked its way through the window. I leaned over, grabbing Llyran's hand.

Just as I went to sink my teeth into his skin, the bathroom door crashed open. Instinct sent my arms over my head in a protective gesture. Beneath my shielding arm, a streak of charcoal arced over my body—a red-eyed, snarling mass that went straight for Llyran's throat.

Brimstone.

Pieces of wood rained down on me, the lighter ones sticking to my wet skin as the hellhound's front claws slammed into its target, sinking deeply into Llyran's chest, piercing his shirt. The beast's sharp fangs clamped the right corner of Llyran's neck.

A high-pitched, scalding scream tore from Llyran's throat, his concentration completely broken. The darkness recoiled from the window as his irises turned from black to a burning, furious blue that latched onto me for a second before the darkness surged back through the window in a storm of wind and gray, enveloped him, and yanked him up and out in a blur.

Gone.

My entire body trembled. I swallowed, slowly reaching up and pulling down a towel from the rack on the wall behind me while Brimstone rooted around the spot where Llyran had just been, confused that his prey had suddenly vanished. The towel flopped down and I held it in front of me, the end under my chin, as Brim stepped over, sniffed my ankle and calf, and then my head where he licked my forehead with his fat, slobbery tongue.

"Mom!" Emma ducked through the massive hole in the door, kneeling down next to me, her arms going around my shoulders. "Oh my God. Are you okay? What happened?"

My hand came up, closed on her arm, and squeezed. Her skin was so warm. My teeth clattered. "Mmm hmm. I'm fine."

Rex slammed into the door next, not making it through the hole, but knocking the top hinge plate off the doorframe. His momentum sent him skidding across the bathroom floor and straight into the tub, flipping ass over end into the basin. I hadn't realized he'd been holding my gun until the shot rang out and hit the ceiling, sending bits of plaster raining down.

Rex's shout of surprise mingled with Emma's scream as I grabbed her, shoving her down and shielding her with the top half of my body.

Small bits of ceiling pinged the tile. The shower still ran. I released my hold on Em. "Jesus!"

I could just see the top of his wet head as it bobbed up. My gun was next as he slapped it on the rim of the tub to push himself to a sitting position. Thankfully the gun wasn't pointed at us. I set Emma aside and lurched for the weapon, snatching it out of his hand and flicking the safety. "What the hell possessed you to get my gun?"

He blinked, sputtering out the water as it fell on him, completely dazed and pale from his somersault into the tub and the gun firing. "We heard you scream. Got Brim . . . Emma said . . . I thought . . ."

A few seconds of stunned silence went by.

"Mom. It's okay."

I took the towel from her, having dropped it when I went for my gun, and sat back down.

Our gazes went from one to another. Rex to Emma. Emma to Me. Me to Rex. And then Emma burst out laughing. It was no time for joking around, but the last few minutes, the shock of it all . . . I started laughing, too, and it didn't make an ounce of sense.

Emma pointed at Rex. "You should've seen your face when you poked your head out of the tub." Her giggles were contagious, but Rex seemed to be the only one who didn't find it funny. He was still in shock.

His pale face finally grew pink. "You're not funny," he said, turning the water off. "Neither one of you. I don't know what I was thinking." He pulled himself over the ledge until he sat on the edge of the tub. "Moving in here with you crazy women." He ran a hand down his face and then slicked his hair back off his forehead, shaking his head in disbelief. "I need a drink." He stood and then shuffled passed us, mumbling about gun-toting women and talking hellhounds.

Once our giggles subsided, Emma slipped her arm over Brimstone's lowered neck and hugged him. "Good boy," she whispered, her face turning into his bald, corded neck. "He knew something was wrong. You did good, Brim, real good. Exactly like I told you."

Brim panted, tongue lagging, totally at ease and, unless I was imagining things, leaning slightly into her. It was the way she spoke to him, the tone of her voice, that wound its way into my clearing mind and set off the five-alarm bell.

"Em . . ." I squeezed my eyes closed against the sudden sting of tears and swallowed hard before looking at her again. "Please don't tell me you can communicate with him."

Her head remained against Brim's neck, but she turned her round, solemn eyes in my direction, looking so young and innocent, so brave and yet so scared. "I was going to tell you . . ." Her small voice held a faint edge of defense. "But I knew you'd get all freaked out and—"

"Here's your robe. You want to tell us what happened, Charlie?" Rex interrupted from the doorway, holding out the cotton robe I hardly ever used.

Brimstone jogged through the doorway and into the bedroom as Emma helped me to my feet. I snatched the robe, turned away from Rex, dropped the towel, and covered myself. Then I made careful steps over the floor, avoiding the sharp splinters of wood and glass. Once on the bedroom carpet, I stopped to brush off the pieces that stuck to the soles of my feet.

"Just got paid an unexpected visit by someone I met once. It's nothing."

"I wouldn't call breaking into a warded house and destroying the bathroom 'nothing.' Unless you want us to believe you two were just showing off powers. You know, like"—he used a deep Arnold

Schwarzenegger voice—" 'my powers are bigger than yours' . . ."

I shot Rex a glower. "That's exactly what it was."

He rolled his eyes and whistled to Brim. "Come on, mutt. Let's get that drink. A Valium would be nice . . ."

"There's some in the medicine cabinet!" I yelled after him, making sure the sarcasm was clear. "Take as much as you want!"

Once the door was closed, I removed the robe, some of the wood pieces falling off my back and shoulder. My skin had dried, so Emma helped brush the remaining debris off my back. I had the shakes, bad, and couldn't control it.

"What have I said for the past two months?" When she didn't respond, I answered for her. "At the first sign or gut instinct of trouble, you run for your room and lock the door."

She gave a guilty shrug and asked, "So what happened?"

I slumped on the edge of the mattress in defeat, still achy in my head and not ever wanting to revisit the horror of having someone violate my mind. "I don't know, Em. He appeared in the bathroom—don't ask me how—wanted to chat, and I wanted him out. How long have you been communicating with Brim?"

"He tried to kill you?"

I shook my head, unnerved by *that* question coming out of my kid's mouth. "No, Em. He didn't try to kill me. He wanted me to listen, and I didn't want to."

"You'll need to shower again, get all this little crud off you," she mumbled.

"Are you going to answer the question?" I went to the dresser drawer as she sat on the end corner of the bed, her hands tucked together and resting in the crook of her bent knee. She stayed quiet as I jerked on a pair of underwear, boxers, and a T-shirt, as though awaiting the firing squad. She, apparently, had the greatest impression of me.

Being a single parent, I always had to be the bad guy, and I hated that. Yes, I was upset, stunned, and pissed off at the universe for giving my child some kind of ability. But it wasn't her fault. It was in her bloodline. In the traces of ancient off-world genes passed down from generation to generation since the time of biblical cohabitation when some of the off-worlders chose human mates and produced offspring.

Those old and diluted bloodlines were responsible for creating powers in humans. Clairvoyants, mediums, shamans . . . The Madigan bunch, however, had the distinction of having not one off-worlder ancestor (which was rare in itself), but two—a Charbydon and an Elysian. It's what made me the perfect subject for Mynogan's gene manipulation. It's what gave my sister her extraordinary abilities. And what had now been passed on to Emma.

I sat back on the bed. "So how long have you known?"

Her lips puckered together, making two dimples in her cheeks, and she scratched the tip of her upturned nose. "I don't know. For a while now, I guess." She shrugged. "But I didn't know I could talk to Brim until a few days after he came home. Well, I mean . . . it's not like we can *talk* to each other, like have conversations and stuff. I can sense what he wants and feels, and he can do the same. Are you mad?"

"I'm not mad, Em," I began, shaking my head. "Shocked? Yeah. But not mad. How could I be mad that you were born with special abilities?"

"Aunt Bryn calls it a gift." Her face paled. "I'm sorry, Mom. She understands, and I knew she wouldn't get upset if I told her. Plus, she kind of sensed it anyway. Well, at least that's what she said."

I pulled a wet strand of hair from my cheek and tucked it behind my ear, then reached up to tie the whole damp mess of it into a knot, trying desperately not to feel hurt that I'd been left out by the two of them. "I'm not upset. And I wish you wouldn't think that's always going to be my first reaction."

"I know. I'm sorry. It's just that you were going through all that stuff at work. And you hate Brim. You hate anything to do with crafting . . ."

I sighed. "Yes, but I *love* you. And hate is too strong a word. I don't hate Brim or crafting."

"You should've told me about Daddy." Her words carved another nice little chunk out of my heart, though rightfully so.

I wanted to back up, to talk more about this communication thing with Brim, but the stark vulnerability in Em's expression told me that would be a terrible mistake right now. It had taken a lot for her to confront me, first in anger earlier in her bedroom, and now here.

I gave her a sorry smile that would never be enough to convey how I felt. "I wanted to. I planned to. I wanted to give you time to get over what happened with me and your kidnapping. But it never seemed like the right time and then the holidays came and you got the part in the Christmas Day play. I thought maybe after . . ." I scrubbed both hands down my face and shook my head. "Look, I don't always make the right decisions, Em. But every decision I *do* make is out of love and wanting to protect you. Everything I do comes from there. You have to trust me on that."

She nodded and then asked the one question I knew was coming. "So, what's wrong with Daddy, anyway? It's like he's a whole different person."

My brow lifted. Yeah. You could say that again.

I took in a deep breath and then let it out. Where to begin? "Well." I clasped my hands together, trying to simplify. "You know how Daddy wanted us to get back together before?" She nodded, and the urge to sugarcoat things gripped me hard. But I had to trust her, had to trust that she could handle this. "I think he was very sad and very depressed and very . . . impatient. He thought using off-world means would convince me to give him another chance, and we could all be a family again. Like before." And I could see in her expression the unspoken thought: *If you would've taken him back, he wouldn't have had to.* "So . . . do you know what a Revenant is?"

"Yeah, it's a spirit being from Charbydon. We learned about them in our off-world studies class at school." Her brow lifted in understanding, and her entire face went pale, the look of devastation widening her eyes unbearable. "Daddy made a deal with a Revenant, didn't he? To get us back."

It was like watching an accident you had no chance of stopping. Her eyes grew big and sad, the tears welling, pooling, until they spilled over in streams that were fed steadily by her broken heart. When her head dropped into her hands and her small shoulders began shaking from the sobs, I stopped thinking and gathered my baby into my arms and rocked her, smoothing her hair, kissing her forehead, and telling her it would be okay, that I loved her, that her father loved her.

When the sobbing stopped, she peeled herself from my arms, wiping her face and then turning around to face me like she had been before. "When did it happen?"

"When he was attacked at the town house, remember? When you were taken. He was dying. He *would* have died, if the Revenant hadn't arrived in time."

Her gaze rooted on the bedspread, but I could see her chewing thoughtfully on the inside of her cheek, a habit she'd picked up from me. "He's still in there." She looked back up at me. "Daddy is still there. I can feel him sometimes . . . like he's his old self, and not . . ."

"Rex," I answered. "Who's actually okay as far as Revenants go, but don't tell him I said that or it'll go straight to his head. He's staying because he cares about you, Em. More than I think even he realizes. And he's been keeping the truth from you because I asked him to." Em nodded, sniffling back tears. "As soon as we can figure out how to fix things, Daddy will be back to normal and Rex will . . . who knows . . . find another contract, be on his way to Broadway or the Food Network."

Emma broke into laughter. "Yeah, no kidding." And then her bottom lip began to quiver and my heart broke. The tears began again, and she leaned forward. I pulled her back into my arms, holding on tight as she cried.

There was no sense of time as we stayed like that, all my senses focused on her and not the outside world. I breathed her in, everything inside of me hurting and loving at the same time. I rode with those emotions, didn't try to fight them or control them. Didn't have to when it came to her. My lips rested on the side of her forehead near her temple, my hand smoothing back the hair from her forehead. Each breath drew her scent inside of me, an instant narcotic that released calming hormones into my system.

My daughter was such a miracle—I wondered if she'd ever realize the indelible impact she had on me.

Sensing that she was coming out of the worst of it, I leaned back and said, "And, for the record, I don't hate Brim."

She straightened, her nose red and wet, her bottom lip sucked in, and her eyes slightly swollen. "So can he stay in the house now? He did save your butt."

I rolled my eyes, but laughed. "I think that was you." The issue of Brim was serious, and I had to be sure. "Emma, you need to be straight with me about him."

"Mom, I trust him with my life. He'd never hurt me. I can't explain it, but everything about him, the way his mind works, his instincts—nothing is hidden from me. There are no doubts in his mind. He'd die for us." Her look held complete and total honesty. And hope, so much hope. "Please trust me."

I drew in a deep breath, reached out, and grabbed both sides of her face, pulling her forward so I could kiss her forehead. When I released her, I said, "He can stay in the house."

"In my room?"

"He can sleep on your rug, but not on the bed. He stays *off* the bed. He'll *break* the bed. And please, please, please . . . next time . . . just run for your room. Promise me."

"I promise." She threw her hands into the air and screamed. Then she was hugging me tightly. "Thank you, Mommy! Thank you, thank you, thank you! You're the best mom ever!"

I'm trying, baby, I thought.

I'm trying.

8

As Emma ran out of the room to tell Rex the good news, I remained on the bed filled with dread. I'd lost her once to Mynogan and his cause. And now there was another psychopath threatening our world. Llyran had come into my home, claimed to be the Adonai killer, and invaded my mind. It left me feeling exposed, weak, and just a little neurotic.

The additional guard of Brim, along with Emma's warded bedroom, was more than enough security, *if* my daughter was actually in her room at the time of danger. To compensate, she had several amulets of protection, some of the strongest known, all made by the Elders themselves, which she wore at all times except in bed and the shower. But was it enough? I'd been told a thousand times that it was, but . . .

I grabbed the phone from the nightstand and

dialed Aaron's number, deciding to put a little more protection on my daughter just in case. Everyone involved would most likely sigh and roll their eyes, both at the League of Mages and here at the house, but I didn't care. He didn't answer, so I left a detailed message.

Next, I called Titus Mott's private line, not surprised that he didn't answer. He was probably off in his mad scientist world working on some experiment—hopefully something that involved a cure for *ash*. I left a message telling him that Llyran was still in the city and asking him to send the Adonai's medical file to my office as soon as possible.

Titus had been studying the once-captured Adonai, trying to find a way to identify and neutralize his powers. Our weapons worked well on almost every off-world species, but the highest of each world, the Adonai and the nobles? Not so much. Titus had been trying to give us law enforcement types an edge over the heavy hitters. Maybe there'd be something in the file to help me deal with this one.

Then I went downstairs with my weapon and returned it to the holster in the hall closet, half amused and half horrified that Rex had tried to protect us and shot the ceiling. We were lucky, to say the least. And I realized I'd have to lay some major ground rules with Rex where my weapons were concerned.

Emma was already in the kitchen when I entered and went straight for the leftover lasagna. Once every inch of my plate was covered, I sat at the table, grimacing as the hunger pangs turned painful. Those first few bites actually hurt. It wasn't until I had at least eight forkfuls in my belly that I began to feel simple hunger versus extreme need.

"Whoa, slow down there, kemosabe," Rex said, entering the kitchen in dry clothes. He grabbed two bowls from the dishwasher. "There's no Valium in this entire house, by the way."

I gave him a sarcastic smile, cheeks full of yummy lasagna.

He ignored me and set two bowls on the table, got some spoons from the silverware drawer, and then pulled the ice cream from the freezer. Emma, I noticed, stayed quiet, standing by the counter just watching Rex as he scooped ice cream into two bowls and then tossed a glance over his shoulder. "You in or what?"

She blinked as though jolted, and then sat down, eyeing him as he ate.

"Okay," he said finally, noticing she hadn't touched her ice cream, "what gives?"

Em grabbed her spoon and pushed the scoops around the bowl as I continued to chew. "Mom told me who you really are." Her voice was quiet and small.

"Oh." Rex paled. "Shit." I kicked him under the table. "I mean . . . well . . . yeah, about that . . ." I'd never actually seen Rex at a loss for words before. He dragged a shaky hand through his damp hair and shot me a glare. "Thanks for the warning." I decided to show mercy and intervene, swallowing my bite and then clearing my throat.

"Can he hear me?" Emma asked before I could speak.

"Uh . . . well, no I don't think so." At her instant disappointment, he hurried on. "But I think he can sense things. You. Your mom. He's *aware*, I guess you could say, just not in an active way."

"So can't you just leave him?" she asked, and it was Rex's turn to look hurt.

"Feeling the love right now, ladies. Feelin' the love." He plopped his spoon in the bowl, looking totally dejected. "Sure I can leave him. Just feed me some arsenic, stick me under a guillotine, shoot me in—" I kicked him again, this time harder. "Ow! Stop kicking me!"

I'm sure my kid would love to hear that Revenants entered at the brink of death and left on the brink of death. Sure, Rex could heal Will's body and stay until old age or natural causes took him, but he didn't *have* to. If a Revenant wanted to leave, because the body was getting too old and decrepit to enjoy life or for whatever reason, he simply put the host into a suicide type situation or was careless enough that an accident would happen. It was the dark and dirty side of possession, and one of the reasons why soul-bartering was illegal.

"It's okay," Em told me. "I know how they leave." She blinked rapidly and stared down. "I don't know why I asked that."

"We'll figure it out," I said. "Right now, Dad is safe. He's not going anywhere. And Rex isn't leaving until we find a way for him to leave safely, without hurting Dad. Right, Rex?"

"I already said as much. I'm not the bad guy here, you know."

Em nodded to no one in particular, finally spooning a bite of ice cream into her mouth.

For a while, we ate in silence. Until Rex cleared his throat and nudged Emma with his elbow. "So, um, me and you . . . we're cool, right?"

The determined gaze she gave him impressed even me. "So long as you keep my dad safe and promise not to leave him. Then, yeah. I guess we're cool."

"Cool."

An uncomfortable few seconds passed before small talk resumed. And when Emma started telling Rex about communicating with Brim, I knew we'd somehow get through this. It wasn't hard to see the relief. Emma finally understood her odd suspicions and feelings, and Rex was able to be himself, which he'd been all along anyway—so much for the *acting skills*. And me, I didn't have to lie anymore or pretend. Still, it was more than odd sitting around the table with my family, with a man that looked and sounded just like my ex-husband, and knowing he was trapped inside there somewhere.

I saw it in Emma's eyes, too. The curious looks, the sadness, and even the hope when we talked about ways to bring Will back. That was the only thing keeping her together, the knowledge that he was in there somewhere; she could see him, touch him, and know he was safe. And one day he'd be back. And Rex, well, he could charm the pants off anyone, and Emma was no exception. She'd been completely taken with him from the start; she just didn't fully understand that the craziness was coming from Rex rather than her dad.

After the ice cream was gone, I stood at the sink rinsing the bowls as they went into the backyard to let Brim destroy the bowling ball. Their muffled voices floated through the window, sounding relaxed and easy, above the soft clink of the dishes.

Without warning, my chest constricted, and my throat swelled. Intense loneliness filled me. Tears burned my eyes and I sniffed, finishing my task and then going upstairs to bury my face in my pillow.

For once I wished I had a warm, hard, male body to curl into, to make *me* feel safe and protected. I had to look out for everyone, to comfort and protect them . . . but where was *my* protector?

I stared at the empty spot next to me, remembering Will lying on his back, one leg bent and one arm thrown over his head. How it was the perfect invite for me to scooch over and rest my head on his chest. His arm would come down around me and his hand, warm from sleep, would rub my arm.

Yeah. Lonely. That explains everything.

★　　　★　　　★

My dreams kept me tossing and turning for a large part of the night and morning, my mind playing over disjointed scenes of the warehouse, the hellhound, and Llyran being pulled through the window and into the darkness.

Aaron had warned me. My blood would make me a target, a beacon to all the psychos and grand-scheming lunatics of the world. Because I was different, seen as an instrument. An anomaly. Something unique and powerful.

Hah. If only they knew how random that power was, and how little I knew to control it.

I rolled over and hit the alarm button before it could ring. *Great potential, my ass*, I thought, returning to my back and throwing my arms wide with a loud huff, wanting nothing more than to pull the comforter over my head and sleep all day.

I turned my head to snuggle into the pillow, catching movement on my forearm. My skin turned paler, almost a creamy white, as my veins became more prominent. Then they moved, making patterns. "What . . ."

I shot up, sitting straight, my heart in my throat. What the *hell*? I blinked hard and then opened my eyes. Nothing. Just my forearm and the long, partially healed scar that ran down the middle where I'd sliced my vein open to bring darkness to the city.

Emma's door creaked, followed by the tap of Brimstone's claws on the floor and then the thuds on the stairs as they went down to the back door.

Just blood vessels and my fuzzy morning eyesight, I told myself. Yeah, blood vessels that moved and made linked, script-like patterns.

Just get up and get moving. Get working on the case.

I rubbed the sleep from my eyes and filed the episode away, making a note to mention the odd visions I'd been having to Aaron at our next training session, then I listened to my inner voice, grabbing my clothes and heading to the downstairs bathroom since mine was partially destroyed.

Once dressed in dark cargo pants and a stretchy white button-down shirt, I twisted up my hair with a clip, put in my diamond studs, and applied a layer of mascara and a quick swipe of clear lip gloss. The aroma of brewing coffee led me to the kitchen where I expected to find Rex tooling around, but he was nowhere in sight. Ravenous, I wolfed down a plain bagel and fixed two cups of coffee, one for Rex, and then leaned against the counter, taking several sips of the thick, hot liquid and feeling infinitely better.

Em came down the stairs in her school uniform—white blouse, Black Watch plaid skirt, knee-high white socks, and black Mary Janes. Her book bag was slung over one shoulder, a Pop Tart in her mouth that she must've grabbed when she let Brim out earlier, and her other hand holding her Cobweb outfit for the play. I set the cup down and pulled the Pop Tart out of her mouth. "Good morning."

"Morning. Practice for the play starts at four." A horn honked outside. "That's Miss Marti and

Amanda. I have to go. It's dress rehearsal, so I won't be home until seven."

"Okay. Have fun, kid. And leave your amulets on when you change." I kissed her and then stuck the Pop Tart back into her waiting mouth. She smiled, somehow mumbling a goodbye as she trotted down the hall, the fairy wings on her costume bobbing, and out the front door.

I finished my coffee, set the mug in the sink, and then went to the foyer closet to get my weapons harness off the hook. I strapped it on, checking all three of my weapons as I walked back down the hall to grab another bagel. I was just snapping the flap over my Hefty when Rex came out of the downstairs bathroom in nothing but a towel around his waist and in the process of drying his hair with another towel.

Two more steps and I would've smacked right into him, but that didn't stop the scent of aftershave and clean skin from springing up all around me—the scents of memories. My stomach seemed to go instantly empty despite the bagel and coffee.

I stood frozen in the hall, mentally and emotionally caught off guard. Will's body appeared as fit as ever, and it looked even better with droplets of water clinging to hard pecs and abs. The one thing I'd probably never get over was the fact that my ex looked really, really good.

Slowly, he withdrew the towel from his head, using his other hand to run his fingers through the wet hair, pushing it back from his forehead. His Adam's apple bobbed slowly, and he eyed me for a long second, frozen like I was.

My mouth had gone paper dry, but I managed a swallow. "Is he in there right now?" Grief burned through my chest. "Do you hear him at all?"

A corner of his mouth dipped, and he shook his head, his baby blues taking on a pitiful look. "Sorry."

Not even a little bit? I wanted to ask, wondering why I felt compelled to keep asking the question; the answer was not going to change. I wanted something, a tiny bit of hope, a sign that would allow me to throw my arms around him, smell his familiar scent, and just hold on to him for a while, but he wasn't in there and—

Rex's arms wrapped around me, pulling me close.

Stunned, I didn't move, but my other senses went on high alert. God. He smelled the same, felt the same, and my reaction was the same—one of great comfort, like curling up in your favorite blanket right after it came out of the dryer. Rex's hand pressed the small of my back and the other hand cradled my head, holding me so that my cheek pressed against his shoulder. For one small second, I let my eyes close.

Why? Why had Will gone and done something so irrevocable? I'd loved him. There *had* been a chance between us. Had he been patient. Had he been thinking about us instead of himself. Disappointment and regret crept into my heart like salt sprinkled onto an open wound. I pushed away, my cheeks burning. "Don't do that again."

Rex stared at me for a long moment. "You wanted me to."

"No, I didn't want you to. I didn't want *Will* to, either. So don't touch me again. Got it?" I pivoted on my heel, forgetting about the extra bagel, grabbed my things out of the front closet, and left.

I parked on Alabama Street and hurried to Underground, stopping at the small grocery store on the corner of the plaza and Mercy Street to pick up some groceries and essentials for Bryn. Then I made a quick beeline for the bakery shop at the head of Helios Alley to get another coffee to go and two gigantic Aeva buns.

The Elysian imps made *the* best baked goods in the universe, and the Aeva bun was like eating a sugary cloud, so light and fluffy that each bite melted as soon as it hit your tongue. Every time I ate one I forgave the imps for their *other* talent—nimble fingers and an extreme weakness to possess shiny objects that did not belong to them.

I placed one of the buns into a grocery bag, then looped six of the plastic bag handles over my left forearm and three over my right, leaving my hands free so I could eat the other Aeva bun and drink my coffee. A little clunky, but doable. I was done with the bun way before I got to Bryn's door, and hit the buzzer.

She met me at the top of the landing in a large sleep shirt. "Here." I held out the second Aeva bun as I scooted past her rumpled form. It wasn't the healthiest breakfast in the world, but the Aeva that gave the heavenly confection its name was very similar to sugarcane, and the sugar-like rush would get Bryn up and moving.

She shut the door behind me as I hurried to put the groceries away. "Did you feed Gizmo yet?" I asked, noticing the water bowl was full, but the food bowl was empty.

"Yeah. He's snoozing on top of the cabinet there." Mouth full, she pointed to the kitchen cabinet, the top end. A small bit of his forked tail hung over the edge. Gargoyles loved to be up high.

I closed the refrigerator and stuffed a few things into the pantry. "You take your dose yet?"

Bryn sat on the arm of the couch, her bare legs stretched out, ankle bracelets dangling. She reminded me of Emma just then, swallowed up in a long, over-sized shirt and her hair a wild mess.

"I'll take that as a no." I shoved the bags into the recycling container. "Where is it?"

"Bathroom," she answered, cheeks full.

I searched for the small packs of *ash*, but couldn't find them. "Where?" I yelled over my shoulder as I bent down to root under the sink.

Her voice came from behind me. "It doesn't come in those powder packs anymore." She stepped into the bathroom, reaching over me as I stood and pulling what looked exactly like an inhaler from the medicine cabinet. "Titus made these for us. You just twist it to your scheduled dose, press down, and it punctures the pack, then you inhale the powder." She performed the actions as she spoke and then pressed her lips to the indented edge and drew in a deep breath.

Her eyes rolled. She took two steps back and slumped against the wall. Her pale throat worked. Her nostrils flared. An expression of ecstasy slid over her features, but as her eyelids closed, a tear slipped out. Her voice was raw when she spoke. "I hate this, Charlie."

My fist closed, my fingernails digging deep into my palm. Goddammit. I pulled my little sister off the wall, gathering her into my arms, taking some of her weight to support her weakened body. "I'm sorry," I whispered into her hair.

Her arms hung limp as the drug worked its way through her system. *Ash* had hit the market so fast, and it had a devastating effect on humans. It was rapture in powdered form made from a legendary, bio-luminescent Charbydon flower, *Sangurne N'ashu*, a Bleeding Soul. It either killed on first dose, or hooked you. After some users who had survived the initial dose began dying afterward, we learned that the withdrawal was just as deadly as an overdose. The only way to keep their body from shutting down was to keep feeding them *ash* in small, manageable doses.

Bryn never had a choice. Her initial exposure to *ash* had come from the fight to close down the Bleeding

Soul farm, and now, like the other survivors, her life depended on the drug.

"Titus will find a cure," I whispered, smoothing her hair. "He will. He'll find a cure . . ."

I held her until she moved her arms and hugged me back, the initial high passing. After a few more minutes, I released her, making sure she was steady on her feet before turning on the shower and then placing a towel on the sink. We didn't speak, both of us too overwhelmed by emotion. Her color was high, but I couldn't tell if that was the drug or because she'd been crying. She turned away from me as I pulled the bathroom door closed and walked into the living room where I sank into the couch cushions, rested my head on the arm, and closed my eyes.

The next time I opened them, it was to see Bryn standing over me, dressed in one of her flowing, ankle-length skirts, her auburn hair twisted up into the usual romantic-looking arrangement, and both dimples indented due to the frown tugging her mouth down. "Charlie, wake up."

Christ. I sat up, blinking away the cobwebs in my brain, surprised I'd fallen asleep in that short amount of time, especially after eating that massive Aeva bun. "Shit. Sorry." I stood, stretched, and pulled my car keys from my pocket. "You ready?"

Her answer was an eye roll, one that showed just how much she was looking forward to this.

"You'll be fine." I passed her, waiting on the landing as she locked the door, and then I followed her down the steps, through Underground, up to Topside, and down the sidewalk to my Tahoe, grateful that it wasn't raining this morning.

We made it to the doctor's office in Edgewood with four minutes to spare. I shoved the gear into park and turned to Bryn, easily sensing her nervousness. "You want me to come in with you for a while?"

She stared straight ahead. "No. The receptionist said no family or friends allowed since it's a group thing, and it might make others hesitant to talk."

"I guess that makes sense." I stared out of the window. "There's a second meeting tomorrow. Two days in a row, and then there's an optional get-together on Sunday at the Java Hut."

We watched the flow of traffic beyond the parking lot for a minute or two before Bryn let out a loud sigh and then pulled her purse strap over her shoulder. "Call me when it's over, and I'll pick you up," I said as she opened the passenger side door and got out.

"I'm a big girl, sis." Her half-smile didn't reach her eyes. "I can take the MARTA back to Underground. Thanks, though . . . for driving me and everything . . ."

I nodded as she shut the door and then strode across the lot, her coral-colored skirt swishing around her and making her stride look twice as long as it really was. She hopped the curb, turned down the sidewalk, and disappeared into the main entrance of the office complex. My shoulders slumped, and I sent up a silent prayer that today would give my sister a new outlook and some hope for the future.

I stayed outside the office building for an extra ten minutes to make sure she didn't bolt, and then I made another small detour before heading into the station.

9

The parking lot at the warehouse had been sectioned off with crime scene tape. A patrol car minded the entrance. I slowed my vehicle and hit the button to roll down the window. After showing my badge, I drove through the barrier and parked near Liz's black ITF van.

A chill hit me as soon as I stepped onto the broken pavement. The skeleton trees swayed in the wind as though reaching for the roiling darkness above. I pulled my jacket closer around me and approached the old brick warehouse, remembering the day before and the horrible smothering sensation that came with it.

The side door was open, the same door I'd damaged, but it had been repaired, the top hinge now screwed back into the doorframe. I hesitated, hugging myself and suddenly experiencing a weakness that I rarely acknowledged. All this raw power in the air, coating the entire city, all these changes happening inside of me, all of it could be overwhelming, immobilizing, if I gave it an inch.

I stepped inside to find the place lit up like a Vegas convention. They'd been busy. Cleaning up the debris, setting up lights and work tables.

I shoved my hands deep into my jacket pockets and proceeded down the long, ramshackle space. The smell was better, and even though I had a firm mental block in place, there was a distinct impression that the malevolence once claiming this area had lessened.

I saw Liz first, standing over a worktable, putting a small, ripped piece of clothing into a baggie with a pair of tongs, her glossy black hair curling beneath her chin as she leaned forward. Her color was good. Her aura appeared normal. And despite knowing that none of us could've predicted that Daya was a Magnus, a stab of guilt squeezed my chest at the memory of what had happened here earlier.

Elliot was farther down, removing small pieces of evidence, one by one, from the debris pile and then putting them into what appeared to be categories. Cloth, small objects, shoes . . .

Liz glanced up as I approached her table. "If you're here for an update, you're going to be disappointed. This place is a mess—it's going to take eons to bag and tag everything. But I guess that's a good thing. It'll keep the Adonai reps at bay while we ID the bodies . . ."

There was no doubt that the remains in the debris pile were our missing Adonai. The telltale visual signs were unmistakable, and every other Adonai had been accounted for. Officially identifying the bodies was just a formality, but it *would* buy us some time. "Yeah, good thing . . ." I echoed quietly. "Pendaran hasn't been bothering you, has he?"

"Just one blustering phone call wherein I was told to treat the body with care and respect. Don't do this. Don't do that. Return her as soon as possible. Yada, yada, yada . . . I actually finished with her late last night."

"And?" My gaze snagged on an open cooler on a nearby table and what looked like a half sandwich in a baggie calling my name. "Hey, you going to eat that?"

She gave a small wave. "Nah, you can have it. Daya's autopsy was a bust; not a single shred of evidence other than what we already know."

Somehow I wasn't surprised. I stepped to the cooler and snatched what looked like a ham and provolone on sourdough. "Keep me posted, okay?"

"Of course."

I continued to one of the side walls where a figure sat at a small table, his silk-clad shoulders hunched, a lone spotlight illuminating the peculiar script on the wall. I stopped next to the table, eating, but my attention on the writing. The letters were in vertical order, not horizontal. The three columns looked similar to many different ancient scripts I'd seen before, but not quite the same either. The way each letter curved, the loops on the ends, the angle of the slashes—they were all different than what I'd come across before.

The more I stared, the more the script seemed to blend together, slowly taking on a linked pattern that looked very much like a complex molecular drawing. My chewing slowed. In the back of my mind I knew this wasn't possible. I knew I couldn't be standing there seeing the script moving on the wall. So what the hell was I seeing? I swallowed the bite and squeezed my eyelids closed tightly, hoping that when I opened them—

"Have you been practicing your breathing techniques, Charlie?"

It never ceased to amaze me that such a scholarly voice could come out of that good-looking package. I cast a glance down to the figure at the table. Aaron *was* a nymph, a loner since he wasn't part of the Kinfolk, and a very capable crafter who'd earned his Magnus level in Atlanta's League of Mages.

I smiled to myself, eyes still on the writing, as I polished off the last bite of sandwich, shoving the odd vision to the back of my mind. "All the time. Doing it right now."

He snorted. "Mmm. Yes, I can tell."

Ancient texts had been stacked onto one side of the table. One was open next to a writing pad where Aaron had started translating. "How's it going?" I asked.

"The writing on the opposite wall is simple. Just

a spell to hide the stench of the place. And we're keeping that one intact while we work. But this"— he motioned toward the wall in front of him—"this is complex. If I'm not mistaken, it's a root language. There are so many elements from scripts of all three worlds, that it makes translating it almost impossible. There could be hundreds of variations. The slightest change of spelling could change the entire meaning. The only thing that seems to be a similar variant is the word *dawn*."

"Dawn. Any idea what it might have to do with our murdered Elysians of power?"

"Not yet, but the winter solstice is right around the corner. Major time for rituals. And what we have written here looks old, perhaps ritualistic in nature. The timing is certainly interesting anyway. I'm also looking into some of those words your corpse used. The ring. The star. Maybe we'll find a correlation."

He shook his head, leaning back in the fold-up chair and studying me. The emerald-green aura around him was bright and energetic. In the short time that I'd known him, it had become apparent that Aaron loved his work. Loved a challenge, too. This kind of thing was right up his alley.

"I got your message, by the way. The Elders said they'd make one more amulet and that's it. Ask for another and you'll have insulted their power more than enough." He gestured to a pile of old crates stacked farther down the wall. "Pull up a box."

I dragged one over, wincing as it let out a nails-on-chalkboard whine. Once I was seated, the nerves set in all at once. We stared at each other for a few seconds.

"What?" I finally asked.

"I sense this visit is more than work-related."

My laugh contained no hint of pleasure at all. "You could say that."

"Well, you *are* changing. Evolving. Things are going to be odd across the board, Charlie. So, what's been happening lately? Still eating nonstop?"

"Carbs and protein, mostly. Can't seem to get enough and I'm *losing* weight. Find out the answer to that one, and the hell with everything else—we could make millions as diet gurus."

"Quite true. That's your metabolism. Inside, your body is working overtime to stabilize itself. This is actually very normal. What else?"

"Well, let's see. An Adonai serial killer broke into my house and raided my mind last night." I laughed inwardly, the words sounding ludicrous. "He's looking for something. Or maybe he found it, I don't know, but I think he's the same one who wrote that script," I said, gesturing to the wall. "I think it has something to do with Mynogan . . ."

His brow lifted at my revelation, and his expression became intensely thoughtful. He nodded slowly, but his only response was, "Mmm." And then, "What else?"

I picked at my fingernails, my mind going back to the bizarre flashes I'd had recently: the hellhound, the mirror in my room, the odd blood vessels I saw beneath my skin, and now the script on the wall. I took a deep breath. "You mean besides seeing a few seconds into the future where my partner kills a hell-hound, seeing straight through things as if they aren't even there, thinking my entire body is trying to tattoo itself with script from the inside out?" I shook my head, avoiding his insightful emerald gaze. "I turned a stuffed bunny into a tiny fur ball, Aaron."

That sort of said it all.

Aaron angled in his chair, the light catching the silk sheen of his dark blue tunic. "I've been studying your case, Charlie, quite a bit in fact . . . and I've made a rather interesting connection. Mind you, it's just a theory, but one I think you should hear." He scratched the short black stubble on his chin, taking his time to choose just the right words. "What do you know about the Old Lore?"

I blinked, not expecting the question. "Not much. I know it's some sort of ancient Elysian legend."

"The Old Lore is a priceless collection of the oldest known writings in our world. These writings are based on a much earlier oral tradition about the pre-history of Elysia, and about the creation of our race and our world. The Charbydons have a similar Lore called the Creation Myth."

"Okay. So what's this have to do with me?"

"We know very little about our pre-history, but thanks to the collection we have, we know a few stories from this time period. It was from these early myths that our belief in a single creator evolved, a belief, in some ways, like your own monotheistic religions." He shrugged. "You are familiar with the One God Theory."

"That we're all created by the same being? Yeah, I've heard about it."

"Being. Deity. Metaphysical entity." Aaron smiled. "Who knows. All we have are myths, and doctrines, and stories, just like you. Some chose to believe in them. Some chose not to."

The theory had gained popularity over the years. The discovery of alternate worlds made a lot of people think or rethink—it was only natural given the circumstances. New theories popped up all the time, and faded away just as quickly, but the One God Theory appealed to many believers. I suppose if you believed your God is the *only* God, the creator of the entire universe and everything in it, then that would also have to include the off-worlders. The theory hadn't put much of a dent into the existing human doctrines, but it did spawn new churches and more places for nondenominational worship.

"In any event," Aaron said, "the coincidences in our religious doctrines and myths are quite compelling. The stories of the Old Lore, for instance."

"How so?"

"One of the myths speaks of the first beings, First Ones, made by the Creator. The myth claims that inside of them was the genetic foundation of all three noble races."

"Wait a minute. Three? I thought there are only two."

"Besides Charbydon nobles and Elysian Adonai, the Old Lore claims that *humans* are the third noble race." He leaned forward. "So one Creator gave rise to the First Ones, and eventually, from them, the three races sprang, evolved—there is nothing in what remains of the traditions to tell us how this happened or even what happened to the First Ones."

Thank God this was all fiction. Try telling a noble or an Adonai that they shared a common ancestor, and you'd better have stellar health insurance.

I wasn't a big history buff, but I did find Aaron's words fascinating . . . until I realized where he was going with all this. My chin dropped a notch and I fixed him with a bland stare. "Please don't tell me—"

"What exists inside of you, Charlie, might very well be the same genetic code that existed in the First Ones: the genes of all three races."

I dropped my head into my hands and let out a deep exhale, then sat back, stunned and a little harried. "You're saying I'm becoming a First One, a myth? You might as well tell me I'm an orphan from Atlantis."

He laughed. "Remind me to tell you about Atlantis someday. Look, all myths are grounded in truth. It's true I have no way of knowing if the First Ones were real or not, but if they were, if the myths are true like some people believe . . ." A shrug was all he gave to finish out that thought. "There's no way to tell what you'll eventually become, no way to know exactly how your body will process the new off-world genes you have. Your entire code is transmogrifying, morphing. It won't happen overnight. You might eventually become a divine being like the First Ones, or something completely unique, something that all three worlds have never seen before."

My mind came to a full and total stop. Just stopped, every thought, every sense replaced by lovely, welcoming white noise.

A singsong echo started. Distant. Two syllables.

"Charrr-leee. Charrr-leeeeee."

Several bright flashes caused my eyelids to close tighter.

"Charlie!" Sharp, loud, to the point. I reared back, blinking rapidly, my brain scrambling to make sense of what was in front of me.

Two blurry faces. Up close. Peering at me.

"See there, she's blinking."

Flash.

What the hell?

"There. She's coming out of it. Charlie!" The sound of snapping filled the air.

"Liz?" The two faces zoomed out and came into focus. Aaron and Liz. "What the hell are you doing?"

"Yeah. See. Told you," Liz said in her no-nonsense tone, bumping Aaron's shoulder and flicking her small flashlight on and off. "Good as new. Yell if you need me." She flipped her hair behind her shoulder and marched back to her work station.

"Just a moment of shock, Charlie, nothing to worry about," Aaron said. "I imagine it's not every day one hears they might be evolving *back* into a divine being."

There it was again, that white noise.

"Head between your knees," he ordered gently, hand on my shoulder as my head went down and my hands covered my face.

Finally, my body started responding—heart thumping as though it had just restarted, chugging along, picking up speed. Chills spread throughout my insides and manifested as a cold sweat on my skin. "Are you fucking kidding me?" I muttered through my hands, not moving, too afraid I'd pass out.

"Like I said, it's just a theory . . ."

"Your theories blow," I said weakly.

Shit, shit, shit.

"Maybe you should go home, get some rest. You want me to drive you?"

"No, I'm fine. I need to get to the office. I'll be okay. Just give me a minute." *Or a million.* I couldn't believe what Aaron had said. I didn't want to be a "completely different person."

"Is there a way to test this theory?" I asked, finally lifting my head. "No *Divine Beings for Dummies* at the library?"

"Very funny. I don't think so. There is no way to test it except to keep evolving like you are." His black eyebrows drew together in deep consideration. "An old Elysian proverb claims that the more at peace you are, the closer to the divine you become. Perhaps try relaxing, putting yourself into a deep state of peace and calm, and then see if you can duplicate these random occurrences you've been having. I'll research more on the First Ones myths. Perhaps then we'll see a similarity or a pattern."

"Okay." I stood. "Thanks, Aaron."

"You sure you don't want to rest for a while? I can take you home."

I've got a Druid King threatening to start a war with the jinn. And a psycho Adonai claiming to be the killer of Daya and the others, one whose next victim will be just for me, I wanted to say, but instead I said, "No, I'm fine." I gave him a tight smile, seeing no need to fake it, and turned toward the exit, letting my feet carry me on wooden legs down the warehouse and out across the parking lot to my vehicle.

The drive to the station cleared my mind enough for me to realize that no matter what Aaron said, there was nothing I could do about it. I had to go on, do my job, take care of my kid, and take things day by day. And despite feeling like I wanted to check myself into the nearest mental hospital, that's what I did. Because when it came right down to it, I really didn't have a choice. People counted on me; I had to keep going. And when my mind kept going back to his words and thoughts of divine, mythological beings, I refocused; I pushed those thoughts aside, pulled into the back lot of Station One, parked my Tahoe, and hurried inside, heading toward the elevator.

I used the small rectangular card attached to my keychain and held the bar code up to the scanner near the elevator door. The scanner beeped and the elevator door slid open just as footsteps echoed down the main hall.

"Well, if it isn't the tri-world reject."

Seriously? My eyelids fluttered closed for a second. I wanted to laugh, toss my head back, and ask the universe if she had nothing better to do than to fuck up my morning. I mean, so far it had been a doozy, so why not add another bit of crap to the mix, right?

Slowly I spun around on my heel, not bothering to hide my distaste or the fact that I was screwing up my nose as though a foul smell had just wafted by. I should just go upstairs and ignore it, but ducking out of a confrontation wasn't exactly my style.

"Hey, *Ass*ton."

Ashton Perry, ITF detective and former coworker, fisted both hands at his sides as his narrow cheeks sprouted red, mottled patches and the superior sneer on his angular face grew by leaps and bounds.

It wasn't a big secret that Mynogan had brought darkness to the city or that Hank and I had been part of the attempt to stop him. The public knew what the ITF told them. But there were some in the ITF who were aware that I'd played a bigger role. That I chose to save my kid, instead of saving the city from darkness. Some understood. Some didn't. But it wasn't really my role that pissed off some of my former coworkers as much as the fact that Hank and I used ITF resources, worked on cases the ITF wasn't privy to, and only answered to the chief and to Washington. And Ashton couldn't seem to get over it. His eyes narrowed to small slits. "I *will* be heading the warehouse murders," he practically snarled. "And you can tell the *chief* that."

I took a moment to indulge in a heavy sigh and followed it with, "I'm really not up for a pissing match today, okay? And we all know mine is bigger than yours, anyway, so why don't you go play Big Man with the noobs."

A nasty sneer drew back the corner of his lip and his head cocked triumphantly. "How's your daught—"

Before I could even think how wrong it was, I had him by the throat and up against the opposite wall, my speed surprising even me. His skin was so pliable under my fingers. I dug them in further, wanting to hurt him, to make him cry.

Ashton's right hand grabbed the hilt of his service weapon just as any cop would do in this situation. And if it was anyone else, I'd trust them *not* to pull it, but Ashton was a hothead and had gotten increasingly hostile toward me. If he pulled his weapon, it'd be all over. For both of us. At least I had my wits enough to latch hard onto his hand with my other to prevent him from pulling the weapon and doing something stupid.

"Charlie." Hank's deep, mellow voice came from behind me, the same moment I felt the pressure of his hand on my shoulder.

My teeth ground together, one part of me knowing I had to remain calm and back off, the other part of me wanting to—"You mention my daughter again," I ground out, "and I'll rip your fucking tongue out and feed it to my hellhound."

Perry's long face was beet-red now, the pressure building as I continued to hold his neck tight, cutting off his circulation. Veins strained, full and angry, along his temples. Satisfied, I eased my hold.

Immediately he shot back, gasping, "I hope you sleep well at night, knowing you've annihilated the fucking planet."

"It's just the city, you moron." I stepped back as he rearranged his shirt, clearly pissed that I'd touched him with my *tri-racial* hands. "And, for the record, I sleep just fine."

"When they start taking over," Perry continued, "don't look for friends here. You damned us all for one stupid kid."

I lunged for him, but Hank was faster, wrapping both arms around my middle, jerking me back and causing my feet to come clean off the floor. "Let it go," Hank breathed into my ear as Ashton Perry had the nerve to laugh, despite his flustered expression, roll his eyes, and then walk out the back exit.

His disregard was a big ole fuck you, and it expanded my anger, pressing against my chest like a balloon about to burst. I swallowed the burn in my throat. "I'm going to kill him."

"And you should know by now that he uses Emma because it's the *one* thing that riles you. No one who counts believes you made the wrong decision."

I knew that, but Perry's words . . . Maybe he was right in a way. Maybe I had damned the whole city, and was just kidding myself that there was a way to fix it. To those like Ashton, the only thing that mattered was that I'd stood in that stupid circle, spilled my engineered blood, and called the darkness to save my kid. I shut my eyes, my body still humming, still experiencing that numb tingling associated with chaotic power. It burned. And it fucking hurt.

"Relax," came Hank's voice, so low, confident, and soothing, like a shot of whiskey spreading through my system. "Breathe, kiddo. You control it, not the other way around."

Even with the voice-mod stuck in his neck, he still had a natural lure. No amount of engineering could snuff it out completely. My muscles obeyed, more willing to listen to him than to the anger that was already beginning to whittle away. I sighed. Then a thought occurred to me.

"You ditched me the other day." I jerked out of his hold and spun to face him, still humming with power, just not as volatile as before.

"So?" He scanned his card to re-open the elevator door. "I needed to cool off," he said, without a shred of remorse. "So did you. I did us both a favor."

"Oh, please." I followed him into the elevator. "Spare me your good intentions. Ditch me like that again and you'll be hurting for weeks."

Hank's smug snort didn't help the situation. He crossed his arms over his chest and lifted a dark blond eyebrow. "You can try."

The elevator stopped at the fifth floor. "Thank God," I said, stepping off. "The ego in here could suffocate an elephant."

Our boss, and former chief of Station One, barreled out of the office we shared and marched down the hall like a formidable old bull in a black leather jacket. "Good, you're here. I'm headed downstairs to—" He stopped midstride, dark eyes squinting and wide nostrils flaring as though he smelled trouble. "What did you two do this time?" Immediately his beefy hand went up. "No. Never mind. I don't want to know. Downstairs," he continued, striding past us and lifting up the file in his hand, "to meet with the brass. Washington pulled rank on the ITF, so we're officially heading the investigation, and that crime scene is mine."

No wonder Ashton was in fine form this morning.

The chief stopped at the elevator. "The guys downstairs have already briefed everyone—this stays under wraps as long as possible. Let's just pray this doesn't cause pigeons to start shitting rainbows over Atlanta. And Sian called in sick today, so I want you both doing the legwork, tracking down that love nest, the warehouse owner, and checking the database for matching MOs on the crime scene." He stepped into the elevator. "Get to work!"

I slid my access key into the scanner. "Pigeons shitting rainbows? Where does he come up with that stuff?"

"Hell if I know. I stopped trying to figure out you humans and your sayings a long time ago."

"Well, trust me, that's no saying I ever heard."

Our office on the fifth floor was, quite frankly, a huge mess. We'd taken up residence in a large suite used as a dumping ground for old or unneeded office furniture and equipment, using the discarded cubicle dividers and desks to carve out a serpentine path that led to a spacious corner near the windows and close to the small kitchenette.

The steaming coffee mug on Hank's desk made the things I should've noticed earlier finally click: the unshaven jaw, the tousled hair, the same clothes he'd worn yesterday. "How long have you been here?"

He plopped in his chair and took a swig from the mug. "Long enough."

"You slept here last night?" I went to the small kitchenette to pour my own mug of coffee, adding half-and-half from the fridge and grabbing a glazed doughnut from the open box on the counter. "What's wrong with your place?" I happened to know Hank kept a very sweet, very expensive loft on Helios Alley.

"Nothing's wrong with it. It's *who's* in it that's the problem."

I added sweetener to the coffee and stirred, coming back to my desk, gesturing. "Continue."

"It's nothing, Charlie." He propped one elbow on the desk and scratched his stubble. "Just a little spat, that's all."

"With Zara?"

Zara was the concierge at The Bath House on Helios Alley. She was also a knock-out siren—weren't they all?—who had as big a crush on Hank as he did on her. She was also part of the group that tried to get Emma back from Mynogan, so she was on my list of folks I'd go to bat for in a heartbeat.

Hank shrugged at my question and downed the rest of his coffee like it was the elixir of life.

"Well . . . ?"

"Well nothing. That's it." He rolled his wide shoulders, faced his monitor, and then started tapping the keys, completely dismissing me. I glared at him, standing at the corner of our desks, which had been pushed back to back, until he finally stopped, lifted his reluctant sapphire eyes, and frowned. "Things have cooled off a little. No big deal."

"See, that wasn't so hard, was it?" I sat on the edge of the desk, cradling my warm mug and polishing off the doughnut, licking a few sticky fingers. "So what's the problem? Maybe I can help. I'm good with relationships." A bland expression came over my partner's face, making me amend that statement. "*Other* than my own."

He leaned back in the chair, swiveling to face me

fully, looking about as enthused as a kid at a financial lecture. The dark shadow of his day-old beard gave him a haunted, rugged look that I found strangely appealing. His throat worked with his swallow and a faint blush crept from beneath the white collar of his shirt. "Just drop it, Charlie. We had an argument. I left, so she wouldn't have to. End of story."

I opened my mouth, so ready to argue the point, when he stopped me. "This"—he flung a hand toward the voice-mod on his neck—"doesn't exactly help, okay? *Now* can we drop it?"

A frown screwed my face as I took a slow drink of my coffee. Surely Zara couldn't be put off by the voice-mod being stuck on his neck. It wasn't like it made him unattractive. Quite the opposite, in my opinion. The voice-mod made its wearer look like some throwback to Viking or Celtic times, when torcs hugged the thick necks of warriors and chieftains.

I slid into my chair and turned on my monitor, letting my curiosity go for now. "We need to talk to Ebelwyn, find out who owns the warehouse, and check out Daya's work—might turn up something on her relationship . . . Pretty sure it wasn't a jinn that killed her," I said, my voice dropped to a mutter, "or any Charbydon for that matter."

"What makes you say that?" Hank asked as I signed into the ITF database.

"Because I think it's Llyran." He scooted around the monitor in his chair, draping his arm across the corner of my desk. "You know, escaped serial killer.

Lays low for a while. Adonai start disappearing and then found murdered."

"I considered him, too. Stayed up last night reading his criminal file. The guy caused a lot of trouble in Elysia. Was officially banished from Elysia by the Adonai Council. Stole something big from the Hall of Records, wouldn't reveal its location, was slated for execution, but killed his guards and fled. That was years ago."

"What did he steal?"

"Officials never said. Then he gets here and starts killing. Indiscriminately. All races. Adonai, too. Every kill was unique. There's no pattern that I can see. It almost seems like he was practicing, trying out different techniques and methods for murdering his victims, you know? The only reason he was caught before is because he didn't try to be careful, or hide what he was doing. Didn't care. Didn't deny . . ." Hank sat back in his chair. "The guy's a lunatic."

Yeah. I could definitely attest to that.

"What's the laugh for?"

"What?"

"You just gave a laugh." Hank's eyes narrowed. "A suspicious one."

He wasn't going to take this well, I knew, so I came right out with it. "Llyran broke into my house last night."

Hank shot off the chair. "He *what*?"

"Mmm." I took a sip from my mug. "Wrecked my

bathroom, too. He didn't hightail it back to Elysia after all. He's been here the whole time. Said he killed our vics. He's looking for something and seems to think I know where it is."

"What is it?"

"I have no idea. I think he just wanted to show me how powerful he is, turn this into a game. Probably latched onto me when I saw him at Titus's lab the first time."

"Like he's stalking you, you mean," Hank said irritably, sitting back down.

"Could be. Who knows? The guy's a Level Ten felon. Totally unpredictable. As you said, nearly impossible to profile. There's no telling why he's doing what he's doing. He did mention a cause, though."

"You think he's our guy? That he's not just taking credit?"

I chewed thoughtfully on the inside of my cheek, rolling around a pen on my desk. "Yeah, but I can't shake the feeling that he isn't alone in this. Whatever he's doing seems grand. I don't know. You had to be there." I met my partner's sober expression. "Something is different about him, about his power," I began as evenly as I could even though my heart rate had kicked up. "He's figured out a way to control the darkness."

The color drained from Hank's face.

"He summoned it, called it into my bathroom. He could've killed me, or taken me, but he didn't . . ."

A low, astonished breath hissed through Hank's

lips. He rubbed a hand down his face. "And you're okay? Em's okay?"

"Everyone is fine. Brim ran him off. You know Emma can talk to him? Communicate with him?" The pride in my voice caught me off guard, especially after having been so overwhelmed by her revelation. Hank just stared at me, totally in a daze. "Yeah, I know, right? Welcome to the Madigan family, where strange is our middle name."

He snorted softly. "You gotta stop with the bombshells this early in the morning. Don't think my heart can take any more."

"Well, lucky for you, that's all I got."

He rolled his chair back in front of his monitor, but I heard his muttered reply. "Trust me, that's enough."

10

Neither one of us had luck tracking the property records for the warehouse. And according to Ebelwyn's receptionist, she didn't know who had asked him to list the property for sale or even the whereabouts of her boss—he hadn't shown up for work, and he wasn't answering calls or his front door.

Unfortunately for us, the one person who had his finger on the pulse of Underground and could probably tell us Ebelwyn's whereabouts was the person I only wanted to see again if it was through a pair of cold cell bars or down the nozzle of my Nitro-gun. Grigori Tennin.

At least it's not raining. I tried to look at the bright side as I jogged down the concrete steps that led to the main plaza in Underground and then proceeded at a sharp clip over the old brick pavers, past the fountain, heading to the shop fronts along the head of Solomon Street. They were crowded with inventory, packed inside and out. Peddlers set up shop wherever they could find space, often in the middle of the street or lurking from the alley shadows.

Once you turned onto Solomon Street, though, the old-fashioned streetlamps became dimmer, the glass covered in soot and grime from the open-air fires and the system of underground tunnels, caves, and homes dug straight beneath the street by the jinn, who preferred living within the earth. Peddlers pushed carts full of food, stones, spells, herbs, and snacks. It was like walking through a dark, otherworldly kasbah in the heart of Cairo.

It had to be pushing ninety degrees, and the choked, crowded atmosphere only made it seem hotter. The smells here were intense, too—earthy and humid, filled with the scents of meats, body odor, smoke, and the distinct scent of tar, which signified a large jinn population.

We weaved our way down the street, aware of the violet eyes that glowed dimly from the darkness. From the moment we entered Charbydon territory, the jinn tracked our movement. They ruled Solomon Street, and I'd guess right about now, Grigori Tennin was being told of our arrival.

We'd planned on invading the Lion's Den, Grigori's headquarters at the dead end of the street, but halfway down Solomon, two jinn warriors in battle regalia—Grigori's personal female guard—stepped out from the shadows. My hand rested casually on the hilt of my weapon as we approached. The female warriors were as dangerous as the males. They were tall, muscular, with the same smooth, sooty gray skin and vicious tempers. The only difference (besides gender) was that the females had hair where the males were completely bald. And who knows, they might've been pretty, in an Amazon sort of way, if not for the scowls.

"Girls," I greeted once we were close enough to speak.

They ignored my sarcasm. "Grigori is not here," one of them said.

Hank shoved his hands into his pockets and glanced around the crowded street. "And I don't suppose you know where he is at the moment."

One of them smirked.

On any other occasion, I would've pressed the issue, but after the morning I'd had, I was a little relieved to not have to deal with Tennin. "Tell him we'll be by later." I did a one-eighty and wound my way back through a thick patch of carts and crates.

Hank caught up and grabbed my arm from behind. It was too congested to walk side by side. "What gives, Madigan?"

"Tennin's not going to give us the info we need." I sidestepped a small jinn boy racing after a stray cat with a homemade bow.

"If it benefits him in some way, he would."

"And if it doesn't—no, thank you," I told the spellmonger opening his coat to reveal vials of colored liquids, "we're out of luck. We won't find Ebelwyn or those missing property records." A space opened up, allowing Hank to fall in step next to me. "His office is up ahead." I pointed. "I say we stop in and look for some property."

"Ah," he began in understanding. "Maybe a nice villa on the coast. Always wanted to be on a cliff by the sea." I rolled my eyes and glanced over to find him grinning like an idiot. "A little siren joke for ya."

I picked up speed and darted between two large stalls selling an assortment of Charbydon fruit and vegetables, and ended up on the other side of the street. I could feel Hank right behind me. A few more dodges and, avoiding a raging fire barrel, I stepped back onto the sidewalk, went a few steps, and then immediately dodged into the alley next to Darkling Properties and Rentals. The sign said it was closed. The main room was dark, but a glance at the apartment over the shop showed a small light coming from the window. I knew that Ebelwyn lived over his shop, just like my sister and many other shop owners.

"Back escape," Hank said, heading farther down the narrow alley.

The brick walls closed in on us as we went. The smell back here was terrible, reeking of strong ammonia—urine of a gargoyle, a few stray cats, and probably a few off-world races taking leaks on the wall if I had to guess. In short, it was lovely, but it was this loveliness that kept the alleys vacant of most folks.

A one-lane street ran along the back of the shops and apartments, used for deliveries, dumpsters, and God knew what else. But by the looks of things, I'd say it was mostly landfill, dumping ground, extra storage . . . I glanced up at the fire escape. "This shouldn't be too difficult," I decided as Hank reached up and grabbed the stepladder to pull it down.

I glanced down the back alley, but all I got was steam from restaurants, a lot of shadows, and noise carried in from the street. Hank and I hurried up the ladder and onto Ebelwyn's landing. The window wasn't locked and it didn't take long for us to duck into his apartment, get our bearings, and search the rooms.

The light I'd seen from the street came from a small office where a heat lamp had been placed over the aquarium of a moon snake, its bioluminescent skin emitting a soft, glowing white light. It was a small one, curled up against a rock. I leaned down and tapped the glass. The thing lifted its head and lunged at the glass so fast, I leapt back. "Jesus!"

"Cute, aren't they?" Hank came around the desk and opened one of the side drawers.

An involuntary shiver ran through me. The glowing white snake was at the glass, half its body raised, weaving back and forth, its cobra-like hood edged in a crown of sharp bony points extended in a sign of aggression. "Yeah." I moved to the other side of the desk to pull open a drawer. "Real cute."

"Not venomous, though. These look like work files. Names. Addresses."

I scanned the file tabs in the drawer on my side. "Taxes, bills, manuals . . ."

"Hold up." Hank pulled a file from the drawer. "Tennin."

I came around the desk to the sound of the moon snake thumping its nose on the glass.

Weave, weave, *thump*. Weave, weave, *thump*.

Goose bumps sprouted along my arms, but it wasn't the snake's neurotic thumping; I had a bad feeling as Hank laid the file on the desk and opened it. "It's Tennin's holdings. All of his properties. Christ, Charlie. He *owns* the warehouse."

Weave, weave, *thump*.

I stood next to my partner, scanning the paper until I found the warehouse address. "Looks like he owns two warehouses in the district." Hank grabbed a notepad from Ebelwyn's desk and wrote down the other address as I bit the inside of my cheek. "So," I began, thinking out loud, "could be coincidence. Tennin owns a lot of properties and businesses. Or he's involved. Or he knows what's happening, knows someone has been dumping bodies on his property."

Weave, weave, *thump*.

"Hell, Charlie," Hank said, "Tennin could've sent Ebelwyn to the warehouse knowing what the guy would find. He'd know Ebelwyn would call you and not the ITF. He either did us a huge favor, letting us know there's a killer on the loose, or he's involved in some way and wants us involved, too."

Weave, weave, *thump.*

Hank let out a sigh and went to the aquarium, searching the table until he found a round Tupperware container. "It's just hungry. Who knows the last time it ate." The moon snake dropped down and began circling beneath the feeding portal as Hank opened the lid of the Tupperware, grabbed a small pair of plastic tongs off the table, and withdrew a small, gray lump.

"What is that?" It looked like a newborn rat covered with gray skin so translucent you could see the organs beneath, and it was covered in what I guessed to be some kind of preservative.

Hank turned the lock to the aquarium lid. "It's a nithyn fetus." He held up the fetus with the tongs to show me. "See the wings? They're like bat wings, but these little guys grow to the size of a goat. The females lay dozens in the Charbydon sand flats. Moon snakes love them." Hank eased the lid open just wide enough to drop the nithyn inside. The moon snake's hood shot out and it attacked the dead fetus with a frenzy that made me look away.

The remainder of our search through Ebelwyn's apartment turned up zilch. There were no signs he'd packed up and left, no signs of a break-in or struggle, nothing to suggest he'd gone missing. The initial discovery of Grigori Tennin's ownership of our crime scene and a second warehouse on the same street was all we had to go on, and as soon as the jinn boss came back to Solomon Street, we'd be paying him a visit.

Hank went down the fire escape ladder first. My vantage point two stories up allowed me to see far in both directions of the back alley, but the steam vents, dumpsters, and other clutter made for some pretty nice cover. As I went down the ladder, I had the very distinct sense of being watched, and it was most likely by one or two of Grigori Tennin's goons.

Oh well. What were they going to do? Call the ITF on us?

Once my feet hit the pavement in the back alley and Hank had pushed up the fire escape ladder, my cell rang. "Madigan." I glanced around, noticing my partner was doing the same and guessing he'd also felt the "eyes" on us.

"Charlie?"

"Yeah? Who's this?"

"It's Orin. Daya's brother."

"Orin," I said to clue Hank in. All his attention zeroed in on me. "What's going on?"

"I've been going through Daya's things." Orin cleared his throat. "I found an address. The client she was freelancing for when she died. There was a meeting time written down for last week. I don't know . . . I thought it might be useful . . ."

"That's very useful." I motioned to Hank for a pen. He pulled one out of the inside breast pocket of his jacket along with the same piece of paper we'd taken from Ebelwyn's apartment. "What's the address?"

"It's a penthouse in Helios Tower. The name is

S. Yavesh. That's all there is, except the date and time."

"Great. Thanks, Orin. We'll check it out."

After I hung up and put my cell phone back on my hip, I handed the paper and pen back to Hank and started walking down the narrow alley. Hank read the address. "That's no jinn love nest," he said, echoing my thoughts. "Helios Tower is occupied by Elysians mostly and some humans."

"Yeah." I glanced behind me, still unable to shake the feeling of being watched. "But Helios Tower has terrace apartments just like Daya told us . . ."

It was a fifteen-minute walk from Solomon Street, across the plaza, and down Helios Alley where the street dead-ended into the swanky underground lobby of Helios Tower, which housed a bar, two restaurants, and a spa. We took the elevator one floor up to the Topside lobby. A good part of the tower was made up of hotel rooms and then apartments and penthouses, mostly owned or rented by Elysians.

We entered the Topside lobby, a beautiful space of windows and light, white marble floors, mosaic wall tiles flecked with silver and gold, and plants, lots and lots of plants. Very serene and very Elysian.

"May I help you?" the clerk at the desk asked as we approached. Human. Male.

I pulled out my badge. "Looking for the apartment of an S. Yavesh."

"One moment, please." The clerk typed the name into his keyboard. "Mister Yavesh lives in one of the penthouses on the east wing. Forty-sixth floor. Number eight. Would you like me to ring him?"

"Please," Hank said.

The clerk set the phone down a few seconds later. "I'm sorry, sir. There's no answer."

"Get a key." Hank's eyes scanned the lobby.

The clerk turned and selected the key from the locked vault behind him, then fiddled with it for a moment, unsure. "Don't you need a warrant?"

Hank returned his attention to the clerk, expression completely bland, but his voice so damn compelling. "No, but you *really* want to help us."

Sometimes I loved my partner.

The clerk frowned, seeming stumped by the tone and the steady gaze that Hank was giving him. It flustered the guy enough that he didn't have any comeback, but he did come out from behind the counter and lead us to the elevator.

Helios Tower wasn't the tallest building in Atlanta, but it had terraces, and if Daya had died on one like her vision suggested, we had a good shot at finding evidence and, hopefully, tracking Llyran. There was no telling what awaited us.

I pulled my Nitro-gun as we approached the door.

"Should I knock first?" the clerk asked.

"No. Just open it. Quietly." I cupped my gun hand, taking position by the door. "Stay out here, no matter what happens."

His hand trembled slightly as he turned the key and opened the heavy door. I executed a quick duck into the open space, seeing nothing but a very clean living space, and then leaned back against the inside wall, trying to sense the same kind of malevolence that had pervaded the warehouse. Nothing.

After Hank was inside and had scanned the place, he shook his head. He hadn't sensed anything, either. "Ready?"

Since I had chosen the nitro Hank withdrew his Hefty. He nodded.

I crept along the wall. The far wall was nothing but floor-to-ceiling windows. The floors were polished dark hardwoods; the furniture looked brand-new and very sleek. High ceilings. The entire space was vast, the living area opening to the dining space and a gorgeous kitchen full of stainless steel, granite, and dark cabinets with frosted glass.

We checked the main living area and then proceeded carefully, going down the hallway to the bedrooms. The first two were empty and pristine. Everything about the place felt . . . wrong. Staged. I shook my head, whispering as I backed out of the room. "It looks like it's never been lived in."

"Or he has one hell of a cleaning lady."

"We do have an excellent maid service," the clerk's voice came from the foyer.

My eyes widened in disbelief. "I thought I told you to stay put," I whispered fiercely, marching up to him and escorting him back through the front door with a stern warning. "Stay. Or you'll be spending the night in a holding cell."

I rejoined Hank at the last bedroom door at the end of the hall.

Last room in the penthouse. I reached out and grabbed the handle. It clicked open. I pushed, expecting to find the room just like all the others, and entered gun first, Hank fanning out to my left.

A gasp made me swing the barrel to the bed.

I'd suddenly fallen down the rabbit hole.

Five seconds went by, and I was pretty sure the stunned face staring back at me had the same exact expression as mine.

"Sian?"

"Charlie? What are you doing here?"

I frowned. "Me? What are *you* doing here?"

Grigori Tennin's only child cast her indigo eyes to the rumpled bed on which she sat, hugging her knees to her chest. Her long, snow-white hair was down, parted in the middle and framing her flawless light gray skin. She was a hybrid, a rare offspring of a jinn father and a human mother. A prized commodity in the jinn world, but rejected by other Charbydons and Elysians, and a fair share of humans, for her biracial blood. Looking at her more closely revealed tearstains on her cheeks and damp eyelashes, and she was clutching a small oval picture frame in her hand.

I lowered the gun, holstering it and trying to make sense of her presence here. "Please tell me you're not involved in this."

"Charlie." Hank's quiet voice made me glance over, and I was met with an expectant look as he gestured toward the picture.

"What?"

His response was an eye roll and a sigh. Obviously I was missing something. Hank holstered the Hefty, walked to the bed, and held out his hand. Sian handed him the picture frame. Hank gave it to me before he went to the small writing desk and pulled out the chair. He sat down, leaning forward to drape his forearms over his knees. "So how long have you been seeing Daya?"

My brow shot up.

Oh.

I flipped the frame over to see a photograph of what had to be Daya Machanna. My gaze went from Hank to Sian. Yeah. Totally didn't see that one coming.

"About four months. If anyone ever found out . . . I mean, I'm a jinn, and worse, a hybrid. And she's Elysian. A nymph. No one would understand." Fresh tears fell, and she sniffed, swiping them from her cheeks.

I went to the dresser and leaned against it, setting the frame down and then crossing my arms over my chest, still stunned. "No one knew?"

Sian shook her head. "No. We made sure to be careful. And if anyone did see us together, we just acted like friends."

"This is why you called in sick, then?" Hank asked gently. "You found out she's gone."

Her body stilled, and then her shoulders hunched and she cried harder. Hank and I exchanged a quick look. We allowed her time to compose herself, not pushing. After Sian finally lifted her head, casting a grief-stricken gaze to the ceiling, she released a ragged breath. "It was all over Underground yesterday."

Not surprising. Ebelwyn was a darkling fae. His office was on Solomon Street, which meant he answered to Grigori Tennin. Which meant, after he called me, he went and reported to Grigori and probably anyone else who'd listen.

"I knew it was her," Sian said quietly. "She was supposed to meet me here after going to the gym that morning. We were going to have breakfast before she went to work."

"So who is S. Yavesh?" I asked.

"He's the guy who owns the place. Daya was doing freelance work for him, restoring some old artifacts. He told her she could stay here whenever she wanted, so we've sort of been using it to meet up. I don't think he ever comes here."

"What's he look like?"

"I've never met him, but Daya said he was an Adonai."

My brow raised at that, and I immediately suspected S. Yavesh was an alias for Llyran.

"She tell you what she was working on?" Hank asked. "Did you see any of it?"

"No. She was working on restoring the items in her lab at the Fernbank Museum." Sian stared at the wall, completely lost. "I just can't believe she's gone."

"Come on . . ." I pushed away from the dresser and approached the bed to help her up. "Let's get you home."

"No. I don't want to go. This is all I have left of her. I can't go."

"You can't stay here, Sian. If your father finds out you're here and what you've been doing here, he'll go completely ballistic."

She sniffed and wiped her nose, looking up at me with round eyes. "No," she said simply. "He'd just kill me and that'd be the end of it. He despises me already for not getting him the things he wants from work."

I took her by the arm and gently urged her off the bed. "I doubt he holds you responsible for that one."

After all, if Grigori was pissed at anyone, it'd be me. I was the one who'd agreed to get his daughter a job at the ITF as payment for a blood debt I owed him. He'd wanted a mole. And what he got was a lot of useless information. Sian had a job at the ITF, but her psycho dad never said she had to have clearance or access codes to case files and ITF documents. Fuck him—not my problem that he hadn't made the terms clear.

Okay, so it *was* my problem. Or, I should say, Grigori Tennin was my problem. And he wasn't going away anytime soon. In fact, my guess was the bastard was sitting back and waiting to see what chaos the darkness wrought, and secretly fanning the flames.

One problem at a time, though.

"Come on, Sian. You need to go home." She gave in without a fight, and walked on her own down the hallway. As we passed the wall of windows, a dark, fluttering blur outside caught my eye. I steered Sian to the open door and the clerk waiting in the hallway. "Escort Miss Tennin to the lobby, please." I told the clerk.

The hairs on my arms stood as they retreated toward the elevator. My hand moved to my Hefty. I flicked the snap to the leather strap that held my weapon. As soon as the elevator doors slid open and they entered, I pulled my weapon.

"Outside. Terrace," Hank said, his own weapon drawn and already with his back against the wall and ready to cover me as I entered.

Carefully we reentered the penthouse, approaching the floor-to-ceiling windows, moving quietly around the furniture to the sliding glass doors. Beyond the glass, a figure sat with his back to us, cross-legged on the ledge of the terrace, knees overhanging forty-six stories below. His black linen shirt flapped in the breeze. Shoulder-length red hair stirred.

Llyran.

I pushed the glass doors apart just enough to squeeze through. Once we were out onto the stone terrace, I nodded to Hank to let him know I'd take the right, but a voice stopped me midstride.

"Hello again, Charlie."

My fingers flexed around the Hefty as Llyran stood on the narrow ledge and turned around to face us. The fact that he was standing forty-six stories up on a ledge as wide as his feet were long didn't seem to distress him in the least. "And Mister Williams," he said. "Brother. *Malakim*. Fellow Elysian . . ."

Malakim?

I fired.

The Hefty's tag thunked into his chest, pinning the linen to his skin. A sound wave–induced shudder went through him as his arms stretched wide. A smug smile grew on his perfect face as though the universe was his to own and operate.

And then he let himself fall backward into thin air.

I ran to the ledge to see his black-clad form freefall at a terrifying speed.

Hank's shoulder bumped mine as he leaned over the ledge. "Holy shit."

Somewhere around ten stories down, a tunnel of darkness snaked down, slicing through the air to curl around his body like a python in a death squeeze, pulling him back up and into its lofty, murky clouds.

Hank and I just stood there, dumbfounded. One second Llyran was falling, and the next . . .

I turned to my partner, mouth open, trying to wrap my mind around what I'd just witnessed, trying to think of an appropriate response, but nothing came.

Hank took a few steps back, dragged his fingers through his hair, and then turned, hands on hips and eyeing me with a stupefied look that instantly shifted to horror. He leapt toward me.

I glanced over my shoulder just in time to see Llyran flying toward me.

No time to react; Llyran grabbed me from behind and jerked me out over the terrace into midair.

II

Through the wind and the frantic pulse surging through my eardrums, I heard Hank scream my name.

There was nothing between me and the ground, except forty-six stories of air. *Oh God, oh God, oh God, oh God . . .*

My mouth hung open in a scream I couldn't voice. I didn't struggle, too afraid he'd drop me. I wanted to turn in his arms and scramble onto his shoulders, to hold on, to have some kind of control, but his embrace was bruising and unmovable.

Llyran's face was against the side of my head, pressed against my hair. His laughter rang in my ears as we shot upward. Higher and higher. And finally into the darkness itself. Into that churning, forty-mile wide mass of primeval Charbydon gray.

Tears leaked from the corners of my eyes as the

earth below me grew smaller and smaller, until it was completely swallowed up.

"Beautiful, isn't it, Charlie?!" His lips moved against my hair.

We slowed, and I was stunned by the thick, dark, undulating mass and the occasional bursts of green zigzagging a thick, random path far out in the distance. Small particles swirled, glowing as though energized, as though somehow giving life to everything around us. The fine hairs on my body stood, and the hair on my head drifted out in all directions as though underwater.

Awareness snaked under my skin. Power. So much power. It hummed through me. My eyelids fluttered. My vision went blurry. My head relaxed against Llyran's shoulder as I was caught between horror and excitement, a heightened response to the arcane darkness and energy surrounding me. It was there, for me. For the taking. It wanted me to throw open my arms and invite it in. It'd be so good, so easy . . .

"There is unimaginable power here, and the one who wields it can be a god!" Llyran shouted.

I shut my eyes tightly, forcing away the fuzz, lifting my head and shaking it hard. After a false start, I found my voice. "Take me back," I barely managed. "Llyran, take me back."

"Not yet, Charlie! I've saved the best for last!"

We shot up once more, the force pulling my insides down. Wind broke hard against my face and those small glowing particles hit my skin like fine grains of sand. My fingernails dug deeply into his forearms.

And then we burst out of the darkness.

Into the light.

Tears erupted behind my eyelids. Too bright, but so warm . . . so warm. After so long, I had the sun in my face.

A shaft of darkness held us aloft, above the churning mass. The wind whipped at our hair, tangling it together. "Isn't it a sight for sore eyes, Charlie? Blue skies as far as the eye can see. Tell me you haven't missed this!"

His arms were still around my middle. The angle at which the darkness held us aloft forced me to lean back against him, my head tucked against the crook of his neck as my face warmed under the glow of the sun. Panic had a hold on my throat, but I forced the words out. "Why are you doing this?"

"Because all this can be yours. Look at it, Charlie." He gave me a brutal squeeze. *"Look at it."*

I did. I did because I was afraid, because I was desperate for the sun, for blue skies. My eyes burned at first, leaving large white dots floating in my vision. But slowly they adjusted to the brightness, and I gazed out over the horizon at the azure sky. Tears slipped down my cheeks, and I couldn't tell if it was the sting of brightness or just me weeping for something I was afraid I'd never see again.

"I can take it all away. Together, we can bring back the light." His hair whipped around the edges of my vision, his voice manic and firm in his beliefs. "I'd do it for you, Charlie. We'd be unstoppable. You can bring about a new era, a new age in which Elysia is ruled by its rightful heirs."

"And who would that be, you?"

"No, not me. The Charbydon nobles. Elysia was once theirs before they were cast out into the dark shithole that is Charbydon, just as Elysia cast me out."

"Yeah, because you're a psychopath."

His arms released me.

I fell, finally letting out a terrifying scream.

He caught me by the ankle, my body whipping around like a rag doll. My entire being trembled as he righted me and held me once again. I had to stay conscious, had to fight against the fear.

Talk. Reason with him. Do something!

His mouth was low against my ear. "Careful with the insults, Detective."

"I'm sorry," I croaked, playing his game, and willing myself to breathe even and deep. "You're doing all this to get back at your home world?"

He thought about it for a second and then shrugged. "Once the nobles are faced with the truth, that Elysia was theirs, they will strike and take it back. And with the star's power, I'll help them wipe out every Adonai in existence, save for me, of course."

"That's genocide. You can't mean to wipe out your own kind."

"I can. They cast me out, turned their backs on me, all because I discovered the proof to the truth they have been hiding for ages . . ." He squeezed me tighter. I glanced over to see his profile as he rested his chin on my shoulder, a wistful smile on his perfect Adonai face. "Now that I have seen inside of you, I have big plans for you. The truth is more than you could ever imagine, Charlie. You have a great purpose in life, a great value, and *I will protect you*."

"Is that why you're murdering people, to protect me?"

"No. I am murdering people because it's necessary. Hold on, princess."

We dropped back. I gasped at the sickening, horrifying sensation of freefalling once more, eyes wide open, my face toward the sun as we fell, suddenly wanting those last few seconds of light before it slowly became swallowed up by darkness.

All too soon, I found myself back in the swirl of primordial chaos and raw power. I couldn't take it anymore. My heart was losing its battle trying to keep up with the shock and fear. Air was not reaching my lungs like it should. And somewhere in the back of my mind was the thought that all this willing power was mine to use and yet I was too fucking scared to even try.

"Please," I burst out on a shaky breath. "Take me back. I'll do whatever you want. Just take me back."

And then I'd kill the sonofabitch.

"Good girl." Llyran rubbed his cheek against my hair. "You and me, we shall be a force of nature like the world has never seen. We shall raise the star and feed off the power. Only you can do that for me.

You will, won't you, princess? You want to see the light again, don't you? The sun, the blue sky . . . I can give that to you, to your beloved city. Consider it a gift."

I nodded, swallowing hard and not caring what I had to say to get my feet back on solid ground. "Yes, I will. I'll do anything."

"I knew you would see it my way."

I braced for the descent, turning my face against the sting of those glowing particles, my hair flying across my face and acting as a shield. Through the strands, I saw the entire city below me, lit with millions of lights. And then, as we drew closer, Helios Tower, and its enormous rooftop arboretum. And closer, I could pick out the individual terraces, and finally, there was Hank standing on the terrace, hands curled around the railing and looking up, his blond hair waving in the wind. And though I couldn't actually see his expression, I sensed it—rage, horror, desperation.

I blinked and he was gone, gone from the terrace as we descended rapidly. My muscles bunched and tensed. Finally after several seconds, the darkness slowed us.

I had to think, figure out my next move. As soon as my feet hit the stone, I'd have to do something because there was no way in hell I was going to be Llyran's *princess*, partner, or raiser of dead stars. Not in this lifetime.

Only problem was, the roller coaster ride through

the darkness had left me a numb, trembling mass. And if we landed on that terrace, Hank was a goner and I was in deep shit.

We glided toward the terrace at a sedate pace. Hank was nowhere in sight, thank God. Llyran was much stronger than the both of us—all he had to do was use the darkness to grab Hank and jerk him off the terrace, and I was doubtful my partner could survive that kind of fall despite his healing abilities.

I pointed my toe, reaching for the railing. Almost there. A breath of relief slid out of my open mouth, and my body relaxed a fraction.

Right before my deranged partner jumped up from behind the railing and took a flying leap toward us.

"Hank! No—"

His six foot four frame crashed into us, knocking us back into midair and crushing me against his chest as he wrapped his arms and legs around Llyran—me sandwiched in between them and utterly helpless.

Llyran shouted in surprise, losing his command over the darkness. We fell straight down, windows and terraces flying by at incredible speed.

"Hold on!" Hank yelled.

Llyran cursed, struggling, trying to shove Hank off as we tumbled, going end over end. My eyes rolled back in my head, and the need to puke or pass out or both made me grit my teeth and force myself to do neither.

Anytime now. We'd hit anytime now.

I didn't want to die like this. Images of my family flashed like a slide projector behind my eyelids, and a moment of calm descended upon me as the power began to coil in my gut.

Screw this. I was not going to go out like this.

"Don't, Charlie!" Hank shouted. "Keep it inside! Trust me!"

The power inside of me ballooned, pushing against my ribs, surging down my arms and legs. I screamed. I couldn't control it.

And then we were jerked to a fast halt. "Now! Let him go!" Hank yelled as Llyran regained control over the darkness. But he had stopped us too fast and when the darkness began to lift Llyran, his grip on me slipped.

Hank and I continued to fall two stories. We nearly separated, but he pulled me close as I flailed to get my arms around him.

We crashed into the flower garden in the center of the tower's U-shaped drive. A loud "oomph" went out of Hank as his back hit first, along with my arms, which I'd somehow wrapped tightly around him.

I screamed as pain exploded along my collarbone, shoulders, and back. My shoulders dislocated, and my collarbone snapped, the sound of my bone break-ing stinging my eardrums. We sank ten inches into the soft soil, the crush of flowers falling in on top of us.

I was immobile. And if Hank so much as twinged, the pain would be . . . unthinkable.

"We have to get out of here," he rasped through gritted teeth; I knew he was injured, too.

"No. Don't move."

He groaned, his heart pounding hard against my temple as I lay there completely still and trying to breathe through the pain. "Charlie. He's coming back."

"I can't move," I muttered, mouth squished against his chest and hot tears wetting the fabric of his shirt. "I'm broken. I can't."

"Heal. And heal fast. Right the fuck now."

"What the hell were you doing—*trying* to get us killed?"

"Trying to prevent it, actually." He hissed in pain. "The only way was to get out of that tower fast and there was no other way but down. I knew he wouldn't let himself hit, and that he'd try to hold on to you."

He straightened his leg and winced. The movement sent a hot jolt through my shoulder blades. "Stop it!"

"Sorry, kiddo, but we've got to go."

I braced as he drew in a deep painful breath and sat up with me on top of him. "*You bastaaarrrddd!*" My vision went blurry. The pain turned my stomach and made my head swim. "Oh God, I hate you."

"I know," he whispered as though it hurt too much to speak louder, grabbing my arm. "You're about to hate me even more."

I gasped, realizing what he was about to do, right before he twisted my arm and shoved the first of two dislocated shoulders into place. I was passing out, but I held out long enough to slur, "You're right . . ." And then blackness took me.

★   ★   ★

I woke to my forehead slapping against my partner's lower back as he carried me like a sack through the Underground lobby and down the well-lit tunnel that led to Helios Alley. My arms dangled, the jarring movement threatening to send me right back into oblivion.

My shoulders were useless and limp, and radiating such agonizing heat that my insides had shriveled. Each jab of Hank's shoulder into my gut pushed a little bile up my throat.

Please let me pass out again. Please.

"Start healing yourself, Charlie," Hank said in ragged breaths, apparently sensing that I was conscious, moving as fast as he could down Helios Alley.

"Go to hell," I snarled, blinded by pain so bad I couldn't think straight.

Hank turned into the entrance for The Bath House, fishing in his back pocket for his wallet and then finding his membership card to slide through the access panel near the large wooden doors. It clicked open, and he hurried inside the massive space built to resemble the baths in Elysia. The air was warm and humid. The sounds of birds echoed in the main entrance area, but all I could see were the blurry mosaic tiles and the edges of palms and containers.

A moan rumbled in my sour throat amid the sound of Hank's low voice and that of another. I was going to puke.

We swung left, went a few more steps, and then

entered another room. Hank laid me on a wide chaise lounge; the jolt of sharp pain that shot through me was the last straw. I turned, my collarbone screaming, and vomited on the tile floor.

After I was through, I laid my head back on the soft white cushion, gasping for air and realizing I was completely alone, left with just the potted foliage and the piped-in flute music that was barely audible over the sound of a fountain.

Now that I wasn't being bounced on Hank's shoulder, I attempted to heal. I regulated my breathing and opened myself to my Elysian power—the side that responded so well to those thoughts, emotions, and images of my loved ones. I healed quicker that way; my Charbydon power was also able to heal me, but hell if I had figured out how to access it for that purpose.

It started small, but built until the energy hummed inside of me, the familiar, cool vibration like a welcome island breeze. Beyond my relaxing mind and body, I heard movement and felt a wet cloth being placed on my forehead. Murmured words passed between what I guessed was a Bath House attendant and Hank. Then all the outside stimuli fell away as I withdrew into myself and let the healing energy take over.

I had no idea how long I laid there in a semiconscious state as my body healed, but when I finally roused and turned my head to the side, it was to see Hank sprawled out on the twin lounge set against the opposite wall. We were in some sort of private massage or meditation room with its own bath, one of many within the complex. The rectangular walls were inlaid with mosaic tiles like the rest of The Bath House, and four columns rose from the corners of the long rectangular pool. Iron sconces held fat-burning candles and two large basins in the far corners held open flames. The faint scent of citrusy herbs made the warm air seem thinner, fresher, and easier to breathe. The only light came from the soft glow of the candles and fires, giving the place a dark, aged feel as though I'd stepped back in time to ancient Babylon.

My arms and shoulders still tingled with healing energy, but I was unsure if I'd healed completely, so I used my stomach muscles to rise and get a better look at the surroundings.

Hank was flat on his back, hands resting on his stomach, his breathing deep and even. There was a gaping hole in his pants leg and blood surrounding it, some deep scratches still on the sides of his arms from where some of the stiffer, thicker stems must have cut into his skin, but other than that he appeared okay.

Gently, I swung my legs over the cushy lounge and very gingerly tested my shoulders, starting with a slow roll. Lots of heat and pain. My hand felt along my clavicle and the tender spot where the bone had snapped, but was obviously now mending.

What was even more amazing, besides sheer luck in landing where we had, was that Hank's insane escape plan had worked. We'd gotten away from Llyran and the darkness. We'd survived a fall from forty-six stories up—a nightmare that would forever join a few others in my subconscious.

And then he'd tossed my broken body over his shoulder like I was some crash-test dummy. The pain had been unbearable.

I let my gaze scan the room once more, pushing the memory into the back of my mind. There was a small pitcher of ice water and two glasses sitting on a table in between the lounges. I poured a glass and gulped it down, much thirstier than I'd realized. I wanted a second cup, but sacrificed the rest for payback—I stood with the pitcher, pausing a second to let my wobbly legs regain their balance and for my head to stop spinning, then walked over to the peaceful form of my partner and dumped the entire contents onto his face.

His arms flew up and he jerked upright, sputtering and taking a moment to realize where he was. Slowly he wiped a palm over his wet face. Then his gaze found mine and went sapphire hard. "What the hell's the matter with you?"

"Don't you *ever* do that to me again."

He wiped his face again and then dragged his damp hair back from his forehead, the muscle in his jaw twitching. "What? Save your ungrateful little ass?"

"Yes." I cocked my head, feeling rank and stubborn. "I had things under control."

"Yeah. The Oh-fuck-I'm-going-to-pee-myself look

on your face really said 'control' to me." He swung
his legs off the bed, and then rubbed his hand along
his shin where the hole and the blood on his pants
were. "Now you're going to have to get me some
water. I'm thirsty."

My hands squeezed the pitcher handle. "Get your
own stupid water."

He stilled. "No. I will not get my own water. *You*
will get me my water." His nostrils flared with anger,
and he spoke through gritted teeth. The flames on
the candles flickered in response to his mood and the
energy being pulled toward him. "You know why?
Because I saved your goddamn life today, and I'd like
a little gratitude." His jaw clenched tightly, but his
gaze did not back down.

I didn't back down, either, willing myself not to
blink, even as my conscience began to feel guilty
for what I'd done. He *had* saved my life. And I was
so focused on the pain, on the way he'd handled
me . . . *Goddammit*.

"Fine," I muttered. "I'll get your stupid water."

"Fine."

I let the door bang shut and then marched down the
hallway toward the concierge desk, hoping to hell that
Zara was off today. Hank's on-and-off-again girlfriend
was the last person I wanted to see. But, of course,
there she was, sitting behind the desk, her perfect blue
eyes staring at her computer monitor, and her long,
strawberry blond hair tucked behind one ear and falling in a sheet of glossy satin that pricked my envy.

I slammed the pitcher on the counter. "Mister High and Mighty wants water."

Zara jumped. "Charlie." She stood, smiling in greeting, rising to her glorious supermodel height, and took the pitcher. "You guys have been out for"— she glanced at her monitor—"an hour and a half? I take it you're feeling better."

"It feels like I just fell forty-six stories. It hurts, and I'm . . . not happy." I turned, leaning my back against the counter as she went to the water cooler and filled the pitcher.

She chuckled. "Don't be too mad. Hank carried you here with a cracked skull, a broken kneecap, and a few internal injuries if I had to guess. And he cleaned up your . . . mess . . . on the floor."

"Oh." All of my ire deflated with that one word. "I thought someone else did that."

Once the pitcher was full, she turned to me and held it out. "He really cares about you, you know." Heat crept into my cheeks as I took the pitcher. She glanced down at her feet and then back up at me, giving me a small shrug and a half-smile. "I don't know if he told you . . . I broke it off with him. For good, this time. I'd been thinking about it for a while anyway."

I set the pitcher on the counter, still holding on to the handle. "But, why?"

"It's hard to explain. I like him. I really do." She leaned closer to the counter, looking like she could use someone to talk to. "Honestly? It's the voice-mod."

Hank's words from earlier came back to me. I shook my head. "I don't get it . . ."

Her perfect gaze fixed on a point beyond my shoulder for a moment as she decided how to explain. "With it stuck on his neck . . . certain *things* are not what they should be . . . um, if you know what I mean."

My brow lifted high in realization. "Oh. Okay. I see . . ."

She breathed a sigh of relief. Her smile was so pretty it made me cringe and want to be her devoted best friend all at the same time. "Yeah," she said. "Sirens . . . well, we *talk*. Murmur, whisper, use our voices to accentuate certain things. It's very powerful. It makes the experience that much greater, and it's way more for the females than the males. That's why you don't see very many female sirens with any other type of males. We almost never"—her face turned pink—"*you know* with other males. I mean, don't get me wrong, Hank is . . ." Her eyes widened and she gave me an incredulous expression of awe. "But without the power of his voice, it's not the same for me. Not what I'm used to."

Just the idea of a male siren using his voice during sex—I was red-faced just thinking about it. "Mott Tech will find a way to remove it."

"I know. And Hank's a great guy and everything. I'm just not sure we were meant for each other. It's all awkward now and . . ." She laughed, shaking her head. "I don't know what I'm saying."

"It's okay," I muttered. "If anyone knows awkward, it's me."

She sat in her chair. "Make sure you guys use the healing pool. It'll speed your recovery." Her fingers tapped against the keyboard keys, her gaze returning to the monitor.

I slid the pitcher off the counter and muttered a lame goodbye, walking a lot slower down the hall than I had a few minutes ago. Hank's irritability, his reaction to my using the word *emasculated* . . . Things were beginning to make a lot more sense.

When I returned to the room, he was lying on the lounge, one arm thrown over his face. I picked up the second glass, filled it, and held it out to him. "Here . . . sorry about earlier . . . it just hurt." Tears stung my eyes. "Really bad."

He turned his head slightly and opened his eyes, staring at me for a second before sitting up and taking the glass. "Thanks."

With a heavy exhale, I sat on the lounge across from him, my attention riveted on the tile floor. "No, I should be thanking you. For saving my life and getting us out of that tower." I glanced up. "And, for the record, I was *not* going to pee myself. I was too damn scared."

Hank finished off the water and then one corner of his mouth lifted into a shadow of a smile. "I was scared, too. Seeing you go flying backward off the terrace and up into the clouds . . . I thought he was going to drop you. On purpose."

"He showed me the sun," I said quietly. "He believes the Char nobles were once Elysians who were cast out. Llyran's got it in his head that I can help him return the nobles back to Elysia."

Hank nodded thoughtfully, leaning his elbows on his knees and rubbing his chin. "How does he think you can help?"

"Hell if I know. He's grandiose, wants more than power. He wants to be in control, of everything and everyone. He mentioned the star, raising the star, just like Daya said. Thinks I can make that happen for him." I rubbed a hand down my face and let out a long, tired moan. "You think he's still looking for us?"

"No. I think he's fucking with you. Maybe he wants to do to you what he's been doing to the others: take your power."

Hank stood and held out his hand to help me up, but I just sat there looking up at him. "Then why hasn't he?" I asked lamely.

"I don't know. Seeing what you're made of? Testing your power? We knew this would happen once news got out about you, what's been done to you. You're going to be a lure, a beacon to anyone searching for a leg up, for power."

"Yeah, and I can't even summon power when I really need it. I can't control it."

"Eh, don't worry about that, Charlie. You're a newborn. The rest of us have had ages to learn how to focus, for it to finally become natural, even in the most hectic, unsettling moments."

Aaron said the same thing every time I got frustrated during a lesson. And it was true, I knew, but when it counted the most, when I needed it the most—sometimes, I failed myself. I could have prevented Llyran from taking me on the joy ride from hell. Theoretically, I was more powerful than he was. I had the genes of all three worlds and access to more power than any being on this planet. For all the good it did me.

"I'm sorry about the water," I said again, trying to think of a way to explain.

"Sometimes . . . pain, or the reminder of it, makes us do rash things. Call it payback for me ditching you the other day." He gave a crooked grin.

Spoken like someone with a ton of experience in the pain department. Curious.

"Come on, we should get into the water. The next time I face Llyran, I want to be completely healed." Hank grabbed the end of his shirt and began to pull it up. My face went hot. He froze, seeing my look. "You know, sooner or later, you're going to have to get used to the Elysian way of things."

I turned my back to him and let out the breath I'd been holding, not bothering to respond. Not sure I'd ever get used to the nonexistent modesty held by the Elysians. In the baths, in this part of their culture, naked was the way to go. I had a healthy appreciation for the male form and had my share of lusty fantasies, but that didn't equate to the reality of standing in an indoor nudist colony and being completely at ease. Hell, even baring it all with the object of one's desire could be a bit nerve-inspiring at first.

Hank's soft chuckle issued behind me as I heard his zipper slide down. "Relax, Madigan. Every private room has the clothing option. I'll wear a shenti. There should be a gown on the chest at the end of your lounge."

I still didn't turn around, though I did cast my eyes toward the lounge and the thick pile of towels and the neatly folded gowns. The clothing option had been made available to the small number of human bath house members and those who had adopted human ways. Once I heard Hank's footsteps retreat toward the pool, I went for the sheer curtain that hung between two of the columns. I pulled each cord and let them swish closed.

I changed quickly, wincing as I pulled the short, Greek-style gown over my head, and leaving on my bra and undies since the material would become transparent in the water.

Hank was already sitting on a mat by the pool's edge, his back to me. I squared my shoulders, drew in a deep breath, and walked forward.

As I drew closer, I dropped my towel onto the nearest table, noticing Hank was cross-legged, posture straight, eyelids closed. I'd seen him half naked in a shenti before, at this same bath house, but it still did nothing to calm the girly spike of awareness at seeing his perfect form, all tanned and hard, and unavoidable, wearing only a linen loincloth.

12

I swallowed again, willing myself to think more like Elysians, entirely comfortable with their bodies, both in and out of clothes.

I was more worked up at seeing Hank than he'd ever be at seeing me. He went to the baths almost every day, frolicking naked with some of the most gorgeous creatures on the planet. So seeing me in my short gown was not going to set him on fire . . . not that I wanted to set him on fire anyway.

"Since when do you meditate?"

"Since when do you think you know everything about me?" he responded, eyes still closed and face not changing expression.

I made a face he couldn't see.

"Have a seat, Charlie. I'll show you how."

"No thanks, I'm gonna soak for a few minutes and

then be on my way." I dipped my toe into the water. It was warm and the herby smell that erupted made me breathe in deeply.

"Scared?"

I pivoted. "Of meditating? No."

"You need practice concentrating, using your focus. It'll help you heal, too. Sit down and I'll show you how to play with water. Unless you're, you know, scared."

I blew a strand of hair away from my face and sat down on the mat, facing him, mimicking his pose. "Happy? What now?"

"Close your eyes, grasshopper." His mouth twitched.

I smiled despite myself. "You're such a dork."

"Ah, but a dork who can do this."

I felt the energy gather before I saw it. It tingled my skin, set me on edge, and I straightened my spine. His aura ballooned, surrounding him in a wash of island blues—azure, topaz, turquoise. The beauty of it was mesmerizing. I lost track of my senses until the air grew cooler and damp. I turned to see waves in the pool, slapping gently at the sides.

Hank lifted his arms slowly. Droplets of water rose from the pool like rain in reverse, following his movement. He held his perfectly formed arms straight out, looking like some Michelangelo sculpture come to life and making it hard for me to choose what to look at, because both male and water were stunning.

Slowly Hank lowered his arms, wiggling his fingers and making the droplets fall like the gentlest rain.

I was smiling, my heart beating a little faster. This was, by far, the coolest thing I'd ever seen him do. Hank hardly showed any powers around me at all. At least not like this, for fun, and not under fire, chasing a criminal down the street.

I tore my gaze away from the pool, struck by the power and the raw, potent beauty of him. I'd gotten used to the way people stopped and stared at Hank, often amused by the fact that even as they looked, they gave him respect and space. Like an unspoken, unrecognized sense of acknowledgment, the same way wild animals give deference to an alpha or a predator among them.

He couldn't have acted any more different, though. Always making dumb jokes, dressing down, and not giving his inborn nature a second thought.

He cracked one eye open. "Stop that." His eyelid closed again.

"Stop what?"

"You're not blocking your aura or your emotions." He dropped his concentration, his hands falling on his bare thighs and his shoulders slumping a fraction as he gave me a frank look. "Keep looking at me like that and I'll take you up on it."

My mouth fell open and then immediately snapped closed. Blood rose hot to my cheeks. I put up a fast block, my pulse beating furiously. Great. When did I suddenly become one of *those* people?

The water in the pool quieted to a gentle, hypnotic wave. "So, the lesson," I prompted, practically burning under his scrutiny.

"That was the lesson. Now it's your turn."

"Riiiight."

"If you have Adonai in you, you should be able to do a lot more with water than the average Elysian. It's an easy element to start with, and you've been focusing too much on the Char side of you."

"That's because the Char side comes easier." Which I really hated to admit. But Hank was right—I needed to practice using the Elysian in me. The more I did, the easier it would be to access when it really counted. And I had used some of it already to fight Llyran. "Okay." I let my eyes close and gave my best meditative pose. "Now what, Sensei?"

I peeked to see his mouth quirk. He tried his damnedest to convey seriousness, but there was only humor gleaming in those gemstone blues. "Don't sound so enthused," he said. "Close your eyes, focus your thoughts, envision the water . . . *feel* it, the wetness, the cool temperature, the way it runs over your skin. You're it and it's you. You become one. You control its flow, its properties. Make it yours."

The persuasive baritone sank deep into my being like languid-flowing honey, turning my breathing into a slow, rhythmic cadence. My focus, however, sharpened, and it didn't take long for me to imagine all the visuals Hank had mentioned.

My skin became electrified, the tiny hairs standing. I raised my arms as he had raised his, ignoring the soreness, and instead thinking of the water he'd lifted and the way thousands of tiny droplets had separated from the mass below, the way they hovered and then fell like the softest rain. I could hear it, and the sound was like tranquil music.

A rich chuckle reached my ears, and I looked to see the water falling just as I'd imagined it. Instant joy erupted in me, a balm of feel-good sensations and energy that made me throw my arms up high in victory and shout. I lunged forward and threw my arms around Hank's neck. "I did it!" The water fell back into the pool as my weight caught him off guard and sent him backward onto the mat. An "oomph!" shot from his lips as I raised my head, gripped by a great sense of wonder and accomplishment.

Pride glowed in his eyes; I could tell by the way they crinkled and lit up. "Not bad, kiddo. Not bad at all."

This felt so much better than using anger and negativity to drive my power. And it had the added benefit of furthering the healing process. I barely hurt at all. I stared at Hank for the longest time, panting and grinning like a damn fool until I realized that my bare thigh rested between his bare thighs, both of my palms flat on his bare chest. Too close, we were too close and nearly naked, and he smelled *insanely* good.

I was in so much trouble.

I pushed myself up, rolling to the side and scooting away awkwardly, silently cursing my ungraceful exit, as Hank pushed to his elbows, leaning back on them and just staring at me with an odd, crooked grin.

The breath died in my throat. His irises had turned the color of blue diamonds. My lungs burned, forcing me to gasp for air. I scrambled up and turned away from him, trying to calm my racing pulse.

Hank's eyes changed on emotions. Lately they'd held on to their hard, dark sapphire color as he dealt with the fallout caused by our fight with Mynogan. But slowly, every once in a while, they would lighten. When he'd forget all the bad things. When the old Hank would shine through, or I'd do something totally asinine. But, blue diamonds? *That* was a new one. And I had known Hank, had seen him nearly every day, for the past three years.

Confusion clouded my vision, and I fisted my hands together at my sides, just standing at the edge of the pool and wondering what the hell had changed. What the hell was wrong with me that I was noticing every tiny detail about my partner and my *friend*?

It had to be the darkness. Being constantly turned on by that kind of raw, primal power was like a drug. I needed an out. Needed to release some of it. It was too much, too much inside of me. Made me start looking at my partner like he could give me the release I needed. At least that's what I told myself.

A groan lodged in my throat. I needed a distraction and quick. "How about we try something a little more dramatic?" I shut my eyes and focused intently on water. Water everywhere. Water that matched my emotions.

"Charlie, I don't think that's such a good—" Hank's voice drowned in the rush of power pounding through my ears like the torrents over Niagara Falls.

Yes, drown him out. Don't listen to his potent voice, the decadent timbre that resonates through your body like a heavy drumbeat. Don't listen, Charlie. Don't. Listen.

Tears rose and closed my throat. I really just wanted someone to be close to, to make me feel secure and protected for once. How pathetic was that? How pathetic that I was so desperate I'd begun looking to my partner for it?

He called my name. I didn't listen. Instead, I wiped at my eyes before he could see how weak and stupid I was.

"Charlie!"

Wet strands of my hair slapped me in the face, stinging me back to reality.

My jaw dropped. Oh shit.

I couldn't move, just stood there in awe, staring at the tornado of water swirling in the center of the pool directly in front of me, writhing and spinning and shooting water everywhere. And my partner going along for the ride.

I was drowning him. Quickly, I closed my eyes again to summon my power, but I was too stunned and panicked to focus.

Come on. Come on, Charlie! Do something!

I tried again. The sound of water was deafening. Plants toppled over. The fires went out. Sconces flew off the wall. How the hell could anyone concentrate in this? I glanced around frantically. My control over what I'd manifested was lost. It should've collapsed the churning spiral, yet I'd somehow given it a life of its own. Hank yelled again. Before I could think better of it, I dove into the spiral.

It sucked me into a wide arc, dragging me in circles around the pool. Fighting against it was useless, so I streamlined my body and flowed with it, moving into the turns as it swept me along.

The panic ebbed. Being inside of my creation was so much easier than standing on the sidelines and watching helplessly. My confidence rose and I became one with the water, not fighting it, not fearing it. Soon I was guiding it, controlling it. Slowing it when I slowed. And up I went, using the water to take me higher, almost to the very top of the dome ceiling, where I swept past Hank and grabbed hold of his outstretched hand. We pulled together and wrapped our arms around each other.

And then I let it all go, releasing my command over the water.

We dropped, along with a few thousand gallons of water, into the pool below.

The water cushioned some of our fall, but we still hit the bottom of the pool pretty hard. Hank's arms tightened around me, and he angled his body toward the concrete just as we hit. Then he was pushing us up, through the water and back to the surface.

We broke through with gasps and coughs.

My legs and arms were wrapped tightly around

him, my forehead pressed into the crook of his neck, and I didn't let go, too afraid I'd sink straight to the bottom of the pool if I did. I was weak, totally spent, in shock at the thought of what had come out of me.

"Why didn't you fight it?" I asked. "Use your power?"

"Because I knew you could fix it, Charlie."

Hank's heart pounded hard and strong against my chest, mingling with the frantic beat of mine. I eased my hold a little, realizing I was reluctant to do so. He felt safe and warm. I, on the other hand, was a shivering, teeth-chattering mess. Reluctantly I lifted my forehead off the side of his neck and looked eye level at him.

I don't think either one of us wanted to be the first to speak, so instead I pushed a wet strand of his hair from his forehead, unsure of what I was doing or why.

Whatever the reason—adrenaline, shock—my blood pressure rose. I licked the wetness on my lips, captured by the blue diamond irises staring back at me, mesmerized, and unable to look away. I felt a tug, a pulse of awareness between my legs. That part of me, I realized, was pressed intimately against his groin, and another bloom of desire rocketed through me.

His Adam's apple slid up and down. His gaze dropped to my lips. His entire body stilled as I held my breath. Then his gaze was back, fixed on me like a burning blue flame.

I couldn't help it. It had been so long since I'd felt

like this. My hand curled around the back of his neck as we moved in closer. My chest and stomach became like an explosion of feathers, so light and airy and breathless. Almost there . . .

And he wanted it, too. I could feel it against me, see it in the way his gaze had locked back on to my lips. The pressure of his hold increased. One of his hands slid up my back and cupped the back of my head. Our noses brushed. His fingers curled into my hair, tugging at the roots as my head angled.

The first bang on the door sent me jerking back with a gasp.

It took several seconds of banging and Zara's voice calling from the other side before I regained my senses and realized exactly where I was and what I'd been about to do. Hank's arms released me the same moment I pushed back. I slid under the surface of the water, turned, and swam to the edge of the pool as Zara entered with three attendants at her back. I hadn't felt this humiliated since high school.

With a weary sigh, I pulled my heavy, wet, shaken self from the water. Zara stopped in front of me, her wide eyes assessing the soaked walls and upended furniture. "Sorry about the mess," I mumbled, grabbing a wet towel and wrapping it around me. "Just bill me if I broke anything."

A splash sounded behind me, but I didn't turn to see Hank hiking himself out of the pool. Instead, I grabbed my clothes and fled.

"Damn it, Charlie," Hank said. "Wait!"

I didn't stop. I couldn't.

Yeah, it was cowardly of me, but I had to get away. Away from him. Away from Zara. Just . . . out of there. I found my way to the large women's locker room, near the main bath, tore off the wet gown, and pulled on my damp clothes, wondering who the hell was controlling my body because it sure as hell wasn't the normal Charlie.

I strapped on my weapons and cell phone and then hurried out of The Bath House, making a beeline down Helios Alley. I didn't need to look at the time on my cell to know that the dinner rush hadn't started. Otherwise Helios Alley would be teeming with lines to the best restaurants and people would already be milling about, shopping, drinking, eating, and enjoying the nightlife in Underground.

My irritation with myself turned to anger with each step I took. Off-worlders just weren't my cup of tea, and I had never thought about Hank in *that* serious of a way before. What was I doing?

For most of our partnership, I'd been happily married to Will. But now that I was divorced and single, free from any chance of ever getting back together with my ex—since, technically, he didn't exist in this realm anymore—I had the freedom to explore other attractions. And apparently, my body had decided to start the explorations whether my mind was ready or not.

God, I felt like an idiot. I never should've *almost* kissed him. And worse, that kind of thing probably happened to him all the time, and now I was just one among many.

Once I reached Topside, I stopped on the sidewalk to catch my breath and refocus my thoughts.

The darkness hung above the skyscrapers, the lights from the buildings illuminating the heavy, swirling mass. Far off in the distance, a green flash snaked through the gray.

Incredibly, I'd been inside of that mass.

How the hell was he doing it? How the hell was Llyran taking control of the darkness? I shuddered softly as my gaze went to Helios Tower; the massive glass dome at its top glowed like a beacon in the dark sky. I needed to figure out the Adonai's interest in me, and how he thought I played into his cause.

I was so lost in thought that I didn't hear the footsteps behind me.

"Charlie Madigan?"

I spun and looked down to see an imp male standing behind me. Three and a half feet tall, wild orange hair, and cocoa skin in a cheap suit and dull dress shoes.

"Who wants to know?"

"I'm with L.D. Collections." He held out a large yellow envelope. Cautiously, I took it. "This is for your ex-husband. He has thirty days." He gave a sharp nod, turned on his heel, and strolled off into the dark shadows.

"Thirty days for what?" I muttered, wondering

how long the guy had been following me around as I tore open the envelope and scanned the cover letter. "Twenty-one thousand dollars?!" I yelled toward the direction the imp had taken, but he was already gone.

Will had been served collection papers.

Apparently, as I read beneath the streetlamp, he was responsible for back mortgage payments on his condo and penalties for defaulting on contracts for the houses he'd been in the process of building. This couldn't be right. And damned if I'd be paying my ex's bills. We were legally divorced.

How the hell had this happ—

Rex.

Following my stay in the hospital after bringing darkness to the city, and during my week at home to recuperate, Rex and I had gone over Will's finances. It was clear from the beginning that Rex lacked the know-how to run Will's fledgling architecture and construction business, so we'd canceled his contracts, found new builders for the projects he'd been working on, and made sure there was insurance to cover crap like this. Rex was *supposed* to have filed the claims. And the condo was *supposed* to have been rented. *Trust me, Charlie,* he'd said. *I've been around for thousands of years. I know how to take care of business.*

My gaze focused on nothing and then down at the envelope, eyes widening on the return address label. "Lion's Den Collections!"

L.D. Collections. *Sonofabitch!* A frustrated groan

burst from my throat. "I can't believe this." Just great. My ex's debt had been picked up by the biggest organized crime boss in Underground. Grigori Tennin.

My fist curled around the letter. I was going to kill them both.

13

I pulled into the driveway and parked. Will's truck was gone. Emma was still at practice. I called and left a message for Bryn to see how the support meeting went, and then I shoved the collections letter into my bag, slung the strap over my shoulder, and got out, but as soon as my feet hit the concrete, I had that feeling again of being watched.

I closed the door, slipped the keys into my front pocket, and then slowly put my hand on the hilt of my sidearm. I turned to scan the park area across the street, regulating my breathing, trying to focus and open myself to my instincts. I took a few slow steps, hand moving to my Hefty and finger sliding the frequency setting to low as I felt an aura prick my senses.

My footsteps brushed the driveway, sounding loud. The aura became clearer. Blues. Greens. The woods. The water. The tangy scent of grass. Then, like looking down a rifle scope, my sense zoned in on it. Nymph. Oak Tree. Across the street. I turned and fired. The Hefty was silent, except for the small hiss the tag made as it ejected from the barrel.

A black shadow the size of a large predatory cat fell from the tree and hit the grass with a faint thud. I jogged across the street, finding what I had guessed, a nymph. A naked male, Orin to be exact, clutching the tag in his shoulder. "Goddammit," he hissed, and jerked the tag out. "Did you have to shoot me?" The nymph whispered the words that would clothe his naked form.

"It was only low stun." I reached down to help him up, but remained on guard, my Hefty still clutched in my hand.

"Did that address I gave you help?"

"You first. You've been following me, haven't you? You were there this morning on Solomon Street. Is this you acting alone or is it on behalf of Dragon Boy?"

"It's part of my service for lying. Believe me, I would much rather be fulfilling the funeral rites than following your ass around Underground."

"So that *was* you in the back alley."

"No, that was Killian. I'm rotating with him. Pen's getting restless. He wants answers. Wants justice for Daya. We all do."

"Tell him to let us do our job. We want the same thing, too, but if you guys start interfering or distracting us from our work then it could jeopardize everything. You need to back off."

He snorted softly. "You try telling the Druid to back off. He wants a report."

It was my turn to snort. "You can tell him that I don't—"

"Charlie," Orin said with a gentle smile, "if I may . . . If one of your family had been murdered, what would you do?"

I opened my mouth and then shut it. I did that twice, my ire completely deflating. "Look, I understand," I admitted. "Believe me, I do. Tell him I have a strong lead on who did this and to give us a chance to do our job. This is what we do. We catch bad guys. He needs to trust me on this."

"Kinfolk trust only Kinfolk."

"Might want to start expanding your circle of friends. You can tell Pen this: it wasn't a jinn. So he can stand his ass down and forget about starting a war." I hiked the strap farther up my sore shoulder, feeling echoes of the horrible pain I'd felt earlier. "I'm beat. Stay out here all night if you want, but I'm going inside."

I didn't look back to see if Orin stayed or disappeared. I meant what I said. I was beat. Falling off a high rise and making water tornadoes sort of does that to a girl.

With Rex gone, Em in school, and the hellhound in the kennel, the house was a blessed space. No noise, no distractions. Just me, my bed, and hopefully a long nap. Before I went upstairs, I rooted through the junk drawer in the kitchen and pulled out a red marker and wrote *FIX THIS* on the collections envelope. Then I went into the guest room downstairs and left it on Rex's bed.

With every step upstairs, it seemed an old ache reappeared. By the time I reached my bedroom, all I could think about was lying down and shutting my eyes. As I sat and toed off my shoes, I saw that Rex had been at work, sweeping up the debris on the bathroom floor and boarding up the stained glass window that had shattered, and my busted bathroom door was gone.

After removing my damp clothes and putting on dry lounge pants and a T-shirt, I dropped onto my mattress and pulled the down comforter over my cold body.

What I got instead of sleep was a good, long look at my ceiling fan.

Aaron's words kept echoing in my head. Divine being. Divine.

What the hell did that mean?

I let out a loud groan, threw my arms wide, relaxed my muscles until it felt like I was sinking into the mattress, and then I began my breathing techniques. My gaze stayed on the fan, turning slowly. Around and around.

Eventually my mind began to clear. My eyelids fell, all my focus on my breathing.

Did you see what Jen wore to school? I'd never let my ten-year-old wear that.

This is Doctor Harmon's office calling to remind you of your appointment next Monday at eleven.

Carrie! Who the hell is running the water? I'm in the fucking shower!

Words became clatter. The clatter of a thousand conversations. Louder and louder. Building and building, until I shot up, gasping, my ears ringing and my head throbbing with leftover vibrations.

Jesus! I rubbed both hands down my face, catching a glimpse of my forearms. "No. Oh, no . . ."

They weren't blood vessels. How could they be? They were faint and blue, though, running beneath the surface of my skin in patterns, patterns eerily similar to the ancient, unknown script on the warehouse walls.

I sat there in a stupor, my arms out in front of me, resting on my legs, as the panic rose higher and higher. My throat closed, so dry and thick it felt like sand had been poured into my mouth.

"No, no, no, no . . ." I started to rub my arms, noticing that the patterns were everywhere, and, becoming frantic, I tried to rub everywhere, erase them, get them off me. And slowly, very slowly, the higher my panic rose, the dimmer the images became until finally my skin returned to normal. I let out a laugh, like some demented old witch. Normal. What the hell was normal anymore?

I lay down, curled onto my side, and pulled the covers to my chin, hoping I'd eventually fall asleep and determined to stay like that until I did.

When I woke, it was to Emma's kiss, telling me she was heading to bed. Must be after dinner, I realized, lifting my head slightly off the pillow to eye the clock. "Did you eat and do your homework?" I asked, half in sleep.

"Yes, Momma," she said, using her best impression of her grandmother. The gentle caretaker, the southern voice. "You keep right on resting now, ya hear?"

"Hah," I slurred and let my head sink back down into the pillow.

"I am *not* moving to the League. And that's final."

I stood at the kitchen counter with my morning coffee. We'd been at it now for thirty minutes. Thirty minutes of trying to tell my kid that, despite the ward room, I thought she'd be safer at the League while I dealt with the Llyran situation. You'd think being kidnapped by a deranged noble would've instilled a sense of self-preservation in her.

But then, I had to remind myself, I was dealing with an irate preteen who could go from fine and reasonable one minute to hellbent and irrational in the next. Though I was the *only* one who seemed to have the ability to affect her moods like this.

"Jesus, Emma. Why does everything have to be a fight?" I asked tiredly. She stood by the table, still in her white tank and plaid pajama bottoms, hair down and in its usual early morning, cave-girl disarray. "I haven't even asked the League yet, but don't you think it'd be best until this blows over?"

Rex sat at the table, silently eating his cereal. Smart guy.

"No. What about school and the play? You just want me to give up everything every time you work a stupid case?!"

"You know, you're lucky I don't ship you off to Orlando with your grandparents," I shot back. I did *not* want to do this. Not this early in the morning.

Em laughed. "At least it's sunny down there."

"Great. You can go to Orlando, then."

Her eyes narrowed and pink bloomed on her cheeks. "No, *Mother*, I will not. I want to stay right here. Not the League. Not Orlando. Here in my own goddamn house!"

"Emma!" Rex and I exclaimed at the same time.

Her lips thinned. The coiled tension coming off of her was palpable. "I can take care of myself. I have Brim. I can take him to school with me. He can be like my bodyguard."

"They are not going to allow a hellhound in school, Emma. He isn't even supposed to *be here*. It's illegal to keep them in the first place!"

Her hands fisted at her sides. She knew she wasn't winning this argument. "You make me so angry. I hate you!" she forced through gritted teeth, and then spun on her bare heel and stomped out the back door, slamming it as hard as she could.

Immediately I went for the back door, her comment only firing my blood even more.

"Charlie," Rex said. "Let her go."

I paused with my hand on the knob, swinging my gaze back to Rex. "I'm not letting her go, and don't you tell me what to do or how to raise my kid! The only thing I want to hear from you is that you have a twenty-one-thousand-dollar wad of cash hidden somewhere!"

I jerked the door open, ignoring Rex's second warning to let her go, and followed my daughter into the backyard. "Emma!" She stopped in the middle of the yard and turned to me. "You can still go to school and still practice for the play. Rex will stay with you, and I'll have Aaron add a warlock to guard you as well. But at night, you'll be safer at the League."

"You have no idea the things I can do. I don't need them. I told you I can protect myself."

The breeze blew her hair, but her entire body remained still and so damn quiet that it made me very concerned. She was trying so hard to be convincing, wanted so much for me to believe her. But I couldn't. How could I when she stood there with her thin frame and narrow shoulders, looking like a hard wind could break her in two?

She doesn't really hate you, I told myself over and over again as her words sank in. "Emma."

I saw it building, her frustrated scream, her white-knuckled fists. I just never expected her to unleash a massive power surge aimed straight at me.

It happened so fast, I didn't have time to move. An invisible wave of energy hit me with such force that it knocked the wind out of me and sent me flying backward to land on my ass, leaves and small bits of lawn flying in my face.

The scent of dirt and tangy green grass filled the air; some of it, I was certain, had gone up my nose. I scrambled up, body shaking, and spit a leaf fragment from the corner of my mouth.

Emma remained still, like a tiny ball of fury. She wasn't done. The only things that moved on her were her hair and her clothes, which fluttered with each strong burst of wind through the backyard. The trees bent and rubbed together. Green flashed in the darkness overhead.

And then her lips started moving.

"Emma . . ." I warned.

A metal clang cut through the morning. I glanced beyond her shoulder to see the kennel door swing wide and Brim bound out. Four blindingly fast, gigantic strides later, he slid to a stop at her side, his claws cutting deep ruts into the grass. He was poised, battle-ready, looking very much like the pregnant hellhound in the warehouse. Defend to the death.

"*Emma Kate Garrity . . .*" I warned again, hardly able to hear myself over the rush of my pulse.

I had no weapons. Not even the protection of jeans and a jacket as I was dressed pretty much the same as my kid. My own hands flexed at my sides. Energy grew from my core and cut a vibrating path through my body. Wind whipped around my child and the snarling beast. Brim made her look so small, his back coming to her elbow.

"I wanted to learn crafting from Aunt Bryn and you said no," she said. "I wanted to learn how to fight and you said no. I wanted to . . . be like you." Tears erupted in her wide eyes. Her lip quivered, and she couldn't finish her sentence, her innocent face a canvas of despair and disappointment. "You always say no."

A dull ache coiled around my heart and a strong, sickening sense of foreboding came over me. I stepped forward. Brim growled. "Emma, please don't . . ."

Her head shook as the tears streamed down her face, making her nose bright red. "I *never* want to be like you."

And with that, she did the unthinkable, the thing that I feared the most.

She leapt onto Brim's back, flung her arms around his neck, and the two bounded out of the backyard.

"EMMA!"

I ran after them, fueled by panic, crashing through the bushes, into the neighbor's side yard and across the street, as my daughter and her hellhound loped over the soccer fields, drawing farther and farther away from me until they were just a dark shadow disappearing into the park.

Still I sprinted until I couldn't see them anymore, until my lungs burned so hot and the air being sucked down my throat so cold that I felt sick to my stomach.

She'll come back. She'll come back, I kept repeating to myself as I finally stopped.

I jogged back to the house in my sweat-soaked tank, hair tangled, a nest for grass and earth and leaves. My bare feet were scratched and cold, covered in dew and dirt. Small pebbles stuck to the bottoms.

Rex was standing on the porch, his face pale. "She'll come back," he echoed as I wiped my feet. "As soon as she cools off, she'll come back." It sounded more like he was trying to assure himself than me.

I pushed past him, immediately going for the phone to put out an APB to every branch of the ITF in Atlanta to be on the lookout for my kid and her hellhound. The order was very clear: Locate only. Engage my kid and her protector and face serious fucking consequences. I was not playing.

I sensed Rex behind me, but didn't turn and instead went for the stairs. "Call Bryn, Aaron, Marti, the school, everyone we know . . ."

"What are you going to do?"

"Look for her. What else can I do?" My eyes burned. "She doesn't even have a jacket."

Rex took a step forward and grabbed the railing. "She won't get hurt, Charlie. You saw what she can do. You're overreacting." He held up his hands. "With cause, though. Who can blame you after what happened with Mynogan? But we have the world's strongest ward room. That kid is loaded down with protection amulets every time she goes anywhere.

Give her some time to chill out. She'll come back. You should go to work."

"Are you out of your fucking mind? I'm not going to work while my kid is out there lost and—" My teeth ground together, forcing down the intense wave of loss and fear rising to the surface.

"Well, you need to do something. No offense, but you're the last person she wants to see or talk to right now anyway."

My fingers curled around the railing as my temper flared, blinding me for a second. The wood cracked under my nails. "Fuck you, Rex."

Ninety minutes later, after I'd driven around Druid Hills, and then tried repeatedly to connect with Emma only to be blocked by her every time, I got a call from Titus. My daughter had gone to Mott Tech. I had to take several deep, shuddering breaths with that one. Relieved beyond comprehension? Yes. But that she'd made it all the way out of the city where a thousand different, horrible things could have happened? Furious.

Part of me, though, was glad for the darkness and the cover it had provided them. Besides Em being hurt, I'd begun to second guess my hasty decision to call in the troops and worry that some noob would find them, fire on Brim, and end up creating a really bad situation. That they ended up making it to Mott Tech unseen was a miracle. I supposed the darkness did have its uses on occasion.

At first, I wanted to turn the vehicle around and race to the lab, but Emma didn't want to see me or even talk to me on the phone just yet, which left me feeling stung, rejected, and hurt.

If she wanted time alone, she could have it.

I pulled my Tahoe to the curb on a residential street and just sat there for a long time. I didn't know what to do, didn't know how to deal with this divide or her sudden anger. She meant more to me than anything else on this Earth, and it seemed like I was constantly doing the wrong things and failing miserably in her eyes. I only wanted to keep her happy. Healthy. Alive. And, yeah, maybe I was smothering her in the process, but under the circumstances, I didn't think I was being all that protective.

The ringer on my cell jerked me out of my thoughts. "Madigan."

"It's me. You find her?"

"Yeah. She's at Mott Tech with Titus."

Hank's sigh blew through the phone speaker like a heavy wind. "Thank God. How you holding up?"

I laughed at that one. "Not even sure I can answer that question. Give me a distraction, Hank. Tell me we have a lead. Something. Anything."

He chuckled. "It's your lucky day then, kiddo. I've got Llyran's medical file. You want to meet at the warehouse?"

"Sure. I'll be there in fifteen."

★   ★   ★

I slowed my vehicle, flashed my badge to the officer in the patrol car, and drove into the parking lot, aimed for the double space between Liz's black ITF van and Hank's Mercedes.

As I pulled into the spot, Hank ducked out of the coupe. He leaned against the car's shiny black paint job, holding the file in front of him with both hands, one foot crossed over the other. He wore tan cargo pants and a long-sleeved, white crew. Calvin Klein could sell an incredible amount of underwear, or anything else for that matter, if they put Hank's photo on a billboard.

My stomach did a light flip. Last time I'd seen Hank, I almost killed him and kissed him all in the span of a few minutes. Hard to forget—

Partner, Charlie, he's your partner and your best friend. Just chill with the hormones.

I shoved the gear into park and drew in an uneasy breath. *No big deal. Just get it over with.* I grabbed my jacket off the passenger seat and then went to face my partner.

"Morning, sunshine," he said, amused at what I knew was a fierce scowl on my face.

I relaxed my facial muscles and made a pretty horrible attempt at smiling. "Morning. That the file?" I reached for it, but he pulled it back, giving me an admonishing look, cocking his head as though waiting for something. I crossed my arms over my chest. "What?"

Satisfied, his arm dropped. "We should talk about yesterday, the pool . . ."

"No, we shouldn't. It was nothing. We have work to do. Now please hand over the file." His eyebrow lifted. Torturously slow, my cheeks grew hot. "Okay, fine. Talk. You have thirty seconds."

A small smile twitched one corner of his mouth, making a dimple in his left cheek. A wicked glow lit a stare that lingered too long on me, a slow, slumberous perusal that made my mouth go dry. He reached out and expertly hooked a finger into the waistband of my jeans and tugged me forward until my hips hit his. "Don't run away from me again," he said in a low, possessive tone.

Oh God, it was sexy as hell.

I opened my mouth, but nothing came out. Yesterday I'd wondered who the hell I was, and this morning I had to wonder what the hell was happening with my partner.

"You and I, whatever this is, is . . ." His hand dropped from my waist to drag his fingers through his hair, looking beyond me for a moment before turning his face back to me. "I can't stop thinking what it would've been like—your tongue in my mouth."

I blinked as heat ebbed all the way into my bones. I finally managed a swallow as a lightheaded sensation made me sway slightly on my feet. "Are you using your siren crap on me?"

"No. But think of all the fun we'd have if I did." His irises turned diamond-blue.

"Did your head not heal correctly? Are you trying to get me in trouble? Trying to ruin our friendship?"

"I'm trying to get your tongue in my mouth."

The rational part of my brain was about to vacate the premises. "Please stop saying that."

"Why, does it affect you, Charlie?" He leaned down and nuzzled my earlobe ever so lightly, breathing his hot breath on my neck, just grazing my cheek with his day-old stubble.

A delicious shiver went through me. "No, no it doesn't." My knees were about to give out. He laughed against my neck, his lips brushing my skin and making me grab onto his hips for balance.

"We should at least explore whatever this is between us. Once and for all."

I looked up at him in a daze. "Once and for all," I repeated. "Explore." Man, that word conjured up all kinds of possibilities.

"I'm a great *explorer*, you know." His lips spread into a broad, white smile as though he couldn't hold it in any longer.

And then I understood.

"You're an asshole." I stepped back, consumed in heat, heart pounding, but relieved that he'd been totally playing me. "And that was the cheesiest line I've ever heard in my life. Does that actually work for you?"

Hank's rich, deep laughter nearly did me in. His grin was absolutely shameful. Then he licked his thumb and pointer finger and trailed them over his eyebrows and said, "I know. Pretty slick, right?"

"Idiot. Who are you and what have you done to

Hank?" I shoved him back. "Just give me the damn file, will you?"

"What? I figured you'd be all embarrassed after succumbing to my incredible charm yesterday. Look, it happens. No big deal. Just trying to lighten an awkward moment."

"You sure it wasn't a little payback for nearly drowning you?"

"That, and the water in the face . . . But really, we should talk about—"

"No. No more talking. I've had enough of your *talking* for one day."

He let out a disappointed sigh. "Fine. You've killed all the fun this morning."

"Fun? You do know my kid ran away this morning, right? And you call getting me all worked up *fun*? Do you know how *long* it's been since I've had any *fun*? 'Cause if you did, then you wouldn't be doing this to me. Oh, no wait. Yes you would . . . because you've lost your fucking mind! Whatever happened to having a little sympathy for those of us who can't go out every night, snap our fingers, and magically get lai—"

Hank's shoulders shook with his laughter, his dimples deep and his eyes crinkling at the corners, and it really bugged the piss out of me that he looked so good while laughing at me while I was sure I was red-faced and frazzled.

"Just give me the fucking file." He handed it over, finally. "Thank you."

"So did I really get you all *worked up*?"

"Shut up, Hank." I leaned against his car, next to him, as he wiped at his eyes, opening the file, my mind gripped with images of murdering my partner in slow, painful, agonizing ways.

It took a long moment for me to calm down on the inside and regroup, to get my head wrapped around work. I flipped through the first two pages of personal health information and vitals, wondering if everything Hank had said, every expression he wore had been a joke. Because some of it seemed completely genuine. Either that or he was one hell of an actor.

I stole a quick glance at him as his gaze turned toward the warehouse, his rugged profile unreadable. I was totally losing it. Losing control over my body, my responses, my common sense, my ability to read people.

Work, Charlie. Focus on work.

Health form. A copy of Llyran's faked visa. Family history, which was pretty scarce. Photos and measurements. EKG. Brain scans. Then I came to the glossy photographs.

"Holy hell."

Tattoos. Small, black script running down both sides of his torso and one hip. Ancient writing.

"Thought you'd like that," Hank said.

"It's the same as on the warehouse walls."

"Yeah, but we don't have a clue what it means. The folks at the Fernbank are expecting us in a little while and we still have that second warehouse to check out. You ready to get to work?"

I glanced at my cell, thinking I'd felt it vibrate, hoping that maybe it was Emma. But it was just wishful thinking.

"Hey, Madigan?"

I blinked. "What?"

"Did you hear me?"

"Yeah, sorry."

"Em's going to be fine." He steered me around the front of my vehicle. "She's a good kid and she has a great mom. It's just growing pains. You guys will work it out." He opened the door for me. "Get in. I'll follow you back to the station so you can park, and then we'll take my car to the museum."

I gave him a half-smile, appreciating his attempt to make me feel better.

Our footsteps clicked loudly along the polished tiled hallway of the Fernbank Museum and down a second flight of stairs where a musty smell hung in the air. We passed labeled doors with names and titles—offices for the curators, archaeologists, anthropologists, paleontologists, restoration department, collections . . .

As we rounded a corner, a figure stood outside of an open doorway, the light from inside spilling over a tall, rail-thin female with pearly white skin that took on a glow in the light, large almond-shaped eyes, and white hair braided down her back. An Elysian. A sidhé fae. And an Elder, if I had to guess as we drew closer. Very elusive and very rare to see outside of Elysia.

"I am Cerise." Her eyes, with their unusual light pink irises, appraised us slowly. "I take it you're the Detective Williams I spoke with over the phone?" she asked, extending her slim hand to Hank. Her accent sounded similar to French, but with an Irish lilt.

"Thank you for opening the lab, Cerise," Hank said warmly. "This is my partner, Charlie Madigan."

"Pleasure to make your acquaintance," she said as I shook her thin, bony hand, surprised to find it strong and warm, and getting a good vibe from her. Her aura was a mix of white, pinks, and purples. "Please come in. We haven't touched anything in here, so it's exactly as Daya left it the last day she was here."

We stepped inside Daya's lab to find a cluttered room with a small desk, computer, and a large center work table covered in dirt traces and small chunks of hardened earth. "What was she working on?" I asked, walking slowly around the room.

"Daya was restoring an eighth-century amphora from a site off the Turkish coast. She specialized in object restoration—stone, ceramics, metals . . ."

"Did you know she was freelancing as well?" Hank asked, leafing through the files on Daya's desk. "Using her lab and museum resources?"

"Yes. We were well aware. Daya was permitted to use the lab and her tools for her freelance work, but only 'off the clock,' as you say. She was very excited about her most recent project."

Hank and I turned at the same time. "Which was?" I asked.

Cerise walked to the table and placed both hands on the edge of the work surface. Dirt clung in the grooves and cuticles around her short fingernails and beneath. "Artifacts with great historical significance." Disappointment settled over Cerise's beautiful features. "I was hoping she'd taken them home with her. We haven't been able to find them here. They were extremely rare. Do you believe this was the reason she was killed?"

I folded my arms over my chest, more intrigued by the second. "They were that important? Rare enough to murder someone over?"

"Oh, yes. The pieces were priceless, in my opinion. Jars, adornments, tablets . . . One fragment, a broken spirit jar, had Solomon's seal etched into its surface, and the carbon dating puts it into the time period when Solomon supposedly had lived. Daya was not through cleaning the symbols and script on the artifacts, but once she was through we were hoping to prove that the items actually belonged to the king himself. If that had been the case, the artifacts would be beyond priceless. And I'm sure you both know how many crafters out there would kill to get their hands on anything attributed to Solomon."

True. Crafters practically worshipped Solomon. Called him the Father of Crafting. He was a legend, historically, biblically, and magically.

"Do you believe the artifacts hold power?" I asked.

"Oh, yes. I could feel it the instant Daya walked into the first level of the museum with the box. It's ancient power. Dormant, but there."

"And the spirit jar," Hank said. "What was its purpose?"

"To house the spirit of Solomon's most powerful demon. Solomon was the master of demons, you see. He created the spirit jar, and the words of power used to capture, contain, and enslave. That's how your legend goes anyway. If you want to know more, talk to the jinn storyteller. The jinn were the basis for many of your myths of demons, Detective Madigan. They have a rich oral tradition. And they claim that Solomon was a hybrid, half human, half jinn."

But none of that explained why there were six dead Adonai and one murdered nymph in a warehouse downtown. None of that explained why Llyran was involved, why he'd hired Daya and then killed her, or what his "cause" was, but the thought made me think of something Llyran had said about raising "the star."

"Do you know anything about a star?" I asked. Cerise frowned. "A star in connection with the artifacts or Solomon?"

Her brow creased and her lips thinned, but she shook her head. "Afraid not. Nothing that I can recall. I'll leave you two to look around. I'm just down the hall in room eight if you have any more questions."

"Wait." I stepped forward, Daya's words echoing in my ears. *The ring and . . . the light . . . mine . . . it's mine . . . into the hand that . . .* Cerise stopped in the doorway. "Solomon is most famous for his ring."

"Yes, that's correct. Most people call it the Seal of Solomon." She frowned. "I believe there were several rings in the collection Daya was restoring."

One of those rings Daya could've restored and given to Llyran. The ring . . . Daya's light going into the hand . . . He'd been using it to suck the life force from Daya and the others—provided my hunch was right. There were other rings of power, but the connection to Solomon . . . It was the most logical conclusion.

"Did the ring have the same power as a spirit jar? Could it contain spirits?" Hank asked Cerise, catching on to my train of thought.

"It was said to have many attributes. To command the jinn, communicate with animals, change his shape, and imprison demons . . . I would think that ring had the power to do most anything."

It felt like the temperature in the room had dropped a few degrees, but I knew it was just me responding to the disturbing idea of Llyran in possession of Solomon's ring.

"I'll be down the hall," Cerise said with a curt nod.

After she left, Hank and I brainstormed, going over everything we knew so far. There was no doubt in our minds that Llyran had the ring, and that he planned to unleash the star during winter solstice. Now we just needed to figure out how he planned to do it, and what the hell he had been looking for in Mynogan's memories. What did he mean by "the star"; some object of power we hadn't seen before?

We took close to an hour to search the room, finding nothing but evidence that corroborated what we already knew about Daya and her work and who had hired her. Once we were done, we followed the same path back to the main level, but this time detoured through the off-world exhibits.

Treasures, thousands of years old, sat in glass cases. Amulets, beaten gold earrings, necklaces, daggers, wands, headdresses, armbands, clay tablets, colorful wall reliefs . . . all quietly beautiful, all with a past that could never truly be known.

A few minutes later, we exited the museum. I stopped, letting the outdoor scent of pine reenergize me and clear away the musty scent of Daya's lab from my nose. The darkness overhead added its own jolt of energy.

Hank stopped a few steps below me. "You coming? We've got time to eat lunch before checking out that second warehouse."

I *was* hungry. "Yeah, I'm coming."

14

The warehouse district was mostly composed of abandoned structures, only a few still in use. There was talk in the city council to revitalize the area and turn the old brick buildings into swank apartments and shops. It was a good idea. The area was going to waste and it drew all manner of vagrants and criminals, derelicts even Underground wouldn't take.

The place was also prime real estate for black crafting rituals and meetings.

My ex-husband, with his secret addiction to black crafting, likely had known this place pretty well.

Hank eased his car to a stop against the curb, near a rusted chain-link fence overgrown with brown weeds. A few feet in front of us stood a light pole with a broken bulb, which gave us a nice spot of concealing shadow. Warehouses lined both sides of the street.

The one where we'd found the bodies sat two lots down from us on the left.

We got out quietly and began moving down the uneven, cracked sidewalk, careful not to trip and staying in the shadows. The constant hum of traffic beyond the district did nothing to alleviate the feeling of isolation here. Even the foliage had an air of abandonment about it.

Somewhere beyond the darkness, the sun was shining bright, but down here, we'd need flashlights just to peer into the buildings. I wanted the sun back, and after seeing it again, the desire to make that happen was even greater.

"That's it." Hank's voice pulled me from my thoughts.

Two stories. Brick. Old. The breeze pushed the unlatched gate back and forth, creating a faint metallic whine that drew gooseflesh to my skin. I shuddered quickly, trying to shake off the prickly sensation, and pointed to a dim light bleeding beneath the heavy doors.

Hank and I jogged across the street and advanced on the warehouse, my hand on my sidearm and my pulse escalating. We didn't slow until we were through the gate and into the empty lot. "Sense anything?" I whispered to Hank. He shook his head. I hadn't, either. "Come on."

We hurried to the front wall of the building. The light beneath the doors was so vague that I suspected it came from somewhere deep within. The doors were ancient, and would wake the dead if we tried to open them, so I motioned for us to go around the side. There'd be a side door somewhere, which most likely would lead into an office.

Bingo.

After taking positions on either side of the door, Hank reached for the knob. I held my breath as it turned, wincing at the slight click as the latch separated from its nest.

We waited.

Nothing. Hank entered. I held my Hefty with both hands against my chest, my back flat against the wall as a weak shaft of light spilled over the threshold. I ducked inside and slid up next to my partner, shoulders touching, and scanned the area. Long L-shaped counter, behind which was a dusty desk straight out of the seventies and a few metal shelving units.

It started so faintly. The softest whisper as though carried on a meandering current. Like a mother soothing a sleepy child. "You hear that?"

"No." He frowned. "What is it?"

"Whispering." I returned his frown. If anyone should hear it first, it should've been Hank. "You sure you don't hear it?"

His brow lifted in question, but I could swear I heard it. I couldn't sense life or anything else to suggest a presence in the building, so I focused on the path of light along the side of a makeshift wall, which separated offices from the main warehouse floor. I led the way toward the flickering yellow light that spilled from an open door far down the wall.

It was also the source of the feminine murmuring still floating inside of my head like an unhurried sigh. The scent of candle wax and sage was strong as we approached.

I did a low duck into the room. Cavernous space. Candles on the floor. Flames made a play of light and shadows over the walls and floor. I flexed my hand on my weapon, drew in a preparatory breath, and then slipped inside the room, Hank right behind me.

Against the far wall sat a massive, rectangular structure on a wooden pallet surrounded on all three sides by pillar candles placed on the floor. Wax had pooled on the concrete, linking the candles together.

Hank stopped, gazing down. I followed his move and found myself staring at an enormous seal drawn in the floor. "Solomon's seal," he said.

We inched closer, weapons at the ready, until we stood in front of what appeared to be an enormous sarcophagus made of a single block of agate. It was smooth and free of design. The lid was at least five inches thick and completely flush with the walls of the sarcophagus. Only the rim of the lid bore any marks.

They were the same patterns on the warehouse walls, and the same odd script I kept seeing beneath my skin.

"It's a coffin," Hank whispered.

I eyed the enormous agate box. "You don't think that's . . ."

"Solomon? No, I don't. If there's a body in there, it could be an old priest of Solomon's, a jinn, or it could hold a very powerful object. Agate is said to mask power."

"Or it could hold the star Llyran has been going on about."

It was obvious the thing hadn't been opened. It was perfectly aligned. No crowbar marks of any kind. Not a single scratch that I could see. But then again, some beings had the power to move things without the use of tools. The stone was incredible, the undulating waves of honey, flaxen, and tawny yellows ringed with jagged cream lines and flecks that sparkled in the light.

"Tennin has to be involved," I said tightly. "Llyran has the ring. Tennin has this . . . whatever the hell it is."

"Tennin *is* a jinn. His association with Solomon is only natural if what Cerise said is true . . . Question is, are they working together?"

"Well, if they're not, Tennin's got his hand in it, playing the situation somehow." And he sure as hell wasn't dumb enough to leave his property unprotected like this . . . unless it was a set-up or he wanted us to find it.

A bang echoed from somewhere in the warehouse.

"Shit!" I whispered, spinning around as my eyes quickly scanned the room. At the far end was a long wall of closets. We hurried over and ducked in the open side as a cloaked figure swept into the room and immediately went to the stone sarcophagus.

Please don't let him sense us. Please.

I did my best to envision my usual black curtain sliding over my aura as I watched the figure kneel down and bow his hooded head. Then, nothing. We stayed like that for at least five minutes before Hank nudged my arm. We needed to find out who was beneath that cloak. I turned sideways and eased through the space. Once out, I squared my shoulders, took a few quick breaths, and then marched purposefully across the floor.

"Put your hands on the back of your head," I said a few feet behind the figure. The head slowly lifted and then stilled. I repeated my request.

The figure stood, rising to a height similar to my own. I felt Hank's presence behind me, and knew he'd have his Nitro-gun pulled.

"I'm going to ask one more time . . ."

The figure didn't listen and instead turned, the face shadowed in the darkness of the hood. Slim bare hands reached up and pulled the hood back.

"Bryn?"

I squeezed my eyelids closed and then opened them again.

My sister?!

Her features seemed glazed over as though just waking from a dream. The moment realization hit her, she went white and tears sprung to her confused eyes, sliding down both cheeks.

"Bryn," I repeated, grabbing her arm, "what the hell are you doing here?"

Her bottom lip trembled. "I don't know, Charlie. I don't know."

During the drive back to the station, Bryn wouldn't speak. She just cried softly as I sat there cycling through fear, shock, betrayal, concern. I finally gave up trying to talk to her, instead shooting glances in the rearview mirror to check on her, to see if that was truly my sister sitting back there.

Once we were back at Station One and in our office, I helped Bryn remove the cloak. Her aura, oddly enough, was completely blank. Totally unreadable. She sat down in the chair that Hank had pulled from the many extras littering our space, put her hands in her lap, and waited as I leaned my hip on the edge of my desk.

"Guess I'll start," I finally said. "Who the hell are you and what have you done to my sister?"

Bryn frowned. "Ha ha, Charlie."

"Okay, then explain to me what you were doing in a warehouse that Grigori Tennin owns, worshipping some sarcophagus."

She squirmed in the chair and her cheeks flushed. "I told you, I don't know. I don't even know how I got there."

I crossed my arms over my chest, in complete disbelief. At her words. At the fact that she was here. What the hell had happened to her? "You really don't know."

"No, okay? I don't. I told you already, but in case you weren't listening: *I don't remember going there.* I don't remember putting on this stupid cloak. And I don't remember kneeling down at some stone box. Get it? *I. Don't. Remember.*"

I let my eyelids flutter closed. I counted to three. "Did you go to the support group meeting this morning? Do you remember that?"

"Yes. I did. We all talked afterward, had coffee and Krispy Kremes, and then I left. I don't remember anything after that."

"What about when you were in the warehouse, in front of the sarcophagus?" Hank said. "Anything? Even emotions will help."

Bryn bit her bottom lip, her brows scrunched together. "I don't know, I felt . . . relieved . . . impatient . . . wanting to see her."

"See who?" I asked.

Bryn blinked. "What?"

"You said 'her.' You wanted to see *her.*"

"Oh." Bryn's face twisted in confusion and she rubbed both hands down her face, leaving her palms over her eyes for a moment before dropping them in her lap. "I don't know. The person inside the tomb, I guess." She suddenly threw her hands in the air. "Don't ask me. I don't even know why I said that."

"Bryn," I said carefully, "I think you should see an exorcist."

She shot up from the chair. "Are you fucking kidding me? You think I'm possessed! No way. Forget it. I've gone to two of those damn *ash* meetings—I'm *not* going to an exorcist." She paced back and forth, completely shell-shocked and disgusted at the thought. "You really think I'm possessed? Look at me. *Look* at me! I'm not. I know I'm not. The only thing that could possess me is a Wraith. Revenants contract first—Wraiths don't. Wraith possession changes your eyes to glow-in-the-dark green. Do my eyes look glow-in-the-dark green to you, Charlie?" She forced down a swallow, her jaw tight as she tried valiantly to stay calm, but the tears were there, they just hadn't spilled over yet.

"Okay, okay," I said, her anguish tugging at my heart. "You're not possessed." I went to her and hugged her tightly because I couldn't help myself. My sister was in pain and didn't know the hows and whys. "Something else is wrong, then. We'll find out what it is, okay?"

She nodded against me, her entire body trembling. "You believe me, don't you? I *need* you to believe me, Charlie."

I stroked Bryn's hair. She smelled the same. Felt the same.

"Yes. I believe you." I looked over her shoulder to Hank. "Let's get a surveillance team on the warehouse, see if anyone else shows up. I'll take Bryn home."

I drove Bryn back to her apartment and escorted her straight into bed. Then I called Aaron.

He arrived on the landing outside of Bryn's door ten seconds after I called, a perk of being a Magnus mage. I let him in, being as quiet as possible. His strong face was pale and shadowed. I had to put my hand on his chest to stop him from going right into the bedroom, but the damn nymph instantly transformed into a black wolf, his clothing disappearing, and loped around me.

Well, that was just great. Usually Aaron was one of the more controlled nymphs I knew, which came from his dedication and study as a Magnus-level warlock. But control obviously didn't have a place when it came to my sister. Those two had a history neither one would talk about.

I followed him into Bryn's dark bedroom. He stood at the side of the mattress, staring at her for a long time before looking back at me, his eyes catching the light behind me and glowing green. Emerald green. With that strong Celtic face, tough muscled frame, and black hair, I wasn't surprised at all that his animal form was a black wolf.

Aaron shifted back to nymph, a process that took less than three seconds, calling his clothes to his body in less time than that. He stood at the bed dressed as before, his head bowed, all of his attention on Bryn. He mumbled under his breath. A current of energy electrified the air, making it waver for a moment. Then he turned to me. "I put her in a deep sleep. She won't wake up until I say so."

"What do you think is wrong with her?"

"I detect no evidence of possession by either a Wraith or Revenant."

"Well, those are the only two beings that I know of that can possess a person. So what now? Mind control? Llyran is powerful, but why would he make Bryn bow down in front of an agate sarcophagus?"

Aaron's brow raised in surprise. Concern settled over his features as he escorted me from the bedroom, closing the door quietly. "Are you sure it was agate?"

"I'm sure, and it had the same script around the rim that's written on the warehouse wall; why?"

He shoved his hands in his pockets, his face shifting into deep contemplation. "That star your victim mentioned . . ."

"Yeah?"

"I've been doing some research . . . The star is synonymous with Ahkneri or the Sword of Ahkneri. Most often these two are interchangeable, as though they are one and the same—the being and the sword."

"Llyran mentioned raising 'the star.' Could he mean liberating this sword? Is that possible?"

A sharp laugh, devoid of humor, escaped Aaron's pursed lips. His head shook. "You think it's bad now with the darkness . . . Supposedly, the weapon is divine, Charlie. Ahkneri was the Creator's chosen one, a First One, his 'star,' but some unknown transgression caused a rift between them. Ever since that rift, she was known as . . . how do I put this . . . as Vengeance. Retribution. Punishment. The sword is a named weapon, which means it is divine in nature.

It's called Urzenamelech, which loosely translates into 'Anguish by fire' in your language. You transgress, and you answer to the blade."

"That's a little dramatic."

"No, that's me putting it mildly. Llyran must believe in the myths. And he might for good reason. Better to believe as he does for now. To think like him. If it is true . . . He'll think he can handle it, but he has no idea what he's about to unleash. Charlie, you need to strike him down, and fast. And if the weapon does, indeed, lie inside that tomb, do not touch it. It'll kill you. Instantly."

"Great," I said. "Then I'll let Llyran open it and when he grabs it, he'll be dead. End of story."

"No, it's not 'end of story.' If Llyran wrote that script on the warehouse wall, then it's likely he knows a great deal about the myths in the Old Lore. He'll know he can't touch it. Only a divine being can wield the sword." Aaron's eyes widened. "*That's* why he needs you. That's why he changed his plans after searching your mind. And that's why you can't touch it, because you're only *halfway* there, if that, if my theory about you is even correct. Either way, touching that sword means you die."

I rubbed my temples and muttered, "God, this is making my head hurt." I looked up. "None of this explains why Bryn was there in that warehouse, and what Llyran's connection to Grigori Tennin is, or what Solomon and his artifacts have to do with a First One."

Aaron shook his head, black hair falling over his profile and obscuring my view. "May I stay here tonight?" His green eyes had become glassier, more worried than I'd ever seen them.

"Sure. I think that's a good idea."

"I'll need to retrieve a few things from the League and then I'll be back." He paused. "How is Emma doing?"

"She's fine. Mad, but fine." I shook my head. "I'm at a loss with her . . ."

"Sometimes, Charlie, the best thing you can do for those you love is give them the freedom their spirit craves. When it's a child, it's a give and take, but she's a *smart* child, and that's because of you. Trust her. Trust yourself. It'll work out."

I gave him a halfhearted nod and then watched him stride to the front door, one second a physical body, and then, the next, a mist that vanished, clothes and all, into the door. For a long moment I stared at the spot, my mind a total blank. I was tired and hungry, and didn't know what to do next. But I could eat.

I grabbed a water from the fridge, and the half-eaten bag of Doritos that I'd bought for Bryn the day before, and then slumped into the loveseat and finished the bag.

15

Aaron shook me awake. I must've been more tired than I thought because I'd drifted into a sleep deep enough to dream—a dream that kept repeating scenes of Emma running away, me falling forty-six stories, and the sunken corpse of Daya sneering at me with bloody lips. A glance at the clock told me that I'd only been out for twenty minutes.

The apartment was so quiet I could hear the muted sounds of Underground from beyond the brick walls. As I roused myself, Aaron went into the kitchen and began cleaning up, packing up the overflowing trash and taking care of business as silently as possible.

I stayed in the loveseat for a moment, letting the fog of my dreams clear. We needed answers. Needed to find Llyran and stop him from doing whatever the hell he was planning. But how the hell did you find a guy who could pop in and out of thin air? I grabbed my phone and texted Hank.

Where are you?

Home. Why?

I'm coming over.

I pushed off the couch and went into the bathroom. The light brought tears to my eyes, a big contrast from the darkness of the apartment. After they adjusted, I washed my hands and then pulled my hair into a ponytail, using a borrowed band and tucking one side of my bangs behind my ear. I straightened my T-shirt, a black stretchy V-neck, and adjusted the charm necklace Bryn had made for me, the small disk nestling in the center of my cleavage.

Once I returned to the living room, I secured my shoulder holster and grabbed my jacket. "I'll be back," I told Aaron as he stood at the sink, washing utensils. He nodded and then returned to his task. "Call me if you need to."

It was a short ten-minute walk from Mercy Street to Helios Alley. I was tempted to stop at the bakery, but kept going instead. Helios Alley was lively, in the midst of the dinner rush, but it didn't have any effect on me; inside I felt quiet and very much alone. After I passed the butcher shop I slowed my pace as I came to Off-world Exotic Pets and next to it, Skin Scripts, a tattoo, branding, piercing, and ceremonial marking parlor.

In the window of the pet shop, a gargoyle pup slept in a cage next to a moon snake, and I shivered despite the distance and safety—the one at Ebelwyn's apartment had totally freaked me out.

Skin Scripts also had a glass front where passersby could watch a patron get inked or branded, but most would agree the ceremonial markings were the best ones to watch. Done with the freshly cut twig of a Throne Tree shaved to a needle-fine point, the inside of which dripped an indigo-colored substance, the mark was scratched into the skin to form intricate symbols relating to vows, religion, or anything that was binding. And once the marks were made, there was no turning back—you were forever bound. Go back on your chosen vow and the Throne Tree ink embedded in your skin turned to poison.

Today, however, the patron inside, a young human male—a college student if I had to guess—was getting pierced in the navel by a darkling fae artist.

133 Helios Alley was accessed by a tall, black door sandwiched between the pet shop and Skin Scripts, the apartment above running the length of both businesses. I pressed the buzzer. "It's open," Hank's deep voice crackled through the small speaker.

With a fortifying deep breath, I opened the door and jogged up the hardwood stairs. At the landing, I paused briefly, about to knock and ready myself, but the door swung open.

Hank stood in the doorway in an untucked white dress shirt, rolled to the elbows and open at the neck, with a tumbler glass filled with amber liquid and ice in his hand. He wore jeans, with a hole just above the right knee and the ends frayed to white threads at his feet, which were bare. He stood aside, inviting me into a professionally decorated apartment that struck me as being more a showplace than an actual lived-in home.

"You cleaned," I said. Last time I'd been here, it looked like a cyclone had hit.

"Zara had it cleaned."

He closed the door behind me. "Just grabbing some dinner. Figured we were going out again after you took care of Bryn."

I followed him across hardwood floors and into the kitchen with its cherry cabinets, stainless steel everywhere, and a smooth cream and black marbled countertop. He stood behind the counter where an entire array of lunch meats, condiments, and toppings had been dumped. After a long drink, he set the glass down. "You want a sandwich?"

My stomach growled. Obviously the Doritos hadn't cut it. "Sure." I removed my jacket and my weapons harness, setting them on the stool next to me. "Just fix me whatever you're making. What are you drinking?"

"Yrrebé."

I made a face. The Elysian drink made from the Yrrebé root was not a favorite of mine. Way too bitter for my tastes. "That stuff is nasty." And strong. "How many have you had?"

"Three. You want a beer or something?"

"I wish." Unfortunately, I didn't have the liver

function of a siren. Alcohol went through their system so quickly that Hank could drink three Yrrebé on the rocks, experience a buzz, and be fine within the hour without any ill effects. "Why do you even bother?"

He shrugged. "Because it tastes good, and it helps me relax. Here, have a soda, then." He pulled a Mountain Dew from the fridge and handed it to me. "How's Bryn doing?"

Hank had to possess the same kind of crazy metabolism I did because he was in the process of making the biggest sandwich I'd ever seen in my life. It didn't seem like he had any rhyme or reason to what he was doing either. Just picking pieces of lunch meats, piling them onto giant kaiser rolls, and building higher and higher . . .

"She's sleeping. Aaron is with her. I've been going over everything in my head and can't make the connection between the star and Solomon's artifacts . . ." I spent the next five minutes filling him in on what Aaron had told me about Ahkneri, and then the next ten trying to eat Hank's colossal sandwich creation.

"I think our next step should be visiting that jinn storyteller," he said, polishing off the last bite, then taking a healthy drink from his glass. "Winter solstice is approaching, and I'll bet Llyran is laying low until then."

"I agree." I finished the Mountain Dew and then dumped my paper plate into the trash can.

"You have a Throne Tree?" I asked, surprised to see the large potted tree in the corner of the dining room. It was obviously pruned and trained to that size because in Charbydon they grew to be over fifty feet high with heavy corkscrew limbs and smooth bark in shades of dark grayish blues.

He flicked a glance at the tree with its thin, leafless branches, the ends of which were pointed and often razor sharp, and nodded. "It was a gift . . ." He dumped his plate into the trash and then began cleaning up the chaos on the counter.

I glanced around, realizing how very little I came here—unlike Hank who was at my house every week, stealing something from the fridge or just stopping by to say hi to Emma—and how very little personal information I knew about my partner.

"A gift from whom exactly?" I slid back onto my bar stool as he turned his dark, enigmatic gaze my way. When he didn't answer right away, I continued. "Why did Llyran call you *Malakim* on the terrace? And why did you leave Elysia to come here? And how do you and Pen know each other?"

He took the three steps to the counter where I sat and placed both hands on the smooth, cold surface. My blood pressure rose. If there was one being with the ability to unnerve me, it was this one. I could handle egos, ranting, fighting . . . but this quiet allure made it difficult to read him, to anticipate his thoughts and actions, and to control my own.

"Full of questions, eh? What's this really about, Charlie?" His voice had dropped an octave, low and confident and easy. And buzzed on Yrrebé.

"It's about realizing you know everything about me, and I know near to nothing about you. It's all surface stuff."

He shrugged, but a small grin tugged on one corner of his mouth, making a nice little dimple in his right cheek. "You never cared before. Why the sudden change?"

Heat shot to my cheeks. "There's no change . . . I was just curious." I sat back and crossed my arms over my chest, embarrassed by how lame that sounded.

He slid his hands across the cool surface of the granite, leaning on his elbows and eye level with me. I held my ground, instantly drawn into the way his eyes started to change from sapphire blue to topaz blue. "You like me. Admit it."

An instant sputter of denial erupted out of my mouth as he withdrew, looking like a damn Cheshire cat. He was trying his best to unsettle me, but he'd have to do more than that to get me unhinged. "Yeah, well, that's the problem with sirens. They assume everyone likes them, and when one doesn't they're just so damned blind and ignorant, that no amount of denial can make them see the truth."

"The truth being that you want me. Don't lie. I can tell."

I laughed without humor. "You're drunk."

A small smile played on his sensual lips as he finished cleaning up and put everything back into the refrigerator and cupboards. "Probably for the best anyway. Wouldn't want you falling in love with me, bugging me at all hours of the day and night. Begging *please, Hank, please. I need you nooooowwww . . .*"

"Oh my God," I said, rolling my eyes.

He wiped the counter, tossed the paper towel in the trash, and then placed one hand on the counter and the other on his hip, his smile fading. "The Throne Tree was a gift from my sister. I knew Pen as a child back in Elysia, but then lost track of him after I'd grown. *Malakim* is something I'd rather not talk about, and I came here to get away from my family because, when it comes right down to it, I'm a selfish asshole. So there you have it. Anything else?"

He stood there, waiting, his irises returning to their familiar hard blue.

I couldn't look away from him, couldn't move, yet every instinct was telling me to run. The air became charged with a dangerous mix of awareness and potent masculinity. I'd become prey—caught, stunned by the sheer beauty and power of his being.

"Jesus Christ," I breathed, heart pounding through my eardrums. "Stop using your siren crap on me."

His jaw tightened and flexed. "I'm *not*." He lifted both hands in an innocent gesture, but his expression said "I told you so." My reaction had just proved his point—I wanted him, and he hadn't done a damn thing except stand there and be . . . Hank. That alone would've made most women cave, but I wasn't *most* women, I was his partner.

"You're an ass. A schizophrenic ass." I hopped off the stool. "One minute you're normal, the next you're all moody, and the next you're doing this . . . *shit*. Sober up already and stop messing with me."

I started for the door, concentrating hard on putting one foot in front of the other. Without a shadow of a doubt, Hank had just completely unnerved me.

Door. Just make it to the door.

Somewhere along the way, my jeans became too tight, brushing faintly against a place that did not need any more encouragement.

The door went fuzzy for a second.

"Charlie." He was right behind me. Why wasn't I moving forward?

Don't lean back, don't lean back.

But I didn't have to. Hank took one more step, his front pressed against my back, his warm hands sliding down my bare arms to encircle my waist, overwhelming me with his scent, his hard body, his heat. The assault cut through my defenses like a hot knife through soft butter.

My body took over, relaxing against him as his head dipped and his lips brushed my neck. My breath hitched. My stomach went light and airy. Holy God. His tongue flicked out and swirled over my skin as his hand glided slowly over my belly and downward. My eyelids fluttered, and my limbs became instant putty. I succumbed so easily.

With his other hand, he reached across and cupped my chin, turning my face to his. My head fell back against his shoulder. His hand delved into my hair, thumb grazing my cheek and lips settling against mine without hesitation. Hank completely swamped me. Took control. Did what he wanted, and I didn't even put up a fight.

The scent of Yrrebé clung to his lips—like newly stripped bark from a pine sapling. His tongue flicked out, warm and soft, trailing idly along the seam of my mouth. My lips parted all on their own. Our breath mingled. I opened to him, letting him in, needing him in. His taste reminded me of Christmastime and roaring fires. His tongue slid against mine in a slow, deep rhythm, making my limbs grow heavy and my body tingle.

Hank kissed like he had all the time in the world, like this moment was the *only* moment, and he controlled time itself.

I was shaking, wanting more, wanting all of him and feeling ready to combust. All this pent-up need . . . overwhelming desperation to be touched.

As though he knew exactly what I needed, his hand slid under the waistband of my pants to cup me, applying just enough pressure to make my blood pool and my pulse beat between my legs. As the pressure built, our kiss deepened. I groaned, trying to move against his hand. I felt his lips smile against mine as his hand dipped beneath my underwear.

That first touch made my knees give out and a

groan erupt from my throat. His arms tightened around me as he moved his mouth back to my neck, a simultaneous attack on two of my most neglected erogenous zones. He swirled two slick fingers around me, slow and steady, pushing me into a state of absolute abandon.

He bit my earlobe, and then spoke words so low and lyrical, so rich and possessive. The words I didn't understand, but the effect it had on me was instantaneous.

Oh my God. My heart pistoned so fast.

"*Jesus Christ*," I rasped out as my body peaked and then exploded beneath his hand.

His fingers kept moving, kneading every last pulse of the orgasm from my body.

I'd never come that fast in my life.

And then he held me, both of us standing in his apartment, locked together as his heart hammered against my back and his erection pressed against my ass. Five minutes? Ten? I couldn't tell. Eventually my heart found its normal rhythm and my mind began to clear, but the lingering effects of the endorphin flood racing through my system left me shaken and weak.

It didn't take long for the realization and total embarrassment to sweep in. I broke from his hold, turned, and stumbled back, my lips achy and swollen, my pulse erratic. I stared wordlessly at him, aware that my face was burning and everything about my reaction had proved beyond a shadow of a doubt that he was right. And I wasn't even under the influence of alcohol; I should've been the one in control.

And I'd become just another siren groupie.

"Stay, *Inanni*. Don't go." He closed the small distance between us.

What the hell was I doing here, acting like this? Like a cliché? "I . . . We have work to do. I . . ."

He hadn't even needed the full force of his siren voice to push me over the edge. A few words, a kiss, a touch . . . My teeth ground together, and I tried like hell to force my humiliation down.

My nostrils flared as my chest expanded with the hum of Charbydon power, like a wakening beast, one that, in my current state, I'd have very little command over. My mind went cloudy again, but this time it wasn't from seduction, it was from the chaos of my emotions and the power they stirred. I blinked hard, trying to climb out of the haze and regain control. I was trembling. My eyes stung.

"You think too much, Charlie."

The disappointment in his tone struck me as condemnation. A short laugh erupted from my throat as I struggled to keep a lid on my power.

Hank pushed my bangs behind my ear. "Stop touching me," I croaked, though I didn't move away.

"You knew this was inevitable from the moment we got into the pool together. Deep down. You knew as I did."

The first wave of tears filtered across my vision, but I kept them from spilling over. "I can't deal with this right now . . ." I went to take a step back, but his hands remained on my shoulders.

I jerked, he held—two strong wills colliding.

It was that tiny, split-second physical war that snapped my control.

It came out of me in a riot of emotion, a bright burst of blue power that shoved Hank back, through the dining room, into the kitchen, slamming him against the huge stainless steel refrigerator. The panel dented, the entire fridge rocking precariously. Shit. I tried to fight my way back to regain control, but it was like swimming upstream in a mud-filled river.

A small, sane part of me knew we were in trouble. I was having a power surge I couldn't manage, and Hank was buzzed on Yrrebé, still nursing a wealth of frustration and anger over the voice-mod issue, having problems with Zara, and now . . . this.

Through vision ringed with blue fog, I watched him straighten and swipe his blond hair from his forehead, his expression one of intense focus as his gaze narrowed and his lips thinned, giving him an aquiline visage, a fierce, dark look that made me extremely wary.

"You don't want to fight me, Charlie," he said, proceeding toward me in a slow, confident, challenging manner. "You want to ride me until you see stars, and that makes you quite angry."

Yes. Yes, I did.

No, wait. No, I didn't.

I shook my head hard, knowing he was goading me, knowing he was just as pissed as I was and was using whatever ammo he had. My face burned. The tips of my fingers flamed and buzzed as a line of power raced down both arms from the center of my body. It pooled in my hands and wrists, weighing my limbs down. *Easy to fix that*, I thought, throwing out my hands and releasing the energy at the stalking form in front of me.

He made a motion as though flicking an annoying insect to the side, and my burst of energy was redirected out the window, blowing the glass and the drapes out above Helios Alley.

It hadn't even broken his stride, and in three long steps he was in front of me.

My eyes widened. Anger burned across my chest. I reached out and grabbed both of his arms, sending thoughts of cold into my hands and daring him with my expression to deflect *that*. I felt it working, the same kind of emotion-fueled abandon that had turned Em's bunny into a small ball, the same kind of inner turmoil that had created the tornado of water in The Bath House.

A glance down told me that it was working. His skin began to harden beneath my grip. Ha! But then it softened and steam rose from his skin.

His hands curled around my elbows, his irises bright like blue flame. "You're an amateur. A child."

"Go to hell."

I kneed him as hard as I could in the groin. *How's*

a little human power for ya, buddy? He doubled over, grunting in pain and releasing me as I slugged with a hard uppercut to the jaw, not holding anything back. I never did. Hank and I sparred all the time. I never took it easy on him. He was an off-worlder. He'd heal. A punch, a cut—hell, even a bullet to the belly— would heal within a day.

I swung again. He deflected, trying to grab hold of my arms and finally getting me into a bear hug amid a slew of angry Elysian curses. I raised back to head butt him.

"Don't . . . you . . . *dare*," he ground out slowly.

I hit him hard, bracing for the impact, but he turned his head and my forehead slammed against his cheekbone. He fell back, taking me to the floor. I tried to roll, but he was quicker, using our momentum to pin me to the ground. I didn't give him time to settle, bucking and twisting beneath him, rolling into the Throne Tree and knocking it over on top of us.

We became a flailing mass of arms and legs, curses and grunts. The Throne Tree scratched my skin. Bits of soil got into my eyes and mouth as we both scrambled to get out from under the tree while remaining the one in control.

I found myself flipped onto my belly, nearly breathless, as I tried to crawl out from under Hank. He snagged my ankle and pulled me back beneath him, his weight keeping me flat against the hardwood floor. Shit. I struggled but couldn't move.

He snapped a branch of the tree, and I threw a glance over my shoulder. "Stop!"

A dark blond brow lifted, and I knew what he was thinking. I hadn't listened to him with the head butt, so now it was payback time. Indigo liquid dripped from the jagged broken edge of the cork-screw branch.

"What the hell are you doing?!" I shouted at him, struggling. He jerked my black T off my shoulder. "I swear to God, Hank, if you cut me with that, I will kill you!"

"You wouldn't kill your lover, Charlie."

"You are not my lover!"

He froze. "Admit it and I'll release you."

"Fuck you."

"Right back at ya, babe." He jerked my shirt harder, leaving a good expanse of my shoulder exposed.

"You can't mark me unless I agree to it, you big idiot!"

"You know the Throne Tree is sacred to the nobles," Hank said. "The Charbydon thrones are made with its branches. Its liquid can link two people forever."

"Trust me, Hank, you'd regret that *link* for the rest of your days."

"I'm sure I would," he said flatly. "But other symbols . . . Ah. Actually, I like that idea." He pressed the tip of the Throne Tree branch against my skin, intending to give me a goddamn ceremonial mark.

I struggled with everything I had, so angry that I fell back on all my human responses, completely abandoning the power humming inside. My chest and lungs constricted as I fought for freedom. Anger had its hold on both of us, and neither one of us cared. Neither one of us was going to lose this battle of wills. I screamed as he stabbed the sharp edge of the branch into my skin, tracing the curved half-arrow-shaped symbol with two slashes and a dot into my flesh as he muttered a few Charbydon words to match.

"Goddamn you!"

The symbol tingled and burned.

Finished, he sat back on my ass. "There. Now try denying what you feel."

The veins throbbed along my temple. My face flamed in fury, and every inch of my skin shook with rage. I could think of nothing but retaliation. And the fact that he *thought* he had won—sadly fucking mistaken.

His decision to sit up was his biggest error. I flipped under him, snatched the branch out of his hand, sat up, and shoved it into his chest.

16

A bloom of dark red spread across Hank's white shirt.

He stilled completely, his face turning pale as his anger bled away. "Don't push, Charlie," he said in a ragged tone.

My fingers flexed on the branch, my heart pounding like a million drums through my ears. "Give me one good reason why I shouldn't."

"Because if that ink reaches my heart, it will kill me in less than ten seconds. No cure. No healing. Just . . . dead."

My mind foundered. I blinked. We sparred all the time. He always healed. Stabbing him with a twig should've caused him an hour or less of discomfort as he healed. Right? For a long moment, I didn't move as the blood continued to spread across his crisp white shirt. Slowly, my anger gave way to the reality of his words. I swear, I hadn't known the ink would kill. "Snap another branch."

"What?"

"You're getting a mark, too. Or I'm pushing." Which was a lie, and he knew it. All he had to do was call my bluff. I'd let go, and he'd come out of this fight without a mark. But I knew he wouldn't challenge. No. He'd crossed the line by marking me. He knew it, and he wasn't the type of guy to shirk away now.

His jaw tightened and his stony gaze met mine for a long moment. Carefully he reached over, wincing, and snapped a small twig from the fallen Throne Tree. "Here."

The liquid pooled at the end. "Unbutton your shirt."

He reached under my hand and began unbuttoning, his face refusing to show the pain I knew the movement caused him. Our collective anger had gotten us into this mess, and we might as well see it through to the very bloody end.

I didn't have to tell him to pull the right side of his shirt off his shoulder. He did it with a glare, offering his skin for my mark.

I placed the dripping edge of the branch against a spot above his right nipple and met his gaze. A moment passed. And then I pressed until the skin broke. I cut the same shape into his flesh and muttered the same words he had, but used my name where he had used his. His dark, thunderous expression never changed; his eyes never looked away from me.

Once I was done, I dropped the branch. I had no idea what kind of mark I'd just given him. My attention returned to the stick embedded in his chest.

He gave me a sharp nod.

I drew in a deep breath, feeling the stark twinges of guilt and remorse for what had transpired. Hindsight was a bitch, and I was pretty certain Hank was thinking the same thing. My hand tightened around the stick.

One. Two. Three!

I jerked hard.

It came out with a slight sucking sound, releasing a fresh blossom of blood. Hank flinched and then lifted himself off my pelvis to sit on the floor beside me. Sweat beaded on his brow. He swiped it off with his forearm before placing his hands flat on the floor, hanging his head low and breathing in deeply.

The mark on my shoulder blade burned, the inky poison sealing the symbol. His was doing the same—but even worse for him, the ink was running through his wound, seeping into his bloodstream with a larger dose than that of a simple mark.

As the last bit of anger retreated, the cold crept in, leaving me trembling and realizing the enormity of our situation. I leaned over on my knees and touched Hank's hand. The skin was *hot*. Sweat dripped from the tip of his nose and his chin. His head remained bowed. "Tell me what to do, Hank." He didn't answer. "*Hank!*"

"Cold," he forced out. "Need to . . . cool . . . down."

I scrambled to my feet and hooked my arm under his, pulling until he made it to his feet. By the time he had, I was sweating, too. I led him into his bedroom and the master bath, the only place I knew to get him cold.

The extravagant bathroom had a shower big enough for a party of five and an assortment of showerheads. It took me several seconds to figure out the nozzle/shower combination. I set it to rain cool water down from the round showerhead on the ceiling and then turned to him to see him fumbling with the small buttons on his shirt.

I took over, fingers flying through the buttons and then removing it carefully, briefly touching hot skin and making me feel guilty again. Once his shirt was off, he straightened, trembling all over, blood seeping out of the small wound and over his flawless skin. Next I fumbled with the zipper and pulled his jeans down.

He held on to my shoulder as he stepped out of them. I glanced up to see he wore black boxer briefs. I straightened, avoiding his gaze, and pulled back the glass shower door.

"I'm fine now," he muttered, but I helped him step into the shower, leaving the briefs right where they were. He gasped at the cool spray, the water thinning the blood on his chest as his arms went protectively up, his muscles tensing.

I swallowed. Seeing him weakened like this—my eyes stung—I'd almost killed him. And for what? Because I had to win? Couldn't admit the truth that he so easily saw? "I didn't know about the ink," I said quietly.

He bowed his head and stepped fully under the rain shower, the water flattening his hair and running over his wide shoulders. "I know, Charlie." He spit water from his lips and then stepped back, using both hands to rub his face and swipe the hair back off his forehead.

The mark on his chest was angry and red, but the cold water washed away the blood as soon as it surfaced. The other wound was worse, but he'd heal. Both wounds, however, would leave a scar. That was another one of the Throne Tree's unique properties. Hank would heal on the inside—most likely in a few hours—but he'd carry the scars for the rest of his life. I tried not to think about my own mark, and the warm, sticky blood that soaked my back and shirt.

"Here, turn around," Hank's solemn voice jerked my gaze from his chest to his face. He held out a washcloth. Mutely I turned as he slowly lifted my shirt and pressed the cold, wet cloth against my mark. I hissed, but the initial sting was lessened by the cold.

He wrung out the cloth a few times, pressing it against the mark until finally it stopped bleeding. "You should take off the shirt," he said. "You can borrow one of mine."

I turned, stepping out of his reach and pulling the hem of my shirt back down. "It's okay." My gaze snagged on the tile under my feet for a long moment before I lifted my chin. "I'm sorry." I frowned and shook my head. "I didn't mean to fight, I just . . . I'm not . . . I don't think I'm ready . . ."

"Don't worry about it." His attempt at a half-hearted smile came out as a pain-laced grimace. "That's the last time I drink Yrrebé around you." He shook his head, quiet for a moment, before saying, "I wasn't thinking straight . . . about the mark."

Two small dots of heat stung my cheeks. "What, um, kind of mark is it exactly?"

A slow exhale whispered through his wet lips as he turned regretful eyes on me. "It's a truth mark." My stomach dropped, my mouth opened, but he continued quickly, "We'll make a pact not to ask each other anything that involves things of a personal nature. And if we mess up and ask, then don't answer. The ink won't respond unless you outright lie."

My eyelids fluttered closed, and I shook my head in total disbelief at what we'd done. "I can't believe this . . ."

"Yeah," Hank echoed, one corner of his mouth dipping into a frown. "Me neither . . . So, pact?"

"Yeah. Don't ask. Don't tell. Got it."

"Same here."

We skirted around the other issue—the intimate one—and that was fine by me. "I should go talk to the Storyteller."

"Wait for me, Charlie."

"We just wasted an hour with all this . . . mess.

You're in no shape to go anywhere. Stay and heal. I'll call you after I'm done." I left the bathroom to the sound of Hank's soft curse, grabbed my jacket and harness off the stool, and hurried out of the apartment.

Only after my feet landed on the sidewalk of Helios Alley did I stop and allow myself to breathe. Holy hell.

Way to go, Charlie. Pop over to meet up with your partner and leave with a freakin' mark. Just great.

I groaned, tucking the jacket between my knees as I slipped my arms into my weapons harness, glad for small miracles—the strap just missed the mark on my shoulder. I left my jacket off, not wanting to stain the inside with the wet blood on my shirt. I kicked a piece of glass off the sidewalk and into the dip of the curb, glancing up at the blown-out window and realizing how disheveled I must look—clothes twisted, hair a mess, soil all over me. Quickly I rearranged myself, redid my hair, and brushed the dirt from my clothes, then began the trek down Helios Alley toward the plaza.

Throne Tree ink could kill an Elysian. That was a little fact I hadn't known, and I'd bet that most people didn't. And I'd bet the only reason I learned of it was because I'd almost killed my partner. I'd seen a few of those trees before, but only in upscale residences and shops—apparently they were high-dollar due to the difficulties in cultivation and the cost of importing them.

I sensed the rain before I reached the plaza. And for once, I was too spent to react much to the raw power that misted over the plaza's brick floor. It still tingled, still spoke to me, but not so intensely as usual. Probably because I'd just spent much of my power and energy fighting with my partner.

Or maybe sex was the key?

I laughed out loud, garnering weird looks from the two darkling fae standing near the soda machine as I headed toward Solomon Street. *Yeah. Just give yourself over to the O and all your problems will be solved.*

I weaved my way through the chaos of Solomon Street on autopilot, lost in thought, my mind replaying events, thinking of all the things I *should* have done and *should* have said.

My steps slowed as I advanced on the Lion's Den, Grigori Tennin's base of operations. It occupied the long row of buildings at the dead-end street—a bar, strip club, and gaming house on two levels. I stopped in front of the door, squared my shoulders, and then opened the heavy wooden door while my other hand came to rest on my weapon.

A wave of humid, earth-scented air and jazz music hit me full on. My boots echoed over the planked floor; the old wood coupled with the heavy timber beams overhead gave the place a dark feel. Typical bar on Solomon Street, though. Steady business. Regulars, mostly jinn. Stripper on stage—this one jinn, undulating against a pole.

The jinn in the room only gave me a passing glance rather than the intent, almost violent regard they'd given me the last time I was here and reeking of a jinn sex-spell. The jinn warrior at the bar, however, fixed a harsh stare on me as he drew beer on tap for the two human males seated at the counter.

I made my way to the bar to the beat of sultry old jazz, which kept the place on a mellow keel, and gave the strippers something to writhe to. Two Pig-Pens—a male nymph and female siren—sat in the back corner. Black crafters. They'd given up their innate Elysian power for the dark power of Charbydon—a very complex ritual with very serious consequences. The thin, dark aura that surrounded them gave them their illustrious nickname.

"Detective," the bartender said, laying both beefy hands flat on the old bar top, his shoulders hunching over and making him look like a water buffalo on steroids. All the jinn were massive, all with smooth skin that ranged from medium gray to dark pewter. Their violet irises ranged in hue, and the males were completely hairless, bald like this one. His arms were tattooed. He wore several rings on his fat fingers, and his earlobes were pierced several times. A typical jinn warrior.

"Your boss in?" I asked.

Jinn males were extremely chauvinistic to any females but their own, so I wasn't surprised when he said, "He's busy."

"He'll want to see me." I turned my back to the jinn, the ultimate in disrespect, and leaned back against the counter, eyeing the jinn stripper on stage wearing nothing but a leopard G-string and deerskin boots. If I had sleek muscles like that, I could do some serious damage. She had to be at least six feet tall, with gunmetal skin and angular bone structure. When I glanced back over my shoulder and saw the bartender had yet to move, I added, "Or I can start asking everyone here for their papers. It's up to you."

The bartender muttered under his breath in Charbydon, but he went to the phone and made the call, returning a few moments later. "You can go down."

Casually I swung around and smiled—the twisted smile I reserved for sarcasm and assholes—and then strode to the door that would lead me into what I liked to call the First Level of Hell.

Damp. Hot. The distinct scent of jinn—tar, and lots of it—assaulted my nose along with the heavy mix of wet dirt and wood smoke as I went down a long flight of wooden steps that led into the jinn's subterranean village beneath Underground. The walls and chambers had been carved straight out of the bedrock beneath the city, supported by massive beams and arches. Long, vaulted corridors curved out of view, the main one leading into the vast central chamber where Tennin held court and the jinn gathered. Ventilation shafts pulled smoke from the rooms. Running water was fed in through pipes. Food was prepared on spits and in pots over open fires. To be in the tribe meant keeping to the old ways as much as possible. Only the jinn who were wanderers or rogues took more to mainstream society, but there weren't many of those around.

A male guard met me at the base of the steps and then led me to the main corridor. Two months ago, Hank and I had made this same journey, passing open rooms where the jinn lived their daily lives, where I'd once seen them picking the petals off Bleeding Souls and tossing the bioluminescent centers into boiling pots—one of the steps to making *ash*. No honey-suckle-like smells this time, though.

As I stepped into the main chamber, I expected to find Tennin sitting at his dining table, dwarfing the female guards behind him. A few jinn warriors sat gathered around the large fire pit in the center of the room, but otherwise the chamber was empty.

One of Grigori's personal female guards appeared from a small archway across the chamber. Not that he *needed* a guard. I'd learned firsthand that the tribal boss of a jinn tribe held absolute rule, and had the power to eliminate any tribe member with a simple thought. The guards were merely for show.

"This way," she said, taking over, and then leading me back the way she'd come.

I followed her down another corridor, past several curtained rooms and wall torches that suggested this was a more personal area of the tribe's abode. Beneath an archway, down another similar hall, and finally the guard stopped and pulled back a heavy multicolored curtain, ducking inside. The chamber was small, and thick with heat and humidity. A fire burned in a pit dug into the far wall.

Grigori Tennin lay facedown on a stone slab, his well-formed, intensely muscled backside completely bare, completely smooth and hairless just like his massive bald head. A human, mid-twenties if I had to guess, very petite and very pretty with chin-length red hair and pale skin that looked even paler next to his glistening, dark skin, massaged his enormous calf.

Tennin turned his head, resting the side of his face on his hands, the three gold hoops in his earlobe winking in the firelight. His violet eyes held a wealth of cunning. "Make an appointment next time, eh?" He sounded highly amused, though I couldn't tell if he found his words funny, or the fact that I was here in his massage parlor funny. "Harder, Missy!" he barked as she moved to the back of a rock-hard thigh. A trickle of sweat ran down the side of her red face. "Good. Good. So, Charlie . . . Miss Detective . . . what you want this time? Shall we bargain again?"

I let loose a bitter laugh. "That second debt, the one where you beat the shit out of my ex-husband, we didn't bargain on that," I said tightly.

He rose onto one elbow. "Ah, but I did. When we bargained, I simply said I hadn't *decided* yet on what the second debt would be. You agreed. Then, I made my decision. End of story, as they say. But he lives, eh? So all is good for you." He put his head back down and closed his eyes.

"Yeah, if you call being stuck inside a body you can't control *living*."

One eye popped open, surprised, and then narrowed in a calculating way. "You don't say?"

"Cut the bullshit, Tennin. We both know you're not surprised. You want to tell me about the warehouses?"

"Which ones? I own many, you see."

I sighed, wondering why I was even bothering. "You sent Ebelwyn into the warehouse. You knew what he'd find."

"So what if I did? I own them, nothing more. You figure it out. You're the detective, no?"

I wanted to hit him. Really, just whale on him until that smug look was off his face completely. "I'd like to speak to your Storyteller," I said.

Grigori's thick head cocked slightly, and one hand came up to scratch his skull, the red gemstone in his ring flashing. "No," he said simply, and that was that.

"No?" I repeated, growing more irate by the second.

"You hard of hearing, Detective? I said no. Now you go away."

"No." Heat of a different kind surged through my limbs, gathering in my chest. "After all the bullshit you've pulled. Supplying *ash*. Getting people hooked to the point where they can't function without it? Working with Mynogan to bring darkness to the city—"

A small grin played on his face. "Now why you think I had anything to do with that?"

"Because I got your fucking flowers. I know you had something to do with it, you sonofabit—"

The guard's blade was at my throat before I could finish the word. Missy the masseuse stilled, her eyes widening. And Grigori Tennin? He just watched me, eyed me so closely that I felt like he could see the angry blood racing through my veins and the chaotic power coiling and screaming for release. I wanted to swallow, but didn't dare.

Another jinn entered, took stock of the situation, shrugged, and then walked to Tennin and whispered in his ear. The hint of victory in his eyes wasn't missed. After the jinn left, he turned his attention back to me and motioned to the guard to remove her blade.

"I change my mind. You can see the Storyteller."

"Just like that?"

He shrugged. "Yes, Charlie Madigan. Just like that." He laid his head back down, dismissing me.

When I didn't move, the guard shoved me toward the curtain, knocking me out of my frozen fury. I nearly tripped, but made it out of the chamber without falling on my face or losing control of my powers—as much as I'd wanted to. My anger was slowly tempered by confusion as I was led through a maze of tunnels and chambers. Why had he changed his mind so suddenly?

We came to another curtained chamber. The guard pulled the frayed material back and I ducked inside, finding myself in a small, low-ceilinged chamber that smelled like smoke, onions, and chili. A small fire burned in a pit in the center of the room, releasing sparks that floated to the ceiling and eventually got sucked into the ventilation shaft. A pallet lay against one stone wall, and a small writing table against another. Shadows licked and danced on the earthen walls.

An aged jinn female stooped over the fire pit, her back to us. With jerky movements, she shoved at the fire with a stick, creating several loud pops and sending an eruption of sparks into the air. The guard dropped the curtain and stayed outside of the chamber, leaving me alone in the room with the old Storyteller.

"Come, come. Come closer," she said, not turning around.

Her long, gray braids were flecked with dirt and pencil shavings, the ends tied off with strips of beaded leather. She wore a brand-new, puffy white ski jacket and a long, stained skirt that had seen better days.

I came around her left side and took up space across the fire pit. There was a pot hanging in the center, the source of the chili smell. "You want a story, eh?" She lifted her eyes, one violet, the other glazed over in blindness. She sighed, her face sinking back into the deep frown lines that curved around her mouth and eyes. "They all wants a story from Vendelan Grist. None comes to see me otherwise." Her head shook in disappointment. "Very well. Sit, sit." She motioned with the glowing end of her stick to the low stones set around the pit, her one good eye gleaming with intelligence. "Once I was this great warrior, ya know? But that is more story, for later times. So what is it? What you want? I haven't got all day, ya know."

I pulled a fifty-dollar bill from my pocket and handed it to her as I sat down on a low stone, pulling my knees closer to my chest. "The story of Solomon," I said, slipping my bangs behind my ears and settling in.

"Ah." She nodded in approval, stuffing the bill into her coat. "That's a good one, yes. The great king himself. The half-breed. Born of the jinn High Chief and a human mother, much like our Sian." She laughed, poking the fire again and making it crackle. "But in those days, he was a god to the jinn. Male of two worlds, ya know? A king who wanted to rule the land, to break the yoke of the nobles, and bring the jinn to greatness."

"I thought he captured the jinn, used them as his slaves, commanded them."

Her white brow lifted and her lips thinned in a scolding manner. "Who tells this story?"

I held up my hands. "Sorry."

She began all over again, and I had the feeling we were going to be here awhile as she started in on who begat whom. I glanced at my watch. Ten minutes later, Solomon was finally begat by the jinn High Chief, Malek Murr, and a human woman, Bathsheba, and was raised as a son of David and a prince of Israel. The story, once again, drove home the notion of truths lost in legends, and the fact that the offworlders had involved themselves in our civilization for untold millennia.

The story continued with Solomon's childhood with his half brothers, his young adult life, and, through the efforts of his mother and the prophet Nathan, his rise to the throne while David was still alive. He was cunning, ruthless, and ambitious, with a lust for magic and power. He reorganized the kingdom of Israel into twelve tribes and built the temple of Solomon.

It was an hour into Vendelan's story that Solomon learned of the First Ones from a jinn Storyteller.

"Since the Great War in Charbydon, when the nobles comes into our land, and takes control of the tribes, makes us bodyguards and servants, many jinn tribes they leave, they make home in the human world. But the nobles, they refused the jinn to stay there, they don't want Malek Murr to raise an army against them. Solomon reacted, ya know? So angry, he was, when the nobles call the jinn back to Charbydon. He learns of the First Ones. He sees, ya know, *opportunity*. Thinks that with this old knowledge of these great beings that he will set free the jinn, return his sire to the throne to rule over Charbydon, send things back to the way they was before the nobles come. 'Cause the nobles never belonged in our land to begin with, you see." She waved her hand impatiently. "Everybody knows this. Solomon, he sets out to uncover this knowledge of the ancients. He makes a cult of powerful jinn and human priests. Some says he succeeds in finding this knowledge. Some says he fails. In the end, he dies anyways. The jinn returns to Charbydon under the nobles' rule, and Solomon is dead.

"But"—her finger shot in the air—"he did great things. It is said he found a star, a star that shone its brightest at dawn. That he forged a ring of great powers to one day give this star life. Solomon's ring, ya know? But who can tell." She shrugged and laughed gleefully, her one eye going bright. "They just stories, right?"

"The star," I said, sitting straight. "He found the star?"

"Oh, yes. And he worshipped it, you see, for the star was a First One. So he makes this new religion. And calls himself the Son of Dawn. They still believe, ya know."

"Who believes?"

"The Sons of Dawn. Oh, they still around. Trust me. New members, sure, but still around."

"What do they believe, Vendelan?"

She leaned forward. "What all us jinn already know and everybody else forgets. The Char nobles and the Elysian Adonai are from the same stock. All were once Adonai. They forget, you see. So much time has passed. Ancient time. But we know. We remember. The nobles, they ruled in Elysia first, but they were no good. No good, you see, so they were cast out into Charbydon. Into our land. So long ago," she sighed, "no one remembers. Sons of Dawn want nobles to remember, you see, to rise up and take back Elysia for their own. And the star is their proof, you see. Not myth, but truth. She is ancestor."

"If it got out that the First Ones were real, and nobles once ruled in Elysia . . ." I said more to myself than to her.

"War," she said with a crazy gleam in her eye. And then she straightened and shrugged, going back to her fire. "Good for the jinn, though."

"How so?"

"Char nobles leave to fight for Elysia. We return home, back to our land, and rule as we did in the old times."

I didn't bother pointing out the fact that Charbydon's moon was slowly dying, that one day there wouldn't be a home to go back to, and, instead, asked a question that I was pretty sure I knew the answer to. "If that happened, Vendelan, if the nobles went to reclaim Elysia, who would be High Chief over all the jinn tribes?"

She glanced over her hunched shoulder, her one good eye taking on a zealous violet gleam. "Grigori, of course."

My stomach went light and cold. Despite the heat and humidity, I wanted to hug myself, to ward off the chill of her words. Even Vendelan, as old as she was, thirsted for war and vengeance against the nobles.

If Grigori felt he had a chance to win, there'd be no stopping him. But why would he want to return to a land that was dying? Why fight to reclaim something already lost?

Unless he knew of a way to stop it . . .

Vendelan turned back to her fire and stirred her pot of chili. "My story is ended, girl." She waved her spoon, but didn't turn around. "All they wants is a story . . ."

I hesitated by the chamber door, feeling sorry for the old Storyteller. "Next time," I said, "I'll bring my uncle Walter's chili and all the toppings. No story. Just food and company."

She turned at that. Her white eyebrow lifted. A grunt rumbled in her throat. "We'll see, Charlie Madigan. We'll see."

I opened the door and stepped back into the corridor where Tennin's guard was waiting to escort me out of the Lion's Den. This time, I didn't pay attention to the chambers I passed or the uneven ground at my feet. My thoughts were on Llyran's "cause" and his "star." He had Solomon's ring. By his own admission, he wanted to liberate the nobles, to start a war in Elysia. The very same thing the Sons of Dawn wanted.

And Grigori Tennin had a hell of a lot to gain if the myth of the First Ones was proven true.

As I stepped beneath the massive archway that led into the main chamber, I saw several things at once. The jinn still sitting around the fire. Grigori sitting like some kind of Conan the Barbarian king in his massive chair, dressed in his snug, triple-X T-shirt, his guards behind him, his booted feet propped up on the massive table set in front of him as he carved an apple with a dagger that was way too big for the job. And Rex standing to the side, facing Tennin.

I took several more steps before I realized what I was seeing.

Rex.

My Rex.

Here. In the Lion's Den. With Grigori Tennin.

I drew up short, so quickly that the guard behind me bumped into my back. But all I could react to was the sight of my ex-husband's body standing there, his profile grim, his hands fisted at his sides as his head slowly turned in my direction. White as a ghost and those stormy blue eyes struck with horror and loss, like he was floundering and disoriented. He blinked several times.

Tennin popped a slice of apple into his mouth and chewed loudly, not bothering to hide the grin on his pitbull face.

Rage flared inside of me, swift and immediate. I burned from the inside out. My mouth was so dry I could barely speak. The hum that tore through my veins drowned out everything else.

Finally Tennin removed his feet from the table, stood, and came around the edge of the table and parked his rear on the corner. Rex hadn't moved. "What? No words, Charlie Madigan?" A deep chuckle echoed through the chamber as he cut off another chunk of apple and shoved it into his mouth. "No disrespectful curses? No insults?" He pointed his dagger at me. "Cat got your tongue?" He chuckled at that, a deep, resonant echo bouncing off the chamber walls.

I blinked slowly, my eyelids stinging. I drew in a slow, deep breath and forced a swallow down my throat. "Rex." My voice broke. "What have you done?"

I expected some kind of excuse. Rex always had a comeback, an answer for everything. But this time he stayed quiet, completely stunned. I flicked my gaze to Tennin. "What did you do to him?"

Tennin shrugged his colossal shoulders and when he grinned, his teeth flashed white and wicked against the dark gray of his skin. He spread his arms and said with a dramatic air, "Opened his eyes." He laughed again, looking down at his apple, tearing off one last bite with his teeth and then tossing it into the fire pit. "I bet you got that collection letter and told him to fix it, didn't you? He comes here. He bargains. And you get what you asked for, Charlie. It's fixed. Debt is paid."

Sweat trickled down the small of my back. *No, no, no.* "Jesus Christ, Rex, what did you do?" I asked louder this time, hearing the panic in my voice, but unable to hide it, unable to sound strong.

He shook his head as though trying to come out of his fog. "I . . . was trying—" He shook his head again, closing his eyes and then opening them, his features taking on a harder, stronger expression, his gaze flicking to Tennin and the rest of the rapt jinn in the chamber, then back to Tennin. They exchanged grave nods and then Rex marched toward me, making me wonder what the hell Tennin had done to him, because the look on his face was one I'd never seen before. And it made me take a step back.

He didn't stop, just hooked his hand around my arm and jerked me along with him and out of the chamber to the sound of Grigori Tennin's booming laughter.

I stumbled several times before regaining my senses, and pulled my arm from his grasp, my ankle turning as I stepped into a dip in the floor. I cursed and fell back, behind Rex. "Rex! Goddammit, what did you bargain? Rex!"

He kept walking, up the stairs and straight out of the Lion's Den and into Solomon Street.

"Rex!"

I ran, weaving through the crowd, the vendor carts, and around the fire barrels, until I caught up with him and grabbed his arm. "Stop! For God's sake, just slow down for a minute." He finally listened. My chest burned from the run and the large draughts of smoke that had entered my lungs.

Something had definitely changed. Rex's eyes were filled with turmoil and though it sounded strange, they seemed to hold more depth, more knowing, more . . . force. Part of me wanted to rail at him, to put my hands on my hips and tell him what an idiotic thing he'd done by going to Tennin, but his grim expression and that look in his eyes gave me pause. "What happened? What did he do to you?"

"I remember, Charlie. I remember everything."

He started walking again. I fell in step beside him, trying to understand exactly what he meant by that, my sense of dread growing with each step as I remembered standing in Bryn's apartment two months ago, discussing the Bleeding Souls that were being used as an ingredient to produce *ash:*

You know why it's called a Bleeding Soul? It was used in the Great War when the nobles first appeared in Charbydon and fought with the jinn for control. The nobles used it as a weapon, the biological warfare of their time. It forced the soul to separate from the body. Myth says that's where the Revenants and Wraiths came from, that they're really the souls of jinn warriors who have wandered so long that they've forgotten who and what they once were.

"Oh my God. You're saying that's true? That you remember?"

"Yes," he said, looking straight ahead. "I remember everything."

Rex was a jinn warrior during the Great War? I stared at his profile, before having to turn back to watch where I stepped. Our insane, goofy, sarcastic Rex was a jinn? A *fighter?* "You're saying——"

"Yes, Charlie. And I was the best." He turned the corner, striding out into the plaza and toward the steps to Topside. "You can close your mouth. It's not entirely out of the realm of possibility."

My mind raced with all the implications, what this meant for him, for me and Emma. He was at the top of the steps before I caught up to him again and darted in front of him, making him stop. "Rex. What are you going to do?"

"I'm going home. I'm going to take a shower. And then I'm going to sleep."

He went to sidestep me, but I jumped in front of him again. "But—"

"Just chill, Charlie," he said tiredly. "The collection debt is paid. I'm not making any decisions right now. You're fine. Em's fine. Tennin doesn't command me. I'm far older than he . . . if only in spirit." He dragged a hand through his hair. "What he gave me to make me remember, it's made me tired. I just want a nap, okay?"

For some reason, I didn't want to let him go. In fact, the urge to hug him gripped me hard, and I realized that I didn't want him to leave us. But I stepped back, gave him an understanding nod, said, "Okay," and then watched him walk away.

I wrapped my arms around myself as cold desolation settled into my bones, followed by a prickle of unease. I scanned the street, getting the feeling of being watched and wondering which of Pendaran's nymphs was keeping an eye on me this time.

17

I shook off the paranoia and sat on one of the benches near the entrance to Underground, beneath a streetlamp, beneath the darkness overhead, and beneath what sure as hell felt like the weight of the world because I was pretty sure I'd just figured out how to get Rex out of Will's body.

A Bleeding Soul.

The mythical Charbydon flower had been used in the Great War by the nobles to rip the souls from jinn warriors. Whatever mixture they used—however they made it and administered it—I bet it would rip Rex's jinn soul right out of Will without Will having to die. And it was just a matter of time before Rex realized it, too, if he hadn't already.

So why did I feel so empty? I should feel joy, triumph . . . something other than this bland, solemn acceptance. I pressed my cool palms to my closed eyelids, trying to reenergize myself. My cell rang, indicating a new text had arrived in my inbox. I shifted my weight and pulled out my cell, surprised to see it was from Emma.

I'm spending the night with the Motts.

I could hear that tiny, stubborn voice in my head and smiled. This kid was going to be the death of me. But at least she was "speaking" to me, and if I could've hugged her through that cell screen, I would have.

U ok? I wrote back.

Yes. srry 4 knockin u down this morning. A sad emoticon accented her words.

My fingers went slowly over the keys. I was not an expert in texting like Emma or Hank. *Some power you got, kiddo. dont run like that again. you scared me to death.*

Ok. mom? i feel weird. i don't want u out tonite.

I tensed. *r u sick? what's wrong?*

Not sick. it doesnt feel right. Im worried about u.

Apprehension stiffened my posture. *ill be fine, kid. ill see you in the morning, k?*

K. luv u.

Luv u 2.

I didn't want to sign off, didn't want to be working this damn case when I could be with my kid. I flopped back and instantly regretted it as my mark hit the back of the bench and sent a hot jolt through my wound. "Damn it," I hissed, leaning forward and waiting for the sting to go away. It wasn't long before the pain shifted to a tingling sensation that sent warmth easing through my system.

A shadow fell over me. I glanced up to see Hank standing there with his hands shoved in his jacket pockets and a grave expression on his striking face. He was still pale, and his hair was still damp.

"How'd you find me?"

He shrugged, staring beyond me. "Wasn't hard."

"Let me guess," I ventured, flatly. "You were going to Bryn's to find me, but hit the plaza and then your new Charlie Sensor started acting up."

"Something like that."

Figured there'd be side effects to the mark. I leaned forward, elbows on my knees, and gazed at the tops of my boots. When Hank sat down beside me, the mark's warmth increased. "I thought it was just a truth mark."

"It is. I'm not an expert in markings. Is yours warm?" I nodded, not meeting his gaze. "Mine, too." After a deep sigh, he asked, "You see the Storyteller?"

"Yeah. Solomon started a cult called the Sons of Dawn. They worshiped the First Ones. Discovered what I'm guessing is the remains of one, and called her the 'star.' "

"And the star is inside of that sarcophagus."

"That would be the logical assumption," I said, not hiding the weariness in my tone. "Llyran intends to raise Ahkneri or gain access to her power or her weapon. I think Tennin is waiting. Waiting for Lly-ran to accomplish his task. If a First One is raised, if the nobles learn the truth that Elysia was once theirs, they'll wage war to take it back. And that leaves Tennin free to take back Charbydon."

"In a few decades Charbydon will be virtually uninhabitable," Hank said. "All of the jinn tribes still there will have to evacuate. If he wants anything, it's to carve out his own territory here."

"Could be," I said, not wanting to believe he'd go that far or be that stupid. "He did help Mynogan bring darkness to the city . . ."

"And now he's somehow helping Llyran start a war." Hank glanced at his watch. "The best time to perform rituals is at dusk and dawn. We have about eight hours before winter solstice dawns."

"Llyran's not going to show himself, he won't risk it this close to his goal. And Tennin won't do anything to compromise his position . . . No word from the guys on the warehouse?"

"It's been quiet. No one coming or going. We could go back, wait out the solstice. He's got to come out eventually. That star is there, and he needs you."

"No, I don't want to give him any more time." I chewed softly on the inside of my cheek, staring down Pryor Street at the myriad squares of light from the skyscraper windows. Determination settled over me. I squared my shoulders. "Let's go tomb raiding."

A slow grin spread across my partner's face. "I love it when you think all criminal and vengeful, Madigan. Warms my heart."

*   *   *

It had started to drizzle again and the air was veiled in a gossamer layer of gray. The entire area took on the atmosphere of a cemetery; the warehouses stood out like gigantic tombstones.

We left Hank's car two streets over, careful with our steps because the "fog" was already settling near the ground. Not being able to see our feet in front of us made our progress slower than usual, but it also gave us time to scan the surroundings. Hank had given a heads-up call to the surveillance team that we were about to enter the warehouse. What he didn't mention was our intent to take the contents of the tomb. That little surprise was just for Llyran. Without the star, his plans were useless.

Still taking precautions, we did a perimeter check of the warehouse, not seeing any lights from the windows or doors, and then took up positions near the side door. I sensed it was empty once again, not protected by wards, which I found odd. With something so precious inside, why was there not a single ward on the place? The side door was locked this time, making me wonder if last time it had been left unlocked by accident or on purpose, and who had locked it since. I used the Nitro-gun to freeze the lock. Hank kicked it, shattering the metal.

We entered quickly, hurrying through the long building to the back room where the sarcophagus was kept. There were no candles burning this time. The room was completely dark, and the whispers were gone, making the room seem even more bereft.

I knew it before I flicked on my light. The room was empty. Completely bare. No agate sarcophagus. No candles. No seal on the floor.

"Shit."

"Now what?"

"Call the surveillance team again. Find out why the hell they didn't see anything." I paced, thinking. "Let's try the penthouse in Helios Tower," I said, already marching out of the room. "Maybe Llyran returned there."

Hank left his car in the care of a valet with specific instructions to leave it in front of the lobby, flashing his badge for added intimidation when the valet started spouting tower rules and regulations. Then we entered the Topside lobby of Helios Tower and went straight for the elevators.

Once inside, I hit the button for the forty-sixth floor and then doublechecked my weapons. Hank and I stood shoulder to shoulder, our game faces on as the floors flashed by on the counter overhead.

Forty-four. Forty-five. Forty-six.

The doors slid open and without hesitation we strode down the hallway to penthouse number eight. I took up position near the door, my back against the wall and weapon drawn. Hank stood in front of the door and got ready to kick.

Inspired, I held up my hand to him, and then decided to check the door handle.

It wasn't locked.

Remembering what had happened here last time made my nerves raw. I did not want a repeat joyride through the darkness. I pushed gently and let the door open by itself. Deep breath and then I ducked inside.

The penthouse was brightly lit, catching me off guard. I scanned the surroundings, feeling the hairs on my arms begin to rise in forewarning. My chest suddenly constricted, and I blinked back tears as my throat closed.

I met Hank's gaze, and his was as confused as mine.

The energy all around this place was not as it should have been. Sadness and grief immobilized me as we pushed into the main living room, our backs to one another, using our senses to scan the open space. Something was very wrong. My throat thickened with heavy sorrow.

"Outside." Hank's voice made me jump.

I turned, weapon trained, to see two figures on the terrace. My eyes widened. "No, no, no, no . . ." I raced to the terrace to find Bryn in a T-shirt and pajama pants, covered in blood, hair up in a ponytail, feet bare, kneeling over a body. The wind blew against me as I approached.

Oh God. No.

My weapon remained trained on my own sister, and I was already blinking back tears. "Bryn?"

Her head lifted and she looked over her shoulder,

her eyes red and puffy, red dots on her cheeks, her lips swollen and wet. She turned back around and wept, her shoulders shaking. I didn't want to step forward. Didn't want to see who was lying there.

But I knew. I already knew.

My friend. My teacher. The nymph with the emerald eyes and beautiful green aura.

His hands were bloody and scratched, obvious signs of a struggle he didn't win. His body was sunken like Daya's, laid flat out on the terrace. My fingers flexed around my Hefty and I raised my hand, using the back of it to wipe at my tears.

Hank brushed passed me, his weapon dropping to his side as his expression paled. My head was shaking in denial. Aaron was not dead. It couldn't be. Not like this. I sank to my knees, letting my weapon go limp on the stone, still holding it in my hand, and doubling over to let my forehead hit the cold terrace, trying to hold in the scream of rage, loss, and guilt.

"No . . . no . . . Goddammit!" I cried to no one, letting my anger out in maddening groans of protest. I had to do something. Had to work. Had to move. I rose, wanting justice for my friend, for a good person who hadn't deserved to die like this.

I grabbed my gun, dragging it along the stone as I stood, my insides shriveling into a tight, searing, breathless knot.

"What happened, Bryn?" I asked, my voice barely a whisper.

Her wide, aching, confused gaze met mine. "I don't know . . ."

"You don't *know*? How the fuck can you not know?! How did you get here?! Did you see it happen?! Did you try to help at all or did you just stand there and say *I don't know?!*" I was shaking hard, crying, tasting the tears on my lips.

Bryn's skin paled and a look of pure mortification passed over her.

"Charlie," Hank said.

"*What?!*" I shouted, throwing up my hands and then turning to my sister. "How long have you been up here? Have you called the paramedics?"

"Charlie, that's enough."

Deep down, I knew it was more than enough, but hurt was flooding out of me so fast that I didn't know how to stop it or make sense of it. I turned away, storming to the terrace ledge, grabbing onto the railing and finally letting it out, screaming until I had nothing left, until my voice went useless, my throat burned, my lungs nearly collapsing.

I had to save Aaron. He couldn't be dead. He was supposed to live a long life, convince Bryn to love him as he loved her. Someone in my family was supposed to have a happily ever after, for Christ's sake. I stretched back from the railing and leaned down, letting my head fall in between my arms as I held on tightly. "We have to fix this," I whispered and then turned, saying it louder. "We have to fix this."

Hank closed his cell phone, and Bryn looked up

from her vigil at Aaron's side. "The medics are on their way. Liz is coming, too, and the chief."

"He doesn't need a goddamn medic! He needs help! He needs *us*!"

Bryn sniffed. "What are you saying?"

"Black crafting. Earth magic. Whatever we need to do to save this body and keep it fresh . . ." The two of them looked at me like I'd finally lost it. "Llyran is collecting their life forces into that damn ring. If we find the sonofabitch, take the ring, and get Aaron's life force back into his body, then maybe we can save him. Bring him back." I stilled, realizing just how insane that sounded. "He'd do the same for any one of us."

Bryn wiped her wet face with her arm and nodded. Her shoulder trembled. Her mouth went tight, trying to stop herself from bursting into tears once more. "I didn't do this, Charlie." Her bottom lip trembled, and I could see the horror she faced, not knowing how they came to be here, what part she played. "I couldn't have. I love him."

"I know." I shook my head in regret and sorrow, hugging her. "I know."

18

"Can't we spell his body so it won't deteriorate?" I asked.

"That's death magic, black crafting," Bryn answered. "You're going against the laws of nature, not working with them."

Okay, so my sister's knowledge was out. I folded my arms across my chest and leaned back against the kitchen counter and watched the activity over Hank's shoulder. The medics were putting Aaron's body into a cold bag to slow the death process. The chief stood over them, issuing orders, and occasionally shaking his head.

"I can reanimate a corpse," Liz said, "but I don't have the knowledge to get the soul back inside, or spell a body to keep it in stasis. I think we need a Master black crafter for that." She glanced around the room. "You guys must know someone, right?"

Since black crafting was technically illegal, most practitioners performed in secret. There was only one Master Crafter I knew, and from the uncomfortable way Hank and Bryn were looking at me, they knew just who I was thinking about.

The woman I commonly referred to as The Bitch.

The chief barreled through the sliding glass doors, pushing them wide so the paramedics could remove Aaron's body. Silently we watched them roll him out. For a long moment, no one spoke as the chief sidled up to the counter on the other side of Liz, sighing heavily and sitting on one of the stools.

"She won't help us," I said. Not since I fractured her jaw with a fury-packed right hook.

"Who won't help?" the chief asked.

Bryn gave him a knowing look. "The O.W."

That was the thing about being beaten to death by a ghoul hired by the Master Crafter who had slept with my husband and ruined my marriage—everyone ended up knowing all of the sordid details.

A frown pulled the chief's eyebrows together. "What the hell is an O.W.?"

"The *other* woman," Bryn said quietly.

I ignored the slack jaw on the chief's blustery face. "She's not going to help. She tried to have me killed, remember? You think she's going to suddenly forget that I punched her in the face for sleeping with Will and just let bygones be bygones?"

The last thing I wanted to do was revisit Will's

addiction to black crafting and the woman who had taught him, spent time with him, and ultimately rose to his challenge one night when he boasted he'd become too skilled to be coerced by anyone. She'd had him in bed and breaking his marriage oath with the snap of her fingers. And the night she ordered my execution was the night Mynogan and Titus saved my life and altered my DNA. All because of lies and deception. Years' and years' worth. It was a wound that I didn't think would ever heal—that sting of betrayal from someone who claims to love you . . .

"What about Rex?" Hank suggested. I met his gaze before he glanced away, but I saw in that brief look that he'd seen my hurt and was redirecting me back to the task at hand. "Will was a crafter. He'd gotten pretty good if he went up against the Bitch herself. Maybe Rex can access his knowledge . . ."

I shook my head. "No. Revenants only have access to the short term memory, and when that fades, that's it."

"So we're going to need a Master Crafter *and* a necromancer," Bryn said. "One to keep Aaron's physical body in stasis and one to reanimate him when the time comes. The soul, though, must go back by itself. We can't force it. But once it's back, Aaron's natural healing process should kick in and repair any damage."

"Can we bring someone over from Charbydon?" I asked the chief.

"Lots of red tape and travel time, Charlie."

"Okay," I muttered, releasing the counter. "I guess it's her, then." She'd surely make us pay for the favor. "And I'll go. She needs to know up front I'm involved. I don't want her finding out when she gets to the station and then backing out."

"With the cold bag, you have approximately three hours to get her to the morgue to spell his body before it begins to suffer damage. Too much damage, and I'm afraid no amount of healing will save him," Liz said. "I'll monitor the bag, and his temperature. Our biggest concern is the brain tissue." She turned to the chief. "Give me a ride back?"

"Sure. And Madigan?" he said, standing. "Don't piss her off. She might be our only hope of saving Aaron's life."

Yeah. That and finding Llyran and getting the life forces back, if they hadn't been used already. If we found that ring in time, we might actually be able to bring Aaron back from the dead.

"That leaves one big obstacle," Hank said. "We need to find our killer."

"What about me?" Bryn asked in a small voice.

"What about you?" I said.

"I was at the warehouse. I was here when he died. I'm being used, and I don't remember any of it. Maybe there's a way to tap into what I'm forgetting to find Llyran? I . . . I need to make this right," she said with a glassy, pained look. "Aaron's dead because of me. I need to make this right."

"Hypnosis might work," Liz offered. "Doctor Berk

is highly experienced. Bryn can come to the station with me and the chief. You guys go get your Master Crafter, and we'll meet at the station."

Are you sure? I asked Bryn with my gaze. She nodded, her chest rising and her conviction firm. "Okay. Hank, you're with me. Bryn's with the chief and Liz. Hopefully we'll meet you back at the station with . . . What's-her-face."

Nuallan Gow.

No one in the ITF would've known she was our resident Master Crafter if not for Will sitting down with me the morning after and telling me everything. He'd been completely stunned by the ease with which she'd coerced him, by the fact that he'd done something with her that he'd never thought he'd do. But he'd been solely responsible for lying, living a secret life, and making that damn bet to begin with. He never should've done it in the first place. And once he'd come clean, starting the twelve-step addiction program for black crafters and pretty much straightening up his entire life, I'd actually considered a reconciliation. And then he'd turned around and made a deal with a Revenant. He hadn't learned a thing.

Bringing up the past like this did nothing for my mood, and by the time Hank drove his car down Gow's street, I was ready to blow a gasket.

"You sure she lives here?" Hank's words brought me out of my thoughts as he parked against the curb and shut off the engine.

We looked out the window at the two-story home

with landscaped yard, porch straight out of *Southern Home Magazine*, white Christmas lights, and a welcome wreath on the front door.

Buckhead was the playground for Atlanta's elite. Extreme white collar all the way and not a place anyone would ever think a black crafter, much less a Master, would call home. But everyone had their secrets. Even in the swanky neighborhood of Buckhead.

"Yeah. She lives here with her two-point-five kids, Labrador retriever, and devoted husband." *While she had completely destroyed my life.* She'd *earned* her title.

"Let me do the talking." Hank got out of the car.

I followed him up the steps and waited as he rang the doorbell. A jingle proceeded the open door, and we were greeted with the Labrador—which had just been a guess on my part—and a slim, highly seductive-looking woman in a white cocktail dress and upswept brown hair streaked with gold tones.

The Bitch herself. Nuallan Gow.

Hurt and anger mushroomed in my gut like a cold burst of wind. My fist curled into a tight ball. She took one look at me and slammed the door.

I leaned forward and rang the bell again, holding it down. When that didn't work, I started making a little tune with the doorbell. "Jingle Bells." It was the holiday season, after all. I could do this all fucking night. And I was certain she didn't want her husband coming to investigate.

No matter how hard we tried, Hank and I had been unable to pin the ghoul attack on her. Her followers were completely devoted, and the creature who carried out her orders to kill me had taken the fall completely and willingly.

There was a huge scandal when I'd accused her of being a black crafter, but she and her husband had the luxury of money and attorneys on their side, and no one believed an upstanding citizen like herself would ever do something so terrible. The ITF was *clearly* grasping at straws.

The click of her heels made me release the doorbell and stand back once more, linking my hands behind me, so I wouldn't be tempted to punch her in the face when she answered.

The door opened and she stepped out onto the wide front porch, closing it quietly behind her. "I am having a dinner party, Detectives."

I rolled my eyes as her perfume reached my nose, perfume that hid the stench of black crafting's telltale scent of wet ashes. She had no aura whatsoever, which was no surprise. She kept a tight lock on her extracurricular activities and hid any and all signs of what she truly was.

Her dark, bewitching gaze fell on me, her lush red lips thinning as they dipped down. Her beauty, I liked to imagine, was a glamour spell, and in real life, when all the crafting was stripped away, she was a haggard old witch.

"We're in need of your skills, Ms. Gow," Hank said. "We're hoping to save a life, a very good one."

My hands twitched, but I kept them firmly locked.

The struggle inside of me was so great that sweat broke out on the small of my back and my heart was pounding from the hurt of old memories, and the injustice that came with it. She never gave a damn about breaking up my family, changing the entire future for me and my kid, or the pain my child had gone through during the divorce. None of that mattered to her. She'd had her fun and then moved on, leaving me and my family to pick up the pieces. I wanted to stab her in the face, but since I couldn't do that, I sent a silent plea to the Powers That Be that karma would come back a thousand-fold and bite Nuallan Gow in the ass.

"Charlie?" Hank asked, leaning close.

"Huh?"

Nuallan smirked, eyes traveling from my head to my toes and back again with an unimpressed expression. "Having trouble focusing, Detective? Thinking about the past, are we?"

I gaped and then snapped my lips closed and did a one-eighty, giving her my back and looking up at the hard face of my partner as he stepped in front of me. "I'm going to kill her now," I whispered. "Please let me kill her."

Hank grabbed my shoulders and turned me back around, saying over my shoulder, "You're the only one with the knowledge to save this man's body until we can return his soul to him. But we need to do it now."

"Why should I help you?"

I cut off Hank's reply. "Because you destroyed my

marriage and broke my kid's heart, you—" *Stupid, dumbass skank*. My heart hammered, pushing the blood around my body so fast it made me dizzy. I was trying really hard to stand there in front of her, but it wasn't working. I couldn't get ahold of my emotions.

"No, Detective, your husband did that."

"And so did you!" I was going to hit her. I committed to it, took a step forward, but Hank wrapped his hand around my arm and pulled me back. "You played a part, and you hold some responsibility, too," I practically growled. "And one day someone is going to rip your heart out and hurt the ones you love."

She pursed her lips. "Perhaps. But not today."

"Excuse us for one second," Hank said, escorting me down the steps and to the curb.

"Let me go," I said through gritted teeth once we were on the sidewalk.

He released his grip, and I yanked my arm away, spinning back to the brightly lit mansion. But I didn't move forward. I swallowed the huge lump of grief in my throat and blinked away angry tears.

"Charlie." Hank's hand landed on my shoulder, his fingers touching the mark beneath my shirt. Instantly dizziness clouded my vision as a warm wave of lust traveled through my body. His hand jerked back. And I knew he hadn't meant to touch me there. "I'm sorry," he said, pausing for a long moment as though he wanted to say more, but didn't. Instead he said, "Stay here. I'll go talk to her."

I paced by the car as Hank and Nuallan's conversation mixed with the sounds of the dinner party inside. Buckhead was a beautiful neighborhood, but all I could see as I looked at the manicured lawns and precisely trimmed hedges and trees was the future. A future where everything green had turned to dust and the darkness continued to roll overhead.

Finally Hank came down the steps, making long strides toward the car.

"What happened?"

"She's coming. She just has to make excuses to her guests and get some things."

"How the hell did you manage that?"

His nostrils flared slightly, and he couldn't seem to make eye contact with me. The muscle in his jaw twitched. "I gave her my ring."

"You *what*?"

I'd never seen Hank without his ring. Ever. Middle finger, left hand. A flat band carved of one entire, flawless piece of Idiron, a rare Elysian gemstone that reminded me of the deepest, darkest red amber. He'd showed it to me one time. I'd always thought it was a plain band, but the inside, where it rested against his skin, had been carved with small detailed script that signified its wearer and the wearer's family. It had been in his family for thousands of years, he'd said.

"It's just a ring, Charlie," he said, shrugging it off.

"What's she going to do with it? Pawn it to pay the electric bill?"

Hank didn't answer. He was already ducking into the car.

Nuallan came out of the house with a large bag, her heels clicking down the steps and over the stone walk, breezing by me as if I were invisible, and got into the front seat. My seat.

Whatever.

The ride to the station was completely silent, allowing my thoughts to drift into those old hurtful memories, regrets, and ill wishes. After this was all over, and Aaron was back—because I had to think that way—I was going to step up my training. Having these powers inside of me was a total waste if I couldn't use them at will like the off-worlders. And plus, being able to wield them meant being able to make people like Nuallan Gow pay on a level she could clearly understand and appreciate.

A glance at the console clock as we pulled into the station lot showed we had exactly one hour and forty minutes for Nuallan to perform whatever ritual needed to halt Aaron's body from decomposing to the point of no return.

Station One was pretty quiet during the night, most officers out on patrol, and the ones who were there were busy dealing with the typical weekend stuff—drunks, prostitutes, spell-mongering . . . the usual.

My mark had stayed warm the entire time Hank had been in my presence, which I was starting to get used to. Oddly enough, it eased some of my tension—the mark possibly releasing some kind of magic feel-good hormone into my body. But my knowledge of marks was seriously limited, so I could be totally off base.

Hank escorted Nuallan to the morgue as I went down the first-floor hallway to Doctor Berk's door, pushing it open after a quiet knock and peeking inside.

Bryn sat in the corner on the floor, her head buried in her arms as they held her knees tightly to her chest. Doctor Berkowitz sat in the cushy visitor's chair, leaning over, her arms resting on her knees and her head low as she talked to Bryn. She glanced up as I entered.

"Charlie. Come in, we're all done."

After a tight smile to Doc Berk, I passed her chair and sat down next to my sister, putting my arm over her shoulders and pulling her close to me. I didn't say anything, just sat there next to her as she relaxed against me, her shoulders bobbing as she cried. I rested my cheek against the top of her head.

The urge was there to cry, too, to fall apart and lose myself in emotions and hurt. But I didn't. It was hardwired into me once I lost my brother and became a mom. If anyone I loved was hurting, I became the strong one. That's how it worked. And my sister was hurting. I had to be the strong one. I *wanted* to be the strong one. It was as comfortable to me as putting on my holster and strapping in my weapons.

I scooted away from Bryn and got to my feet, taking her arm. "Come, kiddo, up you go." Bryn followed mindlessly. I led her to the couch against the wall. She sat and then I pulled her legs up and onto the cushions so she could lie down.

"I gave her something to calm her. It's beginning to work," Berk said. "She just needs some rest."

"What did you find out?"

"Bryn is very serious about helping Aaron, and is open to sharing with you and the others. She has very vivid memories of going to the therapy session, but not much after that. Then her memories returned after she woke up in the warehouse. She has lost entire blocks of time. Filling those in might take several sessions, but she did remember praying at the tomb and knowing she needed to do so before it was moved."

"Moved where?"

"The tower is all she said."

"Helios Tower," I said.

Doctor Berk went around her desk and sat down, removing her glasses and rubbing the bridge of her nose. "Makes sense. I suspect your killer is connected to the darkness in ways that are not only power driven, but emotional, too. He loves it. He thrives in it, delights in it. He wants a stage, Charlie. This is his show. If he has taken that tomb to the tower, he'll get it as close to the darkness as possible."

"On the roof, the arboretum's patio."

She nodded. "Quite possibly. Your guy is on one hell of a power trip. All you have to do is envision it, see things through his eyes, how he views himself and wants others to see him."

I glanced at Bryn, her face not peaceful in sleep, but puffy and shadowed. Still, it was rest, and her breathing was slow and even. I said a quick thank you to Doctor Berk, and then hurried down the hallway to the elevator, which would take me down to the morgue and to Aaron.

19

Nuallan ordered the chief and Hank to remove Aaron's body from the cold bag and carry him into an empty exam room. Liz and I took up space along the wall and watched. There was no way in hell any one of us was leaving her alone with Aaron.

On the floor Nuallan drew a circle, but this one was not of salt but of ashes. "Ashes from a corpse," Liz leaned over and whispered as Nuallan held the container and slowly poured out her circle. I didn't ask how she knew that, just gritted my teeth and tried to remain emotionless.

Nuallan stepped inside the circle and made a seven-pointed star. Once she was done, she set the urn outside of the circle and then turned to Hank and the chief, motioning them to place Aaron's body in the center. After they'd finished and stepped back to the wall, Nuallan faced us with a smug grin and satisfaction lighting her eyes.

I knew then that something terrible was about to happen, that Nuallan Gow was about to exact her price.

"To halt the Dark Mother from taking back what is hers, one must offer a trade in return. A sacrifice." Nuallan pulled a ritual dagger from her bag and twirled it expertly in one hand. In her cocktail dress, heels, and perfectly coiffed chignon, the image was disconcerting. "Someone here must give of themselves. A body part will do nicely." The knife twirled around and around. "A toe. A finger. An ear." Her gaze met mine. "A tongue, perhaps?"

I cocked my head and shot her my best you're-an-asshole look.

Hank stepped forward. "I'll do it." He bent over and began to remove his shoe. "What's one toe, right?"

I blinked. My chest felt funny as I stared at him with a mixture of disbelief and awe. He'd already given up something of great value to him; I wasn't about to let him give anything else.

"What?" he asked me, glancing up, hair falling into his line of sight.

"Nothing. I'll do it. I owe him."

"Yes, Charlie will do it," Nuallan said, cutting off Hank's argument. "How noble. I knew you would. What's it going to be, Detective? The Dark Mother has a special love for tongues and nipples."

My blood pressure rose, and my pulse began a slow, heavy drum in my ears. I drew in a deep breath, my face growing hot. Nuallan cocked her head, watching me intently. "Better yet . . . how about your hair?"

"My hair is not a body part."

"A sacrifice does not always have to be in blood. It is very much a part of you. She will accept it because it's something you love."

That's it? We went from body parts to my hair? My eyes narrowed, and I had an epiphany that Nuallan wasn't doing this for the goddess she worshipped, but for herself. To shame me somehow, to take something she thought I held dear, to make me feel less *me* in some way.

Fuck her. I stepped into the circle, pulled out the band, and shook out my long hair, letting the wavy mahogany length fall. I did love my hair, but she could shave me bald. I didn't care.

Her hand shot out as she stepped aside. She grabbed my hair, wound it around her fist, and yanked me back against her, baring my throat. A sinking feeling swept through my gut. The others instantly tensed, eyes widening in realization.

And then The Bitch cut my throat.

The sting of parting flesh followed the path of the razor-sharp dagger. I shouldn't be surprised, yet I was, and that, coupled with her quick reflexes, left me momentarily stunned.

Hank and the chief leapt forward, but as soon as they hit the circle a wall of protection flew up, blocking their path. A wall of smut. They banged against it repeatedly. The chief fired a few nitro rounds and Hank summoned his power, placing his palms on the smut and sending arcs of muted blue power into the barrier, but nothing broke a Master Crafter's circle.

The scent of warm iron wafted to my nose as blood slid down my neck and over my collarbone. Nuallan used the dagger to roughly saw off my hair. As the last few strands were cut, she angled me around and shoved me toward Aaron's body.

I landed hard, dazed, chest-to-chest with the corpse of my friend as a wave of nausea bloomed in my belly. Nuallan knelt down beside us. "Turns out I didn't even need this." She held up my large clump of hair before dropping it in a heap beside me. "Don't move. Stay on him and bleed."

My eyelids fluttered, brain scrambling out of the dumbfounded haze her actions had put me in. I was still breathing and not choking on my blood. I coughed, feeling a small trickle of it sliding down my throat. She hadn't pressed deep enough.

Nuallan rummaged through her bag and produced a short beige candle, marbled with thin red lines. "This is a candle made from human tallow. Liposuction is such a wonderful thing, much more convenient than butchering and flaying to get to the fat."

The candle lit with the snap of her finger. She made a nest on the floor with my hair, set the lit candle in the center, then picked up the ritual dagger and gave a quick slice to the pad of her middle finger, milking the black blood—she definitely wasn't human—and letting it drop randomly on the candle and my hair. Her red lips moved, and the chant that came from her throat was soft and unintelligible.

She flung her hand, flicking her blood all over me, Aaron, and the circle. "Sit up," she ordered, eyes taking on a faint grayish glow.

The smut in the circle grew denser, choking me as she drew on the dark power of Charbydon and filtered it through her corrupted soul. The power was indifferent, as was the natural energy found in Elysia. Both could be drawn here, and both could be manipulated and used in black crafting. Charbydon's energy, however, seemed to lend itself better to the dark arts, easier to bend to the will of the user, especially if that user was natively Charbydon.

Nuallan Gow, with her black blood and glowing eyes, was not human. What the hell was she? And what the hell had we gotten ourselves into?

My hands were covered in the sticky pool of my own blood—I was always amazed at how quickly the life-giving substance turned cold. I gathered my strength and pushed against Aaron's chest, sliding off him. I sat up near his hip, facing Nuallan as she sat on the other side.

"Take my hands," she commanded, reaching over the body, not looking, mouth continuing to move in her soft chant. *"Now!"*

I grabbed her hands, my blood squishing between our palms, as she squeezed painfully. Her power leaked into me, creeping up my arms like millipedes hunting food. I shivered and swallowed, the movement causing the sting and ache in my neck wound to hurt fresh.

Her chant grew faster, more demanding. A thin cloud of darkness formed from the link of our hands, spreading out over Aaron, enveloping him and then easing down, settling over him like a shroud.

A wave of dizziness flooded my brain and stole my vision. I swayed, knowing I was losing too much blood. I struggled to stay conscious, blinking hard a few times to force the fog away, my vision returning as I lifted my heavy eyelids.

Nuallan's face shifted like a TV losing its satellite signal. I squinted, unsure of what I was seeing. Her human face shifted again, this time a fraction longer and giving me just a brief glimpse of another face—sallow skin, graying in the dips and shadows of sharp bone structure. Bald. Long, pointy ears. Thin, pale lips drawn back from a mouth filled with two tiny rows of sharp teeth on her upper and lower jaw. Eyes that were round and as black as pitch. She looked like a skull with skin and teeth.

A ghoul.

Nuallan Gow was a ghoul.

A moment later, the hideous face was gone, and the Nuallan I knew and hated stared back at me. She dropped my hands, snaked a finger out, and dragged it through the wound in my neck before I had a chance to prevent it. I gasped at the sudden pain as she withdrew her finger, and with my fresh, warm blood, drew a complex symbol on Aaron's forehead—one I'd never seen before.

"And so we halt death . . ." she said solemnly, her attention on the corpse. "It is done."

The gray shroud of black crafting power lay over Aaron, the symbol of my blood bright on his forehead, but dimming as it sunk into his skin.

Nuallan stood, snuffed out her candle by pinching it with her thumb and the bloody middle finger, saying what seemed to be some kind of thank you or prayer to the Dark Mother in Charbydon, took her ritual dagger, grabbed her bag, and then shoved her expensive pumps through the circle of ashes. The barrier of smut dropped immediately and she stepped out, stopping in front of Hank. "Leave him on the floor."

And then she left, the Master black crafter of Atlanta. A very powerful, very deadly, very unpredictable monster.

There weren't many ghouls in the city, most preferring their homeland in Charbydon, but some of the more enterprising of the species had come to our world where they lived in the shadows and maintained a quiet, mysterious existence.

Hank entered the broken circle and bent down to help me to my feet. His scent swirled around me and my mark gave me a fresh zing of energy, but it didn't stop me from swaying on my feet, everything going blurry. "Heal yourself, Charlie," he commanded through tight lips.

My throat burned. I tried to speak, but now it hurt too badly.

I was aware of him and the others helping me out of the room, and of the cool air at the back of my neck where hair *should've* been, of the newly cut ends brushing against my jaw and curving under my chin as my head dipped forward.

"Get her up on the table," I heard Liz say amid the sound of footsteps and metal clanging. Hands slipped under my armpits as I was helped onto a cold, hard table. Then I was being lowered onto my back. Somewhere in the haze of my mind, I realized they'd put me on a stainless steel autopsy table. *Nice, guys, real nice.*

The voices of Hank, the chief, and Liz became lower and more distant until they blended into a low hum and finally silence. My muscles relaxed, and I gave in to the oblivion waiting in the wings.

A surge of heat from the mark on my shoulder, followed by a cool breeze floating over my neck wound and winding its way inside of me, slowly restored my awareness. My mind began to process things again, and after a few tries, I was able to open my heavy eyelids and *keep* them open.

Hank stood over me, one hand over my wound and the other palm underneath my shoulder blade on the mark we shared. I knew what he was doing—giving me his healing energy, and replacing some of my pain with those feel-good hormones from the mark.

I felt drunk. My lips worked, trying to speak, though I didn't know what I meant to say.

"Better?" Hank asked.

I nodded, testing my throat with a swallow to see if it hurt. Yeah. It hurt. But not as badly as before. "Getting better," I rasped out.

"Good, because you know I'm not the best at healing others. Why don't you help me out and start healing yourself?"

"Okay." I could do that. "If you tell me what *Malakim* means."

"It's just a generic term, a greeting from one Elysian to another. Nothing important. Heal yourself, Charlie. We don't have a lot of time."

"You're so full of it," I slurred. But, yeah, he was right. Whatever the term meant, it wasn't important. Not now, and I wasn't even sure why that question had popped into my head to begin with. I drifted into that cool place of healing, thinking of smiles and laughter and my kid, all the good things that sent a familiar hum of pure light energy into all the nooks and crannies, into the places that still burned, and snuffed out the fires . . .

"Charlie. Charlie, wake up," a voice echoed in a singsong tone while a gentle hand shook my shoulder. "Time to kick some Adonai ass."

Those words made me smile.

I woke from what was a very typical healing state— very similar to sleep—to see my partner shaking his head in an amused way. "I thought that would get you up."

It took a few tries, but I managed to ask in a

scratchy voice, "How long was I out?" The weight in my eyelids dissipated as I pushed to my elbows, one hand going carefully to my throat. Tender. A little squishy as the wound had sealed but not yet scarred over. Otherwise I felt okay. I sat up all the way and swung my legs over the autopsy table, giving myself a minute to regain my equilibrium before sliding off. "Don't ever put me on that table again."

Hank tossed me an extra Hefty. "We should double up."

"I take it you raided the armory again. Where're the chief and Liz?" I shoved the extra Hefty in the waistline of my jeans.

"Liz is in with Aaron, getting her stuff ready for the ritual, and the chief is on the phone with DC and the Adonai reps. Now that they know about Llyran, we won't have to worry about them accusing the nobles."

"Yeah, we have enough to worry about," I muttered.

I went to twist up my hair, reaching back and not finding it there. Ah, yes. My unnecessary payment to the Dark Mother. The ends were still long enough to pull back into a barrette or a very, very short ponytail that would stick straight out, but I didn't have any of those handy.

"It looks cute," Hank said. "Makes you look young and innocent and sweet."

My eyes rolled. "Yeah, just the image I want to convey to all the bad guys out there."

Unable to stand the curiosity, I stepped to the small mirror hanging over the sink. My brow shot up. The person staring back did *not* look like me. Same face, of course, but somehow made softer, a little kinder-looking with my mahogany waves falling just past my chin, the front longer than the back where Nuallan had made her cut. I shoved one side behind my ear, the other side falling over my eye.

Gold and copper glinted in my narrow, calculating gaze as I stared at the younger and—dare I say?—peppier version of me. This could work to my advantage. The badasses I hunted would underestimate this version of Charlie Madigan even more than they did the old one. I'd have an edge, and those fuckers would never know what hit 'em.

I shrugged and spun around. "Let's go." Confidence and determination settled over me like a comfortable old blanket as I strode toward the door, but it was quickly tempered by the enormity of what we were about to do: find Llyran, get Aaron's soul back, and stop the star from being raised before dawn. We needed some serious backup if this was going to work.

Once we made it out of Station One and into the parking lot, I grabbed my cell and placed a call.

"The clock is ticking, Detective," came Pendaran's version of a hello.

"Save it, Druid. I need your help."

20

It was nearing 4 A.M., the time when Atlanta's bar and club scene was closing for the night and revelers and waitstaff made their way home. Of course, a few you-don't-have-to-go-home-but-you-can't-stay-here groups and couples lingered in the streets and alleys. But for the most part, Underground had taken on a quiet air.

Hank and I walked side by side down Helios Alley, the soles of our boots echoing in time. Neither one of us spoke. My senses were on high alert, aware of every sound and every movement around us. When the first flash of a shadow fell on the storefront to my left I didn't miss a beat. My hearing trained on the soft pads drumming the pavement. A nymph had fallen in with us.

As we approached the end of Helios Alley and the

Underground lobby of Helios Tower, I felt a moment of apprehension. If Llyran hadn't gone to the tower we were screwed. But the tower felt right. He had to be there. But just in case, I had Pendaran scouring the skyscraper rooftops for Llyran and the sarcophagus.

As we entered the wide tunnel that led to the lobby, two wolves fell in step on either side of us and changed as we went, the air infusing with a quick burst of energy and there they were, fully clothed and armed, and marching beside us. Orin and, I had to guess, Killian. No nods. No talking. Just complete and total focus.

We passed a few late night stragglers and waitstaff, but otherwise the lobby was pretty quiet. Once in the elevator, I hit the button for the last floor, double-checking all my weapons again in an effort to calm myself and prepare as the whir of the elevator cables mixed with the solid drum of my heart. My eyes remained fixed on the numbers as they rose, my finger tapping my thigh.

Finally the elevator stopped and I angled through the half-open door, impatient to get moving. My cell vibrated. Pen. "Did you see him?"

"Candles and sarcophagus on the rooftop. No sign of our guy."

"Your word that you'll await my signal."

"I gave my word the first time you called." The phone clicked.

I shoved it back on my hip and climbed the flight of stairs that led to the rooftop and the entryway to an enormous glass-built arboretum that covered most of the rooftop in an upside down L-shape. The remaining space was a large outdoor terrace. The doors were locked; nothing a low nitro blast into the lock couldn't fix. Gently I used my shoulder to break the lock, wanting to be as quiet as possible.

Hank went in first, followed by Killian, Orin, and then me.

The arboretum opened up into a two-story-high jungle, a maze of plants and trees of every size and color. Condensation misted the glass, and dripped in places, making the air wet and humid. Stone walkways created meandering paths into the darkness of the indoor forest. The artificial sun lights hanging from the rafters had been turned off and the only light that remained came from a few small ground lights along the paths.

The arboretum was a serious ongoing project dedicated to cultivating and growing plants from all three worlds, but it was also designed to be enjoyed. Benches and chairs, hammocks and gazebos were hidden in nooks along the paths and enjoyed by guests and visitors of the tower. But tonight it smelled like tar and darkness. The jinn were here. And someone had left a door to the outside open.

I pulled my Hefty and advanced as I felt the telltale change in air that told me the nymphs had shifted into their animal form and begun the hunt. Hank went to the left, and I took the small path in the center that curved around and disappeared in the jungle.

Through the glass, I could see the hazy outline of the terrace, which would easily accommodate four of my bungalows. There were tables, chairs, lounge areas, and a large pergola heavy with some kind of blooming vine.

I eased my way down my chosen path, my skin already becoming slick in the damp air. The flutter of wings brought my chin up. Canaries and songbirds perched in the rafters and on the limbs of tall, leafy trees. I continued farther and farther down until I felt lost in this artificial rain forest.

As I rounded another flowing curve, light crept up the path.

Candlelight.

I went slowly, sweaty fingers flexing on the hilt of my weapon while my other hand shoved my hair, the roots of which had become damp, behind my ear.

The soft yellow light led me to a round grotto with a fountain built against the wall and a pool curving out in a half circle, the water partly covered in blooming lilies. A few chairs sat on the flagstone floor with a small table between them, facing the fountain. To my left, the path continued to a wide set of French doors leading out to the terrace. The doors were open, sending a breeze into the grotto.

The candles made a path through the open door and onto the terrace.

He was here.

And he was waiting.

The door frame was covered in some type of leafy purple vine. I ducked under, shielding my aura—at least *that* was starting to become second nature—and easing slowly outside.

The breeze was heavier out here, less humid and a welcome relief from the jungle I'd just passed through. The flames of the candles flicked and sputtered, but stayed lit as I followed their path to a spot near the far end of the terrace, where five figures stood over a familiar agate sarcophagus.

Llyran was easy to spot, in the center, his red hair waving in the breeze, rustling in tune with the ends of his black tunic and loose black pants. Flanking both sides of him were two figures, each dressed in hooded black cloaks similar to the one Bryn had been wearing when we found her worshipping the tomb.

I paused, my left hand coming up to cradle my right as I trained the Hefty on Llyran's back. Out of the corner of my eye, I saw Hank easing up along one side of the arboretum glass. I gestured toward our target. There was no way Llyran would be able to handle a double shot of high frequency sound waves going through his sensitive system, at least not for a few minutes. And that was all the time we needed.

Hank and I fired within a half second of each other.

In a blur of speed, one of the hooded figures hooked his elbow around Llyran's and spun, shielding the Adonai. The tags sank into the stranger's chest, pinning the black fabric against the skin. A breeze of disappointment went through me as the figure pulled each tag out with black leather gloves, flicking them away like a mere nuisance.

Obviously our new friend was not Elysian.

I whipped my left hand back and drew the Nitro-gun, both weapons now trained in front of me. I fired a shot of nitro set to hard stun. The figure ducked and rolled with inhuman speed, my shot grazing the edge of the sarcophagus.

The nymphs struck, each taking a target and going down in a melee of black fabric, fur, and growls.

Llyran recovered and was already lifting his hands toward the darkness above, calling it down, when Hank aimed to fire again. A cloaked figure sped toward him. "Hank!" I yelled to warn him, but another stranger popped up in front of me and shoved a hard palm into my sternum.

Pain stole my breath as the force of the blow sent me backpedaling, weapons flying from my hands and clattering somewhere behind me. My attacker pressed the advantage, immediately engaging in hand-to-hand as the scent of tar tickled my nose and bright violet eyes glowed from within the blackness of the hood.

Jinn warrior. But tall and slim, not as bulky as the males. Female. Grigori's personal guard, I'd bet my life on it. He and Llyran were obviously in this together; two beings with common causes. Llyran had the ring, Grigori had the star.

I was on the defensive so fast it was hard to keep up, hard to regroup, gain the upper hand. I blocked several moves in quick succession.

Duck. Punch. Block. Kick.

With every move, I took a step back. My heart rate was now insane, adrenaline masking each blunt hit and block. I didn't have a chance to reach for my secondary weapons. I couldn't take my focus off her for a split second. It was a dance, one I wouldn't be able to keep up with for long. Act. React. Always thinking two or three steps ahead, a confrontation that kept me from even attempting to pull up my powers.

And then in my peripheral vision, I saw it.

A shaft of predawn light, breaking through a hole in the withdrawing darkness and bathing the terrace in a soft blue glow.

It was enough to distract both me and my opponent.

Llyran's hands were still lifted skyward. Wind whipped around him as the darkness above him continued to part, spreading open in a wide circle to reveal a serene violet sky amid the sounds of fighting.

I sensed movement, but it was too late to block my attacker's next blow. Still I put my hands up to block, catching a brief glimpse of my opponent's open palm, head dipped as gray powder was blown into my face.

Honeysuckle blossomed in the air. I gasped, involuntarily.

Ash.

My hand flew to my mouth and nose, even though I'd already sucked it into my lungs. Immediately, the rapture began to run through my system. I raised my fist to take a swing, but my cloaked nemesis crouched low, swiped out a leg, and swept me off my feet. My skull cracked hard against the stone floor. Heat and pain exploded through the back of my head as I landed shoulders and head first. The pain didn't last long, though, quickly replaced by the wondrous effects of *ash* as the faint traces of dawn spread out above me.

My eyelids fluttered, body completely overtaken by pure bliss, a feeling so intense and consuming that there was no way to fight it, no *need* to fight it. It was heaven, and I could stay like this forever, my body sinking, growing roots into the stone, being enveloped in a warm cocoon of light and pure weightlessness. No aches and pains. No body. Nothing.

I didn't know how much time had passed, but the first fuzzy image to register in my mind was the massive hole in the darkness, revealing a sky streaked with purples, blues, grays, and just a hint of orange. No matter how hard I tried, my eyelids would only open halfway. The bliss was still there inside of me, but my mind had come out of the toughest fog— much like a drunkard who no longer had the capacity to stand, but could still slur and see and make attempts at *trying* to think rationally.

My chest rose with the deep breath I drew into my lungs as my head tipped to the side, seeing a blur in the distance. Fighting, though I couldn't tell who. On the other side of me was the sarcophagus, ringed with candles, an altar table sitting to the side with a large alabaster jar and a massive tome spread open.

Why couldn't I feel my limbs?

I blinked slowly, trying to find the right brain command to work the rest of my body, but all I could manage was sight, thought, and breathing.

Stay awake, I had to stay awake. This was important. And goddammit, where the hell were Hank and the others?

It took all my effort to tilt my chin up, to try and see through hooded eyes what lurked behind me. My searching gaze collided with the glowing green eyes of a predator. Orin's name immediately sprung into my mind, but, hell, what did I know? I was high as a kite. He crouched low among the foliage near the door, only a few feet from the table. *Open your fucking eyes, Charlie!* I yelled at myself, my consciousness banging around in my head and growing furious and desperate and mean.

The image of the wolf's face went from blurry to clear and back again. I blinked several times, urging my vision to stop being a fucking weakling and do what it was supposed to do. His image solidified. His gaze held mine for a second and then blended back into the darkness.

Sudden crazed laughter at the absurdity of it all bubbled inside, engaging my stomach muscles, forcing my torso up, and giving me the momentum I needed to turn to the side and push to a sitting position. Once upright, my gut executed an undulating roll and my vision went cloudy. It took several seconds of concentrating on *not* throwing up and regaining my center of balance before I could open my eyes again. This time they weren't so heavy.

My reaction to *ash* was, at first, very human—an instantaneous, blissful coma. And the only thing that saved me from being like all the other human victims was the fact that I was not entirely human anymore. My Elysian and Charbydon genes filtered the effects slowly out of my system, the drug having only a temporary high-like effect on off-worlders.

And what the hell was that sound, a baying echo that seemed to flow through the maze of downtown skyscrapers and empty streets below?

My gaze shifted to the place I'd last seen my partner. He wasn't there, but there was an object lying discarded by the corner. Hank's weapon. Denial hit me hard. No, Hank was fine. He'd simply dropped his weapon just like I had.

"Ah, right on time." Llyran sauntered up to me and grabbed me under the arm, yanking me up. My legs gave out, but he didn't stop—just dragged me to the sarcophagus until it felt like my arm was going to rip from the shoulder socket.

He released me. I fell to my knees, just catching myself with my hands before toppling over and going forehead first into the back legs of one of the jinn warriors who, once again, stood before the sarcophagus.

"I'm going to kill you, you know," I slurred, swaying slightly. "*Both* of you."

Llyran joined his companions at the tomb, his back to me for a long while—which pissed me off because it was a great opportunity to kill the bastard. If only I could stand and think straight.

Llyran pivoted and knelt down, grabbing my hand and shoving a heavy, tarnished gold ring onto my middle finger. Solomon's ring, no doubt. I laughed. It was too big and too wide. The center housed a large oval stone, black as pitch and polished to a mirror-like quality. Mesmerized, I blinked slowly as my hand dropped to my knee, seeing my own hazy reflection staring back at me in the stone. There were symbols carved around the stone. I squinted, swaying every time a breeze hit me. "Denasthr—" I managed to say, trying to read the script.

Llyran spun around. "Not yet, you idiot!"

Slowly I raised my heavy hand and flipped him the bird.

He slapped me hard; the force of his blow tipped me off balance and I fell to the side as searing pain shot over my face and rung in my ears.

"You are a waste of powers!" he shouted, jerking me upright, back into a sitting position. Then he grabbed my chin, fingers digging painfully into my skin and bringing tears to my eyes. "But you won't be for long. The *ash* will cling to your spirit, suppressing it, taking away your will to fight."

"To fight what? You?"

"No, you foolish woman. The king who is about to call your body home."

21

⁓⁓⁓

"That's what *ash* does to you humans." Llyran squeezed my face harder. "Makes you a vessel, prepares your soul and your annoying will to step aside. No struggle. No fight for control. And since you've turned out to be a huge disappointment, we have to do it this way."

I swallowed and lifted my hand, poking him in the chest and slurring, "You're a lunatic."

His lips split into a sneer, and his arctic gaze narrowed, grabbing my hand and shoving the gold ring into my line of sight. "And once he is inside of you, he will use his knowledge to raise the star with this." He dropped my hand. He leaned closer and whispered in my ear, lips brushing the skin. "Then I'm going to take her power for my own, and kill the both of you." He cast his glance to the alabaster spirit jar on the altar table. "Say goodbye to your will and hello to Solomon. He'll be pulling all your strings from now on."

I shook my head as a blanket of sickness rolled through me. "But . . . that's not . . ." No, it wasn't supposed to be Solomon inside of that jar, it was supposed to be his servant, his demon, a jinn.

"Oh, yes," Llyran continued with glee, "his soul is housed inside of that jar, but not for long. Not for long . . ."

Llyran turned back to the altar and began placing candles around the jar. His slap had woken me up, had stirred my anger and my power. Once it was engaged, it went to work, slowly destroying the effects of the *ash*. At least, the physical effects. If what Llyran said about *ash* suppressing my will and my soul was true, making me a willing vessel, I wasn't sure if my off-world genes would fight that or not.

I stayed on my knees, eyes closed, letting them think I was still heavily under the influence. Solomon's ring was on my finger. Aaron's life force was inside of the stone.

I had what I needed. Now I just had to get free and get the ring to Pendaran.

Llyran returned to the sarcophagus and raised his arms, calling out loudly to the darkness. The breeze picked up as a shaft slithered down toward him, wrapping itself around the tomb. An energetic tingle vibrated beneath my skin.

Slowly, the lid began to slide off until it fell onto

the other side of the tomb, with a thud that vibrated the stones beneath me.

The darkness receded. Llyran and his companion leaned over to gaze inside of the sarcophagus. "Incredible," he breathed.

As soon as the lid was off, the atmosphere changed as though the entire rooftop had just become one gigantic lightning conductor and there was an electrical storm brewing. The hum already inside of me from the darkness amplified until my teeth were vibrating. The agate no longer suppressed the power signature in that tomb. It was out. And, holy hell, it was so strong and low and pulsating that my eardrums rang.

Voices poured into my mind. Faint. Confusing. A clatter of noise and broken words. I shook my head. It didn't help. I tried to block it, imagining the usual heavy curtain coming down, but the voices were already inside, the *ash*, maybe, making me weak or susceptible. Whatever the reason, they were desperate, scared, and angry. It was as though I'd gotten a firsthand listen into the depths of hell and human suffering.

I grabbed both sides of my head and bent over.

Charlie!

My name. Familiar. Inside of my own screwed-up mind. Aaron's voice called to me, and I knew I must be losing it. Then a strong female voice. No language I could understand, but welcome and soothing, not at all horrifying like the others. I latched onto that tone, bringing it to the forefront of my mind and shoving all the others back.

Llyran and the hooded figure finally turned from their ogling of the tomb's contents. The smug look on the Adonai's face went completely blank, slowly turning pale. His lips thinned and his irises bled to black. "The Old Lore!"

I followed his murderous gaze to see that the tome was gone. *Orin*, I thought. It had to be. He'd been so near before . . . That tome was the Old Lore? Now it made sense. Hank had said that Llyran stole something big from the Hall of Records. This had to be it. No wonder the Elysian Council had attempted to execute Llyran. No wonder they never revealed what he'd taken from the Hall of Records.

It was their most prized possession. How could they admit they'd lost it?

I laughed. It started small, but grew. "What? Did you need that?"

"What did you do?!" He backhanded me hard, my hair whipping across my face as I flew to the side with a grunt. Slowly, I righted myself, my expression conveying my humor but also my extreme hate. "Fuck. You."

"Go find it." The hooded figure nodded at Llyran's command and blurred down the terrace, the ends of the cloak flying out and making it look like she floated over the ground.

Good. That left me and Llyran.

He had a brief look on his face, like he wasn't sure now how to proceed. I used that to my advantage and punched him in the groin since it was pretty much eye-level with me. He doubled over, cursing as I jumped to my feet, still a little wobbly, and then gave him a hard right uppercut to the jaw. He flew backward, and I turned and bolted for the terrace railing where I flung the ring over the edge as hard as I could.

I glanced over my shoulder, as Llyran pushed to his feet, feeling a rush of victory. He hadn't seen me toss the ring. This might actually work. Energized, I went for Hank's discarded gun, swiped it up, and ran like hell into the arboretum, luring Llyran away from the terrace.

The foliage was so thick I couldn't see beyond my own path or what might lie on either side of me beyond the plants and trees. It was truly a labyrinth, a dark, humid place perfect to evade and hide.

A booming crack made me slide to a stop. Like the breaking of an Arctic ice shelf, several cracks resonated through the arboretum, so sharp and deep I felt it in my chest as they grew, splitting until finally the glass dome shattered, a thousand pieces hurtling toward the stone floor and slicing anything in their path.

I dove into a wide swath of plants, crawling on my hands and knees in the soft, wet dirt as small pieces of glass sliced my shoulders, legs, and stuck into my back and scalp. I burned all over. There! A banana tree. I lurched beneath it, cradling myself beneath its leaning trunk and waiting, calming my pulse, and directing the adrenaline and energy into shielding myself and pulling that heavy curtain down, imagining myself sinking into the soft soil and becoming nothing but a plant with a faint signature of life.

The side of my face ached. Dozens of small cuts stung and bled. The smell of leaves and soil held a whiff of honeysuckle, but I knew that was me. *Ash* had a purpose that went far beyond simple narcotics trade. My new genes may have protected me from becoming a coma victim, but Llyran seemed to think that it still had the ability to suppress my will and soul completely. I hoped to hell he wasn't right. This nasty shit needed to get out of my system pronto.

"Charlie!" Llyran called in a casual tone. "There is nowhere to hide, you know. You come out and finish the ritual, and I'll remove the darkness from the city. I'll walk you through it. We don't need the Old Lore. You and I can raise the star. She'll give us whatever we want. You will be a queen. How can you refuse such a thing?"

He was close. I pulled my knees to my chest and buried my head in my arms, concentrating on my curtain. I heard the shuffle of his feet amid the wind that now blew through the exposed foliage before he spoke again. "The Sons of Dawn are far greater than you or this city. The only way to get what you want is to give us what *we* want."

I wanted to laugh at that. Yeah, and he was just masquerading as a member, using the cult, using their relics and information to get what *he* wanted. He wasn't going to raise the star to worship it; he was going to raise it to kill it, to suck out her life force in hopes of becoming untouchable.

"You know, Charlie, we tested the *ash* theory. Mynogan brought its properties to our attention. Did you know he was a Sons of Dawn member? Thanks to you and your little trip into Mynogan's mind when you killed him, I was able to find the spirit jar that he'd hidden."

My stomach dropped, but not from his revelation about Mynogan and the spirit jar, but from the *ash* theory. I knew where he was going with this, and I tried to stay calm even though I knew the words were coming, even though I knew he was taunting me, trying to get me to respond. "The *ash* victims were test subjects. The survivors are all excellent vessels. In fact, several of them have already proven the theory true."

I kept my head down and willed myself to breathe even though thoughts of Bryn seeped through my control and filled me with the most unimaginable dread. His footsteps passed, and I let my breath out slowly. If I tried to summon my power, he'd know. I had to be still.

"A disembodied soul, a trapped one, like Solomon's, is weak, you see. It does not have the power that a Revenant or a Wraith has. It can't fight, can't win control unless control is given. That's what *ash* does. That's what *ash* has done to your *sister*."

My teeth clenched hard.

There was no more movement, no more talking. And then faintly, very faintly, I heard the sound of

Llyran's low chant. Shit! He was calling the darkness! The wind grew. Leaves and dirt flew up all around me. Louder and louder until it sounded like a wild boar dashing through the woods.

I felt it, all over me, all around me. My body vibrated. I lifted my head as a thick tendril of darkness rose up like some gigantic smoke serpent and dove for me. I darted from my hiding spot and ran, dodging branches and falling over bushes, tumbling head over ass and coming up right at Llyran's feet.

My heart hammered. I grabbed his ankle and sent my power through my hands, not having to hide it now, not having to hold it back. He jumped, his concentration on the darkness lost, leaving it to disperse.

I got three steps away before he grabbed my collar and jerked me back. I punched him in the throat, sending my Char power through my fist as I did. Llyran flew back. I couldn't let up on him, though. I ran after him, leaping as a bolt of power shot from his hands and circled around my waist, lifting me up high and slamming me down hard against the stone pathway. Pain shot through every part of me, leaving me breathless and stunned.

His footsteps approached. There was a crash in the distance. A growl. Llyran reached down and jerked me up only to punch me in the face. I saw stars. My vision wavered. He hit me twice more, holding on to one of my arms to keep me upright. I swung with the other, making contact but not enough to do any damage.

I punched him once more in the groin.

The idiot obviously hadn't learned to protect himself there. He doubled over and I grabbed his shoulders, pulling him down as my knee went up and connected with his face. He screamed and fell backward, his eyes bleeding to black as I turned and jumped into the jungle to the sound of him tearing after me.

My lungs strained. One eye was swelling shut. My face was being cut by every branch and leaf I darted past. Llyran tackled me from behind and I went facedown in the dirt, suffocating. His hand gripped the back of my head and pressed, holding me down, shoving my face farther into the soft soil, and he was laughing.

My arms and legs flailed, but it didn't matter, none of it mattered if I couldn't breathe. My lungs sucked dirt into my nostrils and down my windpipe. I choked, tried to cough, but there was no air. Panic had my heart pistoning like a steam locomotive. The strain and burn in my chest was unbearable.

Eventually I stopped fighting. My heartbeat slowed. My mind became hazy. At least Pen had the ring. He'd take it to Liz like we planned and Aaron would be saved. Llyran's "cause" was gone without the power in the ring to raise the star. He'd lost, and he didn't even know it.

The wild boar sound coming through the forest again. Raging, growling. So close.

A split second of nothing and then an "oomph."

Llyran's hand was suddenly gone from my head. I

pushed myself over onto my back as air poured into my lungs. I wheezed, gasped, and coughed up dirt to the sounds of snarling and curses. And I looked over to see glowing red eyes.

Brimstone?

I pushed to my elbows. *No, no, no . . .*

Fuck. No.

Emma. She'd sent him. The baying in the streets. She'd sent him to protect me.

Llyran's shock wore off and he tore the hellhound from his shoulder and flung him into the artificial jungle.

Oh, Em. Why did you send him?

Llyran appeared above me, bloodied and heaving and furious. He threw his hands skyward and yelled at the darkness. I couldn't see it, but I heard it: Brim's high-pitched scream as branches snapped. Piercing. Terrified. And I knew. The darkness had him.

Satisfied, Llyran snatched my ankle, turned, and dragged me through the undergrowth. The back of my head banged over the choppy landscape. My hands flailed, trying to find something to hold on to. Just as Llyran stepped down onto the stone pathway I saw it—a juvenile Throne Tree. Once he got me back onto the path my chance would be over. I reached and grabbed, snagging one of the thin branches and then letting the momentum of Llyran's pull snap the twig.

The back of my head cracked against the stone as he dragged me onto the path and outside to the terrace and the waiting sarcophagus.

Dawn had broken.

The chasm in the darkness was lit up by orange and purple and the tiniest shaft of sunlight over the horizon, the beauty of it shattered by horror as a flash of movement drew my attention. Brimstone, wrapped in darkness, then tossed like a stuffed animal into the open air beyond the terrace, one last cry echoing from him as he fell.

My fingers flexed on the twig as that distant cry tore into my heart and buried there like a venomous thorn. Hot tears leaked from my eyes, and for a moment I wanted to give up.

Llyran dropped my ankle, turning to loom over me. He leaned over to grab my wrists. My arms were still straight above my head from the drag, making him bend over my body to snag my arm, exposing his chest.

One shot that might not mean anything at all. But I had to try.

As his hands reached for mine, I gathered my last ounce of strength and made my move, jerking down my hand and then shoving the Throne Tree branch into Llyran's heart, using my other hand to push, rising from the floor and screaming in pain as I did, using everything inside of me to make sure it reached the very center of his black, rotten organ.

He gasped, straightened, and then took two steps back and sat down. I collapsed back, breathing hard and teetering on the edge of unconsciousness.

His hand curled around the twig. "Nice try, Detective." Beads of sweat broke out on his forehead and his irises became blue once again.

"Throne Tree ink is deadly, didn't you know?" I forced out through gasps.

A painful smirk spread his lips. He pulled the twig out. "Nothing can kill me." His throat worked with a hard swallow. Thin lines of sweat ran down his pale face. Was it working?

"Your star will never rise," I said. "And the ring will be destroyed. You've failed. And all those people you killed . . . may they haunt you into eternity."

Llyran's eyes darkened. With one last surge of strength he rose, still gripping the branch tightly.

At the same moment a piercing, bestial cry rent the air and shook the tower. Pendaran's great black body shot up in a spiral past the rooftop, soaring high into the sky where his great black wings unfurled. He turned on a wide arc, the abalone shimmer flashing as a shot of sunlight hit the underside of his wings. And then he dove for the tower. In his talons was the small body of Brimstone.

I was frozen in place by the sight, but Llyran paid no attention. His mouth moved. The darkness slowly began to close in around the chasm of dawn as another shaft formed and shot after the dragon. The great Druid King swooped toward the terrace, his wings sending a gust of wind flying across the rooftop as he released Brimstone six inches from the ground. The hellhound landed on all four feet, body coiled, lips drawn back in a fearsome snarl, and eyes bright.

As soon as his paws hit, he was running, fixed on Llyran.

The darkness wrapped about Pendaran as he soared out over the terrace, but it disintegrated as soon as Brim hit Llyran. They went down in a tumble of screams and snarls and blood. Brim tore out a huge chunk of Llyran's shoulder.

Enraged, screaming, knowing his goals were so far out of reach now and determined to take out his vengeance, he shoved Brim back, his face red and straining and gripped with bloodlust. He pinned the hellhound to the ground and stabbed him in the belly with the Throne Tree branch, over and over and over, lost in a murderous frenzy.

An icy scream ripped from Brim's throat, propelling me up even as my insides curled in revulsion. I crawled to the side of the tomb, ignoring the pain firing hot, achy signals through every part of me, and pulled up, catching a glint within the sarcophagus.

No, not a glint—a fucking shining-ass sword.

Without thought, tears streaking down my face as Brim breathed his last breath, I grabbed the hilt of the sword, crying out as flame shot up my fingers, searing a path higher and higher.

The sun broke over the horizon, poured through the hole in the darkness, and bathed the rooftop in white gold.

I turned, raised the divine weapon, and brought it down with every last drop of will and strength in my body. It sliced clean through Llyran's skull, going all the way down to his groin, cleaving him in two and leaving fire in the wake of the wound, one that spread outward and engulfed him.

Gasping, and nearly blind with pain, I dropped the sword, my arm hanging limp at my side as I shoved one half of the burning Adonai aside with my boot and then fell to my knees in front of Brim.

The stupid hellhound had given his life for me.

Hot tears streamed down my dirty face as I gathered him to me using my good arm and cried out in denial. In frustration. In hurt. At the injustice. Everything inside of me, I screamed out into the dawn as sunlight beamed bright and white over us, and as I shut my eyes tightly and prayed. The light behind my eyelids became white, almost painful. Almost as painful as my heart.

I wouldn't lose him. Wouldn't go home and tell my kid he was gone.

Goddammit!

I squeezed his big, hairless neck, burying my face in his sweaty muscle. And then I saw the patterns in my head. The patterns beneath Brim's skin, the patterns like ancient script and molecular structure. I went deeper, seeing those patterns that had been severed, cut, destroyed. Too badly damaged to survive.

Oh, Brim. You stupid beast. And then I let my grief sink me into his patterns until the white behind my lids encompassed everything. And there was nothing else.

22

That voice sounded in my head again. That soothing female voice that I'd heard amid the panic and cries. That welcoming song that blew through me, and drew me, and fascinated me.

"Charlie? Detective, we have to move."

I flinched, trying to get away from the wet assault on my face. The scent of blood and sweat and hound reached my nose. I cracked an eye open and lifted my head. My good arm was draped over Brim's back. I'd collapsed over him. But his large head was turned, his nasty tongue licking my face and neck. My hand caressed his smooth stomach. The wounds were there, raw scars. Dried blood.

"How—"

I tried to shake some mental sense into my head as Brim got up and trotted off, sniffing the stones of the terrace. Pendaran, clothed and back in nymph form, smiled down at me. "I believe you healed him."

My jaw dropped, and I gaped for a moment until the memories began to slowly flow back into my mind. Sinking into him, seeing his wounds, weaving them, putting them back together . . . That had been real?

"But . . . Where? Aaron?" I glanced beyond Pen to see that the hole in the darkness was now gone, cutting off the blinding sun from the city below and leaving us once more in darkness.

Pen's hand slid under my arm, pulling me up. I swayed, my stomach rolling in on itself and sending bile to my throat. I swallowed it down. "Fuck," I breathed out through the pain and nausea.

"The ring has been delivered. We need to get you off this terrace before—"

And then I heard it and understood. Fighting, coming from the stairwell and into the arboretum, the dangerous forest of glass and darkness. Hank and several of the Druid's Kinfolk flooded onto the scene, pushed back by a swarm of jinn warriors.

Grigori Tennin did not intend to lose his prize.

I glanced at the sarcophagus. Llyran had failed. Tennin was another story. I shoved Pendaran away, demanding my body to regain its balance, but I crumpled to the ground instead. I opened my mouth to tell him to take the First One, but as soon as Grigori Tennin himself appeared, marching through the fighting, violet eyes gleaming and chest heaving like a murderous bull, Pendaran's expression went deadly. He ran, leapt into the air, and shifted into dragon form.

Seeing those two heavyweights converge was like watching two land masses collide. Everyone stopped for a second.

Through the chaos, I saw Brimstone attacking and Hank caught against the wall fighting two female jinn warriors.

And I was spent. I had nothing to give.

Tennin grabbed Pen by the leg and swung him around, sending him into one of the steel supports that had held up the glass dome. It bent with a spinechilling whine. Hank had gotten one of the warrior's short swords and shoved it through the belly of one of his opponents, then immediately deflected another. Pen roused, but wasn't quick enough to evade the swift descent of Tennin's vicious axe. It sliced through the Druid's shoulder as the dragon swiped the jinn boss off his feet, gripped him in his talons, and then flung him toward the edge of the terrace.

Hank battled the other jinn. A kick to her jaw sent her spinning around, her back to him as he caught her, pulled her close, brought up his hands, and snapped her neck. She sank at his feet. His eyes lifted, met mine, and he started toward me.

But then his body jerked. He froze, eyes never leaving mine. And then he fell forward with an axe buried between his shoulder blades.

Behind him Grigori Tennin stalked forward, eyes glowing violet red and pinned on me.

Pendaran's wings unfurled as he leapt high over the melee and came crashing down on Hank, his big black wings covering my partner from view, but not before I saw his jaws open and his white teeth come down on Hank's neck. A scream welled in my chest, but before I could let it fly, the dragon's head came up, and his jaws flung Hank's voice-mod into the air.

And then the Druid King's dragon eyes narrowed on Grigori as he came for me. Pendaran let out a furious roar, spun around, took six massive steps, and then lunged for Grigori. The impact sent them flying off the fifty-story building.

I crawled toward Hank, weaving between warriors and ducking weapons. I still couldn't feel my arm, but knew I had to reach him. "Hank," I cried, pulling myself to his body. He didn't respond. Immediately I wrapped my good hand around the axe handle and pulled it out, flinging it behind me and noticing that Orin and Brim had moved closer, making a protective stance around us. I grabbed Hank's shoulder and pulled him over. "Hank!" I tapped his cheek, noticing his neck and the deep, bloody gouges caused by Pendaran's teeth. "Please, wake up! *Hank!*"

The jinn were pushing in; more of the nymphs surrounded us now, outnumbered by Tennin's fierce warriors.

"Charlie?"

I swung my head around to see Hank's eyes open. "Use your voice," I said suddenly.

"What?"

I grabbed his shoulder and shook, though it barely moved him. "Goddammit, Hank! Use your voice and use it now!"

One hand lifted to his neck. Understanding dawned in his eyes, and it was like watching a superconductor draw energy to itself as he realized his power was his once again. His face went merciless, and his eyes went sapphire as he grabbed me, shoved me down, and sat up. Instinctively I covered my ears, knowing that he was about to unleash a word of power, something he had claimed once that I'd never hear in my lifetime. Hah. He should've known better.

The deep five-syllable boom that came out of Hank emerged with the force of a tidal wave that rattled my teeth, flattened everything in its path, shook the building, and—from the sound of glass breaking—popped several windows in the tower.

I waited until there was no sound but the city itself and the constant, heavy beat of my pulse.

When I lifted my head, it looked as though a bomb had gone off. Much of the dirt, glass, and debris had been wiped off the terrace and only some trees and stubborn plants remained. Jinn warriors and nymphs lay where they fell. Brim was next to me, on his side, but breathing normally.

"They're not dead," Hank said in nearly a whisper from behind me.

He was standing, stepping over the bodies, to pick up a dagger and shove it beneath the strap of his belt. It was gray and dark overhead. The wind whipped his bloody and torn clothes and his sweat-soaked hair stuck to his face. He dragged his fingers through it and then gazed out over the skyline.

Last one standing, I thought.

He offered me a hand and I took it, unsteady on my feet at first and my arm still burning and completely useless. "Why am I still conscious?"

"Because you were connected to me," he said quietly. Too quietly. "You had hold of my hand."

"What's wrong with your voice? Are you hur—?" But the answer came to me even as he started to respond.

"I'm controlling my tone. We're not very good at it. Can't keep it up for long . . ."

The voice-mod was gone. There was nothing adjusting his natural tone. But I didn't care. I was in too much pain to care. Maybe even in too much pain to be affected much by Hank's voice. And if not, then, so what? I'd be enamored with him to the point of forgetting I hurt so much. "Talk all you want," I muttered as we picked our way over the bodies, heading toward the agate sarcophagus. "Maybe it'll take the pain away. My arm hurts like hell."

That was an understatement. It hurt everywhere, but my arm overshadowed everything else. It burned, pulsed in an angry, red, infected beat. I glanced down at it. From the tips of my fingers to my shoulder, my skin was pink from the burn and covered in faint blue script.

I approached the sarcophagus, eyes scanning the area. "Where is the sword?"

He turned. "What sword?"

"The one I used to kill Llyran." I glanced over to a pile of ash coating a large pool of blood. "I believe that's him."

A soft whistle blew through Hank's lips. "Uh, Madigan?"

"What?"

"Did you see what's in the sarcophagus?"

"No. I just remember grabbing the sword and swinging."

I joined him at the agate tomb, taking careful steps since my legs were bruised and stiff. At the edge, I braced myself, expecting to see some kind of dried-up remnant of a First One. And then I looked.

"Oh, hell," I breathed.

Hank's hand tightened on my elbow as I swayed. Flawless, porcelain skin. The most perfect face you could ever conceive. Small, straight nose, finely curved nostrils. Lips just as full as my own, but hers were wider and stained red. Black, arched brows. And thick black lashes fanned out against high cheekbones. Glossy black hair. Body wearing a thin linen gown, so simple and fine you could almost see right through it.

Her hands gripped the hilt of the sword, holding it between her small breasts as though I'd never taken it from her.

But what stunned us into silence, what made the breath whoosh out of my lungs and leave me forgetting to breathe again, were the black wings on which she lay.

Fucking *wings*.

"You've got to be kidding me." I finally found my voice.

"That's a . . ." Hank began and then stopped as though the idea was too ridiculous to mention.

But I knew. I knew her voice had whispered through my mind in the warehouse where she was kept, and was the source of the beautiful language I heard when I looked at Solomon's ring and cried over Brim. "Yeah," I said, swallowing, "I think that's Ahkneri, the star . . . a First One."

I let the weight of those words sink in.

"Shit." Hank swiped his fingers through his hair. "Well, what the hell are we going to do with her?"

Wind gusted behind us, making me hold on to the edge of the sarcophagus as I pivoted to find Pendaran standing there in nymph form, bloodied and bruised, a huge gash in his shoulder. "We hide her," he said, walking up to stand beside me and gazing down into the tomb with an unreadable expression. "Grigori cannot have her."

"You didn't kill him?" I asked.

"No, but it will be a while before he can start looking for her."

"You're right," I said. "We can't turn the body over to the ITF. If anyone knew she existed . . . No one can know. She's proof that the myths are true. The Sons of Dawn won't stop, they'll keep coming, keep trying, keep killing innocent people to awaken her."

Hank cursed. "Maybe we should destroy it."

"No," Pendaran said immediately.

Dizziness made me reach for the rim again to steady myself as the voice inside of my head cried, a distant lament that weaved through my mind and wrapped around my heart. No. Couldn't destroy . . .

Flashes hit me then. Fast and sudden, stealing my vision until all I could see were ancient memories bursting in my mind. Sobbing. Painted temple. Columns that rose three stories high. Sun-baked landscape, and the flash of daylight on a river beyond. The dream-like image of this divine woman, on her knees, begging before the flowing white gown of another as tears of sorrow ran down her face. But it was her emotions—the grief, the heart torn into something that was no longer salvageable—that closed my throat and brought tears to the surface. What had happened to her?

"Hell," I swore, throat thick. "We have to keep her safe." I shook my head, trying to get the sense of her gratitude out of my mind.

"She's dead, for all we know, Charlie," Hank said.

"She's not dead." I bit the inside of my cheek, Llyran's words echoing in my head. "You guys do know that she has the power to rid the city of darkness."

For a moment no one spoke.

Then the Druid spoke up. "We'll find another way. What's forty square miles of darkness to an all-out war? I can live with it. Anyone can go outside of the city for sunlight . . ."

"Besides," Hank said, "we'd have no idea what she'd do if she woke . . ."

"She wouldn't hurt us."

"Oh, what, are you channeling First Ones now?"

I gave him a sideways frown. "I realize the lunacy of what I'm about to say, but"—*Deep breath, Charlie*—"I'm going to take her home with me."

Hank's bark of disbelief made me wince. "You have lost your mind. I knew one day it would happen, I did, but this . . . This is pure, certifiable, only-Charlie-could-do-this insanity. You *can't* take her home. It's the first place Tennin will look."

"I have another idea," Pendaran said quietly.

Thirty minutes later, after the chief had been called to round up the jinn and bring Hank a new voice-mod, the nymphs were trickling back to the Grove, and Orin had turned the Old Lore over to Pendaran. Hank and I stood at the edge of Clara Meer Lake and watched the Druid King emerge from the depths, much like the first time we'd seen him only a few days earlier. Only this time he'd whispered the command to manifest clothes onto his tattooed body.

I stared at the water for a long time, my good hand resting on Brim's back as he leaned against me, and my other cradled against my stomach, still uncertain about the decision to hide Ahkneri in the lake. "You sure she won't get cold or wet or—"

"For the tenth time, I'm sure. It's warm down there. That lid is a perfect seal. And she's not submersed in the water, but in one of the largest caves within the lake. The agate, and the depth, plus the bedrock should be enough to mask her from even the most sensitive hunter."

"Only the three of us know," I said, looking at Pen and then Hank. "And it needs to stay that way."

They both nodded. I returned to stare at the lake and the reflection of the cityscape on its surface, the lights twinkling and blinking in the soft ripples. Even the lights of Helios Tower shown atop the water.

"And you'll return the Old Lore back to the Hall of Records once you're done with it," I said, repeating what we'd already agreed upon. Pendaran knew I was placing an enormous amount of trust in him. He'd placed his trust in me during the fight with Llyran, and I had to believe that he'd abide by his word.

"As soon as we study it. If there is a ritual that disperses darkness, we'll copy it, and return the original to Elysia."

"If you have any trouble with the script," I said, with an ache starting in my chest, "you should talk to Aaron. He's pretty good at that type of thing."

23

The sun should be rising, I thought as I held the back door to my Tahoe open and snapped my fingers. Brimstone jumped onto the backseat, and I prayed to God he didn't eat the upholstery while I was gone. Once he was taken care of, Hank and I made our way into Station One and down the flight of stairs leading to the med hold where wounded criminals were treated and detained.

Aaron was lying on a hospital bed, IV in his vein, monitors recording his heartbeat and pulse/oxygen levels. My sister raised her head from her forearm as the door clicked closed. "Hey," she said in a drowsy voice, sitting straighter in the chair and rubbing her eyes. Her face was nearly as pale as Aaron's and, as I drew closer, I couldn't help but look for the signs of possession.

"How's Liz doing?" Hank stood at the foot of

Aaron's bed, his gaze on the nymph, but his question for Bryn.

"She's doing okay. In the cafeteria chugging OJ. The ritual went perfectly. What's wrong with your arm, Charlie?"

I glanced down at my arm, wishing I'd had on a long-sleeved shirt or a jacket. As it was now, anyone who paid a lick of attention might notice the pink skin and the faint blue script just beneath the surface as though my veins had redesigned themselves. They curved from my useless fingers all the way up my bicep and the round part of my shoulder, and the relentless, throbbing pain was almost enough to make me cry. "It's nothing," I said. "Some weird reaction to something during the fight maybe . . ." I pulled my gaze away and stared at the screen to Aaron's heart monitor for a long moment. "And the ring?"

"Liz still has it. The spirits Llyran had trapped inside were released when she read the inscription. At least now they can rest. What happened to the sarcophagus?"

The question was innocent enough, but I had to wonder if it was her asking or someone else. All the outward signs appeared normal. She showed no signs of a typical Wraith or Revenant possession. And that's what disconcerted me. If Llyran was to be believed, *ash* had made her a willing vessel, but for what? For whom? "We destroyed it," I said, turning back to the monitor.

She responded with a soft "Oh."

As I stood there I debated whether or not to tell her what I'd learned from Llyran, but I finally decided against it for the time being. She wanted to be here with Aaron and help right whatever wrong she'd done. Still . . . "I'm going to assign a guard for you," I said, bracing for an outburst.

I expected outrage, claims that I was a bad sister for not trusting her or believing in her, but all she did was stare at Aaron for a long moment, her eyes large and sad, and then she nodded. "We can see an exorcist, too. Couldn't hurt, right?" Her eyes lifted to mine and though her smile was twisted in sarcasm, tears shone in the copper depths.

I cleared my throat. "I'll set it up for Monday."

As we headed for the back door to Station One, several jinn warriors were being ushered inside, causing me and Hank to flatten our backs against the wall to let them pass. The nitro bands around their wrists kept them weakened and allowed the officers to get them into cold cell confinement where each individual would be processed. I'd be happy if the entire lot was sent back to Charbydon, but that was out of my hands.

One of the uniformed crime scene analysts whose name I couldn't recall entered carrying a large container housing the spirit jar, which had been broken in four pieces. Scattered among the pieces were bone fragments—the remains of Solomon, but I guess we'd never really know for sure. Whatever spirit had been in that jar was long gone, probably set free when it broke.

Or at least I hoped so.

Hank and I finally squeezed past several more officers and made our way into the parking lot just as the chief was striding toward the door. "I want a report on my desk first thing Monday."

"What about Tennin?"

The chief rolled his eyes. "Unit picked him up on Alabama Street, laying in a three-foot-deep impression in the asphalt. He was conscious enough to claim he'd come to the rooftop to pull back his jinn, that they acted alone, said the axe in Hank's back wasn't his, and then he gave his attorney's number and hasn't said a word since. He's down in cold cell right now. You want to talk to him?"

I shook my head. "No, it's not worth it."

"He'll walk," Hank said, disgusted. "It's just a matter of time."

The chief's dark frown was followed with a snort. "And when he does, we'll do what we always do—keep a close eye on him until he screws up again. Wouldn't mind if the next time he hits the pavement, it puts him six feet under. For good."

The chief started to walk away, but I stopped him. "Hey, Chief?" He turned. "Make sure Liz destroys that ring."

He gave me a salute and then kept walking as Hank and I went to my Tahoe.

Grigori Tennin had been involved in the making of *ash* with Mynogan. He'd played a role in bringing darkness to the city. He'd aided Llyran in trying to start a war. And the bastard might be derailed, but that sure as hell was only temporary. No. Tennin wasn't through, not by a long shot.

Hank walked with me to my Tahoe. I stopped by the driver's side door, frowning with resignation at the slobber trails rolling down the insides of every single window in my vehicle. Great. I leaned back against the door, finally acknowledging the deep ache in my muscles and bones.

"You should get that arm looked at," Hank said, bracing his hip against the front side panel and crossing his arms over his chest, looking for all the world like some ancient, battle-weary hero with his torn and bloodied clothes, wounds and bruises, and disheveled hair and shadowed jaw.

"Mmm. How's your back?"

"Feels like an axe was planted between my shoulder blades." He rolled his shoulder and winced. "I'll need a good soak in the baths . . ." Images flashed through my weary, unprotected mind. Loincloth. Tanned skin. Siren. Blue diamonds. Heat crept up my neck as I glanced away, eyes on the pockets of light created by the street lamps. "So where does all this leave us, Charlie?" he asked quietly, but directly, and I knew he wasn't talking about divine beings and serial killers.

The drop in his rich tone only heightened the uncomfortable memories knocking around my head. "There is no us, Hank. There can't be."

His expression was blank, completely unreadable, and his voice was even when he spoke. "Because we're friends, partners . . . Because I'm a siren and you're a human? Because you're afraid?"

"Yes, if you want to know the truth. All of that. And because now I've got this damn mark on my shoulder . . ."

"So? I bear one, too."

"And how will I know whether it's the mark or *me* reacting to you?"

One eyebrow lifted as the corner of his mouth dipped down. "That's the biggest load of cow shit you've flung at me in days, Madigan. Might want to lose the excuses and stick to the truth. The mark only reminds you of what's *already* there." A muscle ticked in his jaw as he stepped closer and leaned down, until his bright blue eyes were level with mine. One hand reached out and flicked the ends of my newly cropped hair. "Tell yourself whatever you want. It doesn't change anything. And now that I'm back to being one hundred percent . . ." A grin spread slowly across his face, slicing deep dimples in both scruffy cheeks. "You don't stand a chance."

With that, he winked and strode away.

Very slowly, I released my breath and watched him disappear into the shadows beyond the lot. Damn. Before the mark, and before Hank had gotten his power back, I was in trouble. But now? I was toast.

My eyes narrowed at the spot near the corner where he'd turned, not liking this sense of inevitability one bit. It felt too much like defeat.

Hank Williams had just drawn a line in the sand. He thought—no, he *assumed*—I'd be like any other disoriented siren groupie, but he was about to learn a thing or two about this southern girl.

I could take the heat. Toast, my ass.

My bungalow in Candler Park sat in its fading patch of green like a little piece of heaven in the darkness. Warm light glowed from the front windows, and my expensive down comforter called to me, lured me like Hank never could or *would*, making me yawn three times as I let Brim out of the back of the Tahoe and then shuffled up the walk.

During the short drive, soreness had crept along my limbs and turned them stiff as boards. Everything, from walking and lifting my arm to turn the doorknob, to the excruciating task of removing my weapons harness, was an exercise in grin-and-bear-it. I had to drop the harness and my weapons in a heap inside the closet because my arm wouldn't lift high enough to slip the leather over the peg. And I was too exhausted to care.

The stairs beckoned, but I stopped by the guest bedroom and pushed open the door. Rex lay on his stomach, wearing the same clothes I'd seen him in last and snoring softly. Apparently he hadn't been lying.

Whatever Tennin had done to him to make him remember his past had taken its toll.

I stood there and stared, just thinking and reliving everything that had happened between us. Will and me. Rex and me. Rex and Tennin. With a quiet sigh, I pulled the door closed and went slowly upstairs, saving our issues for tomorrow—they sure as hell would still be there in the morning.

Emma wasn't back yet from sleeping over at the Motts', and though I couldn't wait to throw my arms around my kid and hug her tight, I was glad for the alone time, the silence, and the privacy to strip off my clothes and crawl into bed. My shower worked just fine. Door was still missing, window still boarded up, but the floor had been swept, and the plumbing still worked. But I was too damned tired to care about being clean. I'd have to clean later. The sheets. The pillowcase. My skin. *Yes*, I thought as my head sank into the soft pillow, *later*.

When I finally roused, I wasn't sure if it was night or the next day. I knew I needed to roll over to see the clock on the bedside table, but as long as I stayed completely still nothing hurt except my arm. I stayed like that for a few minutes before realizing I needed a shower in the worst possible way.

Time to move.

I drew in a deep breath and rolled, wincing and

hissing with each flex of muscle and each press of my body into the mattress.

By the time I was sitting, my legs hanging over the mattress, I was breathing hard and sweating. It was ten A.M. the following day. I'd slept for nearly twenty-four hours. I pulled my injured arm close to my stomach. It was hot to the touch and the patterns were still there, still blue, still looking like a combination of ancient script and molecular drawings.

"Shower," I mumbled in a hoarse voice, easing my weight onto both feet. "Shower first."

It was one of the best showers of my life. Waking up. Getting clean. I could even move my arm a little. I put *way* too much shampoo in my hair because I'd forgotten again that I now sported a "cute" chin-length bob. But as soon as I heard the first thump, my stomach dropped and I froze.

A few more thuds and bangs, each accompanied by a soft curse, made me slowly pull back the shower curtain and peek out.

"Does anyone in this house understand the whole shower/privacy thing?" I asked.

Rex held a brand-new door, hinges already attached to the side. He gave me a droll smile and muttered a reply, though the four screws clasped between his lips kind of prevented me from understanding him. I shot him a wide smile. "What was that?"

He rolled his eyes, shook his head, and then lined up the door to the frame. He looked great in one of

Will's soft, baby-blue T-shirts, khakis, and a tool belt strapped around his waist. The shirt color accentuated the stormy blue of his eyes, and his skin looked rich and tan, his hair still kissed by the sun despite the fact that there hadn't been any sun for over two months now.

He matched up the hinges to the depression in the frame where the others had been and then pulled the drill from the tool belt as I let the shower curtain fall back and resumed my shower.

My strength returned as I finished drying off to a newly closed-in bathroom. My stomach growled as I dressed in lounge pants and a T-shirt and then made my way downstairs to raid the fridge.

Talk on the living room television made me pause on the last step. Speculation about yesterday's early morning light show atop Helios Tower, the mysterious collapse of the arboretum dome, and the amazing display of nature as the darkness parted to reveal the dawn of the winter solstice.

Nothing about First Ones or the Sons of Dawn.

I let out a breath of relief and kept moving toward my destination. Rex came through the back door, tool belt gone, and washed his hands in the sink. "Didn't have a chance to shop, but there's cereal and one everything bagel left. Emma's out back with Brim."

"Thanks." I made a bowl of Lucky Charms and sat down, watching him tool around the kitchen before he finally turned and faced me.

"Before you start in on me," he said, "I want you to

know that . . . I need some time to figure all this out." He dragged a hand through his hair and let out a deep sigh. "It's getting crowded in here. Feel like I'm three different people."

"Sucks," I said quietly. "Rex, I need to know you didn't make a deal with Tennin that puts my family in jeopardy."

"The deal is over and done, Charlie. Me taking that potion, or whatever the hell it was, in exchange for the collection debt being paid." At my disbelief, he said, "He wanted me to remember. Apparently, to Tennin, that was worth twenty grand." He slid into a chair. "Let's just get through Christmas and then we'll talk more. There's a lot I have to tell you." He paused, letting the weight of his next words settle into his tone. "I know how to fix things. I know how to fix everything."

My spoon paused in midair. I held his gaze for a long moment. "Okay."

He blinked. "That's it? Just okay? No shoving a Nitro-gun in my face and demanding I leave Will immediately and tell all about my jinn past?"

I gave a light shrug. "We shouldn't rush things. We'll need to be certain whatever you're thinking of will work. And besides, you'll probably need to find a new host body first, right? Unless, you're changing your mind . . ."

"No. Not changing my mind. I want Em to have her father back."

Relief flowed through me. I tipped the cereal

bowl and drank the milk. "Good. I'm going into the backyard to play toss-the-bowling-ball with Em and Brim." I set the bowl in the sink and then headed for the back door. "Oh, and thanks for fixing the bath-room."

He looked at me like I'd lost it. "I like the hair, by the way."

I smiled. "Thanks."

That evening, I sat on my kid's bed and told her the entire story of what really happened on the tower—everything *except* the fact that a First One was lying beneath Clara Meer Lake. She laughed. She gasped. She cried. She hugged Brim and begged me to take her to the Grove so she could see Pen, the Druid King, transform into a dragon—which I considered doing just for the fact that shifting for the amusement of a child would really annoy him.

We talked for hours.

And then something extraordinary happened. She started talking to me, telling me about *her* feelings, her thoughts, her hopes and dreams, things she'd kept from me or didn't think I'd want to hear.

I listened.

And it made all the difference, sharing with my kid.

She'd begun a journal the day Brim came home, which she called *Hellhounds Rule, Parents Drool*. She'd been writing in it ever since. After showing it to me and letting me flip through a few pages, I realized my kid had a knack for the written word, a beautiful way of expressing herself and looking at the world.

Amazed by her and the individual she was becoming, I kissed her, leaving her lying on her bed with the journal open, Brim curled up on the rug.

I went downstairs to the sounds of Rex cooking dinner, and out onto the porch, making my way barefoot into the cold, dry grass in the front yard. I shoved my hands into my pants pockets and stared at the thick, churning darkness overhead, knowing that somewhere beyond was a sky filled with the last light of day, a beautiful rainbow-colored sky painted on a canvas of blue.

I bit softly on the inside of my cheek, eyeing the great expanse of gray as conviction and inevitability settled deep into my bones.

Despite Grigori Tennin, despite the hardships to come with my sister and the other *ash* survivors, despite whatever the hell happened between me and Hank, and the complications sure to arise with bringing Will back, I'd do this one thing. One day. Soon.

I'd bring back the light.

Acknowledgments

For expertly guiding me through the trials and tribulations of the second-book "experience," for believing in me and bolstering my confidence when I needed it most, *enormous* gratitude goes to my editor, Ed Schlesinger.

For the most amazing cover art on the planet, Chris McGrath. I bow down to your insane talent.

For being two of the most coolest and helpful women in the biz, Erica Feldon and Miriam Kriss, publicist and agent extraordinaires.

For eating all those microwave meals and dealing with one seriously distracted mind, eternal thanks and love to Audrey, James, and Jonathan.

Because I didn't last time, shout-outs to Dylan, Ryan, and Isabel Long. I miss you guys. When are you going to move closer to me?

For reading like the wind, Kameryn Long and Jenna Black. Thanks for the last-minute critiques and assurances. And for Vicki Pettersson, Lilith Saint-crow, and Jackie Kessler—thank you doesn't sound adequate for the help you gave me. You ladies are awesome.

And finally for all my family, friends, followers, and readers who gave Charlie Madigan a chance. Thank you so much for your time, your emails, and for spreading the word. You have made this journey incredible, and I am humbly in your debt.

Desire is stronger after dark...

Bestselling Urban Fantasy from Pocket Books!

Bad to the Bone
JERI SMITH-READY

Rock 'n' Roll will never die. Just like vampires.

Master of None
SONYA BATEMAN

Nobody ever dreamed of a genie like this...

Spider's Bite

An Elemental Assassin Book
JENNIFER ESTEP.

Her love life is killer.

Necking
CHRIS SALVATORE

Dating a Vampire is going to be the death of her.

Available wherever books are sold
or at www.simonandschuster.com

 POCKET BOOKS
A DIVISION OF SIMON & SCHUSTER
A CBS COMPANY

23521

KICK SOME BUTT

with bestselling Urban Fantasy from Pocket Books and Juno Books!

SHADOW BLADE
SERESSIA GLASS
Sometimes you choose a path in life.
Sometimes it chooses you.

DEMON POSSESSED
LAURA BIKEL
Detroit is burning…but it's just the beginning.

EMBERS
STACIA KANE
Is she going on a dream date…Or a date to hell?

AMAZON QUEEN
LORI DEVOTI
Being an Amazon ruler can be a royal pain.

Available wherever books are sold
or at www.simonandschuster.com

 POCKET BOOKS
A Division of Simon & Schuster
A CBS COMPANY

JUNO

23849